I0735302

Published in 2019 by
Kinetics Design, KDbooks.ca
ISBN 978-1-988360-37-9 (paperback)
ISBN 978-1-988360-38-6 (ebook)

The artist: images by Vicki Easton
The editor: Matthew Godden

The designer: cover and interior design,
typesetting and printing by Daniel Crack,
Kinetics Design, KDbooks.ca
https://www.linkedin.com/in/kdbooks/

Contact the author at
gaycheesethebook@gmail.com

GAY CHEESE

A NOVEL

Lorne Eedy

A nutty and somewhat cheesy story.
A tale filtering through a city perspective.
A trail that lands up country.

"I MUST PLAY JIMMY! This is a character an actor could get his teeth into, charming, complex and amusing. His life seems quite removed from my own, in that I am coming from an urban to a rural environment while Jimmy is small town all the way, but it's always fun to play something, as an actor that is somewhat removed from one's own experience, and we both have a few things in common, including our love of goats and our excitement at the prospect of owning a '53 Ford pickup. (A vehicle I have always coveted.)

I would love to be a part of this project.

— Robin Ward, Film and Television Actor

Chapter 1

Location, location, location!

Start with some rural-route GPS on an insignificant dot on the Canadian Army Survey map. A magnifying glass may help. This tiny dot is named Transvaal. Transvaal is off the map, at least the Ontario Highway Map. The tiny dot interrupts the barber-pole stripes that signify the grey gravel roads on the back-country survey map. The striped path follows the southwesterly path of the Upper Thames River, not to be confused with the Lower Thames and/or East Thames Rivers.

"First gravel right, south of Town."

To the east, in a universe that's far away but still part of Canada, stands the great City, graceful under the heavens, steadfast by the side of a Great Lake. Distances get shorter, from sixty kilometres an hour on gravel to ninety on the uneven hardtops that carry commerce and day-trippers to the 401 highway corridor, and the speed gets up to one-twenty. Tick-tack, tick-tack, homes pop up, toadstools surrounding the big international airport.

Follow the path of solo drivers leaving the rows of wheat-, barley- and straw-coloured vinyl siding. City commuters pass cross-over highways, packs of strip malls, and those temples for serious shoppers at Yorkdale and Sheridan Mall. Down toward downtown, where an eight-lane ribbon funnels traffic toward an avenue and a destination, both named Lakeshore.

Pass those creamy ice-cream vendors, comfortable fat-tire bicycles, shirtless joggers and skinny dogs sparring for space along the two-lane lake path.

Ding. Ding. "On your left. Passing."

"Thank you."

Cyclist glances back. *"What kind of dog is that?"*

"A Portuguese water Dog."

"Hello, buddy. Good dog. What's your name?"

"Pedro."

Backing up from the lake path, the lineup of row-on-row, tick-tack homes is replaced by a common forest of apartment condominiums.

Up and up and away, these high-risers.

Up from Mother Earth and the city-created sandy shore of the Great Lake, herds of City folk make their nests in their condo birdhouses. The city altitudes flown by these highly evolved birds put them at the height of civilization, a pattern that takes them from high home to high work. Balancing the uppity *trop haute* of the City is the wonderful cosmopolitan nature at its heart. Look around at the Benetton flavour that criss-crosses the greater City in paint-patch swatches.

Here in the City, above bumpy streets, uneven sidewalks and concrete curbs — high up in their condo with the million-dollar lake view, the dream has blown a tire …

"It sucks."

John slams through the condo doorway onto the tiled foyer. *Click, click.*

He tosses one bike shoe, takes another double step forward. *Click, click.*

He tosses the second shoe, a nice flip to the sidelines. His helmet lands like a Frisbee on the hall bench. The Italian gloves fly off onto the marble floor.

"It sucks."

John sweats, fumes under his sunglasses as he takes a dark view of himself in the hallway mirror. "My God, look at my hair." Plastered to his head. My God.

His partner, Greg, comes in from the kitchen; slows the drama down.

"What happened?"

Temperature still rising. "Bike stolen. It sucks."

Greg asks the obvious question about John's birthday gift. "What about your lock?"

"Locked tight to a post. Tight and gone. Lock, stock and bicycle. Gone. It sucks."

Greg waits for the police-record rewind on another bicycle event. The worn script demands an understanding nod or two or three.

John rants at the empty wall of the foyer. "That's the third bike in three years," John says.

"At least this one was used and cheap."

"That's not the point."

Greg can't help himself; he wants to brush John's hair and dry off his forehead. What a mess. Instead Greg bites in. "What is the point?"

"I have to take the streetcar, then walk. Walk in tights down Queen Street, with a helmet — and the worst, bicycle shoes. I am never going to the police station in that getup again. Thank God for my Zende sunglasses. My God, my eyes must be bloodshot."

Here we go; John will never go to the police again. Here we go, past the wait, the indifference to John's plight and the injustice as John describes the cast of criminal characters in a common waiting room. Here we go.

"I felt like we were penned together, all sorted in an unsorted manner. They took all the seats. Can you imagine walking all that way in clipped bicycle shoes?"

And here we go with the grand finale.

"My feet hurt."

Greg stops nodding it up as John reaches down for his aching soles. Here we go … will John say it? Yes.

"And one of *them* may have stolen my bike."

At the first bike MIA report, an unusual bunch of characters was described over and over in Audubon jailbird detail. Second time around, Greg took notes as the same script unfolded again. How many times does an unusual thing have to happen before it starts to be usual? Now, with thirdsies, my God, here we go again, Greg tells himself as he snaps to with a few more head nods toward John.

Of course, John would always be polite, no matter how sordid and unusual the characters. But how many times can he repeat the same verbatim details? First,

Greg must remind himself of his partner's mind, that of a combination chartered accountant and lawyer. Second, and more important, Greg must remind himself to just wait it out. He knows the script — time to let John just blow out the steam. And, my God, look at John's face as it puffs up crimson. Nod your head, Greg.

"Click, click," John says. "Those shoes are like cat bells announcing my arrival. Click click, everyone. Everyone stares with this same look: *Hey idiot, where's your bicycle?*"

And here we go again with the moment of partner intervention, a touchy thing. Greg steps up. "You're no idiot. Not my bestest friend John. Give Greg a hug."

Here we go, as John stands stiff, sweating and red-faced to be taken in a soft embrace by his bestest friend. The friend indeed taps a chorus of back-pats. "Now, does that make John-boy feel a little better?"

Greg can feel a tension release as John's hands rise to Greg's hips. Yes, those are the same wet, sweaty hands, unwashed from a common police room. The sun always rises after a nightmare.

John relaxes enough to reflect some sunshine on his rough ride. "At least this cute guy offered me his seat. Said he liked my Zende gloves."

Greg has stopped any nodding and hugging and moved to a big smile. He drops the subject of stolen bike number three for the task at hand: his not-so-hidden agenda. Things may move well ahead, with another bicycle gone. The real estate agent's already in play, with one big condo set to go.

Here we go. Maybe.

When the second bicycle disappeared, Greg made the call on his own to Stevie.

"We've talked about changes," Greg told him. "But John's not quite ready. And he's so pissed. Let things settle a bit."

"Well, the market is not settled. Up, up, up."

"John still has a tether to the City. But it's getting shorter."

"Stevie's your best agent man. At your call, Greg."

Third bicycle gone now. Perhaps this final incident has lifted the veil on John's insight. Greg drops the small-catch, loose change for a trophy-mount reel-in for the big cash-in. "How much do you think this condo is worth?"

The next morning, they are joined on their deck by their guy in real estate, Super Agent Man Stevie. Lake Ontario spreads out as a backdrop.

"Best lake view in downtown Toronto," Stevie says, "when you consider that you can have a sit-down dinner on the deck. Twenty for supper."

John piques at an underestimate of their big deck's appeal. He clears the air with hand movements expanding toward outer space. "We had an eightieth-birthday catered brunch for Greg's mommy, with forty guests. Right, Greg?"

Greg nods in earnest. The lads are comfortable with their Super Agent Man in real estate.

"Happy, happy little sardines we were, weren't we, now?" Greg lets his two pointer fingers swim out together.

"No one has the panoramic that you guys do," Stevie says. "It's size that matters here. Number one selling point. This place will be gone in two weeks max. Our price is a perfect hook and sinker to generate a bidding frenzy. It's the deck. There's nothing like it in the City."

John is back from outer space to the change in home space. "Greg, are you sure about this?"

It means more than a sale — it's a whole change in life. John — the legal expert, the auditor — is struggling with the big change. He's rocking back and forth, almost off balance.

Greg looks to Stevie while he speaks to John. "We asked Stevie over for his advice. So, ask him." No response. "Big cash, John boy. Big cash."

Still no response. Greg cashes in on the dream concept. "Our dream come true. With big returns. Big cash."

Greg isn't sure whether it was the big dreams, big cash or big returns that did it, but John turns back to Super Agent Man. John is caught in a gold-rush thought.

"Stevie, are you sure we should do it?"

"Up, up, up. Ad will be in the *Globe* on Thursday, with open house on Saturday. Your super agent will have you a firm offer by five in the afternoon."

"Greg? Stevie? Are you sure?"

It sure happens fast.

On Saturday, as promised, all Stevie's super-agent hands are on deck for a full-day open house. The full-colour eighth-page in the *Globe*'s "Homes on Parade" did the trick. He has full- colour blow-ups in plastic easel frames in each show area, including the black marble bathroom with steam shower, heated towel racks and bidet. "Your best agent man got upper-right page, eh? Want a great spot? Count on Stevie."

Squirt. Squirt. "A little eau de lavender here and a little there. John, the muffins warming in the oven can be put on the counter now."

Squirt. Squirt. Stevie flits past the kitchen to the parquet draw table in the dining room. "Greg, you need the glads here, centre shot. The muffins will hold down the aisle counter."

Squirt. Squirt. "Whoops. Those two vases on the deck are just wrong." *Squirt. Squirt.* Off the Super Agent Man flies to save the moment.

The advertisement has spelled out a simple process for making offers on-site, in sealed envelopes.

Squirt. Squirt. At nine on the button, the bottle is dropped in the hallway half-bath and the front door swings open.

Stevie turns to the crowd off the elevator; some of them have been waiting in the lobby downstairs since seven-thirty. "Be a Boy Scout, everyone."

Couples and strangers exchange confused looks. *Boy Scout?*

"Come prepared. Prepared to buy. Because Super Agent Man Stevie will sell it today."

Greg turns to John. "The muffins in the oven."

"On the platter."

The owners stage the peach-strawberry examples of mini-decadence. (Miss Vicki delivers mini-muffins or maxi-decorated theme cupcakes.)

Stevie calls out to the group. "Small mouthfuls, please. Let's not track a crumb trail across the slate floor."

The open oven has filled the air with fresh baking, a draw back to the dining area. No one touches the platter. John and Greg look at each other and quickly retreat to the master bedroom.

"No one wants to be the first."

"I need a pee."

"You're nervous."

"No, it's that third capp that's doing it."

Greg taps his foot on the Persian hand-knotted carpet. John shifts through the door of the ensuite bathroom.

"Oh my God. There's someone in our bathroom."

The surprised Boy Scout retreats back to the hallway door.

"Is this not an open house?"

"Sorry. Owner needs a pee. In his bathroom."

Greg pulls his partner aside. "John, take your pee before the next one comes in." He smiles at their guest. "Yes, it is an open house."

Bang. Bedroom door swings open, with Stevie leading the charge.

"Seven hundred — *seven hundred square feet* of master bedroom. The custom Aurora hand-crafted bed in Brazilian cherry … stays. Including those side tables and two, yes two matching highboys. Same mid-century design, same builders … all included in the sale."

The Boy Scouts line up. John and Greg head for the hallway and hit the deck next. Even from outside, they can hear Super Agent Man lay it all out.

"Seven hundred square feet, not including the walk-in closet."

He slides the floor-to-ceiling mirrors on coasters to reveal the core of the apple: Greg and John's *American Gigolo*–style staging room. The Boy Scouts chorus an agreement.

"Hm-m-m-m."

"Aa-a-a-ah."

"Ni-i-i-ce."

The partners sneak back in to the untouched platter of mini-muffins and grab one each. Stevie arrives with the master bedroom groups in tow. Super Agent Man anchors himself to the kitchen aisle, waiting for his group to line up.

The floodgates open as the kitchen crowd closes in on the treats, with commentary.

"Did you see the James Snow original oil above their gas fireplace?" someone murmurs.

"Forget the Snow oil," Stevie says. "The stone surround rains down."

"*Rain?* Rains down?"

"A gravity drip down the stone facing of the fireplace. Look at the moss growing, man. On a fireplace."

"Wow," someone gushes. "Never seen that."

"Super wow."

The piranhas devour the platter of mini-muffins.

"Nice," one prospect remarks, licking his fingers.

Stevie has their attention; he face-shifts to a look of intensity. "Here is something that's not just nice — it's gorgeous: commercial glass-door fridge. Hand-pounded copper vent. Norwood FourStar gas and convection range."

Stevie puts his hands down on the marble-top island, which begs to be touched. "Marble. Looks like black suede, yes. Marble."

He moves in close on the audience, quiet-like. "The current owners have such a tasteful style about them. Who cares about condo fees? If you own the cabin cruiser don't fret the price of gas."

The visitors take in the Hanover blue slate floor, Italian marble counter, hand-hammered copper kitchen backdrop, and teak-infused dining room area. The partners have moved to the farthest corner of the deck, looking back at the sales performance. Greg's having fun.

"Standing here gives a super-perspective on the size of our deck. Just smile, buddy — here comes Stevie."

And now, as the group reaches the south side of the condo, Stevie utters the inevitable first words uttered by every visitor to Greg and John's pad: "Look at that view."

All visitors offer a similar exclamation as they step out onto the deck and behold the panoramic view of the island off the City harbour, a leafy blob that blocks the invisible expanse of Lake Ontario. Stevie's rolling on.

"Wet bar, smoker, and look at the Broilchief barbecue."

A little note from one Boy Scout who apparently never got his Water Navigator or Bronze Canoe badge — a non-swimmer with a horror of unknown waters: "The lake is rather dark."

Lake Ontario is indeed all dark, stretching out behind the clear definition of a boardwalk following the outline of City Island, a blur between heaven and water. Stevie as Super Agent Man keeps an inside view on the blob, lightening up the dark comment. "Lights up really nice at night. A jewel in the lake. Lots of definition. And people action."

"People action" brings up thoughts of Hanlan's Point, a known nudist beach, getting a few winks or grimaces from a number of prospect faces. No matter, Stevie turns on the logic and charm.

"Not *too* much action, though. The ferries, sailboats and aircraft are fun to watch. Have a look through the binoculars."

Greg and John stick to the far corner of the deck's vast open space as the group proceeds to the foyer.

"No. Condo. I've. Seen …" (Attention, Boy Scouts: all eyes on me as Stevie's hand waves expand to take in the capacious entry.) "… HAS …" He hacks the word out, then lowers his voice with more waves in a ta-dah fashion: " … a foyer entrance like this."

And that look of astonishment that only a Super Agent Man could give. "You could fit a Christmas choral group inside."

John watches, but he can't quite picture the choral set decking his hall. Greg listens, almost ready to count the repeats in the Super Agent Man pitch.

Greg and John last through four full Stevie tours on his set loop from bedrooms, bathrooms and dining area to the million-dollar view, then back to start at the entrance. As the afternoon stretches on, they eye each other with that half-dumb look used in couple conversation, the look when there's no need for words. Half-raised eyebrows and that cocked head say it all: *We have seen it all.* They look in silent acknowledgement back across the deck chairs toward the dining area and kitchen.

Over and over they said it, how many times?

"My God. What a view."

"Oh my God, will you look at the view."

Over and over, with "my God" uttered somewhere in proximity to "will you" and "the view," accompanied by a chorus of ohs and ahs, repeated and repeated again.

Stevie, a real Super Agent Man, is always one step ahead. In between tours, he flies out to the edge of outer space, reading their minds.

"You'll see," he says. "You'll see it all the way to the bank. I saw you, with those skeptical looks. First on the muffins. And was Stevie not right? No trail of crumbs following the tours."

If Greg is a wanderer and a wonderer, John is the GPS anchor of their relationship.

John gives off an unassuming façade at first glance, but he's a law partner with a CA earned later in his career. He specializes in the full gambit of estates, foundations and trusts, with particular expertise in contracts. Pulling this together, he hires out as a phenomenal expert witness.

In the corporate world, John turns up as the worst expert witness for or against the prosecution in audit testimony. He can cough up reams of correlations and conclusions with his photographic memory. He out-details Revenue

Canada, bringing up whole sections and paragraphs of the *Tax Act* verbatim from his photographic memory.

"Oh no. There's that John Georges in court today."

"The guy's a data beast."

"Tore my best defence to shreds."

"My strategy in a case? Call John the Auditor. Best when he's on side."

"Or busy on some other case."

If the Canadian tax auditor had an Avoid List, John's phone number would be featured on it, along with his picture (the salt-and-pepper shadow hair and beard all neatly cropped, matching the signature bow tie and tortoise-shell reading glasses).

In fact, John could be on the Please Ask list, because John can play for both sides if the pay is right.

"Slam dunk," he boasted when he got his first expert witness gig. "Five thousand retainer. Another five if it goes to court. Six hours at six hundred an hour for ten minutes on the stand. Nice."

Greg can do the math.

"Super nice."

And yet Greg is a surprise on the financial front, when it comes to the take-home. A combination of small wages and big tips challenges his CA partner's cut in the paper chase. A mighty attempt by a mere server, indeed.

After years of free board, horse stalls and no university loans on his parents' Kingston farm, Greg headed to the City for an easy hire in the restaurant trade. His sommelier designation followed, allowing him to move up the rack from simple wine recommendations with unintelligible terms to some delicious drops. More satisfying for Greg, but unintelligible to most unwashed occasional diners:

"The acidity has been balanced by a higher alcohol," Greg tells the client, with trained honesty.

Greg rolls his empty Vidal stemware. Looks at the tasting client. Monkey see, Monkey do. Greg holds up his empty wine glass with another roll back and forth. Monkey see and do again. This time Greg points for the customer's focus.

"Now look at those legs. That's alcohol." The sommelier smells his imaginary sample, in sync now with the diner. *"That bouquet. Crispy fresh; winter clothes closet; maybe some cinnamon. Sir, you have made a wonderful choice."*

The customer can't smell any clothes closet that he's familiar with, so he bails. *"Thank you, young man."*

But Greg is not quite finished. *"Now roll it over your tongue. Apples, cashews, maybe an orchard."*

"Very nice, young man. Thank you."

And for the reds:

"With gravity feed, the fruit is not over-handled. The Pinot Noir is magnificent. A wonderful complement to the American oak."

The tasteless rich know how to taste their wine. Greg follows the action with some background.

"No bottling for one year. Then three full years in the bottle. Sir, you have made a wonderful choice."

Greg has moved up yet another tier at the toney downtown establishment that guarantees without guaranteeing: *"The largest wine selection in the City."* Hits you in the face in 14-point type on the menu under the wavy logo.

Other restaurateurs whisper their corrections, coloured in jealousy.

"The largest whine group in the City."

"Their customers are that tasteless kind of rich people. Have you looked around the room there?"

"Looks like a lot of people that have money. Look close; it's not a beautiful crowd."

The operative word is *rich*. Wages have stayed minimum, but tips are off the scale for a smart young sommelier.

Greg is quick on the draw, shooting ahead of the market and current tastes.

"This Napier/New Zealand blend is a French Bordeaux killer."

"Please have a taste. If it does not please you, we have —"

"The largest wine selection in the City," the prospective customer interjects.

"Guaranteed, Sir."

"Delicious. Can this be bought?"

"We import it."

Greg has more finish on the great drop.

"Why pay four hundred dollars for a wine ..." (He has his customer's full attention.) *"... when we offer a better selection. Imported by us, all private. And best, it's a better drop for a quarter the price. I will leave tasting notes if you're interested."*

Greg presents the label for the customer's inspection. Customer rolls the wine around in his mouth.

"Greg. Can you get me some of this?"

"Sir, you will leave tonight with all our importer's information."

Time moves Greg from over-barrelled Aussie reds to overpriced California Cab Sauvs, then close-up to out-of-their-league reds from the County. In Greg's pre-sommelier days, he had a penchant for big French reds.

Right now Greg has the best of gigs on the go. For the show, he opens up the gates on choice Oregon Pinot Gris and Pinot Noirs. He was first in the City to push whites from Quails Gate in Kelowna. He was first to put a finger in the dike on the tsunami of chewy Australian Chardonnays; now everyone who's anyone agrees that they have sailed away from popular taste.

"No, Greg got me off those dry-mouth Chards — those sugary Rieslings! — years ago."

These days, as his reputation expands, Greg's been sourcing some dry, late-harvest Rieslings from both Alsace and a generational winery from Victoria, down under.

"That's sure nice on the palate."

"Greg from the restaurant suggested this."

"Hey," Greg would complain to John at length. "I get the *terroir*, temperate, region, the gravel backed by a thousand or two years of viticulture. But explaining that to a customer? Their eyes water."

First there's the wine-varietal idiots:

"Where's Bordeaux?"

"Where's Beaune?"

Stupid is what stupid does, adding in some geography.

"I rented a house in Provence. Where's Avignon?"

Are cat people stranger than dog people?

"I have a terrier. How does that fit in?"

Greg doubles down on the dumb-dumb. Bite in:

"And what is your terrier's name?"

"Rolfie."

"Very nice, Sir."

Greg leans in for a discreet address:

"Terroir, Sir. French for territory."

Another big tip from Greg, for Greg.

Along with New Zealand, anything, an Aussie something or two, South American Sauvignon Blancs and Chardonnays, and a hinterland Sparkler from the County, the well-known sommelier always brings a smooth style to the deck with the awesome view when friends come over:

"Wow. That Torrementes varietal from Salta Argentina. Delicious deck wine."

"Can you get me a case, Greg?"

"Vintage section at the OBALB."

"No kidding."

"The wine store always hides some gems."

The tours of duty end in late afternoon, and the downtown City three-bedroom condo sucks the bids up.

Greg has popped a pink sparkler held in reserve for just in case. Count John in.

"Wow. In like flint, smooth and crispy."

"A Blanc y blanc with a touch of Cab from the barrel. Dry, crisp like green apples, with that touch of royal pink."

John leaves the tasting notes to his partner. "Wow."

Greg has a flute stretched out as the Super Agent Man flies onto the deck for a smooth landing.

"Whoa, Greg. What's this?"

"Special special from the cellars of Greg."

"Guys, it's more than cheers," Stevie says. "I have a substantial cash offer."

Ever since Tuesday night, every time Stevie has told them about the big cheque they're going to receive, Greg goes all doo-woppy, putting on his imaginary Ray-Bans while easing both hands back along the brush-cut sides of his head just below his curly crop of hair. Elvis lives in the City condo with the awesome view.

"Doo doo. Doo-o-o-oo … doo. Doo-doo doo-oo … doo, doo doo …"

John and Stevie are always a little astonished by the act. (John would rather not encourage Greg with his unrecognizable covers, but nonetheless there's this part where Greg does this pocket-reach for imaginary cash that he kind of finds attractive.)

John whispers into Stevie's ear. "I don't do karaoke."

Stevie doesn't miss a beat. "You can characterize *that* as karaoke?"

"Buddy," John says, "I think you've mixed up Deep Purple's *Smoke on the Water* into some ABBA."

Stevie can't help himself. "Did ABBA do acid?"

John sips his wine, then pulls his nose up from the effervescent charge and looks at Stevie.

"So there was a Boy Scout."

(Stevie has a scouting past, giving him a knowledge of the number one designation for a Canadian Boy Scout: Queen's Scout.)

"Lads." The drums are beating a ta-dah. "A Queen Scout." Stevie beats on. "A Queen Scout prepared to buy."

John and Greg shrug their shoulders with little surprise. A long day may have created second thoughts and some indifference from John.

Stevie lifts his flute to the sky with a come-hither look, and heads inside to the mini-muffinless dining room table. The silence reverberates across the slate floor as the partners sidle up for decision time. John fidgets in the Lucas Larson teak chair. The movement of legs is the only sound.

Stevie becomes silent super agent as he pushes a folded piece of paper across the parquet draw table. Greg's reach-in reaction, a snatch for it, is blocked — not by John but by the firm command of the Super Agent Man.

"Stop."

Greg and John look at each other. They are caught slow-footed with a couple of half-dumb looks. Stevie has one quick word to fill in for the lack of response.

"Think."

The partners look to each other.

"Think, guys. Think before you look."

Both look at Super Agent Man.

"The figure," Stevie says as all three hold their concentration. "Think about it. Because it's all here."

Eyes narrow at "all here." John and Greg pause, look at each other. Stevie fills in the silence as his head turns side to side.

"Stop and look around." Stevie nods his head. "Everybody's happy." Another nod for well-being. "We are all healthy. So what will change your address?"

Stevie is bobbing his head up, and down, up and down. He stops.

"We are wealthy," Stevie says.

Greg finds himself nodding while John stares straight ahead.

Another pause; looks are exchanged between the agent and Greg, then John, then Greg again, and John. Stevie cuts into the uncertainty.

"Cash." Pause and look. "I am talking wealthy. The big retirement. And even more. Enough more that there will always be money in the bank. What kind of big amount could possible motivate you guys? How much cash turns into a big move?"

The Super Agent Man is flying, on fire. "Big enough to invest for your retirement. Still big enough to have a ton in the bank."

John's indifference disappears for the show-me moment. He turns to Greg. "Bring it on."

They leave the paper on the table for several seconds before Greg does the reach. He pries open the fold just enough to squint to see the amount. His eyes widen as he slides it with a half-turn toward John. John takes his squint with a short pause for an inhale.

Both partners look back at Stevie in a chorus of amazement. They could have been Christmas carollers in the foyer. "Holy shit. Are you serious?"

Two chairs kick back after their chorus with a holy yell and a serious scream. The third chair joins in without pause. The train of thought speeds toward the light at the end of the tunnel.

Greg is all in for the ride. "Serious shit."

Stevie knows his Super Agent Man stuff. "Right as rain."

John stops the express train. "What's the catch?"

"Nothing," Stevie says. "No strings attached. Clean as a whistle. All easy peasy."

"Furniture inclusion?" John asks. "Or auction?"

"Auction, boys. Doesn't want the furniture."

Two up-front guys have dry throats.

Stevie has reached the sky with mental high-fives all round. The deal is real.

Greg has moved from flutes to three Vidal wine glasses with a cold bottle out before anyone can say Sold.

The down pour is on with a sip of Pinot Gris.

"Congratulations," Stevie says. "Nice drop, guys."

Greg is too distracted to dip in to a review of a fave varietal, though he does remind himself of the superb finish fashioned by those New Zealanders.

"Listen up," Stevie says.

The Super Agent Man has a sum up, glass down on the day. He returns to the pause points of a great sale.

"The key point is motivation." Pause. "Get this, guys. His wife's brother has been here for a party."

John and Greg look at each other. Pause.

"She's seen his photos," he continues. "He showed her his Bronies at play."

"Wonder who that was?" Greg muses. "What a great party."

"Couldn't believe how many of our friends were Bronies," John adds.

Stevie pulls back to the pause points. He has always been more into Smurfs himself. "She only saw the view," he says. "She wants the place no matter —"

John interrupts him. "What brother?"

Pause. Business is business first with Stevie.

"Forget the brother. We have the cash. Check? We have the motivation too. Check?"

"Check?"

"I mean check off the list. This is a cash offer."

John speaks up for the pair. "Hm-m-m. Motivation? Motivation is that number preceding the six zeros. Greg and I are motivated."

Stevie adds on more motivation. "Big cash is a given. She wants to pay that. Or almost anything, I guess. And that's just from looking at *pictures* of the place."

Greg nods. John the Auditor becomes lost in the direction, as Stevie lowers his voice and repeats, "Or almost anything."

John looks to Greg. "Double hm-m-m, I'd say, Greg. No, it's even more than that. It's ten times the hm-m-m we paid for it."

Greg is lost in thought, but winks. "Hm-m-m-m-m-m."

Ridiculous thoughts have opened up on big ideas that resound back and forth from partner to partner. Greg dreams a plan. John plans a more reasonable dream. Easy peasy, when a dream is backed and lubricated with the big Boomer bucks.

Chapter 2

The incident incendiary to our story starts on a farm in Transvaal. Spelled with a double "a," a dot on the survey map a few kilometres south of the Sunriser, as the crow flies. Even locals (but never those in the know) repeat the same question:

"Transvaal?"

"The Kember farm."

"Jimmy and Barbara?"

"First gravel right, south of Town."

The nutty part of our cheesy tale starts up with a daily quest — the quest for food to maximize the chances of winter survival and comfort.

Transvaal is just one more roll of the countryside beneath the beautiful Town of St. Marys. Up, up we go for a bird's-eye perspective, high above the valley that follows the Thames River downstream. That ribbon of asphalt heading east and west is Highway 7, located a few convenient concessions farther south. Between the black highway and the browny-blue river, a canopy of green marks the borders of patchwork fields. The grid sheet of pioneer-built concession roads — gravel byways that mirror the lay of land and hug the winding river.

This summer's record heat sizzles up into the dust plumes pushed by busy pickups and the occasional errant car. The ballooning mushroom permeates the giant leafy canopy, rising to the treetops that reach out into the universe. The dust replicates a rather grey, early-morning mist, but this is no dawn reprieve: the slap of heat on your face tells you different.

Above the U-shaped, hardtop pathway, a nut quest unfolds up in the wilting treetops that front the Kember family Century Farm. A perfect patch of walnut trees and a few oak converge to lay out a big buffet in the nut-diet world.

Treats surround the stone house and porch. A bulk market of nuts and tasty perennial bulbs fill the expansive garden trimming the yard. Treats! — topped off with the platform bird feeder filled with black sunflower seeds, an easy swing from the spreading dogwood.

None of the Kembers' strategies for warding off vermin are particularly effective, especially considering their track record with one very special squirrel. Here on their greener acres is one smart, fat furball, Chase of Kember. Chase, the brown squirrel whose longevity alone — not to mention his tenacity and ingenuity — makes him almost a household member (well, in the large squirrel's small mind). In the animal kingdom of critters, Chase would be the equivalent of Grandpa Squirrel — a toothy patriarch to generations of sturdy-pawed furballs, spread through a string of leaf nests up and down the gravel Sixth Line. When Grandpa speaks, the young listen.

"Listen up, young Kits. Wherever you climb, jump or run" — he looks around the furry circle in his large oak-tree hollow — "be decisive, Kits."

Grandpa points to the ground below with a toothy grin.

"Look. The gravel road under our nests is covered with flat brothers and sisters — Kits like you who couldn't make a decision."

Kits have all seen the blotches that were once family.

"Be decisive," he urges.

It's not hard to imagine the Kember generational farm as a nutty Versailles for Chase of Kember — Grandpa joined by his extended network of rodent families in the string of nests.

Most activity for Grandpa lies in the lower canopy, with a great view of his domain's DMZ, the Kember front yard. Known qualities are the quantities of bulbs and birdseed. Unknown danger, though, may wait on the large farmhouse porch on a piece of worn burlap.

The champion challenger limiting Chase's dominance in the yard spreads out on the porch with one eye open, the keeper of the gate. This predator, who's welcome inside the house, is Max, the German shepherd. Here lies an aging beast of potential terror to squirrels, slow cyclists and any stranger, even neighbours.

"That dog. Have to remind myself he's on the porch. Scares the crap out of me."

"Seen those teeth? I swear that dog gets dental cleaning."

"Yeah, it cleans its teeth by grabbing pant legs, high boots and low bicycle clips."

To the Kembers, Max is a caution light and a doorbell, one that displays incredible natural algorithms in sound and movement on guard duty. *Bark, bark. Calling all Kembers.*

Chase looks down now for dark eyes looking up. "Kits. Look close to the beast. One eye looks."

Furball Grandpa Vegan might be the direct opposite of the long-in-the-tooth carnivore, but they do have farm longevity in common.

"Young Kits," he continues. "Even if the beast is sleeping, that does not make the seed-tree safe. The beast must be in the human nest."

"Does not being decisive work, Grandpa?"

"Here, young Kit. When stealing the human feed, a Kit has the need for speed."

The gang of furballs wait for elder nut direction.

Jimmy Kember steps outside, with his customary ponytail and bib overalls. "Max needs some shade, Barb. I'll let a little extra off the chain." He moves the dog's burlap mat back into the shade beyond the porch, in anticipation of a record day of heat. "Max, here's some fresh water. Last night's leftovers, too."

The good life of a porch dog on the farm. Max's viewpoint on Transvaal in the heat of the moment is shade and water.

Max positions himself with old-dog experience to gain the perfect panorama of the tree-lined double lane and front yard. Max has learned all the tricks to an expedient and extended canine life.

Why work hard when I can work smart? Master and the Missus want it simple. Old dog tricks practiced over time. *Familiar vehicle, one bark, maybe two.*

Unfamiliar sounds brings Max into full barking action. At any unfamiliar sound, the old dog barks it out like a bad cough, waiting for the Master or Missus to come out. (*"Max! No! Porch, Max. Porch, Max."*) The Max job is complete when the humans take over contact. Usually the Missus answers with leftovers, which helps Max forget the reasons for his original barks.

Max helps the Missus. Now Missus helps Max.

Grandpa Squirrel can see in those large, dark eyes what the Kits do not recognize. "Cross the beast's boundary, he'll chase us down. So Chase stays up."

The green light comes only when the old dog is inside the farmhouse or in Town on a pickup ride with Jimmy. At such a time, Chase may choose the garden buffet for a relaxed breakfast or lunch. When Max is on the porch, red light.

Right now it's yellow light. Max is still problematic when he's near his dog house with the extra-long chain, farmhouse stage-left. Max can still reach his mat and bowl at the limit of the tether — a half-circle of danger off the front of the farmhouse that prevents any approach.

This year the fading summer has seen bulb genocide. The large brood of spring squirrel kits has grown into a vortex of need over a shrivelling stock from the heat. The bird feeder fills in the corners of the squirrels' hunger. But at this moment, the motherlode is about to pop on the old walnut tree.

"Kits," he says now. "Forward to the seed tree."

"Need for speed, Grandpa?"

"No, young 'uns. It's be-decisive time."

These players are set in place, ready for the action to unravel. Four main characters: the old dog, the fat squirrel and the goat-raising odd couple. You could almost hear Grandpa Squirrel crack his paw knuckles in preparation for a hustle à la *The Color of Money*. He shoots into action, racking up the Kits in anticipation.

For the fat, lead furball, it's an established routine.

The same furry flight pattern carries Chase on his worn bark route from his leafy maple loft. First, off the branches on the yard's edge, comes an Olympic long jump to the telephone wire. This manoeuvre is what separates the older squirrels from the Kits and remaining caboodle. The jump keeps survivors at least a branch's length away from any predation.

Predation?

Lying in wait may be not just Max but weasels, mink, or possums, as well as climbing feral cats and nasty raccoons. (The hydro-wire route, it should be said, eliminates the four-legged bunch, but not attacks from above. Mr. Hawk always has a great view from above the barn, a clean lane to strike.)

Grandpa chatters as he dashes.

"Speed, lads, speed. Do not look up. Don't look down. Do not pause. Look to your claws. Speed, lads — speed."

The Kits can watch the action with no danger. The high wire leads the alpha grey squirrel to the 125-year-old walnut tree right by the porch. A mammoth pantry of nuts.

Chase scurries along the wire. He keeps his eyes up even though he could run the route blindfolded. All eyes, all efforts to avoid that slow but nasty German shepherd. Max is the only danger constant on Chase's mind. He still hasn't been able to locate the dog. *Where is the beast? Is he lurking below?*

Business as usual and no worries, with no burlap mat in sight. The line of furballs backs up along the hydro wire, back to the long jump-off branch.

"Does Grandpa see something?"

"Smell something?"

"Or hear …?"

"Shut up and pay attention. Wait for the signal."

Yet something is off on this one squalid, simmering summer day.

Chase may have been careless out of squirrel hubris. Maybe he's just slower with age; add in distractions of yummy thoughts or the excitement of having no dog in sight. Maybe for Grandpa it's just the wrong time, just the wrong place.

For the Kits, the moment reels out in slo-mo, frozen frame by frozen frame.

His four paws attached to his fat frame stretch out in flight — a flight that takes Chase to a lower wire running along the right side of the house. The wire belongs to Zorra Internet & Telephone (ZIT). His paws pull in for the grab, a synchronized hook-on.

Whoopsie.

Chase of Kember isn't that limber off the timber, today. His rear quarter fails to line up with the short front paws. The paws' reflex misses the landing target. The backup line of younger furballs on the hydro wire, and the Kits higher on the branches, make a chorus of family support.

"Thut. Thut. Thut. Thut."

Group realization. The chorus slows down in a squirrel alarm.

"Nut-thick. Nut-thick. Nut-thick."

The horror of it all.

Desperate for a balance on the high wire, Chase digs in. Sharp claws up front hit copper, while back claws dig in with a flurry, all in such a hurry. On the front-paw action, the telephone wire is a low current, but Chase hits silver on the hind-end grab. A power charge takes the opportunity for a furry detour. Houston, we have lift-off.

Sparks shoot three feet in the air.

It's ZIT for Chase.

Max has listened to the squirrels increase their chatter. The German shepherd's head lifts from the backed-up snooze spot.

Pop pop pop.

Max looks up and sees a black tennis ball with a tail of fire traversing his universe. An historian might call it a Greek fire; for a person of letters it might be a Greek tragedy. The flaming ball bounces with an explosive crack-of-a-whip.

Pop pop pop.

Onto the yellow lawn.

Chase is no more — no more than a charbroiled fluffy exaggeration, smoking at ground zero after the flaming swan dive.

The hottest temperatures on record have turned the Kember front lawn, a pride-and-joy green lawn in June, to brown, sawed-off midget fescue by August. Barbara's worst lawn in years is about to get much worse.

Smoke rises and more fireworks follow. The turf is a yellow carpet leading to an inferno. The panorama is as apocalyptic as an old dog could ever imagine. The dog greets Hell with a painful and horrendous howl.

"Ow-w-w-w-wa-a-a-a."

Max is not moving off the dirty mat.

"Ow-w-w-w-wa-a-a-a."

Barb's concentration on jars, lids and canning stops in a pickle. "Never heard that bark from Max before." The complete unfamiliarity of this dog doorbell rings a warning. Barbara doesn't let the second howl fade before she jumps into action. She turns to the window and cries out. "Jim-m-m-m-me-e-e!"

Jimmy never realized how loud his wife could get. He stops in his tractor tracks, swivelling his head from the shed to the 1865 farmhouse. He recognizes the unfamiliar sound of stress. An automatic reflex, he turns off the machine, turns, dismounts and runs.

"Jim-m-m-m-me-e-e!"

Entering through the back door, Jimmy runs through the mud room and kitchen, words and actions melting into the diorama of horror on Barb's face in the hallway. She shouts and points out the screen door. Jimmy sails forward as Barb reconfirms.

"Out front!"

Max is standing by his mat, face-forward beyond the front steps. Jimmy throws open the screen door with Barbara looking over his shoulder.

"Holy focking shit," she says.

Coarse words, to be local honest, that are not unfamiliar coming from the Missus, a retired high school teacher, or the Master right behind with speed, a professor emeritus indeed.

"My God Almighty," Jimmy says.

Off the mat, Max retreats behind Barbara. *"Ow-w-w-w-a-a-a!"*

There, splayed out on the front yard, the scene in flames sparks out a Dante Chip 'n' Dale horror story. (Jimmy would later recall hearing Jack White's frantic song about the "Fire in the Disco" ringing in his head.) Take a few seconds for the unconscious crisis-management skills to kick in. Bells are blasting. One. Two. Three. No time to relax and reflect as if water were boiling for no-hurry morning tea. The pot whistles like the Royal Mail for action.

Jimmy appeals to a higher authority. "Call the fire department! I'll get the hose."

Barbara, always practical, always a teacher, offers common sense at the worst of times. "Remember to turn the hose on!"

Off past the boundary of the yard, off on the sidelines, introductions are in order for the largest group in the nutty cast, a gathering that ignores and is ignored by all incoming participants — the Kember champion goat lineup. This crowd knows all about electricity. They stand a few hooves back from the single-wire fence. The bearded crew has never seen the likes of this before. The largest, calf-sized in black-and-white splendour, speaks up.

"Na-a-a-a too good for Cha-a-a-a-se. Na-a-a-a."

Forty-plus respond to their queen.

"Na-a-a-a. Na-a-a-a."

　　　　　　　　　　　　　　　　　　　　　　　　　　　　　LORNE EEDY

The nutty action is about to move up to launch stage two, with unfamiliar but official visitors.

Barbara's mix of home spills, school drills and farm thrills is the book on action. Past common sense it begins with the end in mind. In the end, she is not about to see her gardens up in smoke. Boundaries are set. She ignores 911 for a direct call to the home of one of her former babysitting charges. That's how rural things work. It's not the fire department; it's the local lads from Blanshard and Nissouri Townships.

"Bob, we've got a bit of a problem with the grass on fire."

"Grass on fire," Bob echoes.

"It's the front lawn — it's in flames."

Chief Bob knows the voice of his former part-time caregiver, his wife's current ride to choir practice at the Methodist Hall. She's chatty with a focking edge. But today, it's all edge, no chat.

"I'll be right there, Barb."

Bob slides into action mode, adjusting his boots and equipment belt while he shifts gears in his one-ton stake truck. He cradles the buzzing cellphone under the shoulder of his shifting-arm. He's an experienced hand at fire response, recognized and respected throughout southwestern Ontario.

Bob rose to city fire captain in a first career before taking over his family's Century Farm milk operation. The only son feels good every day, repeating the chores and path of his forefathers and foremothers. It's common experience Blanshardinians and Nissourites can count on. *("He's a lifer.")*

The Chief's experience makes the difference between a good ending and a worse one. No need to add a local disaster to next week's happy coverage in the *St. Marys Journal*. Bob, equipment and crew are several wasted kilometres south of Highway 7, while St. Marys is just minutes from the Kember farm. The direction of Bob's approach does help with the personnel and equipment pickups on the same concession road. He clicks his CB mobile as his deputy chief, Mike Pender, packed and waiting at his gate mailbox, jumps into the cab. Anybody might be calling on a cell, but the emergency frequency gets an immediate reaction. A direct radio call to his neighbours, the St. Marys Volunteer Fire Department, improves the odds for a good story in the newspaper.

"Sandy, we need your tanker. Grass fire at Jimmy's."

Bob omits the distinction of lawn versus pasture to keep things simple.

Chief Sandy McLean of the St. Marys Fire Department lets Bob take the lead out of respect, recognizing the experience on hand. Country knowledge runs both ways. Chief Sandy holds regular coffee court with Jimmy on Saturdays. The advantage of local knowledge is no need for winding address numbers; the call to "Jimmy's" is all the GPS he needs. Everyone knows the Kember Century Farm, with its two St. Marys High School prodigies who later became the Professor and the High School teacher.

Chief Bob has trained neighbouring volunteers for years and years. Every member of Sandy's fire team knows Chief Bob from Nissouri.

"Cavalry on the way, Chief," Sandy replies.

St. Marys adds an extra water tanker to the balance heading down-country.

Grass fire is the name of the flame, no matter a front lawn. Big Bob talks to himself more than to his truck-mate and 2-IC, Mike. "Have to nip it first. If the fire skips or jumps to the paddocks?" He answers his own question. "We'll set a fallback burn line second. That'll contain any breakthroughs. Two teams, Mike, divided in two. You take the boys to the fence lines. My guys will set up hose and tanker."

"Yes, Chief." Mike's good humour offers some relief. "In any case, I love barbecued goat."

The Chief runs the checklist. He considers dry grass this time of summer to be kindling set for surefire ignition.

Bob has a moment of wonder in the organized response to crises. "How the hell could a fire start at Jimmy's?" Both the Kembers are non-smokers, and it's still too early in the day for any barbecuing.

No matter, he sees wild potential for disaster in the record-breaking heat. This will be a test of all his experience and resources. Fast fire needs fast response. Bob heads for Pumper #1 at the B-N Fire Hall, still barking on the radio to get the water tanker up and going. He has six volunteers already on the way to the fire, in six different trucks.

"Mike, call Eddie and have him take charge of the parking. It'll be gridlock."

"Especially if the rubberneckers come out."

"We need to lock down the site ASAP."

The Kembers are in the northeast corner of Nissouri Township; across the concession line lies Blanshard. The response has to be orchestrated from one direction. Fortunate, considering how the Thames River divides the Townships. Transvaal is south of the Thames River and St. Marys but north of the highway. The Town's fire hall has convenient access to the highway, Town and most of the two Townships. For a response to a fire in Blanshard Township, which is a donut that surrounds St. Marys, the Blanshard fire route would need to cross a number the bridges on a ride through St. Marys.

Mike can read the boss's thoughts.

"Thank God we don't have to tour through Town. Jimmy's in our furthest Nissouri corner, but we aren't crossing into Blanshard."

Chief humour. "Unless we park on the north side, then we're in Blanshard."

All six pickups head north, followed by an equipment convoy. Nissourites can hear the equipment's progress. Ian has #1 growling and spitting out exhaust across the yard in front of the B-N fire hall. He rolls up front beside the Chief, who sparks up his team.

"Good work, lads," Bob says into the hand-held CB mobile. "We may actually beat Sandy and his crew to the Kembers.'"

Mike is off to the warming pumper, the Chief to his red super-cab, with the flashers burning yellow and orange. He passes the growling beast, #1.

"We may be first," Ian says back. "But their tanker will beat #1."

Two disadvantages for rural fire departments are age and size. The Township's limited budget explains why the capacity of #1 is only two thousand gallons. The manufacturer is all-Canadian Western Star, while the engine is a hard-core Cummins.

Tally-ho as Ian motions to the sky. Bob knows the gesture is a thank-you that the 1963 classic runs on the raptor power of high-octane gas versus sluggish diesel.

"Let 'er rip," Bob says. "Mike's behind you in the pumper."

Ian pounds the gears up, rams the shift and pushes the gas pedal to the metal.

R-r-r-r. Bang. *R-r-r-r.* Bang. *R-r-r-r.* Bang. *Cr-u-u-unch.*

Third needs work as it grinds the metal.

"Whoopsie."

R-r-r-r-r. Bang.

The straining metal and rubber gain traction in a northerly direction as #1 steers onto B-N County Road 57 north. Neighbours, along with pulled-over traffic on 57, can smell the burning launch. The in-the-know drivers react to the siren call and park at the side of the road. No wants to miss being a witness to the parade.

"Roll up the windows, honey. I'll put the AC on."

Add some marital knowledge: *"You're a little close to the ditch. Put your four-ways on."*

Mike pounds the clutch and rams the gears in an automatic rhythm. He is northward bound, set in his direction. He's off without hearing the Chief mutter as he steps up into his ride.

"I have no idea what shape the Kember well is in." Bob cradles his mobile radio for hands-free as experience goes into review. "The facts are incomplete. We need that information to act upon before we land on site."

The first spectators all stare in wonder as their seats shake while #1 blows by.

"My goodness, the noise that thing makes."

"The smell! A new experience in burnt rubber."

"Smells worse than a fire."

Bob is back, juggling his radio handset and cellphone while he steers. Experience tells him the farmhouse is the first concern. Most important for Transvaal and nearby St. Marys, the fire will not be allowed to move past the double laneway or down the barn path. Worst case would be losing the barn. Best is a brown lawn and a crispy garden. Boundaries are predetermined through years of training and experience in grass fires.

Back in Town, St. Marys' finest volunteers charge up. Chief Sandy lives four blocks from the St. Marys Volunteer Fire Department's well-stocked station. (*"I can see the entranceway when I mow the boulevard lawn."*)

This morning, the Town chief had his own home fire on the go. He was smoking his fresh lake salmon from Friday's day off at Goderich when his buzzer alarm went off. Automatic for Sandy — when alarm goes off, the smoker goes off. Alarm buzzers continue a web pattern across Town in order to pull the whole team together. Like the B-N, members of his Town team will take eight to ten minutes to the 6th Concession, beating the equipment. Not one but two state-of-the-art pumpers follow, minutes behind. Impressive stuff to their country cousins.

"Man, those guys have all the best in everything. Two pumpers?"

"Town of St. Marys has a great tax base."

"Two pumpers?"

"Fire is an apple-pie-and-motherhood issue. So they spend it."

"Size of their tanker? For Town?"

"Money, money."

Chief Bob wants the Town's tubby tanker, Big Red. "We will need those five thousand gallons," he tells Sandy.

Chief Sandy accelerates two-team cooperation, juggling his cellphone and mobile radio.

"Scottie, get Big Red up and going."

"Right, Chief. Beam it up in four minutes."

"Randy. Report to Big Bob. He'll be on site and in charge."

His group of lads are second to none in their response time. Time is a point of community pride among the thousands of volunteer firefighters in Ontario.

Time contains damage. Time saves lives. They're volunteers, so bragging rights come with the territory, along with the satisfaction of working with one's neighbours to limit a grass fire.

The Town volunteers have their own set of well-practiced routines for Town and Country. But it's not often that Big Red makes a guest appearance. Is she quick? As quick as a five-thousand-gallon tub can be. Sandy is giving his final orders from the front lot of their fire hall.

"Rev 'er up, Scottie. Don't let the RPM drop below four thousand or she'll stall."

"Never a problem, Chief. Big Red knows the feel of my spurs."

The close-by Town neighbours can just walk out to their shaded front porches, hot sidewalks or yellow lawns to catch the drama unwinding from this end.

The alarm siren over the steeple of the castle-lookalike town hall wails warnings. After the pager buzzers go off, pickups across St. Marys light up with their green blinkers. In a choreograph of fire hall and town hall, sirens are followed by the wailing of a convoy in motion. First, up from the fire station, then from the town hall steeple. The emergency sound from high up can be heard ringing around the confluence valley on which the Town sits. Jimmy, Barbara and Max, if not distracted by a flaming front lawn, would hear the echo all the way down the Thames River south to Transvaal.

Radio, TV or lawnmower may block out the warning, but not so lucky for the Town dogs. All the sirens cause a cacophony of barking:

"Luna. Baby. What's wrong?"

"Don't cry, Teddy."

"Spike, Mommy's here."

After the official sirens, the emergency convoy passes through Town.

The Chief's blazing truck and the two wailing pumpers offer conventional warning, but those in the know wait for Big Red.

If someone was playing loud music or mowing the lawn, they might miss the siren call — but no one, deaf or distracted, misses the eruption of Big Red firing up.

The coordinated emergency response is automatic. Country polite comes to Town. Driving Citizens pull over to avoid the racing volunteers in their assortment of pickups. New residents, visitors and aliens would think one thing:

"Crazy driving."

Quick local justification for the means of driving:

"Never been an accident."

Volunteers and Chief Sandy drive pickups, period. Dobson Ford is in the lead as the source for choice rides. The Chief drives the only red one. The assortment of trucks all have tiny green blinkers that give a soft glow accompanied by flashes under their windshield.

"My girlfriend thinks it's kind of sexy. I leave them on when we park."

"Park? You idiot. You have your own apartment."

"I'm telling you. Can't hold her back when that green goes off."

"Apartment."

"Well, not after hockey practice. Warms up the cab quicker."

The two pumpers bomb down Queen Street on the path of the rocketing pickups. A ways back, heard long before it can be seen, comes Big Red. Big Red's siren blows different, a sick-dog howl recognized by all those in the know. Or is it a sick Canada goose?

O-o-o-o-huh-huh-huh. *O-o-o-o*-huh-huh-huh.

Seven minutes is the average get-to for Chief Sandy's lads. Transvaal takes four extra minutes. "Chief, Randy and most of the lads will arrive first. I have Pumper #1, #2 behind. Scottie's kicking our rear end through Town. Big Red is full and ready. Add another three or four minutes."

Locals having their Saturday morning coffee in the downtown can hear it a-coming. They stop slurping to marvel at Big Red doing a power left on Water Street.

R-r-r-r-ri-p-p-p. R-r-r-r-ri-p-p-p. Rub-bub-bub-bub.

Scottie prays no one's in the accessible parking in front of Dick's Milk & Variety. The coffee witnesses across the street hold their noses with a gasp.

"Look! The back two axles are off the ground."

"That's an awful stink."

"Hey, it's Scottie!"

"Scottie?"

"Driving Big Red."

Everybody waves at Scottie. Scottie smiles and nods with two hands reining in the beast.

Bang. *Gr-i-i-nd.* Bang. *Gr-i-i-nd.* Bang. *Er-r-r-r-r.* Bang. *Er-r-r-r.*

Scottie drops into third, then to second at the exact turn of the wheel. He lets the clutch up, hoping to slide around the corner. Once Big Red's nose is pointed south, he pounds up two gears. *Gr-i-i-nd.* Bang. *Er-r-r-r-r. Gr-i-i-nd.* Bang. *Er-r-r-r-r.*

St. Marys keeps its streets paved and dirt-free for no dust-up. But Big Red nonetheless fluffs out a cascade of burnt rubber smoke. And Big Red runs on stinky diesel too. The oohs and aahs follow it all through Town.

More impressive than Formula One, the five-thousand-gallon Big Red negotiates the hairpin turn without taking out parked cars, Nosey Parkers with their java drinks and the variety store on the corner with its owner, Dick, watching as usual in the doorway.

Out front in a reckless lead, the flock of pickups hit a hundred kilometres plus, passing through the thirty-kilometre-per-hour recreation zone at the south edge of Town. Next is Chief Sandy, followed by the brand-new Pumper #1 and the older but reliable Pumper #2. The vehicles pound the hot asphalt south to the edge of Town, past the Swim Quarry rubberneckers. All windows are down in the double-cab fire trucks, so the Quarry swim crowd wave at friends, neighbours and relatives in response. Nobody can help but notice what's bringing up the rear.

Whoop. Whoop. Whoop.

Big Red shakes the high dive as it chugs by at an amazing eighty-five clicks.

"That's my Uncle Scottie. Wave, guys."

"Tell Uncle Scottie that truck stinks … and the noise it makes."

Sandy's on his CB, checking on the team. Scottie's concentrating on speed. "Chief, my boots would be dragging on hot asphalt if I pushed them any harder to the floorboards."

Big Red passes the cement plant to drag up the incline named Dickie Hill; it's tricky. Ian feels gravity drop the velocity to thirty-five kilometres at the crest. Scottie lets the tanker coast up with full throttle, then he shifts down two gears. *Gr-i-i-nd.* Bang. *Gr-i-i-nd.* Bang.

He watches the RPMs drop to four thousand as he crests the hill. He shifts back up.

Bang. *Gr-i-i-nd. Er-r-r-r.* Bang. *Gr-i-i-nd. Er-r-r-r.*

Scottie can see the dust clouds ahead on the first right south of Town, heading west on Concession 6.

Whoop whoop whoop.

Coming from the south, Big Bob has his Dodge Work Wagon's pedal rammed to the floor, lights a-blasting. Without slowing down for the Highway 7 crossover, he powers a right onto the 6th Concession, where fading dust tells him his team is on site.

Bob has the planned work delegated for grass-fire containment. His cab-mate, Rolf, part-time deputy co-chief (a Swiss dairy farmer by day), instructs the incoming extra help. Town participation gives encouragement to their country cousins. The B-N lads need few instructions under their talented Chief.

Rolf finishes a boot zip and buttons up his jacket. Helmet on and adjusted to look up. "Bob, there's Jimmy on the porch. With his garden hose."

The Chief powers past the double laneway, right into the ditch, then up on the fence line. He freezes a look on his deputy. "Kind of limp, eh?"

Both doors open, they're out on the run.

"Don't underestimate the hose on an old goat," Rolf says, then splits off to the left to join up with Randy. "Maybe something's on the barbecue?"

Sometimes a little humour lightens up hard work.

Even the water from a soft hose helps with the containment plan. Jimmy's saving the porch, if not the Century Farmhouse. Forget the front lawn and gardens, though — they've been burnt to a crisp by the furball critter.

Big Bob is on with his big response plan. Cavalry arrives with the *big* advantage of that plus-size tanker truck. Big Red pulls in two minutes and thirty-five seconds after the first and second pumpers, parking off the concession, up close.

Chief Sandy joins up with both teams of volunteers gathered on the farm. He stands in the expanding dust with his CB mobile in his pocket. "Focking great. Freeze our nuts in winter. Choke breathing the dust in summer."

B-N's #1 is on the west driveway entrance, pumping hard. Four firefighters on the Town pumpers wait with hoses in hand as Big Red slides in. The St. Marys team attaches four hoses, hitting the ripping flames dead on. Four double teams direct the water power, all nozzles blazing. Scottie and two others are on the dials, gauges and valves. All participants get at it in a practiced drama under the direction of Big Bob.

At Sandy's direction, Big Red has landed in a perfect position beside the two pumpers.

Max is quiet, backed up on the porch, his job complete. All this action, all these strangers are past his treat grade.

The first responders always attract fans to their siren call. The larger cast of fire-chasers has skipped the 6th Concession today, though, in this record dry summer. With a lack of visibility through the entrails of dust, what's there to see?

The first right on bad gravel south of Town restricts the adrenaline for a gravel-road adventure.

"Just washed my car."

"Another field fire. Lots of smoke, nothing substantial burns."

"What about a barn fire?"

"Not pretty if the animals aren't out."

"Remember the MacKay hog barn last year?"

(The room fills with silence at the thought of a complete hog operation gone.)

"Worst dust I've seen since summer of '73."

The goats have little curiosity about that which does not fill their gut. They give a bare glance at what seems to be human chaos unfolding, with the masked volunteers, that terror Max, and the Missus and Master, not to forget a few Transvaal neighbours, all drawn into the inferno of activity. There's so much red, with the five mechanical beasts that roar and spew a mass of snakes that spit both water and fog. Over on their right, the gravel road in front of the paddock is clogged with the smaller metal beasts that brought the humans. Back in the fog of the yard, masked humans wrestle with those horrid serpents. Another set of humans stand still out of the action. *"Na-a-a-a go-o-d. Na-a-a-a go-o-o-od."* All beards point forward in amazement at the vast supply of two-legged animals running hither and thither. The goat team have never, ever imagined that humans existed in these numbers.

Herd consensus is unanimous. They have never seen such a shocking display of fire, flame and brimstone. Her subjects wait for royal assent. The calf-sized queen of her subjects shakes the white beard on her black face. *"Na-a-a-a. Na-a-a-a, ne-e-v-v-e-er-r-r be-fo-o-r-r-r-re."*

The response by all her subjects ripples down the fence line:

"Na-a-a-a go-o-o-od. Na-a-a-a go-o-o-od."

This oral vote of affirmation goes unheard by Max, the remaining squirrels in the canopy, and the masked and unmasked humans. The herd moves on. Queenie knows the annual Royal Winter Fair trip will be kid's play compared to the donnybrook unfolding here today. She also knows something about the fresh straw in the back pasture paddock:

"Still moi-oi-oi-st."

Both fire chiefs work their sides of the yard, congratulating their individual teams on their efforts. (Later, back at the Town fire hall, Chief Sandy will leave his crew with bragging rights, losing two minutes off their ETA. Big Bob, back at the B-N fire station, will remind his guys how they came farther but still got there first.) The persistent fire attempts to move toward the barn buildings, forgetting the house. The firefighters counter any moves. Big Red and Town Pumper #2 cover the centre stage of flames and smoke before the wide porch. Their country cousins' equipment, the complete inventory, dampens down the opposite borders; first order are the outbuildings and barn. Town Pumper #1 helps with a grunt of power.

"Randy. Arch the water toward the pump shed. Connect up with the B-N water line."

Pumper #1 responds, sucking on Big Red's reservoir of five thousand gallons. An impressive display of water power by any fire department's standard. One Town team has saddled up to help the two B-N groups in play on the east side.

"Ian, big man, haven't seen you since the Nissouri Fair."

(The lads aren't thinking about the flames at hand but a past tug-of-war competition between neighbours.)

"Wes, buddy, thought you Town guys were trying to forget that one."

"Night before, too much time boating at the Summerfest beer tent. Not next year, though — take the warning, my friend."

Wes, Ian and their fellow warriors look up, without orders, to the porch. Ian yells above the din, accompanied by thoughtful nods to the distraught Kember farm family.

"Good job, Jimmy. We have it under control."

A group of masked men push anything turned crispy or gone to charcoal back toward the fire epicentre with their specialized rakes. Another team damp-pads the risky borders with the precision of Danny the janitor at St. Marys High School (a principled man, famous with a wet mop). A border has been created. For the first time in the last hour, Barbara thinks the front flower gardens and side vegetable garden might have a future.

The neighbours have one thought. *"Glad it's not our place."*

Rubbernecking Nosey Parkers drive by in droves:

"Jimmy doesn't smoke, but he does barbecue."

"Haven't seen any lightning today. Or was it wet hay?"

"Where does Jimmy dump his used charcoal, eh?"

Jimmy has moved past the stone house and outbuildings to work on saving the treeline, including that big old oak tree. The volunteer firefighters' support gives him dim hope for a burnt but still shady front yard. He consoles himself beside the old oak tree.

A little ahead of expectations, with teamwork, the good story is working out. The former grass is soaked as the smoky fire fades to a steam-room simmer, then to wisps of mist. It's all fog to the herd, who've never seen so much smoke before. Everyone but the Kembers can start to relax, with the air clearer around the farm. The goat herd have headed off to greener pastures, nodding their little beards to royal decree.

"Na-a-a-a so ba-a-a-ad, na-a-a-a-a ba-a-a-ad. Wo-o-o-rk like a her-er-er-d."

Jimmy congratulates himself. Although his garden hose lacks well pressure, it helped keep destruction at bay. The front porch's pine floor and steps have taken more than enough water. He's stunned by the apocalyptic action but satisfied with his small contribution.

"I told them the well is low," he reminds himself. "Bob called St. Marys for a second tanker."

Max stays back on the porch now with Barbara. Both are silent witnesses to the horror of it all. Not often is Barbara Kember stuck for something to say. Max wonders if this somehow means the end of dog treats.

The height of chaos passes a breaking point. No one has seen the goats head out, all beards down on the job at hand, oblivious to the outcome of the day's events.

"*H-m-m-m-m. Wet grass not ba-a-a-ad.*"

Their focus is past the foggy pandemonium and on to thoughts of food in greener pastures — the back paddock down the fence line near the water tank. They leave the breakfast theatre to enjoy a contemplative lunch.

"*Ni-i-i-ice.*"

Goats look for greens in the same way that the coffee klatch relishes the bean. Goats first must look to the large Nubian, their queen, who's the size of a Holstein calf.

"*Moo-o-o-ove along, ladies. Moo-o-o-ove along.*"

Chapter 3

Back on the home front, the crisis calms from flames to smoke, to steam and smoulder. The well pump has dried up, but Jimmy still stands, holding the dry, limp hose on the porch.

Barbara takes action. "Boys will need something cool. I'll bring out the ice-cold lemonade."

The boys would rather have a few cold brewskis instead, but those closest to the porch give a polite nod of acknowledgement. Jimmy comes to, watching his wife disappear through the screen door. By the time the volunteers and a few nosey neighbours have gathered around the porch, the screen door opens again.

"Jimmy," Barbara says. "Pass the cups around. Mother will pour." A few chuckles in the group. "Make sure the boys have a seat."

Jimmy plays a stiff traffic policeman, with stacked plastic cups in both outstretched arms. His hands make slight moves, directing left, right and a final sweep across the wide steps. The boys grab a cup as they line the vast porch.

"Thanks, Mrs. Kember," some of the men call out.

"Who said anything about my mother?" she replies. "Focking *Barbara*, boys."

A full chorus. "Thanks, Barbara."

Over ice-cold drinks in plastic punch cups, the nutty story is refreshed.

Cut to the Chase. For the front porch group, he's done gone to the finish line. For the Kits, no more Grandpa stories. The second generation looks up to the first generation of uncles and cousins. The horror of it all permeates the canopy over the front yard, while the humans sip their lemonade. The 6th Concession extended squirrel family is confident nonetheless, knowing they've learned their lessons well from the greatest of all furballs, Chase. Max is not alone on the porch in sensing the great sadness in the air, from the heirs apparent, up above. Jimmy is sad too, as he grabs a pail and stick to whisk the sad remains away. Ground zero is a dark reminder of a wild day that needs to disappear behind him. The first witnesses over by the barn are now indifferent to anything but their stomachs. The herd thought has moved to greener, moist pastures, back in the shade of the old oak tree.

Max can hear the one voice from the herd:

"Moo-o-o-ove aaa-a-along, La-a-a-dies. Moo-o-o-ove a-a-a-a-along. Na-a-a-a to-o-o-o ba-a-a-ad. Too-o-o-o the grea-a-a-at tree-e-e-e."

And the chorus from the herd agrees:

"Na-a-a-a. Na-a-a-a. Na-a-a-a."

The herd has a group consciousness on what the great tree means. For over a hundred years, the old oak tree has sheltered the sweetest of grass, soft enough for a pre-toddler. The taste of wet, fresh greens under shade, away from the human heat. To human ears, the volunteers and neighbours, the goats remain in the background, silent witnesses. The goats are quite the conversationalists, though, if you understand their meaning. Ask Max:

Dumb beasts. They never shut up. A good nip would straighten them out. Love to bite into that big bossy calf.

Max, in his canine, quiet way, holds the full story. He hears the chatter, the change in tone. With one eye open even from the back of the porch, he saw it all unfold. From the countdown and the ignition to the flame-ball landing, all is seared in his memory. His lips, though, are sealed.

On the human side, Jimmy takes a sip and pipes up on the porch. All seats taken, he's a standing witness.

"Gentleman, thanks for the quick response to our family farm."

His punch cup reaches across the expanse of the great porch.

"The lawn can be fixed. The flower beds replanted. We'll buy new bird feeders from Doug's."

Jimmy cracks a smile and gets a little laugh all around, followed by head nods. "It's all stuff. All replaceable." More heads nods with sips. "Gentlemen, you saved our home, our outbuildings and old Frankie out back."

Smiles and chuckles at the thought of the fat pig who's always a highlight for tour groups on the Kember farm.

"Thank you."

For the moment, Barbara is another silent witness, letting her husband set the tone.

"I was about to start the tractor," Jimmy continues.

"Jimmy," Barbara pipes up. "The tractor was going."

"I had just started up the tractor. I heard Max moan."

"No, Jimmy. I first heard Max moan. And called you."

"I turned the tractor off."

"After you heard me yell your name."

Jimmy turns to Barbara with a blank look. Barbara leans back and lets it rip. *"Ji-i-i-i-i-m-e-e-e!"*

Max gives an unnoticed yelp of surprise, and the whole porch gets an imagined shot of Jimmy coming to attention on the tractor.

Jimmy looks back to his audience of lemonade-sippers. "I could hear Barbara call me. I turned off the tractor and came running."

Chief Bob, who already knows the story from the kitchen call all the way up to the limp garden hose, fixes a look on the centre of the front yard. "You say the black stretch there is from a flaming squirrel?"

Max can agree that those details were accurate. The Master is an academic.

"Hit the electric wires somehow, digging in," Jimmy says.

Barbara is not out of the technological loop. "Jimmy, I think it was the telephone wire."

That blank look returns. "Wire or wires. Stuck his paws into the wires."

Big Bob shakes his head, looking back and forth at the front porch lineup. "Telephone wire. ZIT."

"ZAT," is the automatic fun-bunch reply from the group, the conditioned local reply. A men's chorus of silent chuckles, head-shakes and pursed smiles backs up the tragedy.

The Professor ignores the group muse. He is fixated on that black skid mark. "Chase hit the dry grass in a burning ball."

"Chase?" someone asks.

"Don't ask," Jimmy says. "We have one big fat squirrel raiding our birdseed feeder."

"Focking thing is into my tulip bulbs," Barbara chimes in. "Thinks they're escargots."

The front-porch group collect their thoughts, take another sip on the lemonade. Someone has to ask the question:

"We can see the fried squirrel, burnt ground zero. But how can you tell it was Chase?"

"My goodness," Jimmy says. "Did you see the size of that tar ball? That's Chase for sure."

If anyone were to look, they would see Max nodding his head at his Master.

Chief Sandy steps into the conversation, drawing from a surprising vault of experiences. "I've seen raccoons, groundhogs, skunks … squirrels … fried on generators, conductors and a few high-voltage wires. Can't forget that badger caught in the utility substation. Generator burned all the fur off him — he walked out steaming. Looked like an ugly baby seal."

One of the volunteers pipes up. "I was there, Chief. Ugly fat Chihuahua."

A chorus of grand laughter circles the porch. Chief Sandy is not finished, his eyes pivoting to two o'clock while he continues the inventory. "Even a few reptiles, with assorted snakes, tree frogs, various turtles and one huge iguana getting zapped. I've seen seagulls, crows and sparrows. Even owls and one bald eagle fried."

"Chief, they should profile you on *Animal Kingdom*," someone says.

Another volunteer pipes up. "Remember Al's dog that fell through the ice?"

Sandy grinds on with his description of the Noah's ark of volunteer rescue. "And yes, lots of chipmunks and squirrels."

"We don't do cats in trees, eh, Chief?"

"Cats," Sandy scoffs. "We just tell the owners. When the cat is ready, the cat will come down."

Sandy doesn't stop before making the big point. "Never ever, in thirty years in St. Marys and surrounding Townships, have I seen a grass fire — that's the qualifier, grass fire — never seen a grass fire started by a squirrel."

The porch crowd nod in unanimous agreement.

The master gardener can't continue to hold her silence when it comes to *her* garden. "It's not just my lawn. It's my garden, too. Gone. And all because of one big old, fat" — the chorus of volunteers lean in as they listen in anticipation — "*focking* furball, at that."

Barbara points to the centre of death.

"That's what you get when you eat my tulip bulbs."

She adds in a few finger shakes for a Barbie poke.

"Focking rat."

Sandy knows, Big Bob knows, Max knows, and most on the porch know Barbara's preference for dropping the f-bomb. Even Sandy's wife, who works at Doug's Hardware, has mentioned Barbara's f-preference, so the St. Marys chief has a little background understanding. And Evelyn's a Newfie.

"She uses the f-word right in the store, talking about those squirrels," she told Sandy once. "It's more like a Newfoundland 'f,' which rhymes with *stock*, or *stocking*. That takes a bit of the bite out of that horrid word."

Marital humour when Sandy looked out their back kitchen window at the scurrying below their bird feeder. "Focking squirrels," he chuckled to himself.

"Sandy, stop it. You know I don't like the word."

Now, on the Kember Century Farm, with the day marked as a success, the firemen start to hand out the "best in squirrel" lines.

"Sure was a fat one. Is there Weight Watchers for squirrels?"

"Should have pushed back the tray of nuts, eh?"

"Too much time watching *Chip 'n' Dale*."

"No, Chase preferred *Rocky and Bullwinkle*."

"Chase, buddy, you should have stuck to pumpkin seeds. Those walnuts, acorns and sunflower seeds are high-calorie."

And the volunteer gardener. "Those tulip bulbs are cholesterol beasts."

A few more quips and quacks follow the small groups as they waddle in their wet boots out the double laneway. Big Red and #1, last of the arrivals, jump off first, leaving their dust and exhaust trails for others. Through the din of engine starts, the two tankers can be heard fading in the different directions. Bang. *Gr-i-i-nd. Er-r-r-r.* Bang. *Gr-i-i-nd.* Bang. *Er-r-r-r.*

Pickups back up onto the concession and take off left and right into separate dust trails. *"Whoa. Careful with the u-turn there, Randy."*

Barbara cleans up the dishes amid the distant rumble of equipment moving off. The ashes stoke her thoughts on a direct rural route to *the* sore subject.

"Focking enough is too much," she says to herself as she leans against the kitchen counter.

Master and dog still stand at their silent posts on the porch. Jimmy can feel the heat rising behind him in a lightning rod also known as Barbara Kember. Max holds out small hope for a treat. His stomach growls. He wishes that he could be a goat and walk off.

The screen door opens and Barb barks it out. "Jimmy. This is *the* sign. The focking sign to sell the farm."

Barbara has had enough after years and years of trials and tribulations on the farm. She's left a trail for change, leaving the real estate paper around, complaining about the strain of doing laundry with the iffy well and whatnot, and bringing up evidence of happy neighbours who have moved off their farms.

"The Neals bought up on Douglas Drive," she announced a few months back, bringing that day's *St. Marys Journal* into the living room. "Nice lots."

Jimmy just burrowed deeper into his novel.

"They have a garden," she persisted, "and look — here's one for sale with a hot tub. Norman Morrison is having an open house next door this Sunday."

No reaction from the armchair. Never a reaction at the breakfast table or in the bedroom, either.

Barbara began to shift tactics, attacking her husband's tight purse. With a good accounting of what needs to be done around the Century Farm, she waded in on future infrastructure costs: cracks in the foundation, lack of insulation and curling shingles. And what about wiring? *They* could be the next burnt critters, after all. So she hit him on the cost of well-being.

"Have you asked Dan Graham for a quote?"

Ding. Got him well in the pocket again.

"The chimney will be a problem. Need to call Ed on the pointing."

Ding ding.

Today the goat train has come to a crashing halt at high noon on the porch of the Kember Century Farm home. Barbara stops at the steps' edge and sets down her tea towel. Jimmy is trying to retreat with the refreshment leftovers through the screen door but Barbara turns to full body contact, pushing a finger into his shoulder. She grabs and squeezes the imagination of her husband's tight purse.

"Ever since retirement, there's more goats," she says. "And more goats. An army of goats."

"A herd, Barbara."

"There's an army of them. Look out there."

The goats have kept to the faraway back paddock in all the commotion. She points out there anyways.

"They are a focking army of them, eating up our pasture. I am seeing more milk. I am doing a focking shift on the milker every afternoon. But where's the cheese? Jimmy, where's the focking cheese? The labour commitment gets bigger. The product gets smaller."

Jimmy's chances of retreating behind the screen door are fading.

"Matter of time, Barbara."

"Your time has come, Jimmy. The dream is bigger. And your energy is getting smaller." She shakes her head at him. "Where's the cheese, Jimmy?"

She hits hard. "Down with the farm."

The Kembers have always lived on the farm, but never relied on the farm. The Professor has a full title: Professor Doctor James P. Kember. Jimmy taught Mathematics at Western University, a thirty-five year stint, followed now by two years of retirement. His father, James B. Kember, milked a large quota of Holsteins full time.

"Dad died with his boots on," he says. "Where he wanted to be, on the farm."

Barbara is a realist.

"Focking died mucking the stalls."

A point well taken by Jimmy, stuck in a farm tradition passed through generations on the Century Farm, that of shovelling shit.

Goats are easy labour compared to cows. Further, the farm is a pleasant distraction from academia. Jimmy has had fun massaging a few kids into a growing family of Nubian goats. A small effort before and after school has now expanded in his retirement.

"Jimmy, you might be the morning man," she says with a head jerk toward him and a point back to the milking shed. "But I'm the one milking those focking goats in the afternoon."

"It's easy stuff compared to all the bull and cow stuff." Jimmy has both hands stuck out upside-down as he gestures with a set of horns. Barbara drops the red-cape challenge from her husband.

For years and years, Jimmy has milked the idea of the goats producing cheese.

As the math and business Prof, he's processed the manufacturing side of things into an impressive case study that works out the goat equation on the Century Farm.

As the farmer, though, he never gets to the cheese.

Yes, he builds a great milking herd. The goat team approaches sixty members, surrounded by the latest in Swiss technology. While Barbara combs out and curries the ladies, with mixed results in baby socks and toque-and-mitt sets for the hospital gift shop, Jimmy takes pride in his prize breeding of the herd mix.

Yes, he's rejigged a barn shed into the new milking shed. He's had it plumbed for the stainless-steel washing equipment, with new concrete floors to support the state-of-the-art cooling tanks, the tiles sloped for power-wash drainage. More stainless steel surrounds the room to chair-rail height, then green plaster to a hunter green ceiling, crisscrossed with pipes of all sizes. The viewer perspective is interrupted by six smart TVs. It's a showplace for future cheese.

Jimmy would never confess this under torture, not even toe-tickling, but his tight back and arthritic feet sigh in relief at the thought of surrender. The new well and the new roof to come — the biweekly payments on the shiny MotoMotion tractor in the shed — all weigh down his thoughts with costs. Those five-kilo-metre drives to Town seem so long on snowy nights when Barbara has a meeting or a choir practice, or needs some shortening at the IGA. (Jimmy stops to wonder why she can't run to the IGA on her own.)

His mind makes an easier adjustment to the short drive to the Sunriser. He could catch the coffee klatch seven days a week if the mood struck him.

"I could walk," Jimmy sometimes says to himself. "All pavement. Drive the convertible."

Later that afternoon, as he stands, staring out his study window at the Dante panorama of charred turf outside, Jimmy shuffles forward then back on his heels, in silent acquiescence.

"A come-and-go yack. And a coffee. Every day."

Hm-m-m-m.

Max can see the smile on Master's face as he gets up from the rug and heads for the porch for a drink of water.

Barbara, meanwhile, is ripe and ready for the urban life of the small Town. She's joined up to a big list of activities already, which include the quilting club bicentennial project and the horticultural club's civic gardens. There would be convenience, with feta cheese a walk away at the IGA, the Curling Club without a stormy drive, dog-walking just out the door on the array of Town pathways or a close-up interaction with her beloved Methodist Hall.

All in all, it looks better and better being in St. Marys than getting into a frozen or bake-oven car for a five-kilometres drive.

"I could walk and get milk," she says to herself on the porch in the late afternoon sun as she knits Aldert a Maple Leafs logo scarf for his birthday. "No more focking goat milk. Nice to forget chores. And that focking fat squirrel."

That focking comment on the squirrel moves her to a millisecond of respectful silence over a dead adversary.

"My God," she reminds herself. "There's a focking colony of them on the concession. There'll be Chase II no doubt."

Max lifts his head when he hears "Chase." He waits for the Missus to make the next move.

Bigger thoughts rise to her field of vision than the apocalypse of a burnt and dusty front yard. Barb looks at Max from her rocker.

Max looks up at her. *Missus is talking to me.* Barbara wades into his wide-open eyes.

"Jimmy needs to part ways with those focking goats."

Max understands the name of Jimmy, his Master and the name of those dumb beasts.

"Goats are in disposition mode." Max notices the Missus raise her tone. No *focking* necessary with the way she looks out at the pasture.

Max and the Missus are both caught off guard when the screen door opens with a groan and a slap.

Jimmy shuffles onto the porch, both dazed and confused after a big day, nodding his head.

"A sign, yes. To sell. Yes. It's time, Barb.

Barbara plans to dial up her favourite read, the Toronto *Globe*, to pay for a word ad she has contemplated and refined over a long time. She always knew the *Globe* would be the venue. She and Jimmy both enjoy the thick Saturday edition Jimmy buys at the IGA after his coffee klatch. (She has that figured out too: *"Nice getting delivery in Town. Or pick it up at Dick's."*)

Barbara, in a possible marital balance with Jimmy's secret on the pig trough whey, never confesses to a secret life with the *Globe*'s Business Opportunity classifieds. She can hide out with her interests at the Carnegie Library reading room. For thousands of page turns over the years, Barbara has lived through dreams hocked in the City newspaper. As a retired high-school teacher, an avid reader, and a *Globe* Opportunity ad addict, she now jumps at the chance to craft a selling message. Jimmy is stuck on a proper burial stop for Chase while Barbara rolls full-throttle ahead on a green light to exit the black landscape.

That evening, in a classified word daze, the Professor just nods his head at all the wording variables. "I'd say it all in the first two words. 'Say cheese.'"

Barb gives a big nod to her husband. Are they in sync on her select choice of a cheese header? He's dazed.

"Say cheese," she echoes. She puts more pucker into it. *"Say cheese."*

Jimmy is not in the mood for any more massage of the message. Barbara pounds it out with pluck and pucker, with an exclamation mark.

"'Say Cheese! Presto, you're out of the Big Smoke.'"

She's out there on a marketing rocket. After years and years of waiting to roll out the final sale, it's finally down with the farm. Barbara might delete the word "you're." Maybe keep the "presto" part out of the Big Smoke.

Jimmy plugs in his nickel to stop her thoughts. "Barbie, you've been ruminating on the focking sale for the last ten years, at least. Just give me the ad, please."

He picks up pen and paper and adjusts his bifocals in an academic way.

"Okay, now listen up," he says, reading over Barbara's copy. "'Say Cheese! Presto, out of the Big Smoke. IN.'" He looks up. Barbie has never seen her husband anywhere close to the concept of a life change, and now here he is in dictation. "*IN* in caps. IN in caps leads to the next line. 150 Acre Goat Farm, idyllic Transvaal near St. Marys. STOP. Sixty plus prize goats. STOP. Show, dairy proven. STOP."

Barbara interrupts. "Stop the STOPs. You're not taking a telegraph. 'Period' works."

"Okay then. 'Restored 1865 home.' Period. 'Registered Century Farm.' Period. 'Opportunity calls to Norm Morrison.' Period. 'Black Aces Realty 519-555-5555.' Period."

"There's a few *ins* we could omit," he goes on. "And it's not *Norm*; never has been."

"Stop," she says. "I think you got them all. Period. And Norman, okay."

"Stop? I've already cut the *please* before *call*, and if I'm spending dollars on up-marketing words, *idyllic* and *Century Farm* stay. Period."

"Stop there," she says. "Let's not quibble over per-letter costs for *Say Cheese*, but *Big Smoke* is two words. *Toronto* will work."

In the end, the couple want the same thing: to add personal flare to fire up interest. Barbie has Jimmy in full motion now, so she gears down to listen and nod while Jimmy gets sentimental.

"We want fresh but respectful stewardship," he says, setting the pen and paper on the coffee table. "These are generational lands we have loved for so long."

He is lost for a moment. "For generations."

"Amen," she says.

"And we'll get your buddy Norman on the search ..."

The Missus begins to sing.

"For a little cabin in the west, for our little nest..."

Jimmy has a few more wrinkles on his furrowed brow than he did the day before. "In St. Marys, right?"

Barbara has one thumb down while her left hand points to ground zero. "Down with the farm."

Max watches the Missus pound at her talking machine. Second call on that eventful day, after the Country 911 to Big Bob. The front yard has now changed from a yellowy brown to ash black. Jimmy's face is somewhere between those two colours — a brown ash. The Kembers and their front yard are showing a dry face forward after all that morning drama and lemonade.

"Norman. Are you out and about?"

Norman Morrison, known with affection in St. Marys and environs as "Stormin' Norman," is the most eclectic roustabout of real estate sales in Town and all about. An in-the-know high on the gossip chain. A regular stool-warmer stage left from the pass-through window at the Sunriser. Norman Morrison has the skill to balance Town and rural. The fifth estate comes first, he knows. He's the man who knows all, almost before it happens.

Norman answers right away. "Sorry to hear about the fire, Barb. Are you all right?"

Norman never asks about or refers to the squirrel incident. Even if it had been murder, robbery, kidnapping or arson, he would damper any heat. Stormin' keeps it simple.

Free hand on her forehead, eyes closed, Barbara sums up the motivation.

"There's been fire enough for me. Fired up enough to list the focking farm, Normy."

Chapter 4

"Greg, I never tire of the great view."

"It's a view master."

"More like a dominatrix with condo fees."

John settles with his cappuccino and the newspaper into a woven lounge chair, as Lake Ontario stretches out behind. Greg ignores the read for now, concentrating on a delicious coffee in the delightful beams of the morning sun.

Great digs down and close to central City action. It's a smooth-flowing life.

Their *Globe* arrives fresh at the brushed-steel entrance door in their climatized hallway at seven-fifteen sharp each morning. It's a natural process. Don't forget the rubber trees in plastic ochre pots that garnish the doorways.

The favourite sections are sorted on the granite countertop. Top of the list is dragged to the expansive deck with the awesome view, weather permitting. All sectional residue from the *Globe* will be left in the kitchen for a late read or early recycling. The number-one read all week is *The Report on Business*.

It's not so much a paper chase as a paper seduction.

Opportunities in the *RoB* do not state "For Sale" but rather "For Investment," which sucks the reader in. Forget thinking of money up front — this is an opportunity to invest. John is first up, mornings, dictating his personal sort. The business section is held in his left hand, balanced by the sheer power of contemplation, while he coddles his John-crafted cappuccino in his right.

John studies the bean with academic resolve, searching, sampling for that high-above taste. Every morning starts with reflection on the quest for the perfect result, followed by the *Globe.*

The Bean Book of John starts with Rule One, far from any coffee bushes. It's off the farm, no matter the cow, as long as it's 3% milk. John always goes for the cow that fills those returnable jugs unavailable in the organic grocery. It takes a safari search of best-before dates in the large coolers of the worn variety store downstairs.

Rule Two is supply management, with the internet order of raw cane sugar: Anita's natural cane sugar, hand-milled in Kelowna, British Columbia.

Rule Three in the Bean Book is right off the cover: the bean. Medium-roasted, Central American, in vac bags chosen either from a lineup of walk-up roasters steps away or pre-bagged from a distance, now on the organic grocery shelf. Greg offers his geography graduate's input off the roaster's label:

"Where is Baden? It says Ontario. Southern Ontario?"

The proof is in the first sips. Notwithstanding Rule One and the 3% milk, it's Rule Two that's the deal-breaker. John quotes from the book.

"Beans provide *the* taste, and 3% is the perfect complement." (Greg is relieved John does not also milk the topics of filtration, cream content, and coffee-to-water ratio.) "But the secret of success is sweetness."

The secret is Anita's, an exotic hint of sweetness that makes the capp more complex. The dash of milled cane sugar in John's steaming milk gives the capp a hint of caramel.

"Mm-m-m-m," Greg says now as he soaks up the view of the long leafy island off the downtown lakeshore. "Caffeine and contemplation."

"The machine, the bean, the cane and voilà." John gives himself an imaginary pat on the back. "Hm-m-m-m. John, you da man."

"So good, John my man."

For a Monday, John is sticking around with his capp in his comfy lounge chair for an unusually long time.

"John, shouldn't you be off to work?"

"Got to get that last lick on my capp." And then the unexpected answer. "Booked a sick day. Seems important."

Greg almost coughs up his last licks. His partner is in, all in, for the big leap. John sips away over the top of the *Globe*, reading their future instead.

"There's a lot of big when this deal gets done," John says.

Both partners know the big balance in the 1% savings account energizes a big dream. The partners spent all day Sunday with the weekend edition of the *Report on Business* — and its whole fat shopping list of opportunities — taking a big, expedient neck-up check-up re-evaluation of their past, present and future lives:

"My God. Forget any Tech stocks."

"A short on Blackberry. The long-term on Apple. Don't underestimate the power of technology."

"Anything serving coffee, food or ice cream is a Not."

"Be prepared for Craig hitting us up. Remember his idea on 'Alley Cats Smoking BBQ'?"

"Remember the Turkey Jerky Take-Out?"

"Wow. That idea really sucked."

"There were a few who got jerked off on that deal."

"Forget any investment with the word turkey in it."

"Craig's list of dumb ideas never stops."

Stepping back from the restaurant follies, they considered all possible coffee-related investments. The cup floweth over.

"I'm not investing in a franchise named after a dead hockey player."

"A very talented defenceman."

"Couldn't drive defence in that Ford muscle car."

John shook his head. "Exotic. 1972 De Tomaso Pantera. A piece of art destroyed."

"Detroit muscle car with an Italian name, that's all."

"Still difficult in any car to change your lane going 250-plus kilometres."

"They're too expensive anyways."

"Panteras?"

"No dummy, the franchise."

Greg and John are masters of personal duality that play off each other. Everyone wants John on their quiz team. Everyone wants Greg for Charades or Pictionary. He is the entertainment between questions and during smoke breaks. Greg is never picked for win or place, just show. Greg dreams; John plans.

Greg looks up from his phone. "Remember, Friday we're guests of Super Agent Man Stevie for dinner."

"That Stevie can really do a brilliant job on *osso bucco*. *Cena perfecta*."

"John, *osso bucco* is Italian, not Spanish."

The high-rise style of lakefront Toronto has percolated a panorama of great friends and after-hours spots, and a "Hey, what about that new place, (fill in the blank)" approach to most evenings.

Up for a morning capp at Balzac's or maybe an early sidewalk sausage, and then out late with tickets for one or another of the world-calibre events drawn to the perfect City.

"John, I think we've done every restaurant on the Danforth."

"And most of the Annex, too."

Out to lunch in the Distillery District, off for evening drinks at the Tosh. (*"Not the Tosh. Last time that old guy at the bar was looking at my tush."*)

These daily drop-ins become crossroads of City life through their repeated routines and activities. The downtown warren shows off well-worn rabbit paths after all the days of going here and coming from there, which end in a little whoopee most nights. Lately, though, John and Greg have been wanting off the party-party treadmill. More and more often, the lads feel more like pumpkins than carriage princesses.

John whistles as he turns the page now. "Oh my goodness, look at that Molson Bank stock go."

"Go for that 4.5% dividend!"

"Go bank, go!"

Unbeknownst to these two wealthy partners from the Big Smoke, they are about to embark on a nutty and cheesy rural adventure. The listing jumps right out of the thin Monday edition.

"Greg, it says Say Cheese."

"Who says …?"

"No, this ad, in bold type. It says SAY CHEESE."

"I like it. But what are we saying Say Cheese to?"

"Say Cheese to a 150-acre goat farm."

"Not horses? That would be the same as …"

"Okay," John says, "it's not Dad's hobby horse farm. There's sixty goats, show and dairy proven."

"Proven for what?"

"Greg, just 'Say Cheese.'"

"And where?"

"Get this: 'Idyllic Transvaal near St. Marys.'"

"Is that near Baden?"

"Hope so — we can buy our beans from the source."

"Costa Rica? A vacation!"

"Ha ha. No, the roaster."

Greg moves off the capp, grabs his tortoise-shell reading glasses. "Here, let me read it …"

John has laid the bait; now he passes the hook. Greg's head moves forward between the *Globe's* covers.

"Look, it's karma. It says 'For opportunity call Norm Morrison.' At some real estate agency called Black Aces …"

"Lucky opportunity, dropped in our hand."

"'Restored 1865 farmhouse included,' John. No renovations."

"Eliminations, Greg. A lifetime of mid-century modern from the City does not fit a century home. Is the opportunity worth the sacrifice? How important is this opportunity?"

Greg gives John the closest thing to an intense look he's able to do. "How important-important *is* this?" His mood switches to joyous. He opens his arms up as wide as the great view of the dark Great Lake and hugs John.

John gives appreciation its moment, then asks, "How important on the important-important scale?"

In a fit of serendipity, Greg had ordered a manual called *The Successful Goat Herd* off Amazon. He sizes up the opportunity to present the case. There's no need to start up the subject on the lounge chairs with their distracting vista. Maybe over the marble counter? Nah, that setting works better during lunches — or after, with iced coffees. Greg stands and reaches both hands out to John.

"How important-important, John? Let's just say, skip the caffeine drinks." Greg does a joyous pirouette on the Hanover slate floor. "Get this boy a Champagne cocktail."

"Whoa!"

John-boy's off to the stainless steel dual-temp wine cooler. He is off to the races on his side of the opportunity. There's nothing quicker than liquor to bring the partners together.

Greg has signed on; now he needs to get his serious suit on. If he wants to up this opportunity into an actual working plan, he'll need to deflect John's missiles of practicality, responsibility and reason. He knows a fortified bubbly refreshment will give John a good chin-up or bucking up. Greg fears John firing missiles of sense into what John will call "another of Greg's dreams," or *Gregzdream* for short. More than a word, it's an idea that has morphed and been amalgamated into the couple's vocabulary. Say it like it's one word. Say it in a slur:

Gregzdream.

That's the word that came to describe Greg's idea for franchising concierge travel agencies, or selling massaging chairs to the Tosh and other night spots. John had to remind him of internet travel booking, and club-goers' possible activities on fake leather.

"John," Greg responded, disappointed. "You have such a dirty mind on how low people will go."

Greg doesn't want this new venture to be just one more chapter of Gregzdream. Maybe this time the ignition of the nutty story will launch the dream into a seventh-heaven orbit of cheese.

And true to form, John can't help himself, as a driven lawyer and auditor.

"Gregzdream!" he says. Both hands rise to the heavens above the vast patio vista. "What the hell do you know about goats?"

Greg was a Boy Scout growing up, a perfect preparation for the impractical. Over many restless nights, not to forget comfy hours of lounge-chair inactivity, he has mulled over a possible rural adventure for the partners. He has dreamed up a bank vault of reasons to combat John's audit on practicality. Now, he starts at the beginning.

"Father had his farm north of Kingston," Greg says. "It was 150 acres, remember?"

"Hobby farm."

"It was work. I slopped the barn every Saturday until I was twenty-four."

John has heard the Kingston story over and over, so he pounds in a nail of sarcastic humour. "Sloppy thinking."

"Ha ha. Never discount the time to plan and think when on chores. A full day with a pitchfork, running through one of our barns? That's a lot of slopping."

John adds some practicality. "Sloppy dreaming."

The Boy Scout is prepared to cross that street. "Quality time to think."

John piles on the poop with both hands digging down, then a toss into the wind. "You were stuck in sloppy thought."

Greg picks up his CV. "I helped from ten years old."

John has a few more nails in the arsenal. "Whoa! How come so long on the old farm, buddy boy?"

"I admit it. I lived at home until I graduated from Queen's."

"Whoa."

Greg deflects the nail. "Just couldn't say no to Saturday chores, with Dad and Mom paying the freight on school. Got a few extra bucks. Had Mother's car to drive back and forth. At least until I moved to T.O. But I got there debt-free, with a little extra cash in hand. Had to say *adios* to Mom's homemade breakfast, though."

John recognizes the draw of bacon and eggs off a wood stove. Breakfast from Greg's mom was a big draw into their relationship. John likes this part of the dream life. "I couldn't say no to that, either. Irene's knee-breaking breakfasts. I miss them, and her."

John comes from City folk, people who walk or take public transportation about their high-rise domain. There is nothing rural about John. He holds in jest Greg's rural-route rearing.

"You must have been quite the prom queen from King Stone."

Greg is prepared for all questions on Kingston. "It was Mister for me that night. Better when your prom is a Muster."

"Muster? That's a military term?"

"You bet I mustered it up for my prom. They had it at Fort Henry."

"At Fort Henry?"

"A full prom muster in all that history."

"What did you wear?"

"Cadet suit à la 1867. My grandfather's original pillbox hat and black jacket with white beading and red buttons. Mother made the red pantaloons. God, they were resplendent, with two wide white stripes."

John is stuck for words. Greg is eyes up in memory.

"I was a big hit."

John forces himself to return from the vision of his partner at his school prom in a cadet costume. "But what the hell do you know about goats?"

Greg always makes time for the dream. So he's given tons of thought to all possible what-the-hell, where-the-hell and how-the-hell questions. It's all part of his dream, Gregzdream, to give a practical answer.

"I am not a complete idiot when it comes to farming. Farming business is farming business."

John cannot help an upgrade on simple axioms. "Sure you don't mean 'Stupid is as stupid does'?"

"Real mean, buddy." John looks as if his head could start to spin at the marvel of this dream business. Greg ignores his ignorant expression. "All we're talking about here is 150 acres. Same as Father's."

"Farming, farming, farming. That's important, important, important. Listen to you!" On the deck with the awesome view, John waves about like he's the Wizard of Oz standing in dust-covered rural Transvaalia. "These aren't plasticine dreams in a playset or horses in stalls on your family's hobby farm. You didn't milk horses. I never saw a stallion at that farm of your parents'. And fifty of your family's hundred acres are rocks and scrub brush. Four SkyDomes' worth of crappy land. Then another four to six for the house and outbuildings."

Greg starts to do the math in defence. "They're called barns! Who says outbuildings? And two sheds." He's almost counting with his fingers. "And the two-door garage back of the house."

"Don't forget the outhouse."

"Forget the outhouse. It's a garden shed now." Greg moves in to deflect, counting off fingers. "We had cows, chickens and pigs."

John has his index finger pointing east to Kingston. "Whoa. A real Old MacDonald's Farm, eh?"

Greg is flustered, caught by the novel comparison. "All the animals had to be cared for ... Had to learn from that."

John loves the debate, but he still finds himself thinking about back bacon. He remembers the brilliant wood-fire breakfast at Greg's parents' farm. His easy tours around the barnyard even came with a campfire-percolated coffee. John the Auditor has a superconductive memory for nailing the details.

"That one cow you had. Daisy. Those lazy-laying chickens that came up as dinner guests on our visits. The two fast geese, Ginger and Gander. A big chase in order to finish as two great Christmas dinners. And that stuck-up pig."

"He made a delicious choice as our guest."

John smiles as he remembers. "The pig took all the ground apples and corn husks we gave him and hoovered the abundant harvest of tomatoes, squash and cucumbers. Without an acknowledgement of our donations, snout stuck to the trough bottom. Rude animal."

"A fiesta pig, barbecue or wood-fired oven ... sumptuous."

"What was his name?"

"Gordo." Greg can't leave humour out of his dream. He snorts it up with a few guffaws. "*O-o-o-o*-huh-huh-huh. *O-o-o-o*-huh-huh-huh."

"Good, Greg. Now try to ignore the elephant-in-the-farm question."

That stops the comic.

"Yes," John goes on. "Sixty *plus,* the ad said. Goats." John looks up, in counting mode. "That number must be equivalent to the needs of a fucking elephant. Probably two or three bulls, with that number of goats. That is not a herd, that's a bearded nation loose on the range. Are you a fucking veterinarian?"

"Not to worry. I have a fucking chemistry degree."

"This is herd biology, not country-ass chemistry."

Greg does not flinch. "We have the cash."

John throws the notwithstanding card on the table. "But it's nice to hold something back to fatten up our portfolio. The cookie jar. Rock Fund Investments."

"Rock Fund?"

"John's rock-solid investment strategy."

"And now you have a degree in investing?"

"Okay. Let's see the profits milked out of those fucking hollow-stomach goats. See how rock-solid that is."

Greg has the quieter voice. "Artisan goat cheese."

"Let's be clear on cheese. I have never seen Say Cheese Artisan Goat Cheese at the organic grocer or The Cheesy Way on Davenport. Where's the cheese? That's the big question."

"Never seen it on any restaurant cheese plate," Greg concedes.

John is in a serious stop. Greg moves in close. "Who knows more about cheese than we do?"

John is in a dead halt. Greg closes in. "What does Patrick always say at the cheese shop?"

The partners do duet. *"You guys should be cheese sommeliers."*

"And what do my customers say at the restaurant?"

"Greg …" But John relents, joining Greg in another duet. *"Are you a cheese sommelier?"*

John is stuck in the cheesy reasoning. He has bought into the life-changing adventure, adding up the practical and subtracting the impractical.

Greg fills in the cheese gap with some fun strokes.

"You know what they say about Brie!"

Both break out in laughter. It's a classic naughty party play on the bouquet of Brie rising above the cheese board. Greg seizes the moment with another assault on the naming.

"'Say Cheese Company Artisan Chèvre.'"

Stop the record. John climbs back on top with a repeat on sensibility. "Do people know what chèvre is?"

"Chèvre!" Greg says. "Shit, they can read the label, John. You're the label guy, Mr. Detail."

John is spelling it mentally out with a Sharpie in big block letters. "Well, I still like 'Say Cheese Artisan Goat Cheese.' Simple. That's what I'm reading."

He dabs the marker for punctuation, then looks up.

"I do not do camping," John says.

Greg stops for a good stare as John continues his list of boundaries.

"Is there indoor plumbing? I will not walk to an outhouse. My God, think about that in the middle of the night."

"That's why God created front porches," Greg says. "To pee off." Greg points his zippered hand to the wind.

John is horrified by the call of the wild. "I want to hear a flush."

"Before I hear the flush, I want to hear this Black Aces dude."

"But first, the Champagne cocktails have made me hungry"

"Hungry? For what?"

"Dim Sum. That's what I'm in the mood for."

"Order up from Suki's. We'll pick it up. Faster."

"Dennis will deliver it."

Greg orders in. John calls up the Black Aces.

"Would Mr. Morrison be in? Yes, Mr. Morrison, Norman Morrison. Stormin' Norman? Same person. He is in. Who's calling? John, about the advertisement in the *Globe*. The *Globe*? Our national newspaper. You don't have the time to read. Yes, it's long distance."

Greg leans in, all ears to the speakerphone.

"Normin' … Nor-r-r-r-min-n-n-n."

The partners back off as the assistant yells into the phone.

"O-o-o-o-kay Bonnie. I've got i-i-i-i-it."

The partners close in, back on speaker.

"Aargh. Aargh. Aargh. Norman speaking."

Both look at each other with shrugged shoulders. Greg whispers. "He's a pirate."

John waves Greg off, flashing the phone at him and pointing to his ear.

"I'll give you Jimmy and Barbara's home number. They can answer any technical questions on the farm, the goats and Transvaal. *Aargh. Aargh. Aargh.*"

"This *Aargh, Aargh* stuff," John says as he hangs up. "Is there something we don't know?"

"John, just think how much fun this will be."

"Fun being led around by an old pirate. *Aargh. Aargh. Aargh.*"

"I love it. A treasure hunt."

The City couple gets in sync with the Country Kembers. There's a torrent of quick, short phone calls in the first twenty-four hours, then more detailed calls to cover more ground. John the Auditor and Barbara switch over to emails, which build up to a verbal agreement and a Saturday appointment.

"I put the Kembers on speed dial under Say Cheese."

"Clever, Greg."

"Barbara seems to wear the pants, eh?"

Chapter 5

The parking lot is full at the Sunriser for Mull-Over Monday.

"It was a squirrel."

"That started it all?"

"Yup, fried itself hanging up on the telephone wire. The furry flameball hit the dry grass and poof."

"A squirrel?" somebody else chimes in.

"Fire chief told us. He could see the charred remains dead centre atop the fire."

"Geez. Have to check the ground on our ZIT wire."

Incident on the Saturday, details on Monday. Two words circle back and forth around the S-shaped counter at the Sunriser:

"That's nuts."

Fire sirens always generate more interest in Town than ambulance and police do. The Transvaal neighbours' report went all the way to the Sunriser for fact refinement after the weekend. Transvaalites have claimed that they could hear Chief Scottie screaming out his open fire engine window: *Wo-ah. Wo-ah, Red. Wo-ah. Stop, baby, stop. Wo-ahhh.*

"*Wo-ah,* maybe," someone decides now. "But he never said *baby.*"

"How do you know?"

"Jimmy told me."

"Jimmy was holding his limp hose on the porch," someone else says.

"Never mind. It's *Big Red* or *Big* or *Red, wo-ah.* Never *baby.*"

One of the dimmer wags snickers in a back booth, away from the inner-counter discussion.

"Sounds like old Hap mounting the Widow Foster."

Where there's one dummy, there's two.

"Fostering up her furry little animal. That's our Happy Hap."

Enough of too much is heard in the kitchen. Braedon stretches his neck out of the pass-through to catch the dummies' attention.

"Ronnie. Donnie. Shut up."

After Braedon withdraws, the closer stools could hear his conclusion:

"Should have kicked them out. Pair of idiots. What's the diner become? Hiding dummies in the back."

Braedon guards the protocol of his elite coffee group. Not to forget that he serves the best shoestring fries, foot-long hot dogs and milkshakes for Town and Country miles.

From his look-out vantage over the great morning coffee crowd, the sit-in and take-out lunch, plus late nights, Braedon, the good captain and short-order master, knows the ebbs and flows of his diner clientele. Running the diner deck, check floor and the S-counter are a sister tag team. Who better to do the job than his two main servers, Jayne and Jacqui? (*"Hey, youse. Where ya been? Coffee coming up."*)

Braedon has laboured over fresh coffee pots, hot stoves and deep fryers at the Sunriser for over thirty years. Keeping an ear on the room and a hand on the griddle takes Olympian balance. It's a quartet in the kitchen, with back-up cook Angie, then Jacquie and Jayne, all standing behind Braedon.

Braedon sits up with a smile for the wild ride. "They'll be working the mirth out of this for the next forty years," he tells Angie. Never did he expect to hear about a disaster as nutty as this one.

Nuts *are* the backdrop to our cheesy story, as Chase of Kember will of course tell you.

Just as edible nuts vary in grades — whether they're legumes dug from the ground or shells picked from a tree — human nuts vary in grades on the Town tree of life. (Locals will argue all day about the distinctions between Crazies, Daisies, Nuts and Kooks.)

"Remember Dougie Smith? He took the bus to Plains Georgia. Hung out with Billy Carter?"

Dougie's grade is Plains, Georgia–certifiable but local harmless. Crazy stuff that's neither harmful or hurtful.

Bobbie Bynck, often referred to as Booby Dink, is another easy-peasy target. Hear the snickering build, a swirling smirk that touches down here and there around the S-shaped counter.

One patron makes a puffing movement to his mouth.

"Pf-f-f-f. Pf-f-f-f."

Everyone gets the joint connection.

Bobbie is the kind of local nut who snow-blows his laneway with a joint hanging out. That vapour trail you see is not the MotoMotion exhaust.

A typical exchange:

"Did you see the six o'clock news last night?"

"Nope. At a Moose Lodge dinner."

"Get this. Of all the people in Town to interview, guess who? They catch Booby Dink on the street."

"What would they ask that idiot?"

"Get this. They ask him about NAFTA."

"What did he say?"

"He blew vapour trails up their television ass."

"What?"

"You know. The corporate global conglomerate generate an exhaust choking our world. Then he points to the sky. Right on camera."

"They left that nonsense in?"

"Amazing what you see on TV."

Above all the distractions of Kooks, Crazies and Daisies is the more positive spin on the sense of nuts:

"He's got nuts."

And, in a usage that's unique to St. Marys — where Stonetown Cement uses steel balls to crush the limestone, multi-sized steel balls called Arnies: *"Guy's sure got ten-pound Arnies."*

Or consider this example:

"The Schoenfelds started with ten milk cows. Cows of suspect breeding, I might add. Skip to the third generation today. Look who's on show with the milk producing, plus Grand Champion at the Royal Winter Fair last two focking years." (A look to the room.) *"That's Arnies. I am telling you."*

Day Two at the diner, Tuesday, adds up more information and one big surprise.

The regulars around the irregular S-shaped counter can't believe it.

"He *sold* the farm?"

Braedon's head bumps the side of the pass-through for the second time this week. "Ouch. He *sold the farm?"*

The announcement had been whispered then announced by the Pirate Captain on his reserved stool, Stormin' Norman. Mull-Over Monday led to a parade of chiefs, their volunteers and Transvaal neighbours all joining in to fine-tune the rounds of information.

"That Jimmy sold the family jewels, he did."

"Yup, Century Farm."

"Make an offer like that."

Wink, wink, nod, nod, all pretending to know the price.

"Big City money is big money."

The gamey aroma of big City dollars clouds their imaginations at first.

"Still, family farm. A hundred and seventy-five-plus years."

"Tells me he has the family Canada Company deed. It's framed in the hallway."

"Lucky the house frame didn't burn up."

"It was a high-rent fire sale."

The room stops.

"You know, City money."

The room goes on.

"A few flames on Jimmy's arse. That'll get him into a house in Town."

Someone in a back booth broadcasts in a low voice. "Barbara put the focking flames to his balls."

The room erupts into laughter.

Greg and John, unbeknownst to themselves, are introduced *in absentia* to the stool crowd.

"Investors from the Big Smoke."

Third stool over from the cash register:

"Background in farming. Want out of the City."

Stool at the back of the S:

"Big bucks."

And an in-the-know source from one of the booths:

"Sure is. My brother-in-law Frank at the Molson Bank told me almost eight figures."

The heads on the stools at the S-shaped counter and the booth benches nod to a big calculation of zeros and decimal points. "H-m-m-m."

Back to the third stool:

"Easy peasy with the price of City real estate."

Back stool:

"He's a lawyer."

Neighbouring stool:

"And her?"

Third stool seems to know a lot.

"She's a he. They're a couple."

The diner masses respond in a low hum.

"H-m-m-m."

One known character, Stormin' Norman, sits at his usual place in a back booth. For the moment, he lets the embellishment flow for the entertainment.

"Same-sex couple," someone else says.

Braedon watches the coffee klatch. From a side stool, a new topic changes the theme: "The Jays optioned Pablo Forio."

"Who's playing short?"

"The kid. His job to lose."

All the morning crowd, at least the sports fans, have waited for the Jays' top prospect to be called up from Syracuse. Braedon personally can't wait for the hockey season to start. But his room will be safe running the bases on baseball, so the head reverses to the skillet for eggs and bacon. Braedon picks up the familiar introduction on his tuned–out-front ear.

"Aargh. Aargh. Aargh."

The room is silent.

"Ask him yourselves. Jimmy takes his seat on Saturday. *Aargh. Aargh. Aargh.*"

"Get your seat," Stormin' calls out as his back disappears through the grease-smeared glass door.

Braedon turns to Angie and the sister servers. "The counter will be a lineup. Even the booths will be stacked. Saturday will be an event."

Every day, the story is questioned, filtered and fluffed up according to the Sunriser's natural refinement process. By Wednesday, signs of fatigue are beginning to show.

"How much more information can Jimmy add? My lawn will need mowing on Saturday."

Thursday, moving to Friday, the doubts get more specific.

"Car wash in the morning; afternoon, wedding."

And the overall know-it-all's conclusive answer:

"I've heard everyone's details — Stormin' Norman, most of the volunteers and neighbours, and both chiefs."

The in-the-know rebuttal:

"Then skip the #1 witness. But my butt will be on a stool."

"Anything important, drop round the house."

"That'll cost you a beer."

The wind-down to Jimmy approaches a silly point in the discussions.

"Just don't ask Jimmy about the goats."

"Goats?"

"The goat farm, goat cheese, the kids in the barn. You'll get a long lecture."

One odd but reasonable question arises from the S-counter, cash register side: "Who wants to be a goat-herder?"

Slurpy head nods around the room indicate a consensus on the unknown territory of a conversation stopper. The sum-up on anything in herd management, for this diner gathering, is what's on the barbecue.

"Jimmy Kember can sure barbecue a goat, though. Better than Zorba the Greek himself."

An in-the-know with more GPS depth steps in. "Have you tried Mykonos down in the City?"

"They do a goat on the spit?"

"Saturday nights."

Angie the short-order cook can almost hear Braedon's contemplation at this last idea.

"I'm not too worried about Saturday nights," she tells him. "Don't complain, Braedon. We're up to our yin-yang in take-outs. If somebody wants to drive to the City for goat, so be it."

Not once in the first week — a daze leading to Jimmy on his Saturday sit — does anyone broach the subject:

"So, where *is* the cheese?"

Yes, Jimmy could drive on to process excellent cheese from his state-of-the-art milking shed, but the proficient Professor is stalled, with his hands frozen on the starter. Barbara leaves the best alone, cooking up odd cheeses in the back kitchen, including an excellent Brie. The close-by neighbours are more sympathetic, practicing the golden rule of rural roots: support thy neighbour. The un-knowledgeable speak their support combined with heavy head nods.

The shed?

"Looking good, Jimmy."

The herd?

"Looking good, Jimmy."

The shepherd?

"Looking good, Jimmy."

And who knows anything about the state-of-the-art Swiss equipment.

"Looking good, Jimmy."

The knowledgeable, who know better, keep in line.

"Looking good, Jimmy."

Ne'er a Transvaalite would show anything but support for Jimmy. They follow the standard gossip protocol on avoiding harmful or hurtful comments but take it one further with a neighbour: no comic comments about thy neighbour. Farther-away farmers and certain Town folk, however, would not give any slack to the generational, albeit part-time, farmer and full-time professor.

"Jimmy's a business suit wearing goat's clothing."

"Aren't them academics at Western smart enough to learn the cow business?"

"Bovine. It's the bovine *business, buddy."*

A smarter view spins things more into the positive.

"Who's the goose and who's the gander here? Jimmy's retired with an eighty-percent pension. Guaranteed health benefits, too. No farmer gets that deal."

And there's always a few who think with their stomachs:

"Does a wicked goat on the barbecue."

Indeed, in order to cull the underutilized herd, a number of unlucky young male goats periodically take one for the team. They part ways for greener pastures in the backyard barbecue. The Kembers donate and cook up a taxi squad of team extras, young unwanted billies who join the St. Marys Volunteer Fire Department (and tug-of-war team) annual fundraising barbecue. It's a go-to event in the small Town.

"Yummy. I ask for the ribs."

"Ask him about the sweetmeats."

"At the barbecue?"

"Yup. Ask him. Jimmy always has something special on the side."

The full squad of extras are basted in thyme, rosemary and mint over the hot coals. Always a group of men to watch the turning subject in a masterpiece of barbecuing. Jimmy can prep the spit, prepare the billy and apply the baste. But a tip of the hat to Barbara, the lady of the house, who makes that secret sauce.

"Wonderful baste."

"Barbara's family recipe. Secret stuff."

"They barbecued goats?"

"No, but her dad was a barbecue and smoker genius."

Chief Sandy overhears the discussion, knows the ladies, adds on the sauce:

"Focking great baste, eh?"

A chorus of chuckles.

"You're terrible, Sandy McLean."

But the story is about cheese, and in this barnyard action plan there is a little cheese, after all. The stainless steel urn of fresh milk that Jimmy leaves by the kitchen sink now and again is more than needed to show a little product. It's a show that demands a lot of cleaning and scrubbing for just a little cheese. And of course there's little spare time available, with the herd expansion and cleaning up. But Barbara can prepare soft-rind cheeses to show off for friends. The triple cream is a barbecue hit.

Jimmy held off for years on ordering the last of the state-of-the-art-equipment, but in the meantime, the automatic milking equipment and cooling tanks allowed for Barbara's kitchen-made cheese and a few specialized customers' goat's milk. Ontario Regional Children's Hospital has a standing order for two sterilized cans.

For years now, Jimmy has dreamt of becoming a farm-gate producer of goat cheese. He's just about worn out the plumbing on throne time thinking about the future of his boutique goat cheese business. Whether it's on the throne, the stuffed armchair or the tractor seat, or while carrying those endless focking pails of surplus goat milk back to the pigpen, Jimmy rolls the ideas over in his head:

Artisanal? Artesian? Nope, that's a well. Artisan? Hm-m-m-m.

Then, later in the evenings:

"Barbie, what do you think of 'Say Cheese Artisan Goat Cheese'?"

She drops her knitting needles, resisting the urge to shove the ball of yarn into his gob.

"That's a lot of cheeses in one name, dear."

"One cheese, Barbie. It's in the name. The other is corporate."

Barbara ignores the lecture.

"Seems too cheesy to me."

That was weeks ago, just weeks before the farm was sold. The sale, which took days to negotiate, is now under Town review.

When this Saturday morning rolls around, Jimmy can feel the hot breath from wagging tongues all the way across the Thames, over the dusty 6th Concession. He tries to do the walk of shame into the Sunriser without anyone noticing.

Mull-Over Monday is now five days back. A full set of weekday mornings has added hours and days of fresh details to the nutty story. Everyone in the room is familiar with the two-alarm response to the grass fire. They wait with burning ears and dry tongues for Jimmy's arrival on his regular Saturday visit to Town.

All mirth and chuckles stop with Jimmy's grand entrance.

The entire lot, jammed into booths and knee to knee on stools along the double-horseshoe counter, all turn in one motion. They rhyme out a pithy welcome for the doorway sneak:

"You did *what*?"

Jimmy knows the gathering is impatient, right ready to prime the pump of the prime witness to the farm incident. He feeds them cake.

"Yep, we're moving to Town. We bought Faye and Ben's house on Thomas."

The coffee klatch sets aside a back-to-Ben file. (That Ben who has been short-shifting his stool at the Sunriser for over a week.) A wag offers up Ricky Ricardo: *"He'z got-sum splainin' to do-o-o-o."*

Benny-baby will be saved for a future morning special on the grill. (The protocol book at the Sunriser dictates nothing harmful or hurtful on Gentle Benny. He will get no comic mercy from the coffee klatch, but all in good fun.)

Town and Country GPS, it should be noted, remains oral. No matter what address Ben runs off to, he leaves the house its permanent name — a name that will never change no matter how long the Kembers pay Town taxes. The small brick house at 138 Thomas Street South, to most Citizens, will always be identified as The Andrews House.

"Which Andrews?"

"The original on Thomas."

"Where are Faye and Ben moving to?"

"Kind of quick, isn't it. Hope they can keep all those moving boxes separated with the address changes."

The GPS in St. Marys, it should be noted, is a technical oddity unlike anything in the entire Canadian postal system. The postal codes are based on an arbitrary system that matches addresses to a series of boxes in an algae-green building on the corner of Jones and Wellington Streets. So, plugging in your GPS is problematic, leading to misdirection and confusion for visiting relatives and parcel deliveries. Locals are always in question from half-open vehicle windows and doors.

The system limits the usefulness of house numbers.

"Where?"

"Steve Bailey's, on Maiden Lane."

"Todd's son. Beside Skip's?"

"Right. He'll leave his laneway clear."

"Where?"

"Nifty's."

The oral GPS turns up historical, sometimes hysterical terms of reference. The imagination stretches for a reference to the original builder, the most famous owner, the longest term of ownership, an inventor, or a member of Parliament. A large, well-kept Queen Anne–style on Queen Street is called The Queen Mary. (*"Six apartments. All large. Some two stories. Big as a ship."*)

Another big-as-a-boat pioneer merchant home, Underwood Park, is named after the family's original in Britain. It's an uppity B&B with an outstanding breakfast served to whispering pairs on linen-covered, padded chairs.

A cramped and worn-out six-plex with bad parking becomes The Club — the name given for an array of bad behaviour behind battered closed doors in need of WD-40.

"My goodness, you say the daughter is living … there?"

"Deliver the fridge to The Andrews House."

"Underwood Park needs the order right away."

"Across from The Roger House."

"Beside the Grand Trunk Hotel." "A hotel?" "You know, the building with the Black Aces office." (Why-didn't-you-say-that look.)

The Andrews family have their original homestead nailed. One hundred and fifty years in the same house helps almost every Citizen to know the oral GPS. One of the first that newcomers learn in their new hometown language.

"Whose?"

"The Andrews House."

Never a number will be mentioned, founding families continue on in name only. Mass GPS is a work in progress, address direction amalgamation.

"Whose?"

"Becketts. New City people moved onto Thomas Street."

"Where on Thomas?"

"Across from Carmen Snead's. Green roof, yellow brick with nice green porch."

A lifer reaches back in time past.

"The McCutcheon house. Gotcha."

When Jimmy and Barbara come to Town, they will live in The Andrews House built by Benny's grandfather. In the opposite direction, the Kembers leave a generational Century Farm with the same name forever. They leave The Kember Farm to live in The Andrews House on Thomas.

Today the crowd keeps it light with the goat-herding Professor, trying to wrap their heads around the moving arrangements.

"What about the boxes?" someone wonders. "With them moving in while you're still moving out? You'll have to empty most of the house."

"Upstairs, downstairs," Jimmy says. "We have a plan to work. Two bathrooms. Share the kitchen, front room, share the porch, the farm during the transition." Jimmy's on a smooth move. "We get to share their expensive Italian coffee machine. And Benny has his drive shed empty and available for our boxes."

"So, Jimmy. What's up with the squirrel battle of Transvaal?"

"True words, Bobbie. Always a battle."

The whole room sucks in a collective breath with fresh nuts thrown out on the table for roasting. All coffee slurping, conversation snorts and arse shuffling pauses for more on the nutty tale. My goodness, any in-the-know is dying with impatience to fire up the big two-alarm incident. Jimmy's just tiptoeing through the tulips with a fat old squirrel.

"I gave Barbara some of those Canada Day white-and-red tulip bulbs. Nice gift for Valentine's. Planted in April and gone by May."

The room fills with impatient silence as the leader of the back-booth dummies takes the floor. (As stated, Booby Bynck is not the brightest local, some say not even at the level of a dim-wit.)

"Lots of them squirrel folk, eh?"

Yup, Braedon's head is out the pass-through window, checking off his back-booth dim-wit list. Back in the kitchen, Angie the short order cook listens in on the accounting for morning theatrics.

"Booby, Trip, Ronnie, Donnie. Have to get rid of those twin dim-wits. There's Little Al tucked in the corner. And Stinky Stuart. Haven't seen him in a while."

Back up front, third stool from the pass-through, Jimmy's all Country class. The Professor never condescends to dim-wits.

"He was one fat and old, crafty creature, Bobby."

Booby assumes the posture of a deer in the large morning group's headlights. He's frozen on the floor, fascinated by the furry story. Jimmy releases the poor fool, turning his stool to the back booth.

"Barbara calls him 'that focking animal.'"

A wag next to the dummy group barks back with a wink.

"What about that mean old dog? Sure likes the rubber on my car."

"Max," Jimmy says, nodding. "Well, Max is just like many of us in the room …" — the room stops slurping — "He's old. Max don't move too fast or too far from his mat and bowl on that shady old porch."

Booby has planted his ass back on the bench. Never underestimate a fool with his mouth open. He spouts some expert drivel on squirrel psychology. "That focking squirrel. Made a fool of the dog."

The coffee klatch laughs at who's-the-fool. They slobber away with double and triple sugar on their tongues, washed down with high-octane coffee, fuelling the need for fresh information. The pause in conversation brings the smell of burnt caffeine and simmering impatience.

Jimmy pauses. No point defending an old dog's smarts to a young Neanderthal. The caveman runs headless back into the conversation.

"Did the poor focking thing ever get a name?"

An important question never imagined by any member of the Sunriser's seven-day regulars. The Saturday morning audience turns to hear Jimmy's answer.

"I called it Chase."

A thought chorus from the room. *Chase?*

"Well," Jimmy explains, "I'm always yelling to Max. 'Go chase.' So I call him Chase. The focking squirrel seems to know his name."

The gathering enjoys the academic's insert of some focking into the conversation. A question from someone a little closer to Jimmy:

"What about Barbara?"

"Hey, she calls it what it is. 'That focking furball.'"

The laughter burns a trail back and forth through that morning's gathering. Some classic comics are offered:

"Rocky's flying cape didn't work so good, eh?"

"Rocky should have worked out a little more. Maybe Jazzercise."

"I think they call it Squirrelcise."

"*Nut* your regular squirrel."

"Flaming furry."

Jimmy has always kept a tight lip when it comes to naming Chase. Now the floodgates have opened to nutty jokes. Jimmy can give thanks that Barbara, the tulip defender and birdseed provider at war with that clever creature, bears no witness to this silliness.

"More like a cheeky monkey up in the canopy," he adds.

The morning group at the Sunriser want to eat more cake, and how about some icing?

"Jimmy, when were you going to confess your secret enterprise?"

Jimmy is slipping, sliding down on the roller coaster rails toward full disclosure.

"Jimmy, how about the real goods? Tell us about the goat cheese universe in orbit on the farm."

Muse moment from a booth. "Captain Jimmy, beam me up."

Jimmy, with beyond a doctorate in math, plays a double advantage. He's a 100% farm boy who can do the math of the rural man-humour. Today is just the usual grind from the Sunriser morning coffee gathering. Jimmy's got one word to shut them all up: teats. Use "teats" in any context and the room goes quiet.

"Three hundred fat teats ready to squeeze. Squeeze ourselves into the production of goat cheese."

Jimmy gives it all in Western University fashion to a first year, first day class. He ramps the roller coaster back up to startle all with his passion on teats — sorry, cheese. He announces with pride:

"The Sunriser will be our first customer. Right, Braedon?"

Braedon's head is in position. No bump necessary to comment from the pass-through.

"Squeeze those teats, Jimmy. Greek salad will be on the menu for sure."

Braedon casts an eye round the audience.

"No need for City Greek," he says. "Maybe we'll barbecue a goat. Greek Night at the Sunriser."

"Now that's a start," someone chimes in.

Braedon is not finished. "Bring the two gentlemen in for coffee, Jimmy. On the house. Meet the locals."

Jimmy nods. "I'll bring them in myself. It's a quick close. Four weeks."

Braedon makes a note to bring Angie, Jacquie and Jayne in earlier on the introduction day for the extra help. His wife, Lisa, may need to get a babysitter. It's showtime at the Sunriser. A Jimmy regular Saturday could be good, but now with the farm sold, the sooner the better. "Any time would work. Let me know. Folks want to meet the new owners."

Jimmy knows Country showtime. "Right as rain."

"Jimmy, do you mind me asking?"

Jimmy nods.

"Tell me, Jimmy," Braedon says. "Which is the husband?"

Braedon is not looking at Jimmy. He sticks his entire neck out the window, watching movement along the stool lineup and back on the booth benches. The stools freeze, the benches straighten up to the direct query from an unusual source. Braedon's neck retracts through the window, the opening framing a huge kitchen grin.

"Ha ha," he says. "Just pulling your legs, lads." He canvasses all reactions. "I could not care less."

The smile is gone into the back.

"So, Jimmy," an in-the-know says. "What are the lads going to call their enterprise in cheese?"

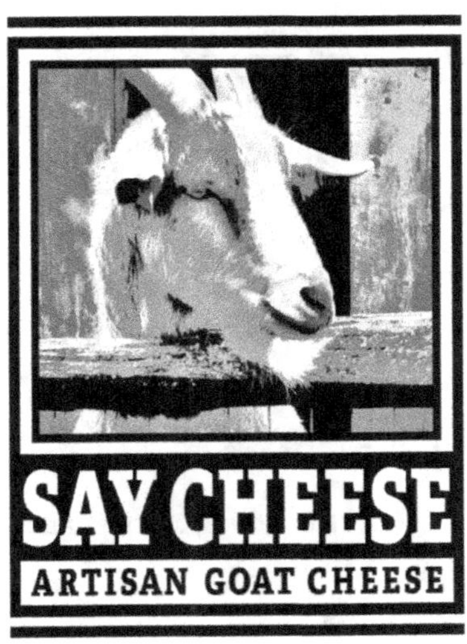

"Barbara and I always agreed on the name Say Cheese Artisan Goat Cheese. John and Greg loved the name from the get-go. The partners decided to keep it — with our blessing, permission and full support."

That singular voice pipes up from the back.

"Gay Cheese, right. You did say Gay Cheese?"

The chorus line breaks out in snickers. Braedon returns to the pass-through with the darkest of eyes but no wagging finger for the crowd. He is the king of his coffee court.

"Careful. Careful, lads." The dark eyes dart about the room. "These are investors in our community, no matter if they're from the City or from Timbuktu. No matter who's the husband."

A voice from the back lightens it up. "That's Tuesdays at Tim Hortons: Tim Buck-or-Two Tuesdays."

The coffee crowd is quick to move on, push that City button.

"Just don't mention World Cup tennis or MLB soccer."

"Football. Everyone else in the world calls it football."

"American football, rugby football, Australian football, Canadian football. Soccer works for me."

The true nature of the Canadian sports fan comes out after the nurtured failures of the long, recent past: true north pessimists.

"Not important. No Stanley Cup in fifty years. Nothing high-calibre about that. The world would call that losing."

Here in St. Marys, the folks shorten up the long distance from the City with Country wisdom, the wags taking the complete piss out of any big-city bluster.

"Aren't those City folk close to God? They do live up in the sky. Some of the perches are up forty, fifty floors."

"Some even higher, I'm told."

"Aargh. Aargh. Aargh." The gathering swivels stage right (Braedon left) to the old codger who's back, smiling, on his stool. "Close," Norman says. "Just ask them about their view. *Aargh. Aargh. Aargh.* I think I'll puke if one more Citiot moving here tells me about their condo view."

"Isn't it about what they got?"

"That's the first thing they always tell you. Right off on the first call." Stormin' has his hands up with tiger paws, squinting eyes, a real cry-baby look. He starts up a whiny baby talk. *"Look how much we got!"*

A back-booth wag pipes up. "So what, couldn't pay me to live there. Why the attitude?"

"Aargh. Aargh. Aargh. That's the attitude from altitude. High-up living makes them dumb."

The cluster beating continues.

"Pretend gods there. Real-life Citiots out here."

"Here, they're on a wild safari. Back there, it's nefarious."

"Nefarious? What the fock's that supposed to be?"

"Most perfect City in the world. Just ask them."

"… after the crime report on ETV news."

And a spiritual review. "When they have a party, are they hosts from heaven?"

And the practical stomach. "Do they have barbecue in the City?"

The round of chatter, mirth and slurping sounds hits a crescendo. A group that may never push an elevator button to a fifty-plus-storey building, ever.

"On Toronto elevators there's a floor. They call it S-2-S-G-F."

The room stops.

"Shoulder to Shoulder with God Floor."

Even the newly-minted import residents catch on quick to the protocol of tittle-tattle. Citiots are open game on an open range in Town. Chris from a booth has bought one of the new estate homes back of the old lime quarry.

"My new neighbour from Toronto tells me he smells pig shit."

The locals listen up.

"Focking Citiot doesn't know the difference between pig and chicken shit and Shinola. Can't tell any of that from his fat wife's bowel movements."

City boy cracks off a good one this morning. A big nod all round for the newbie.

A crowd that has a few dim-wits, some silent in-the-knows, and the regular gossip sponges fill the stools for their caffeine constitutional. No one seems to care about shit conversation. Few are paying attention to any continuity on the subject of Citiots, whether import or outport.

Slurp. Slobber. Slurp. Slurp. Someone in the back asks the question:

"What's your neighbour smelling?"

"It's the rubber brake factory off John Street."

Another back-booth dim wag lights a summary for the morning:

"Citiots. More moving to Town every day."

And if there's one, there's always two local dim lights:

"What can you do, eh?"

Chapter 6

"Goin' up the country. Goin' up the country. Takin' a friend of mine."

"Greg. Lay off the Canned Heat. Woodstock was fifty years ago. Your music choice has an overdue date on it."

A sensitive issue in modern times, a pokey subject tossed back and forth between life partners.

"Don't you label me."

City grit from the Big Smoke's burnt rubber and exhaust has been left behind. That intoxicating industrial mixture, added to the cocktail of concentrated humanity, unique to the City. The gritty path that commuters are drawn to as they listen to the same old bad news on the AM on the 9s, during the AM-PM traffic drive. John busts his buns on the bicycle to the office; Greg is good for a short walk or a taxi to the restaurant. The non-commuters keep their exotic electric plugged in, reserved for weekends.

"Robbie and Matty have invited us up to their cottage."

"One-thirty kilometres. There and back, no worries."

"We don't have to plug it in till we get home!"

For ten months of the year, life's path is weather dependent, so they wind through subterranean tunnels for subway, sushi or dry cleaning, always surfacing into the City grit.

But Country grit? That's the dust cloud that blocks rear-view mirrors, that plume of grey barrelling out behind our Country adventurers.

Unbeknown to the City pair, their rural route has taken them past a right turn, down a cattail-lined concession.

"Look," Greg points to the ditch. "Wienies on a stick." Nothing to despair for our natural comic on a drive. "Where's the campfire party?"

Serious observation, too: "Wow, the whole ditch. Full of cattails."

With the fading signal of AM 570 on the 9s, the traffic report disappears around the same time the dust appeared.

"Greg. What happened to 570?"

A smarmy voice speaks up.

"Right turn in five hundred metres."

"I didn't think our route off the expressway included gravel," Greg says.

The GPS answers. *"Turn now."*

John turns the wheel. "Here we are, buddy. Back onto the pavement …"

Greg is caught in the window wonder of rural routes.

"Greg. Some tunes, man. Dial up some tunes."

"I told you that if you didn't buy the satellite option, you need to bring your iPod."

John drives on in electric bliss, the careful accountant. He wants to change the channel, but he refuses to join a long list of dialling disasters. A careful driver does *not* take his hands off the wheel. The lucky driver does *not* break Country Driving Rule #7: *Do not dial the radio while you are behind the wheel.* Greg gets to choose the score to their magical mystery tour. He reaches for the dial.

"Baybee. Baybee. Stay ya here, here here. Baybee. Baybee, stay ya here, here here …"

"Rap, rap, rap," Greg says. "Is that all Country people listen to?"

"Greg, you need to get out more. That's dance music. How about some classic rock … and not 1969. The seventies work."

"Gravel run, gravel fu-u-u-un. Loose surface, careless fun. Come on Baybee …"

"Greg. No country and western. And what's all this *baybee-e-e-e* crap."

With City choice gone, the selection includes the livestock market report, coming events and today's obituaries on AM 1280.

"My God," Greg says. "Listen to this."

　　　　　　　　　　　　　　　　　　　　　　　　LORNE EEDY

The driver squeezes the wheel. Again he strains *not* to reach for the dial. Heads up to the road; his mouth is down with pursed words. "Tunes. Tunes. Anything. Not this."

"No, John, listen. Pork stocks are up. Corn futures down. That's different shit than Van Halen's greatest."

Surrendering to the rural, Greg lets it off again. "Ung-*huh-huh-huh*. *O-o-o-o*-huh. *O-o-o-o*-huh."

"What you doing that for?"

Greg snorts again. "I'm calling Fred Ziffel."

John the smart guy is caught flat-footed. "Who?"

"Fred Ziffel from *Green Acres*."

John is stuck in a Ziffel cramp. Ziffel? All he can do is grunt. "What?"

For once his partner has the upper hand on useless knowledge. "*Green Acres* is this TV show that my dad used to watch in reruns. We had some great father-son laughs over that silly show."

"My parents watched *That '70s Show*."

Greg ignores the useless input, beaming himself up into the local theatre. "Norman can be Fred Ziffel. He's the local go-to guy for anything and everything."

Just as John is starting to recall the old sitcom, Greg blurts it all out, first choice. "I want to be Zsa Zsa."

Everybody loves Greg in party mode. Don't count John out, though, coming up smarter in the details. "Greg, heartbreak time. Sorry. It was her sister, Eva Gabor. *She* played the ditzy blonde."

And then John joins the casting. "I'm in. I'll be Oliver Wendell Douglas. What a name, what a role."

All of a sudden the partners look at each other.

"My God, Greg. Did you pass one?"

"Not me."

"My God. That smell is searing my sinuses."

They turn from each other to the outside.

"Not me. That's from … out there."

The stink of humanity has been substituted with the stinky things humanity eats. Chicken, beef, turkey, pork, sheep and goat crap. All of Noah's ark, it seems, in one heaping pile of shit. A natural but horrible stink, a modest drive from the City.

Ears on the radio, nose on the landscape and eyes ahead.

And the change in road surface begs the obvious:

"John, why are we back on gravel?" Right away, Greg has his answer. "Crap. Turned off the GPS fooling with radio. Wait …"

The smarmy voice comes to attention.

"Make a U-turn now. Make a U-turn now."

A blast back from the driver. "Okay, o-o-o-ka-a-a-ay. I'm turning around …"

Whoops. An incoming dust cloud rises ahead to blot out the gravel road. The grey plume pushes forward a red pickup truck. Coming in at sixty kilometres, incoming toward them, and then gone, the vehicle is responsible for a massive mushroom filtering up into the walnut-tree canopy and floating toward them. The dust tsunami camouflages the road ahead. Hypnotic.

"My God, it's apocalyptic."

"John, keep more to the right."

John's fist tight on the wheel, the car slides right. The cool air-conditioning seems clammy. Greg wants to drive. But it's not his car, the driver has told him. (The new exotic in their City high-rise garage was John's therapy for dealing with the second bike theft.) Still, Greg feels a need to drive. He can't contain his excitement about driving.

"No," Greg says. "No-o-o-o. Not the ditch."

"Make a U-turn now. Make a U-turn now."

"Will you shut the fuck up?" John tells the machine. He squeezes a touch back from the right and the car swims onto the gravel. "O-kay-y-y-y," he says, relieved.

"Stay. In your lane. Stay. In your lane."

Greg is a frozen deer in the passenger seat, caught in the spotlight, staring into the horror of it all, their own particular apocalyptic journey into rural-route darkness.

Greg understates his concern, which is the best way to make your point to a lawyer. The comatose deer jumps to life. "No. Not okay, John. I do not want to meet my new neighbours … in a *head-on.*"

"Make a U-turn now. Make a U-turn."

Never one to miss a rare chance to lecture the genius auditor and careful-but-lucky driver, Greg picks up on the road surface.

"It's gravel," Greg says. "You did *not* grow up on these back roads."

John never says no to an opportunity to lecture, at any lectern, bar or kitchen table. And not in the driver's seat, either. "You did *not* grow up raising goats."

"Horses."

"Goats, Greg. That's the real rearing question."

It's animal crackers back and forth.

"There," John says. "Right there, a laneway." The car owner, driver and partner turns to the passenger. He covers false confidence with a spin on funny. "You are such a ditch," he says. "Ditch lover."

His deer passenger stares into the dust, shakes his head. "Want to feel those furry wienies? Rubbing on your fuzzy wuzzy face?"

The dust cloud has drifted off to the adjacent corn fields, allowing John to make his three-point U-turn. The GPS directs them back to county hardtop.

"Continue on the current road for eighteen kilometres."

The partners are dusted off from the gravel, back onto the straight path to a new life. Greg has returned to his passenger window view, stumbling back in his mind on the horror of the journey. He will never confess any heart of darkness toward Gregzdream and buying a goat farm — but a head-on crash in a cloud of obscurity on the way to buy a goat farm? There has to be a message here. His journey might come to an absurd end rather than a fortuitous beginning. Here in southwestern Ontario, just east of St. Marys, they've almost spun out on a tributary of gravel to their heart of darkness, a new and unknown opportunity. John is drifting off the hardtop, back to staring at the radio dial.

"John, eyes front," Greg says.

Greg sees John's grip tighten on the wheel as his concentration returns.

Bang. Thump. Thump.

"What the fuck's that?" John asks.

Thump. Thump.

"Hit a pothole, man. Flat tire."

John cries for help in the mirror from the long-gone pickup.

"Whoa," Greg says. "Get the car over. On the side here."

"I never had a flat tire before."

"That's why we have roadside assistance. Put your flashers on."

Greg touches his driver's shoulder. "Relax. We'd better phone Norman. Tell him we'll be late for the appointment."

"Look at the GPS. We could walk to Town from here."

"Call Norman."

"You call him," John says. "He's on *your* speed dial. You're the one with the dream."

"Relax. I'll call him."

John takes in a breath of his surroundings without dust. Beautiful. Bucolic. Bull.

"There's a bull staring at us. In the field. There."

A big black Bossy chews and stares over the fence line.

"That's an Angus steer," Greg says.

"Heifer? Named Angus?"

"That's the breed. And a steer is a bull without balls."

John stares back at the cow in pain; his left hand is automatic, grabbing his parts. He offers some manhood sensitivity. "Oh, you poor thing, you."

"Better on the barbecue," Greg says as he puts the phone on speaker. "Shhh. Norman's on the line."

John can't imagine which part of that heifer he's been enjoying on his patio barbecue.

"*Aargh. Aargh. Aargh.* You've got a flat."

John and Greg hold their hands up in a silent *huh?*

"Jamie Crawford's your man. I'll give you his number."

"Norman," John says. "We have roadside assistance. Included with our car."

"*Aargh. Aargh. Aargh.* Get your pen out. Jamie's it, with the Little Hooker."

"Norman," Greg says. "Hooker?"

"That's his tow truck. That's it for at least thirty kilometres. He's your man. And the Little Hooker."

John gets antsy. "Next it will be the Bates Motel."

Greg holds up three fingers, mouthing the words *Aargh, Aargh, Aargh.*

"*Aargh. Aargh. Aargh.* No worry about a motel, boys. Call Jamie. He'll hook you up."

"Norman, it's a flat, not a tow job."

"*Aargh. Aargh. Aargh.* Blow job then."

That stops the pair with a moment of shoulder-shrug reflection. Norman talks on.

"Jamie has a compressor. All the tools to do the job. See you at the office. Say thirty minutes."

"Thirty minutes," the partners reply.

"Jamie's the best Little Hooker anywherezies." Norman ends the call with a mirthful three Aarghs.

Greg has P for puzzled plastered across his face. "Your turn," he says to John. "I can hear the banjo music. *Aargh. Aargh. Aargh.*"

John gets the Hooker number teed up.

"J-j-j-amie here. The Lil-li-lil huh-huh. The towing service."

John explains the predicament and location.

"F-f-f-f. The gravel road p-p-past Charlie's gas bar. See you in f-f-f-f. See you soon."

Greg looks at John. "Bates Motel. We're goners."

"I need to stretch my legs."

As they step out of the car, the roll of the landscape east of St. Marys, along the Wildwood basin through the Gore of Downie, takes their City breaths away. A cool and moist late summer's night has generated a mist covering their field of vision. Four eyes adjust as a light wind cleans up the view. In his moment of contemplation, John touches on his recent driving trauma.

"At least it's not more goddamn dust."

Greg gets it. "It's a John Constable painting. Bucolic …"

Greg's voice fades off in the distance as John takes a few steps down the road.

"What's that?" John asks.

"Where?" Greg asks.

"There. On the road."

Greg and John approach the splotch on the concession road.

"Is that fur?"

"There's a tail."

"A raccoon?"

"Way too small a splotch."

John moves in close to the splotch. "It's a squirrel."

"This is a tough neighbourhood for squirrels."

Honk. Honk.

The guys jump to attention, ambushed in the middle of their roadkill forensics. A massive yellow hood pulls up behind their car, and a goofy guy in a cap waves at them. He rolls down his window. "B-be-be-be right there. T-tah-tah-told you."

Greg and John stay fixed in place, mesmerized by the Country Hooker with her lights blasting, blinkers flashing and that windscreen over the pitted chrome grill.

The gravel dust floats away to reveal *The Little Hooker*, in red script. Out from the yellow door pops a pock-marked face with a big toothy grin. A disheveled large man wears a nifty black baseball cap, screaming out in red with gold shadowing in large script: *Rogers*. A smaller line underneath is bold enough to state *Does It*.

"I'm J-j-j-j. Jamie."

"I'm John. This is G-guh-guh-greg."

Greg can't believe the words out of his partner's mouth. "You're quick," he says. "We haven't even found the spare yet."

"My goodness this is one f-fa-fa-fa, one nice car. The ca-a-ah. A vehicle that needs no ga-ga-ga-gah. Buy it at the mall."

The three stare at the electric exotic.

"Let's h-ha-ha-ha, let's take a look."

Jamie doesn't need the Little Hooker's hook or chain — just a spanner and the fancy spare.

"Expensive car. G-gra-gra-gar. Good spare."

John and Greg move back from the site of the fur splotch to watch as Jamie bends, fetches, fixes, showing off amazing angles of his ass-crack as it peeks out from the cleavage of his buttocks. Above the man's diligent dexterity, the partners place bets with silent looks: *Will the pants fall to the knees?* Jamie picks up the spare with a muscled pirouette, then mounts it on the lugs. It's a full set of nuts from his left pocket, on with the charged-up socket drill. A reverse pirouette, a flat toss to the trunk. As the lid drops with no time for a dust-off, Jamie has an invoice already stretched out in hand.

"Whoa, Jamie." John, super auditor, prepares to get into let's-make-a-deal mode. "Cash?"

Jamie retracts his steel invoice folder, tucking it up under his armpit. His toothy smile widens. "Thirty cash will do it."

Greg cannot help himself. His mind is running a credit card smack down the crack of this arse. Alas, cash payment limits his response. "The Little Hooker takes care of its John," he says.

Jamie is up quick, back up in his cab, a Christmas light show-off, waving.

The couple return to goodbyes. Greg returns to humour.

"John has always paid first for any pull job."

It's official. The City couple has been introduced, live, to the first two characters on their rural route: a major personality in Stormin' Norman Morrison, a minor one in Jamie Crawford. And a great theatrical prop, the Little Hooker. (The stories a Hooker could tell.)

The exotic couple and luxury car are stand-outs in Town. The heads in the front window of the downtown Tims comment on the parking job.

"Automatic parking."

"Mine has a back-up camera too."

"No, it's auto-*ma*-tic. Parks *itself*, dummy."

The front-row-standing group inside the window at Scott's Barbershop also stare at the electric car. All thought is wired the same.

"Don't see too many of them in Town."

"We don't have a shopping mall. That's where they sell them."

"A shopping mall? No garage?"

"Buy 'em off the internet. Deliver it to your house."

"Automatic parking."

"My car has a backup camera too."

One common and clear conclusion from the local point of view. The visitors, landed aliens, stand out, with their tanned faces, legs and arms. The observers would fail at identification of alien clothes brands, which include Maui Jim. They can see the aliens point down the street. All heads stretch left from the barbershop, right from Tims, leaning out in wonder.

"Salesmen?"

"They never come in twos."

"Consultants for the Town?"

"Not with those tans."

"Lawyers?"

"Not with shorts and tans."

"Citiots."

Not necessarily negative, the reference to "Citiots." Citiots could mean they're looking for Country property, or they may have relatives in the old folks' home. Out of nowhere, a know-nothing is ignored:

"Pair looks like Hackney breeders to me."

"Nay, they're theatre visitors."

"No way, that bunch? They're actors."

"Notwithstanding their electric car, I can tell you that pair is not on a bus tour out of the City."

The in-the-know barber, Scott, pulls together the alien crumb trail.

"Bet they're dealing with Stormin' weather."

The heads-up lineup in the barbershop window nod in agreement.

Across the street, the lads head along Queen, an easy walk downhill to the broker's office two blocks away.

"Jeez, thirty bucks for that Jamie," John says. "He's one character. That was a deal."

"In the City you'd be lucky getting anyone to come at all. Look at that building up there. My God, it's a castle. Do they sell soft ice cream there?"

"It's the town hall. Have you not read anything?"

A stinger after a long ride. Greg continues past the castle toward the Black Aces offices.

"No Starbucks?" Greg says.

John wonders at the naïveté of his partner. Did he not read the Town and Township brochures they received as attachments?

"Greg, I think the one other franchise in Town is Torpedo Subs."

A kid stunned by new Country wonders halts on the sidewalk. "Wow. The frontier of civilization. No wall-to-wall franchises."

And no Walmart either, but if the lads would walk one block past Black Aces, they could marvel at the Town's awakening to independent coffee. Capp support comes with three independent baristas within the downtown but off Main, on the side streets.

Of course, the number one spot for caffeine is the coffee klatch that gathers at the greasy spoon diner in the east end. The Sunriser is open at five in the morning, when the Portlandia barista gang are still in bed dreaming of customer reward cards.

Reaching the corner, Greg whistles with excitement as he reads the name of the street. "The main drag is Queen Street. Wow." A wow barely uttered before a sidewalk interruption from that familiar phone voice.

"*Aargh. Aargh. Aargh.* Nice car, boys. Is it German?"

The prehistoric, chisel-faced man introduces himself in a crackly voice as Norman Morrison. His square frame extends outwards above his tight belt, accenting the overhang of a kettle-sized beer muscle. The partners are stuck with silent handshakes and half-dumb looks.

"Timed it perfect. Little Hooker, eh? *Aargh. Aargh. Aargh.*"

Silence.

"Don't see too many German exotics 'round Town."

They do look back one block on the left to where their car is parked.

"No," John says, "it's built in California."

Don't let the Golden Earring ringtone on his cellphone fool you: Norman's a surfer boy. "Jan and Dean have never seen anything like that."

Greg and John look at each other. Norman listens to the same music as their parents.

They keep to the topic of transportation. "Jan and Dean would love that it's electric," Greg offers.

Norman doesn't know how to react so does what he does best. *"Aargh. Aargh. Aargh."*

"We're Green supporters," Greg continues.

So they eat vegetables? Norman cuts back to what he knows. He's still on transportation. "Won't do well on the gravel. We'll take my pickup to the farm. *Aargh. Aargh. Aargh.*"

He looks at the lads as if they've never been in a pickup. Could be true for John. A distant memory for Greg as a boy.

"It's like four La-Z-Boy chairs on wheels. *Aargh. Aargh. Aargh.*"

"La-Z-Boy will have to wait," John says. "Us City boys need to get back tonight. We'll drive so we can leave right from the farm."

Norman seems a little disappointed not to be able to show off his La-Z-Boy captain's chairs to the City boys. This old horse, although cracked, creaky and chiselled, runs for the win. There's no place or show in his race for the deal. Accordingly, Norman never cheaps out on transportation. Norman-normal is a Concession Cadillac with no irony, a Ford Super Duty King Ranch. His brand-new current ride even massages the king's arse and back. All is a set-up for the grandest of entrances.

The Super Duty King Ranch has extendible sideboards that move out, reach out, for loading passengers and driver, and then tuck and hide away when the mission is complete.

"Feel like Moses stepping from the Mount when I step down off those running boards."

"Stormin', don't you mean Jesus on the Mount?"

"Aargh. Aargh. Aargh."

Barbie Kember was classmates with Norman from Grade 1 to Grade 10, when Stormin' cleared out.

"My Dad needs my help at the auction barn. What more can I learn here?"

School never teaches horse-trading, carpetbagging and tin-cupping. Norman's old man was known as the General. He never served in the army, but in general, the General knew something in general about everything.

"Go ask the General. He'll know if pygmies are monogamous."

And a four-star auction appraiser alongside his partner:

"These figurines." (The General shakes his head.) "Overvalued. It'll be a heartbreak for the Widow O'Hara."

"Nobody buys oak."

"8-track tapes? Box 'em up for the garbage."

Little Norman soaked up yards of experience instead of school life. In contrast, Barbie went on. She sought higher learning in a grounded form by continuing her education in Home Economics. She took the Sunday night train all the way to the Royal Agricultural College in the wonderful limestone City of Guelph.

Stormin' is neither a Daisy nor a Crazy, but he's still a definite character. One might say the best example of eccentric, our Norman.

"Aargh. Aargh. Aargh."

A combination of oddness and gumption, with the nutty nuance of repeating his *Aargh* and *Aargh* after anything said. All this behaviour merges with a real set of Town arnies for local business. Norman pulls the eccentric character traits into his real estate sales approach.

"Watch the old bugger's feet with customers. He shuffles back and forth. Leans in and out."

"Like Muhammed Ali, the old codger. Can float like a butterfly and sting like a bee."

"Get stung by his honeybee commission check."

"Codger, yeah."

"He ain't no butterfly. Stormin' Norman's more honey badger."

"Stinger."

"No he's a digger. Most big houses in Town. Lots of farms."

Stormin' Norman keeps a finger on, and his long nose in and around, all Town and Country real estate business.

"Forget those fancy coffees. Sunriser coffee comes black, thick and with information. Aargh. Aargh. Aargh."

Everybody knows you can never have a real estate agent as a good friend, but as a drop-in guest? (*"Susie would love me having a piece of her birthday cake."*)

Doesn't matter to Stormin' Norman, as he just shows up, invited or not. (*"Can't deny me a piece of that anniversary cake."*)

And those Christmas Open Houses with the shrimp wheel. (*"Is that Norman Morrison beside the shrimp?"*)

Norman circling the pink crustaceans seems like a given for the in-the-know:

"He just shows up at clients' barbecues, Christmas parties, christenings and bar mitzvahs."

"Do we even have a Jewish family in Town?"

Because of his prehistoric birth, Norm is not clear when he meets John and Greg. He puts his first step into *it* right at the Black Aces office:

"Will your wives be working in the cheese manufacturing?"

"Well I don't know about *your* wife, Norman …"

John hangs onto the word *your,* then *wife* pops out, with a final punch out with a strong *Norman.* "Or in fact I wouldn't have a clue about *any* wife. What about *our* … wives, Greg?

John looks at Norman. Norman feels the tables are turning in an unwanted direction.

"Tough question, Norman, when Greg is *my* partner. Greg and I both like the term 'partner,' or 'life partner.'"

Greg pipes up with a big smile toward John. "The one and only husband for me."

The Pirate Captain heads back to a safe harbour. *Keep it to the matter on the platter,* Norman says to himself. *Easy peasy. Follow the money. Move it forward in engagement and forward to contract signatures.* It's a winning deal. Greg and John can see his lips move, but they hear nothing.

"Having a cooperative partner is great for any business," he finally says. *"Aargh. Aargh. Aargh."*

Wow. The boys are gobsmacked by that Country-tactful answer. The Citiots note an innocence about the sharp-nosed, wiry-haired broker. Norman grew up on the farm. Nothing in his Country rearing accounts for the nature of same sex.

"Well, I'm all for lady farming," he says next. (A nasty shot, in the same ballpark as "hits like a girl." Or, after a bad tee-off: "Buddy, suggest you try the white blocks next hole.")

Norman goes on. "Do you partner lads have any goat experience?"

"Partner lads," at least, for the Citiots, is safe and familiar. Partners could mean any combinations of genders, whether married, dating or living together.

Greg rows right along for the cheesy ride. "I grew up on a farm north of Kingston. Helped my father rear the herd."

Norman lights right up on this image. John swears each grey eye moves in different directions. Greg rows on, leaving out horses and the words "hobby farm" and "non-skilled barn labour."

John pipes up. "Slopping, Greg. Slopping the barn."

"We had a Bobcat."

"Shit is shit, Greg."

"Nice shit, on 150 acres."

"Fifty of scrub, fifty of roll and rock."

"Log fires, Mother's wood cookstove, campfire coffee in the morning ..."

"The best in memories, partner."

"Why wouldn't Dad have raised goats?" Greg asks himself. "Our land was so rough. Too tough on Holsteins." He's knee deep in memory. "Goats would have been better."

John decides to leave Greg's best years alone.

Norman senses an unease between the couple, hidden under their expensive sunglasses. A lost look needs to be pointed in the right direction. Money. "So you think there's a big opportunity in producing goat cheese? Here in Transvaal?" Norman is the silver-haired, grey-eyed Pirate Captain, and cheesy comments are left off-board his ship. Business is business. He shifts foot to foot while his nervous twitch sails forth. *"Aargh. Aargh. Aargh."*

For no reason, Greg blurts out, "I'm an honours chemistry grad from Queens."

John winces. Norman winces too, without their notice. The Morrisons are no slouches when it comes to education. He doesn't bother mentioning that his eldest son is a professor at Western University's prized business school, a young contemporary of Professor James Kember's.

Norman is desk-ready for a winning deal. He has all in place: the latest stamped survey, well capacity, water quality, an inch-thick pile of Swiss manufacturers' receipts, a three-page inventory list, a structural report on the outbuildings, well-above-paid Township taxes, clear property deed and a zero balance on ZIT. All in their place, ready for show, looking for a winning deal. John goes for a final audit on the originals, having already read the copies sent by attachment.

Meanwhile, Greg can't help himself with curiosity. "Norman, how did you get the name Black Aces? Why not Black Aces?"

"*Aargh. Aargh. Aargh.* That's a story. The skinny version is that I won the brokerage in a poker game. Wish I had four aces, but all I needed was one. Had the two red aces. Drew the ace of spades. Bingo, I'm in the real estate business."

End of story. John has completed place and show.

"Any more questions, gentlemen? Here's the offer, as discussed."

Time to deliver, sign on the dotted line.

But.

"Boys. There's a 'but first' with the closing. But first, the timeline is tight with youse on the quick sale in the City and the Kembers waiting for Thomas."

The partners turn on this.

"Thomas. Saint Thomas?"

"*Aargh. Aargh. Aargh.* Relax. Everything will work out."

So the legal start to Gregzdream crosses the line of never-return inside the Black Aces office of Stormin' Norman Morrison, on Queen Street in St. Marys.

They turn to Norman. Greg almost hugs him but reverses to a heavy handshake.

"Welcome to the artisan goat cheese business," Norman says. "Welcome to Town, boys."

Everyone heads out, Norm to his truck and the boys to their parking space up the street.

Ten minutes later, Greg is pointing to the screen. "I told you. We could walk to here."

"Two kilometres on gravel. No thanks."

Greg dabs the computer screen. The screen answers him with its smarmy voice.

"*Your destination has been reached.*"

John is still driving straight ahead down the concession. "Here?"

John's mouth drops open. The GPS's red arrow flashes left for a quick turn right onto a hard-surface laneway. John slams on the brakes.

"Greg. The front lawn *is* completely burnt." All eyes on the battleground. "Is this a joke?"

"No, it's biblical."

"That's not a burning bush," John says. "That's the front lawn."

"It's apocalyptic …" For once in his comic life, Greg, the Queen of cheesy torts and retorts, is unable to press the embellishment button. "This is nuts."

Norman dismounts from the Super Duty Moses electric sideboards, as a big bad old dog shoots out from behind the back of the pickup. John backs up as Greg moves forward. He recognizes the old dog discussed in phone detail.

"Max," Greg says. "Maxy. Maxy. Maxy." Love at first sight, consummated with a left-pocket dog cookie. "Good doggie. Like your ears flopped?"

Norman has his ears to the ground for a win on this deal. He *has* met a Citiot or two. He knows the partners have ne'er a clue about the setup of a milk operation, the condition of the outbuildings or the quality of the land. But Norman would never sell a pig in a poke, no matter how dim the local wit or how far-off the Citiot. Norman has some relief in that goats are hard to kill; they can survive in the Sahara Desert. The farm boy feels Transvaal may be a charmed environment that fosters a novel enterprise. There's a milking herd sufficient to meet the needs of cheese production.

And he knows the Kembers. The outbuildings include the huge barn, with accommodation to double, triple the herd. And the milk shed is complete now, with Swiss equipment for cheese production recently installed. Of course, the big question remains: Where's the cheese?

Wandering the front yard, Greg does a Mickey Rooney. "We'll decorate the shed. Open bar will be in the gazebo. Snacks on the porch. We *will become* … *Green Acres*."

John pounds a nail. "We might want to use our green back yard lawn versus the front yard apocalypse."

"Back yard, front yard or barn, it's *Green Acres*."

John lawyers up. "Contractual, trademarks, copyrights, naming. Problems, problems, Greg. We need a first-things-first approach. You have the list in an email and a copy was put under your Capp this morning. We need to learn how to use the cheese equipment in the drive shed, not install bunting."

Greg is not over-matched. "Buddy, relax. We'll keep it to a local match with the show characters, even add a few. *But* … the best of all, John. Everyone can keep their local names. It's Country live reality."

John thinks release, privacy concerns and more contracts. No matter, Greg starts his own list for a story that began with a burnt furball and an opportunities word ad in the *Globe*. "Stormin' Norman is Fred Ziffel. I want to be Eva Gabor as Lisa Douglas."

John is more impressed than concerned by Greg's surprising and possibly weird secret knowledge of *Green Acres*. His partner rolls on.

"There's Mr. Haney. Oliver Wendell Douglas, of course that's you, John. Hank Kimball and Sam Drucker? We'll have to find their local match and use that local name. We need a local yokel with their name but the characteristics of Ralph Monroe."

John lights up. "Oh my God, Mary Grace Canfield as the clumsy carpenter." His load of insignificant quiz-night detail is mind-boggling.

Greg switches back to load up the humour. "And we can have some Howdy Dowdy in Transvaal. We can get all the look-alikes together in one big party, party, party."

John goes all quiz-night hardball with a *Green Acres* fact slap. "What about Newt?"

Greg gives a full ponder with that half-dumb look. "Who the fucking hell is Newt?"

Norman takes advantage of a pause to steer the partners back toward a literal reading of their farm transaction. "New roof on the double-wide drive shed."

Norman points to the shiny MotoMotion front-end loader, side by side with the junior tag-team member, a Bobcat.

All Greg can think is how easy slopping has become since he was a boy.

"Did you see the creek along the back property line?" Norman goes on. "Paddocks have proper fence. Good drainage. Well-maintained buildings …"

Check.

For the entire week, Greg has been showing off his Google satellite piloting skills to facilitate John's City-view audit of the Country property. Greg steps up, again, into Gregzdream. "Norman, let's make cheese." The drone plotting has really lit the fire on his Gregzdream. "The milk shed looks ready for the makings."

"One step at a time," John reminds him.

"*Aargh. Aargh. Aargh.* We need to work on the timelines, but first we need to meet the Kembers."

Norman shows off his dexterity by shuffling backwards to the porch while pointing the opposite direction.

"Just wait till you see the state-of-the-art equipment. Jimmy imported it from Switzerland, eh. Had a team of factory technicians here for a whole week; flew all the way over here. The Professor had it all installed according to his own measured plans, drawn and engineered, now framed on the wall."

Norman slows up, allowing the partners to move in close.

He whispers as a couple appears over his shoulder through the screen door.

"You *have seen* the receipt. Impressive, eh?"

John the Auditor is most impressed. Less cash needs for the process to get up and going.

Max watches, smiles, as the love-in unfolds between Master, Missus and the luxurious dog cookie attached to new human scents. Again, he is the first witness. The old dog can't fathom the number of back-and-forth calls between the City and Transvaal. Dog senses register a higher buzz in the last week from the human ZIT line. No introductions necessary with these new friends.

Jimmy smiles and shakes hands with the lads. "How would everyone like an ice-cold cup of Barbara's homemade lemonade, eh?"

"A nice tall glass with well-water ice," Barbara says. "The mint is from my garden. Just right, after that long drive."

John feels like he's back at Greg's parents' farm, north of Kingston. Greg just feels at home. Max is up on his feet, pointing to the outbuildings. Jimmy is pointing too.

"Let's start with the Say Cheese pride and joy, our state-of-the-art milk shed."

Jimmy's eyes sink back into his forehead. Much, much more than just a milk shed. It's been a long, long path, with little cheese to show for it. He comes up for a breath. "We are now up and ready for cheese production." Jimmy lays the shine on the deal. "Ready and waiting for our new owners."

You couldn't take the shine off Greg's face. John is thinking immediate cash flow. Norman, he's in a wonder on how one fat squirrel could turn all these lives around. John has his clipboard of lists and questions, most of which have been covered on those ZIT calls.

Max marvels at the speed of the tour. Master is so much slower than this, most days. No slopping this time around, no feeding, no milking, no moving the ladies. Most of the human talk takes place in that sour-smelling room where the goats line up for their release outside. But no goats today. A peek in the stalls, Master pointing around at everything, lots of human head nodding. But no goats today.

"Norman discussed the tight timelines on closing?" Jimmy asks.

"Greg and I have some things going to storage, most to the auction house. We have lots of friend invites to stay over. But, as we discussed on the phone, having us stay on site could make for the smoothest of transitions."

"Barbara has a plan for *our* living arrangements, and more ice-cold lemonade. She calls her plan Upstairs-Downstairs. Sorry, questions?"

Greg has a big one. "Where's Frankie?"

Everyone laughs; even Norman knows the pig.

"Let's finish up on the porch," Jimmy says. "Norman discussed a timeline with hold-back."

"Yes," John says. "Greg and I are in agreement with 250 thousand hold-back till cheese is in production. We also agree to share the house for up to two months on the Upstairs-Downstairs plan."

Greg can't help it. "So what about the pig?"

"Greg, after we dot the i's and cross the t's, we'll visit Frankie and his gang with a big basket of ground apples."

As simple as God's green apples, Gregzdream seems to be coming true. The partners head out the 6th Concession to Town with the sunset glowing in their mirrors and warm thoughts of a Normy-recommended bed and breakfast.

"All this signing; I'm beat," John says. "Marie's Gentle Dreams B&B sounds great."

Greg is still in Gregzdream. He snorts the pig call to John.

"*Ung*-huh-huh-huh. *O-o-o-o*-huh."

Chapter 7

The next day, as they're heading back to the City, Greg takes note of a massive sign on a barn on a side road leading cross Country. The black and red plastic letters read Mike's Auction Barn.

"Check this out, John. 'Auctions every other Tuesday night. Two Saturdays a month.' There's one tonight!"

Greg peeks into the back of the electric. "How do we fit anything in this car?"

John's turn to be Boy Scout–prepared. "With the fold-down flat, my car has sixty cubic feet of storage."

The owner of the exotic electric gets a look back from the passenger in his life. "How do we fit anything *extra* in your car?"

"Let's preview," John says. "Then decide."

Inside the Auction Barn, Mike is about to hang up on another gigantic Victorian sideboard.

"Don't want it," he says. "Sorry. Everyone says that. Yup. Make it a bar. Well, the bar has dried up on that idea."

After Mike ends the call, he says to no one in particular: "Too big. Who has a ten-foot wall these days without a window or door or fireplace?"

The caller on the other line is selling an unbelievable carved fireplace surround from some sad former pioneer merchant home under conversion to apartments.

"Sorry," Mike tells him. "Have three on the go. Yes, I have marble. And tiles. Yes, but no." (Billie already sourced out a beauty, currently stored out back toward the November sale. *Those tiles are outstanding, no damage. The surround is cherry. And look at the cast fire box, stamped 'Ingle — Brantford.'*)

Phone rings again, somebody looking for a special gift for a certain occasion. Mike shouts out to Billie for an idea.

First impression on Billie, ignoring the pencilled eyebrows and frizzed blond hair, is that he's a little trashy, a little bit of a stand-off. The major-domo of the sales barn skirts the show tables, pulling out a raft of keys. He fingers the exact one to open a specific cabinet with the correct high-end goods.

"This bisque Art Nouveau pen-and-ink set will knock 'em out, Mike."

"Huh? Pen-and-ink set? Knock 'em out, Billie?"

But Mike has learned to drop the questions, let the expert talk.

Mike's Auction Barn has its niche with boatloads of sought-after collectibles from long ago. He mixes vintage furniture with decorative original art and trims the hall with a flash of intriguing paraphernalia.

The high-school part-timer looks up from a stack of boxes in the corner. "More LaserDiscs, DVDs. All HD. The eight-track stuff. Cassettes."

Mike points to the big door on the right behind his auction help. "The bin."

With a magnifying glass hogtied to his neck, Billie goes back to sorting a lot of Royal Doulton figurines, Wedgwood platters and Lladro angels purchased out of guilt at the Las Vegas Airport gift shop.

Vintage, skinned Country furniture in oak, maple and pine goes cheap. Cherry and other exotic woods hold their own based on the quality of the piece. The real movement in taste these days is mid-century modern, the bailiwick of a certain couple of Citiots.

The sales barn shows off a parade of antique sideboards, corner and flat-wall cupboards, lamp tables, candle-stands and shelves of whatnot. They stick to a prioritized list, which does not include gigantic Victorian sideboards.

Earlier this week, a James Nesbit 1864 four-sided, swivel magazine stand gave a star auction performance. The craftsman's mix of cherry inlay, bird's-eye maple panels and walnut burl pilaster brought raves all the way from the appraiser to the auctioneer. *("Billie. It was a wonder passing three thousand. But my goodness! Over eight thousand dollars.")*

And neither Mike nor Billie caught the *Batman 3* misprint piled in Lot #142 of a dozen comic piles. Within twenty-four hours, the lot hit eight hundred bucks.

"Take a picture. Get the laptop out."

The current projection for #3 is sitting at three thousand dollars US. Today, the staff of four at Mike's Auction Barn are all hanging on for the ride.

Billie's antique knowledge is rural reared, a generational surprise, from the gravel concessions of the Gore of Downie. True knowledge comes from driving collectible old aunts.

"Aunt Betty had a Comet convertible," Billie tells people, "Margie, a Fargo pickup truck with three-on-the-tree. Neat stuff to drive."

The downside of the ride was Auntie repetition.

"Look, Billie, this pickle cruet is complete and undamaged."

"Look, Billie, a bird's-eye maple butter bowl with no cracks!"

"Look, Billie, over here ..."

Three aunts at the same sale make Billie want to say uncle.

"Look, Billie, yellow wildflower dessert comports. A full set."

Billie's gang of three still repeats almost every Saturday. He's grateful to drive and manages to flip the repetition around to appreciation. He soaks up the walking Auntie antique dictionaries, happy to be a chauffeur at their bid and beck on an auction morning.

"The bubbles in pressed glass are good." Aunt Margie rolls the goblet in the sunlight. *"Means it's old, Billie."*

Aunt Helen pulls the drawer right out of the dresser: *"Best view, back of a drawer. Unique dovetail. Top-drawer piece, Billie."*

Billie is loved by his large Gore of Downie family in his difference. He didn't always get such a warm reception in the rest of the world. He still remembers coming across an odd note at the Methodist Hall in St. Marys during Junior Choir and Sunday School. A crumpled ball that missed the trash can. *"Don't put me beside him."*

The odd note stayed with him through Stonetown High and confirmation. That glance up from the church pews at the special Sunday service. *"Why am I still sitting beside him?"*

"Him," young Billie, was smart enough to get a four-year bursary at the wannabe Ivy League Western University.

Billie would peel off the veneer of politeness for his Western buddies. *"They have to call their dances The Homophile Club. What's a homophile? A gay person who goes to the library?"*

After graduation, he stayed in the University City to teach elementary school, doing the social circuit by attending late-night party clubs. After twenty-five years, and an early retirement buy-out, Billie came home. He honours his ailing parents with personal care on his family's worn-out Downie Township farm. The combination of home life, St. Marys and the Gore of Downie, university, and staying on in University City has churned his mixed vision into a bit of a kaleidoscope. Billie keeps reeling in the sheaves of a distance past. He gets back into the auction flow, a natural at appraising. Flow Blue flows in Billie's veins at Mike's bimonthly barn auction. Miss Part-Time Help mines his employment source for take-home material, with a discerning eye for the rarest of rare — especially when it comes to the blurred blue glaze made famous by the Davenport Factory of Longport, England. Billie scours for the rarest scenes in octagonal teepee-shaped bodies. He tells Mike, "They speak to me. The oldest, oldest of all Flow Blue from almost two hundred years ago. I have three sets of pitchers and wash basins ..."

It's all a win-win for auctioneer Mike, who depends on that discerning eye. (*"Junk or treasure, Billie divides all. Most of the junk fills the bin out back."*)

The wonderful blend of rural, university and city inspires both happy and campy. Billie the appraiser works under the rhythm of quiet words of self-motivation:

> *"Billie Billie filly filly,*
> *The pile goes up and up.*
> *Billie Billie silly, silly,*
> *We've had 'bout enough.*
> *Billie Billie filly filly,*
> *No room for more stuff.*
> *Billie Billie silly silly,*

Billie stands near Mike and Mike's mother, Lorraine. "Who are the gentlemen in Bermuda shorts? Curly Head is cute. The other one looks too serious."

Mike has never sat on a Sunriser stool in his entire life. Lorraine knows all as a top Country in-the-know. She has already updated Mike on what she's heard about the lads in the Bermuda shorts.

"Goat cheese. City money."

Billie recognizes a common trail. "More drama on who's the husband."

Mike quotes Lorraine. "Whoever writes the cheque, Billie. That's the husband."

"Well, write me a cheque, Curly Top."

"These guys are above-budget bidders," Lorraine says.

Mike is on the ground. "They need vintage furniture for a Century fieldstone house. Let's load them up."

Billie goes back into silly, silly, Billie Billie, filly filly mode while quietly shadowing the City customers.

And the partners cruise the auction lineup unawares, ready to match the furnishings to their new lifestyle.

"John, that cherry flat-wall is struggling at two hundred bucks."

"I love the matching lamp tables. Cherry, too."

"The Georgian highboy may be a little over the top for a Country farmhouse."

"It *is* top drawer."

Greg stops, looking over John's shoulder. "Ps-s-s-s-t."

"What's up?"

"Don't look, but we have Gollum tracking us."

"Gollum?"

"You know," Greg says. "Frodo and Sam on their adventure. *That* Gollum. The way he's followed us around the preview. He's standing behind the showcases."

John turns. Billie stops. Greg looks back over John's shoulder. Billie catches the stare, smiles and waves.

"My God," Greg says. "Gollum is staring and smiling at me." Greg is stuck cringing and waving back. Reviewing his extensive list of required new-lifestyle items, John rescues Greg from his feeble freeze with a left hand on his upper arm.

"Come. We have some reserve bids to decide on, so let's get a number."

Lorraine watches as they approach the counter.

"So you bought the old Kember Farm, did you. Gonna make cheese, they say. Old Jimmy never made any; now what do you think of that. Jimmy and Barbara have a household of antique furniture. Suppose they could be sellers; never were buyers. No Kember address in the system. I know it's Transvaal."

Lorraine does not wait for any replies but moves to a new position on her desktop.

"In that case, I will need your proper domicile. Mailing address, if different from the domicile. I know you City folk like box numbers and stuff."

She zeroes in on John, up from the computer, up over her reading glasses. "And no American Express."

"Just a minute," he says. "I'll call it up on my phone."

The maternal leader of the generational auction family knows technology. She holds up a large smartphone. "Message me."

John looks at her, on pause. She points her phone at his phone.

"Message me your information."

When John finally complies, Lorraine reviews the information, talking to the screen. "I knew it wasn't Transvaal. It's the 6th Concession 527457, RR #3, Thorndale N0M 2V0."

That stops John and Greg on the spot. "Thorndale? We're in Transvaal."

"No sirs, your post office calls it Thorndale. Transvaal is just a square red dot on a survey map."

"Thorndale is twelve kilometres away. Why not St. Marys? It's three kilometres from us."

Lorraine can be mother-firm with patient bidders, dim-wits, lookie-looks and Citiots.

"Can't fight the Post Office. Thorndale. Be thankful you still have rural delivery ..." (another look off the screen over the readers) "... in Transvaal."

Lorraine misses nothing at her age.

"Now, sirs, we have your address, email, you're on our newsletter. We need your number on file — MasterCard or Visa?"

John and Greg know the drill for auction bidding registration; get the credit card out for the guarantee. Lorraine notices Greg's constant stare at a piece of furniture tucked in a corner.

"A no-show for payment," she clarifies. "Yours for a hundred bucks. Cash please."

Before John can flip two fifties on the desk, Billie is standing with the chair waiting for Greg to open the exit door. At least, he's smiling at Curly Top, with a head jerk to the exit. In amazement, they follow the chair out to the parking lot and right to their car.

No one-trick pony, Billie helps shove a mission-style comfy chair in the ass end of the exotic electric.

John pushes the Close button under the hatch, getting an immediate sound reaction. *Ding Ding Ding ...*

"Lid doesn't quite catch," Billie says. "The car sensors are picking up the problem."

Both Greg and John look at the slight, blond man, stunned silent that Gollum talks.

"Press the Menu icon," Billie goes on. "Scroll to the Door Hood Trunk icon. Press. Then press Off on the Alarm Warning."

Billie takes no awkward pause as a problem.

"My dad subscribes to *Motor* magazine," he explains. "Electronic systems get big coverage. Your electric gets the most."

Still nothing.

"My name's Billie Ball," he smiles. "I'm chief appraiser for Mike. Anything you're interested in, just ask me. I have first eyes on all that comes in that door." Billie jerks his neck back toward the auction barn. "See something on the web listings or in a preview? Just ask me."

His stare pulls a question from Greg. "Well, then. I can put Billie Ball in play with a question on a vintage dress. A dress in your auction preview."

"Billie gets lots of vintage clothing from collectors and wearers."

"Wearers?"

"The dress-up crowd, a mixed salad of interest, all *la couture* label chasers."

"I noticed a Rico Letang wedding dress that would have been one expensive bill for the father of the bride. Twenty thousand plus."

Billie focuses on Greg as he replies. "Good label eyes, says I's. And a big story that goes with it. A nightmare story that can be addressed with that dress."

John is apprehensive, not about the story but the fact that Billie his leaning is elbow on his car. Worse, Greg is leaning in with *his* elbow, too, on the opposite side of the car.

"Did you hear the story about Allin Douglass?" Billie asks.

"Who?" Greg says.

"Careful on spelling Allin, with two *l*'s, and an *i* instead of the usual *e*. And the last name has two *s*'s on the end of Douglass."

"Sorry," John chimes in. "We haven't even moved in yet, so we don't know anyone."

Billie moves close in, with his elbow still on the roof and an all-knowing look from an in-the-know. Greg's feet stay planted, but his head leans back to accommodate Billie's proximity. Billie presses on.

"He *had* a second-hand store on Bank Street. It's the thrift store now."

"Wait, so what's important about this Douglass guy? Two L's with an I on the Allin. Ass on the end his name."

Billie ignores alien sarcasm on a fab story. He moves closer, lowers his voice. "Allin liked ballroom dancing." He holds his eyebrows up with an ask-me-why look.

"More to the point," he continues, "he liked to wear his vintage gowns." Billie is almost hissing in Greg's ear now. "Dresses from the store. Off the rack."

Greg can't help himself. "Must have been quite a queen — you can bank on it."

Billie puffs his face up in a frown, eyebrows down. "Better! He was a roamer."

"A roamer," the Citiots both echo.

Billie's eyebrows are up and down, down and up. "Flitting about. A bird of paradise who flits about in the night."

John is spinning gears to get traction on small-town dress-up. "A bird in a couture dress?"

"Cocktail dresses, prom dresses." Gollum hisses it out. "*Wedding* dre-e-e-sssss-es. Allin, Miss Dress-Up, keeps a better schedule than the train. In fact, he's stuck on a timer clock, same place, same times." Gollum agre-e-e-ees with himself. "Ye-e-ssss. Ye-e-ssss, he comes out at night in his dre-e-e-ssss-e-sss."

Greg and John are lost. Is this a Hungarian art movie, or is this guy for real? They look at each other for help. They blurt out questions, questions:

"Roamer?" "Dresses?" "On a time clock?"

"Ti-i-i-ime clock, Greg. Sho-o-owtime, Friday nights at eleven. On the clock, the time clock. Roaming, he is."

Greg goes all Western. He returns a silly volley in song, slapping his hips and moving back from the corn-haired appraiser. *"Roamin' roamin' roamin'... Get this wagon train roamin' ..."*

Billie is stopped in his story tracks. Both John and Billie come out with an echo. "Huh?"

"Allin is roaming with a dress train. Get it?"

"Huh?" John says again. "Don't you mean rolling, not roaming, Greg?"

"Okay, John, then 'rolling along.'"

Greg turns away from his partner and toward the frizzy-topped man smiling at him. "Rollin' along in his dress-up gown, did Allin with two *l*'s and one *i*, at the chime of midnight, give up this ..." (Greg pauses with a stare back at John) "... roamin' wagon train and turn into a pumpkin, like Cinderella?"

"Turn into a *pump*-kin. That's so fu-un-n-n-e-e-e-e."

Both partners stare in disbelief at the conversation coming out of Cornhead. Time to stop roamin' and start rollin' along.

Greg leaves all boundaries on gossip protocol behind. This Friday night special in a roamin' dress breaks all the rules. He can't believe the strangeness of the truth, so he rises to the dumb occasion. In turn, Billie is smart enough and exasperated enough to know when to bail. The interruptions, the quips, the quirks are too over the top, over the Curly Top. He retreats to the auction preview on show.

"Did you see that Philco 1954 TV console?" he asks the Citiots, his elbow off the roof, heads up, back to the entrance.

Greg puts on the brakes, returning to his normal tact. "Sorry, Billie. Squash the pumpkin jokes. Skip the auction tour. What *happened* at eleven on Friday nights in Town like clockwork, with this Allin all dressed up for roaming and flitting about?"

Billie gets back on the wild horse tale.

"Allin was on parade. Just dressed in something off the prom, bridesmaid or even couture rack. A pass through the alleys of downtown St. Marys in a passed-on gown off the rack."

This is nothing startling in the odd file for Greg or John, but it still piques their curiosity.

"And what happened to Dougie?" John asks.

Billie hits back. "He became a *pump*-kin!" Both laugh as Billie adds on oddness. "No, actually, the parade ended in a pumpkin shootout."

Greg exhales. "No-o-o-o-o, Mister Billie. No-o-o-o-o!"

Billie is cheek to jowl with Greg. "Ye-e-e-e-sssss."

The Citiots are both incredulous. "A shootout?"

"Yup, ambushed in the dark alleys of St. Marys."

Greg cannot help himself again. "*Roamin' Roamin' Roamin'*… The wagon train is ambushed."

"Yessss," Billie says. "Ambushed with his ass blown off late one Friday night. And, might I add, on a full moon."

"No more ass on Mr. Douglass," John says.

Greg needs to fill in the details. "Ambushed by who? Local police? Here in St. Marys?"

"St. Marys Constabulary at its best. The Sergeant." Billie winks in-the-know. "Also known as the Chief. Plus Supercop Russ rained on Dougie's singular parade. A storm, that one night, in his Rico Letang couture wedding dress." The corn head gives another jerk back toward the preview.

"Dougie?" Greg asks.

"Douglass. Dougie-Ass." Billie winks. "Better known as Wedding Girl."

The partners stare at Billie in astonishment.

Billie continues. "Yup, rained down rock salt. Dougie comes floating around the stone stables. Right back of Thames Pizza. Get this. He's wearing a known dress off the rack." This time, two winks in-the-know. "He's decked out in Cindy Davies' wedding dress. You know, the Rico Letang — Cindy dumped the dress in a rage. She caught Jack Junior in the laundry room …"

John is having a quick audit on the couture dress. "Someone from *here* wore a twenty-thousand-dollar —"

"Married into the Rogers Family …"

"Who …?"

"You know, 'Rogers Does It.' This time Jack Junior was doing it — in the laundry room."

Greg cuts him off. "Billie. Some other time in the laundry room. Tell us about the shootout!"

The interruption is ignored.

"On Saturday morning, the very next day, the coffee klatch gets started. Right off, the first swivelling stool swings with details. The Sunriser crowd renames

Allin" — one wink — "with two *l*'s and one *i*, right then and there on the spot. Renamed him there."

"Renamed? Renamed him what?"

Billie can't hold it back. "Wedding Girl."

Billie gestures understanding by rubbing his palms together toward Greg and John.

"Wedding Girl is right on the mark, I'd say," John says. "Saved poor Mrs. Douglass and family a direct connection to the scandal and embarrassment."

Greg winds it out with one more reference to the sixties TV show.

"Was there any connection between this Douglass and the other one, Oliver Wendell in *Green Acres*?"

Billie appreciates the crafty script effort. "One Douglas there and one odd ass here, Greg." He has more. "Sorry, should have mentioned. The Chief planned his assault with his salted double-barrel .24-gauge."

"Shotgun?"

"Salted. Gauge of twenty-four on a shotgun makes it more of a squirrel gun. With the salt it stings but no injury. Supercop Russ did the actual dirty business."

Billie cradles and then blasts a pretend shotgun, all from the hip. John is hands up in response. "So why did the municipality take this interest in Wedding Girl?"

Billie steps back for local on-the-ground education of the ways and means.

"Small-town conservative values. What would the children think? Downtown neighbours having a late-night beer on their deck — what would they think? What would Cindy Davies think with her Rico Letang jilted wedding dress parading around Town? This prom parade was *not* hidden. It made stools swivel in snickers at the Sunriser."

"The Sunriser, that's the diner …?" Greg asks.

Gollum leans in. "*Tha-a-a-a-t* place is the Town's school of scan-n-n-n-dal. Anyway, the Chief and Supercop get primed up with a few brewskis. Cheers to Wedding Girl's final act."

Gollum gives his version of a Boy Scout salute. "The Constabulary, our finest in blue, have done their detective work. They know Dougie's parade path. They pick their strategic ambush spot."

Greg and John can't wait to debrief on the car ride home with this wild stuff. Billie is almost out of breath.

"The coppers themselves tuck up in the hedge. The one along the stone wall, left side of the old livery."

"Liver?"

"Liver-e-e-e. Behind the back corner. In the bushes. Hidden."

"Okay," Greg says. "Ambush."

"An ambush point which allows Supercop to blast off Dougie's arse."

John is horrified. "Blasts his arse off?"

"Remember, shotgun with salt, no big damage. But go figure. He was shooting for his knees. Stopped him dead in his tracks. Or rather, arse-end backwards to the police. Buzzed by the fuzz."

Greg picks up the horror of it all. "Buzzed dead in his tracks?"

"Salt, Greg. Just salt. But old Dougie had lots to say."

"What did he say?"

Gollum stops, then takes it up an octave for a Betty Boop. *"Ga-a-a-a-ad!"*

Curly Top turns to the large barn to see if anyone else is watching this charade on the parade, as Billie continues:

"You've *ruined my Rico Letang couture gown."*

In a lower voice for the pretend Chief:

"What?"

Back to Betty Boop:

"This is *not* off the rack. You've *ruined* my couture house gown from Paris." Billie doubles down as Betty Boop to make a GPS point. *"Not* Paris, Ontario."

John is touched. "Was Allin okay?"

"He went dumb. He fell to his knees, sobbing."

Greg wants more plot. "What did the Chief say?"

Billie wags the Chief's naughty-boy finger with the official Town word: "I *catch you* prancing around like Cinderella *one* more time. *One* more time, Allin Douglass … I'll *shoot your fucking* balls off!"

John has lost any thought of litigation. He is having a heifer moment for the second time in less than a week. He's flabbergasted at the idea of losing one's balls. "And Allin?"

"Dougie, our boy, has style, perspective and off-the-rack verve. Did not back down from the cops. He just sobbed, repeating *You ruined my Rico Letang couture creation*, over and over."

Billie repeats in the crowd-catching voice. *"Ga-a-a-a-ad. You-ruined-my-1965-Larson-couture …"*

Greg leaves the pantomime to go back to the beginning.

"Clockwork? Friday nights? What happened next?"

"Parade got rained out."

Greg pauses in thought — a party thought.

Billie brings him back in thought to Town alleys on a late Friday night, possibly early Saturday. "The parade did stop then and there on that late Friday night, possibly Saturday morning, but not the drama. They say Dougie and the missus still play Mrs. Allin and Mr. Missus, ballroom dancing back in Toronto."

Greg and John both search their memories of big-city venues, wondering if they've ever seen that dress pair.

Greg pulls John aside. "We have another theme-party idea."

John is caught off guard. "Another party? What theme?"

"Allin with double *l*'s and one *i*, Douglass with an ass on the end. A dress-up party."

"A dress-up party?"

"Even better, John, so much better than just the dress-up."

"How much better, buddy?"

"A Wedding Girl party."

"Wedding Girl party?"

"Yes, yes, yes. It's a shotgun affair." Greg looks up to the sky to put a high finish on the proposed event. "A heaven-sent theme. Dress up in vintage wedding and prom dresses, bridal gowns and couture if you want. And party!"

John interrupts. "Couture?"

Greg has one up on the master quiz partner. "High fashion, handmade in Paris — Paris, France."

Billie sneaks up between them. "Can I come? I have a peach chif-f-f-fon that Mother wore to her sister's wedding in 1958. Did not last a year, that marriage. It fits me at knee length." Billie giggles, or is it a Gollum cough? "Flooo-z-z-zy. Makes me look like a real f-f-f-f-looo-zzy."

Greg and John give a corner-eye glance back and forth and think in sync. Where else in southwestern Ontario would a lad come out in peach chif-f-f-fon? Say Cheese, eh?

John has all elbows off his car, the driver door open, ready to power off.

"Let's not set a date for anything, whether Dis Tress or Green Acres. Most important right now is the launch."

Greg, the hospitality queen, steps up for the team. "A *successful* launch. We want a Big Launch. We need Jimmy to barbecue a goat. That'll be a home run."

"Not for the goat."

Greg is ready to howl, but John interrupts. "Not that pig call, Greg. Please no."

The server-supreme sidesteps his dance partner and goes for the goal posts. "We need caterers, a bartender, a rental company for chairs, tables, glassware and flatware. Oh my God, and someone to clean up."

"You need a *list*, buddy. We have just a few weeks to launch."

"Oh, my God. Where do you start … in the Country?"

John the Auditor likes fun, too. "First, let's hit the Buckatoo Store in St. Marys for decorations."

Greg is on for a dusty drive back over to Town. "Cheesier the better."

Chapter 8

But there's still the magnificent deck with the awesome view to say goodbye to.

The lads will miss the order-in fresh spring rolls made with love by Suke Lee or his wife, Linda, delivered by son, Sam.

And the best baba ganoush, an easy pickup from the Lebanese bakery around the corner.

"Forget the carbs, Greg. NO bread. Some of those ancient wheat or seaweed rice crackers would be nice. The expensive store has a great selection."

Greg knows that John's referring to the trendy organic grocer with aisles of unknown labels.

"But the falafels will be hot out of the wood-fired oven?"

"Greg. NO Carbs. Crackers."

Not to forget a few Champagne cocktails.

Chin-chin.

"Top me, buddy."

"Greg, buddy. What a treat for a Monday afternoon. The best of life from our porch." *Chin-chin.*

"To a better life past the porch. Out there in Transvaal, southwestern Ontario. To our partnership in cheese, buddy."

John and Greg look over Mike's auction newsletter in comfy chairs, in between packing up their wonderful collection of mid-century modern. Forbes Bye-Bye Auction's bruised steel vans are hauling out the big stuff.

"Wrapped up like mummies."

"Hope there's King Tut bids."

They now look forward to surveying Mike's inventory online before each auction, every second Tuesday and Saturday. The last couple of weeks, when visiting the farm, they've made GPS-dependent Country detours through Haysville to stock up on raw-milk Gouda at the farm-gate cheese shop. Over to the Theatre Town to buy fresh sea-salt focaccia from Ed's Bread. Then, if there's been bid success or there's a necessary preview, Mike's. Greg works the shopping list through his stomach:

"I can't wait for poached brown eggs and maple-cured smoked bacon on Ed's focaccia. With a touch of your aioli, John."

The couple that shares together stays together; take the aioli, for example.

"John's secret aioli recipe is all yours, Greg."

Mike's is an easy, on-the-way excuse to do a lookie-look for furniture to fill the old house.

"Accoutrements, John. It's the total style package."

"Sounds expensive."

"John. Do the audit. No one wants this shit no more. And cash rules for the cheap bidder."

The frequent fly-bys to the Auction Barn build up to full disclosure. Billie provides a *Green Acres* new-age seed bank of ideas for the party shelf.

The Country appraiser relays a magic carpet ride, 1001 themes. Curly Top stands amazed, visit after visit.

"Billie taught elementary school for twenty-five years," he tells John later. "He was a regular at the Wing Bang Club."

John shows little interest. "That was University City. He Wing-Banged only on the weekends. Never met him."

"All it takes is one weekend and … You won't believe this, either. Billie dated Super Agent Man, Stevie." This increases the limited interest. "Before our time in the City."

"Some twenty-five years ago," Greg continues. "But you're a City boy. You knew Stevie from high school."

"I honestly can't remember Billie."

Greg seems to have the line on Billie's City lineage. "He was at one of the first Dis Tress, Dat Tress parties."

"A frightening party parade."

"No, great stories. And he has the local scoop on *things.*" Greg holds double fingers in parentheses to the side of his Ray-Bans.

"Things?" John goes all audit. "We need to stick to the work-plan list. Cheese before furniture, and furniture before Billie goes gruff."

"What about the Big Launch party?"

"We need to build the ship before we launch it."

Greg is ramping up to his role in goat management. He's enrolled in a one-week course called "The Art of Artisan Cheese-Making," at the Richard Baird Culinary College. The timing dovetails like heated Velveeta with the farm closing.

Best, the college is a four-block walk from their condo, not counting the elevator ride down from the heavens. He passes the sidewalk investment and real-estate offices to arrive at a comfortable school of hospitality. The mixed bag in the lightning-in-a-bottle course includes four bored housewives, one struggling couple, four serious types and a handful of students along for a free ride.

"Do we get to eat the stuff we make?"

"My mother thinks it's cute."

"Weird, dude. My girlfriend thinks it's cute."

"Cool, dude."

All seem to question the direction of this stylish *bon vivant* in what we know as Gregzdream. He's a sophisticated gay gentleman — an old person to the barely post-pubescent students who whisper out of Greg's earshot.

"I hear he's a *bon vivant.*"

"What's a *bon vivant?*"

"Doesn't have to work. My sister is a server at his restaurant."

"Dude owns a restaurant? Which one?"

"No. My sister and the dude work at the same restaurant. He sold his condo for millions."

"So two million. For a condo."

"Twice that. Have you seen the photos? The awesome view."

"So he bought the restaurant?"

"No, he bought a goat farm near Michigan."

"What the hell does he know about goats?"

Greg can't hear the comments, but he picks up on the intent. He turns to face the classroom gossips:

"I learned when I ran my father's horse-breeding farm north of Kingston."

Size is everything. So Greg upsizes for a little fun with the younger urban hipsters:

"Yup, three hundred acres. Learned the horse business before moving to Toronto."

He has the student dummies tuned in now, so he boosts a few more for the home team.

"Three hundred goats. Two winners from last year's Royal Winter Fair. Number one, or was that the number two, goat cheese in Canada."

The students make notes on their smartphones about googling Transvaal. Greg thinks that the Royal Winter Fair will make his must-do list. One small step for City-kind in the wild projectile called Gregzdream.

Meanwhile, deskbound in the move to a new life, John plumbs ahead. He audits every source for small business agricultural start-up and cheese grant money, whether federal, provincial or county. The pair don't need a loan, but they still want to suck up some free money.

"Write the Town tourism development committee," Norman advises.

"We're in Nissouri," John protests.

"Town has the budget, Township does not. *Aargh. Aargh. Aargh.*"

John sends a letter of introduction to the mayor of St. Marys, Bob "Chico" Appleby. The Town has an innovation trust fund set up through the sale of excess land. John receives the application by file attachment.

"'To promote visitor traffic to Town & County.' That's what the app says." Here, Johnny on the spot, in a great program for free money. John gets ready for another visit to Transvaal for some Town presentations.

"These Country folk have never seen a PowerPoint with video highlights." John jabs at his touchscreen.

"Never with goats in action, anyway."

Teamwork follows a strict timeline, according to John. Greg has to let go of the editing, tweaking and fussing about for the right quality videos and photographs. John has all the graphs projecting maximum success for cheese. John insists on a solid deadline in order to make a big point at a scheduled appointment. Greg insists on quality presentation.

"John, this is *not* rocky, bushy, lumpy eastern Ontario. These people know agribusiness. It surrounds them. Maybe soften them up with Frankie at the trough," Greg suggests.

"Huh?"

"Rural folks love those cute farm shots. It's not birthing season, but Frankie and his porky pals are in the photo can."

Greg is hands up, clawing at the air with his nose up. "I have a pano shot, the whole damn family snouts up."

John feels a partner leg-pull. Gotcha.

Greg lets a few loose. "*O-o-o-o-huh-huh-huh. O-o-o-o-huh-huh-huh. O-o-o-o-huh-huh-huh.*"

John has to admit that he loves Greg's hog call, even if he can't tell whether it's supposed to sound like the swine itself or just a call to swine. The presentation is serious stuff, though, so Frankie gets a pass.

On other desk duty, the responsible one reviews the sales agreement, the environmental assessment, the Transvaal Township bylaws, and anything contractual or potentially legal including the propane service and the Zorra Internet & Telephone (ZIT) billing.

"ZIT has already replaced all wires and the server and input boxes," he brags to Greg. "When I told them I used to work as a lawyer, the service rep couldn't do enough."

John digs on for full disclosure, while Greg ponders his imagined dream list, with Country potholes of distractions.

"How can a telecom, no matter how small, be from a point on the map that no one has ever heard of?" Greg wonders out loud. "Nissouri Township! Not even my spell checker has that one. Then you add Transvaal into the mix. Do you know that our neighbours call themselves Transvaalanians?"

John is head down to the screen. "Transylvanians?"

Greg rolls his eyes up. "Transvaalanians."

John is stuck.

"No matter," Greg says. "Dracula could never find the place, let alone fly through all that dust."

It may be Gregzdream, but it's John who has the nightmare. He sticks to a serious daytime path but cannot kick a certain recurring dream. He confides in Greg, his life partner, once again.

"Everything ends up in shit."

"Shit?"

"Farm poop. Manure. The dream doesn't start out that way. It starts out with the goats. But I'm in the middle of them, and they move in closer, and closer …"

"Then move your arse out of there."

"Dummy, it's a dream. I'm surrounded. And they start to bite me."

"Bite you? Goats. Maybe they're zombie goats, eh?"

"Well, there's no blood — maybe 'nipping' me is more to the point. So I run, run, but my path is shit, a brown ground cover. I'm slipping, sliding, sailing through shit but not skipping it. I look down, lose my balance.

"That's when I wake up."

Greg knows that his sensible partner, no matter the matter, welcomes the distraction of humour. "That's not exactly true. You're doing that heaving-breath thing in your sleep." Greg squeezes John's nose for effect. "Snorting with your nose. That's when I roll across the bed and give you a nudge."

Greg cups his hands over his mouth and nose, snorting like a pig.

"*Ung-huh. Ung-huh. Ung-huh.*"

John looks at him like he's done a fart. "It's goats, buddy. You're snorting like a pig." John sticks to silence, with a half-dumb look.

Greg does not let the comparison die and snorts some more.

"*Ung-huh. Ung-huh. Ung-huh.*"

One of Greg's talents is doing animal and bird impressions. Greg rolls across the silence to new territory. "Frankie is going to love a little Pig Latin with his Master, Greg."

John returns to the matter at hand. "I wake up at night in a cold sweat. I find myself screaming the same tired lines."

Greg vamps it up. "*Goats! Fucking Goats! How did I ever get into this mess?*"

John stops and looks. "How did I — sorry, how did *we* — get into this mess?"

Greg, for once, holds up some sensible support. "Buyer's regret, partner? Or buyer justifies the purchase all the way to the bank?"

John gives Greg a little wake-me-up in Gregzdream. "Except *we* paid *cash*."

"I suppose the satisfying rub is that we still have tons of cash in the bank."

John comes back practical again. "Cash? Our cash is in our investment portfolio. Stocks, Greg."

Greg can counter-account-attack too. "If our bank account is a little light, don't forget that Walter talked you into those marijuana stocks. And, when we signed that hold-back for the Kembers, *you* said all was 'good' ..."

"Good to make cheese. All set to go, partner."

Both minds go to pause with the image of their little nest in the west. Most of their assets are indeed tied up in the Say Cheese statements.

(They both know that at this moment in the far-off west, Frankie is waddling through the muddy pen to bank on his cache of unlimited milk: *"Rub-a-tub-tub grub. Tons of grub in the tub, tub, tub."*)

"Along with a prizewinning herd of goats," Greg offers. "*And* a generational 150-year-plus Ontario farm."

John's eyes roll. Greg notices and re-confirms: "With a beautiful fieldstone farmhouse."

John subtracts the dream from the assets. "Roof pointing, insulated windows — who knows the expense of this old house," he says. "Goats? More like eating machines that produce milk. That's the milk we need to truck over to the back of the barn every day, where back out of sight we feed bigger eating machines that do *not* produce an ounce of milk."

But Greg has bought in. "Frankie's a cream puff. I think he already knows me."

John adds up Frankie's market future. "The family swine can dine on someone else's portfolio. Frankie does not want to end up as two hundred pounds of milk-cured bacon."

Greg's eyes tear up at the thought of eating Frankie for breakfast. John switches back. "Goats, Greg. Cash guzzlers. They are just eating up the cash flow."

Greg straightens up, throws cash to the wind. "We'll get the cheese operation up and Adam, John. Soon enough."

"The purchase is complete, and excuse the pun, but I'm not *ki-i-i-ding*: we need to make cheese ASAP. We need to get a quick sort on our plan. Number one is moving."

"Moving in with the Kembers will be kind of like a B&B … on a goat farm."

"That will sort itself out but we need to sort, sort, sort. A big reduction in stuff. You have a lot of stuff, so sort, Greg."

Greg is handy. "Lots of boxes from the LCBO. I'll give Judy the heads-up. Save the ones with the handles off to the side."

John is realistic. "Lots of garbage bags to sort your shit out. I'll make a shopping list for Canadian Tire."

"My stuff has value."

John stays religious to the plan. "Dump it, or you can carry it. Out of the condo, down the road all the way to Transvaal. Your choice, buddy."

"The Rick's Café tokens we mounted in the shadow frame?" Greg protests.

"*You* mounted. How drunk did you get at that bar?"

"The card keys for our special hotels?"

John pushes his hands to the side in a shovelling motion. "Gone."

"The coaster collection?"

John has his thumb going back behind him, whistling. "Gone."

"And the antique corkscrews on the custom Portuguese cork frame?"

The auditor goes still. "Okay. That comes with us."

Greg can do math. "That's a one-in-four ratio, John. To cut seventy-five percent, that's a little severe, don't you think?"

"You sort it, you carry it."

"The matching CP train travel posters from the thirties?"

"Why in the world would locomotive art fit into a century stone farmhouse?"

He ignores Greg's pouty silent rebuttal.

"Great auction item," John offers.

John's thought pattern runs back to the nightmare. Nipping goats chasing him through thick and thin, slippery poop. The shit show is everywhere. His fall in shit on waking reboots him. His imagination sidesteps to an art image hanging out behind the bar of their deck with the view, a vintage purchase at a Tim Cotter Auction in Napanee.

"It's horrific," John says. "That circus sideshow poster of the four-horned goat. You bought it as a joke. Now we're wearing the dream."

Greg defends his ironic art purchase. "It's not a joke. It's a classic Robinson Brothers Circus original."

Greg has a full-on half-dumb look plastered across his face. That does not stop him.

"Forget the dumb poster. It's coming with us to the farm. But it's *not* your nightmare. It was your fourth margarita last night combined with too much hot tub, John. You cannot do more than two of those margaritas."

"I *was* one dead soldier by number four."

Greg snorts off. *"Ung-huh. Ung-huh. Ung-huh."*

In Gregzdream, Greg will be down in the barn, milking those ladies 24/7. John will find comfort in his farmhouse office, taking care of the books.

In the meantime, working the deal brings out John's in-house due-process persona. What a partner! John knows contracts, conditions, attachments, appendices, agendas and regulations, and loves a search through the fine print. Their investment deal, though it starts as a dream, needs to be farm-legal.

The auditor lifts his head up, readers down, from the laptop. "Did you know there's no burning without permits in Nissouri Township?"

"No furry wienies for a bonfire. Boo hoo."

Greg takes the course, reads his newsletters and books. John shadows the reading while grinding the figures. The partners come together with John Capps until late at night, sometimes as late as four o'clock.

"John, I found this beautiful coffee table book on Nubian goats."

"Maybe they have goat colouring books, too."

Partner's firm voice. "John."

"Actually, I did bring you a find. From the library, which does not have colouring books." He pulls the specimen from his briefcase. "Look, *Small Goat Herd Management*. And voilà number two: *The A, B, G on Making Goat Cheese*."

Partner hugs all round.

"You know, from the course I've been taking …"

"You mean the short course?"

"Yes, from the short course, my long-confirmed understanding is that two personalities make up the goat cheese model."

"Let me guess. Smart John and Gregarious Greg."

"Sure," Greg says. "You keep to the Excel and I'll do what I'm trained to do."

John's turn for a full-on half-dumb look.

Greg beats an imaginary drum. "Ta-dah! My talent is?"

"Slopping the barn."

"Yes, I'll slop the barn. But I'm talking about the goats. We need one person in the barn and one in the milk shed. A shepherd for the herd, and a cheese-maker to handle the milk."

"You learned this at that short course?"

"No," Greg says. "Read it. It's in the book I gave you."

Greg is right: two very different personalities are needed in the goat business, aside from barn-slopping and Excel-calculating.

A shepherd manages the herd, administers to the flock. A shepherd listens and is kind, intuitive and proactive toward their herd. He or she recognizes the queen of the ladies and the sequestered king.

A cheese-maker makes the cheese, manages things from the teat end to the store shelf, including the IGA by the Thames River in Town.

And the two partners celebrate the dream. *Chin-chin,* by candlelight on the massive patio.

"Thank goodness for you, Greg, and your dreaming. I would have never followed up on that goat ad."

John raises his flute while grabbing another slab of Mountain Oak wild nettle gouda. With a third hand, he could have patted the dreamer on the back. Instead he reaches for the clink. "Never would I have imagined the impossible, Greg. Not without your quest for adventure. Here's to my life partner — I love the dream."

Hands down, hugs all round.

"Thank you, John. Thank you for being the perfect partner."

Release me, please release me, for there's a going-away party, on the perfect patio space, highlighted by a glorious sunset, for the City couple in their condo with the awesome view. John and Greg shine on, in the final curtain call on City life.

"Greg, it's Philip. He made it."

"The Great P himself."

The couple can look back from the Great Lake refreshed with a wonderful wave of friends at a point-break to a new life. John sits up on the edge of his lounge-chair comfort perch.

"Dan the Man. Haven't seen him since Scary Gerry's party."

Greg is counting heads. "There lots not to miss here."

John is on, on to the chilled flutes with the sparkling drop. "Lots of misses. Here's to our new adventures. Here's to new friends."

Ching. Ching. Greg can't help himself with an extra *ding.* "Country folk, eh?"

Both laugh. "Look at the crowd at the cheese table. Let's get hospitable, meet and greet."

The partners can work the room, excel in their own awesome space. They start at ground zero, the cheese table.

"Is that some of your chèvre, Greg?"

Patrick and Paul, the two-peas-in-a-pod pair, are up on cheese.

"Patrick, we haven't started any cheese-making."

Paul scarfs down a cheese cracker smothered with Brie while he makes talking points with the free hand. A question falls out his mouth through cracker bits. "You do have goats, right?"

John straightens the pair out. "Yes Paul, and the equipment installation is complete. We just need to make the cheese."

Deep pause as the crowd gathers. The best interruption for John comes in the door.

"Hey, there's the Human Highlighter. Where does he get those colours …?"

Greg confesses to his partner. "Colour me dumb, but I find myself always saying 'Hi Human' or 'Hi Highlighter' …"

"Aaron," John says. "His name is Aaron. Just say 'Hi' … watch me." John is off the cheese spread, into the marble foyer. "Hey, Highlighter! Looking … colourful, buddy.

Greg holds down the cheese fort. The cheese question that never stops: "Any more of that great chèvre?"

Greg points toward the kitchen. "Cooler in the pantry, Paul."

The best of going-away parties is going on, *and on*, a sold-out must-do in the condo with the awesome view.

"There's Chanty and Maddie. Woo-hoo!"

John partners up back at the zero point. Chantelle and Madeleine, neighbours from down the street, grace the marble foyer with an arrival wave back to the cheese masses. As the couple in question seem to pause in the spotlight from the cheese table, Dan the Man starts it off.

"I love Chantelle's choice of theme, Dis Tress. Forget the little black dress."

Greg is in stitches remembering the ladies' big dress-up party, where every outfit had to come from the very back of the closet. (*"Wear it out, baby. Wear your most outrageous dress. Your worst disaster."*)

John adds in his cheesy memory of the big soirée. "How lucky I am. It's in the family. The velour thing from the kitsch wardrobe bank cultivated by my sister through a life of bad taste."

Greg pipes up, both hands to the heavens. "Thank God for Linda."

Patrick joins the dress parade, a style charade. "Did you see Agent Stevie in his mother's third wedding dress?"

Paul joins in partner thoughts. "Thank God he did not inherit her bad style."

More laughter. The cheesy chatter rounds the table.

"And Walter in his fat sister's prom dress."

"Well, old Walter needed the extra girth."

The gathering digs deep, down into stitches.

"Oh my God, were people not *still* going Sunday morning?"

Both hosts with the most awesome Great Lake view rush forward, turn on the grand entrance in unison.

"Maddie. Chantelle. Kisses. Kisses."

More friends are escorted to a welcome round the cheese table talk. Easy stuff on the pick-up with the official hosts at the table. Dan's on the good times.

"That Dis Tress party was some event."

Maddie joins in. "Thanks, boys. Love opening up the home runway."

"Runaway success."

Off the table, Aaron leans in. "I've already bought my next year's Dis Tress. It will be the highlight."

The table turns back from the future. "Maddie dresses up so well."

The group nods in agreement. John, in an aside to Chanty, adds up the partner picture. "Never could get Greg to consider wearing a dress. Until your party."

Chantelle turns the conversation back to Curly Top. "Greg. What's the problem?"

Greg comes to attention with a salute. "That would be a horror show, Dawn of Dis Tress. I kind of go in for little cadet soldier. You know, the pillbox hat and all."

Chanty likes the schtick. "We loved it. Do you have a little baton, too, Greg?"

Greg has a pinched face while his right hand beats the left palm with imaginary schtick. "Chanty-baby, my baton is long and stiff. For extra discipline."

Out of nowhere Jacques, AKA Pepe le Peu (don't ask why *peu*, little, versus *P.U.*), hops his hobby horse across the kitchen floor, whacking his butt to the hip-hop soundtrack. Jacques has known attributes to all who have come in for close encounters of the third kind. "Did someone call for long and stiff?"

More cheese goes round off the long teak table.

Chapter 9

The last few weeks have been a flash, up to the point of the big Saturday move-in. The City partners have two rooms off the front living room. Behind the staircase, across the central hall from the back kitchen area, the Kembers clear out space for John's office.

("Yes Greg, I know how important social media is," John reassured him. "I'll have space for you to work on your computer.")

With the partners due to arrive in just an hour, the Kembers have cleared out the downstairs completely, except for some living room furniture and the complete set of front porch wicker.

"Greg said it would be nice to use the sofa and chairs while they looked for a replacement."

"Translation: another delivery from Mike's."

Greg and John have more pieces moving in from Mike's Auction Barn than the delivery van from the condo with the awesome view. The Kembers have pieces moving out to the so-called double garage in the back of their soon-to-be home on Thomas Street.

"Town folks — go figure," Barbara says. "The building is almost the size of the drive shed and they call it a focking gayrage."

"Barbie, be grateful Ben and Faye have emptied it out for us."

Barbara leans into Jimmy's ear. "The lads didn't have a lot, eh?"

"Barbara, the lot is lots, auction lots from Mike's."

"Thank God I purged the kitchen. They have that baler-sized cappuccino machine. First thing in the focking door."

With all farm extras gone to fill the oversized Town garage, an empty house creates a hunger for life-change contemplation.

"Jimmy, was I supposed to offer them two bedrooms? They are a focking couple, eh?"

"They're focking adults. We told them there would be two rooms plus one office downstairs. They'll figure out the sleeping arrangements."

"Well, looks like two beds have come off the moving truck."

"Two rooms, Bar. Two choices."

In August, sunny lazy days push the goat herd to cooler ground. The goats have no idea how tender their teats will feel in a matter of a few weeks. They lift their beards from the beaten grass to move up to the old oak tree. Shade and a chew on the hawthorn bushes that line the sides of the border fence satisfy their urge for an easy life.

Chew. Chew. Chew.

Queenie looks back to the outbuildings.

"Na-a-ah. Too bizzz-e-e-e-e. Na-a-ah."

The front west corner paddock cannot be seen, but there is a familiar smell. The massive barn blocks the view down the grade. The drive shed and modernized milk shed, now ripe for cheese-making, block most of the Century Farmhouse. Max is out of sight on the porch, another known smell.

Backing up to the arse-end of the fenced corral, a pack of pink backs squeeze up to the far side. That's Frankie and the gang — snouts down, with little notice about busyness, gorging on unlimited fatty goat milk. The pigs, smarter, feed in oblivion with fewer ideas than the goats about the big changes afoot. Pigs stick to what's important.

Max the German shepherd, Frankie the pig and the army of goats are confused by the unfamiliar humans with their silent-moving machine. Max has learned to listen for the loose gravel of the concession.

All ears for any Max signal. Queenie assures the ladies, as always.

"Na-a-a-ah. Na-a-a-ah bother till the beast ba-a-a-arks. Na-a-a-ah."

Two barks means an incoming friend, such as the known fuel oil, feed and fertilizer trucks. Even ZIT's service van gets that kind of familiar indifference. It's the resonance of off-the-porch barking that gets farm-animal attention. Heads, tails, beards, noses line up along the solid-slab wood fence. Not too close, though. Jimmy has a waving string of barbed wire on the top bar.

Up in the big top of the lower canopy, the next three generations of squirrels take notice, along with a nervous rabbit down behind the rose bushes, abundant mice in the barn and the milk shed, and a nesting crow family up on the unused stove chimney.

From the first time City met Country, Max got in close. Max has gotten closer on the follow-ups; two muffled barks and he's off. Off the porch for guaranteed head-scratches from both John and Greg. The goats are confused, with a happy Max off to greet the silent machine. Queenie cautions her team.

"Na-a-a-ah. Na-a-a-ah the beast we kno-o-o-o-ow."

The dusty plume disappears them as they approach their nest in the west.

"Jimmy says the hybrid's silence confuses the animals," Greg says. "Max gets excited. Jimmy says give 'er a pump or two when we pass the property fence."

"Hello, *ding-dong*, Avon calling."

John has never had a pet, period. On the farm near Kingston, Greg always had a dog. Even the most loving of them, named Jennie, remained an outside farm dog, however. Greg also grew up with nastier ones, including Bad Jake and the appropriately-named Ripper.

"That Ripper was a handful," he muses.

John met the dog once and was terrified of him. "No, he was a mouthful. That dog had the most teeth. I'd get a beer out of the side garage, and Ripper would not let me back in your house. Your nasty dog."

Dog ownership is standard business for most Country folks, including at the Kingston hobby farm. Big old Max, though, is a charmer from the start.

"I can't believe it," Greg says. "What a pussy-wussy Maxy Waxy is."

Max will tolerate pussy-wussy names like Tinkerbell, Ruby, or even Baby or Fluffy, if there are four hands scratching. He's had the privilege of watching Lassie, Rin Tin Tin and his favourite, The Littlest Hobo, on the dancing box. "Lucky" could be his name.

John is nervous with all pets but canaries and budgies. Greg touches his partner's elbow.

"Didn't you have an ant colony, a turtle with a green plastic palm or the sea-flea circus mail-in from your comics?"

John has a sad puppy look as he considers. He does remember a few incidents with large angry dogs when he was a boy delivering Simpsons catalogues in the 1980s. Size didn't matter to him, whether miniature, toy or standard poodle. John has continued to reflect on his canine nightmare on their multiple visits to Transvaal. He tightens his grip on the wheel now.

"Maxy Waxy started off as Mad Max. That dog scared the bejesus out of me. Remember?"

The first time, Greg had to reach out for John's hand, joining it with Max's nose in a helpful introduction.

"I remember," Greg says. "We drove up a laneway featuring a recent apocalypse on the lawn."

"I was driving. We both were looking right when Max bounced off my window. A black snarling beast from Hades slapping my beautiful car door. Thank God, no scratches."

Greg's rural upbringing has taught him one thing about dogs: Wait. Wait out a farm dog like Max from inside the vehicle; wait to see the farmer's eyes. Another piece of knowledge picked up by rural-reared Greg is to bring a treat. One big City advantage: treats from the famous Dog Gone Good on Danforth. (To John the Auditor, it's that Goddamn Expensive Store.)

With his new owners having retreated to the Country, Max will hate to kick that expense. *(Mm-m-m-m. Crunch. Crunch. Chew. Chew. Crunch. Better treats than the Missus gives.)* Thanks to Greg, the pleasure will last some time, though, with two five-pound gift bags coming up-Country.

This time round to Transvaal, John gives the horn a toot-toot.

The army of goats hears the honks even before Max. They stand head down and unregistered until Max makes the call off the porch. At two barks, they lift their beards from the grass to the arrival of their new masters.

Greg's Max connection tells him the old dog already recognizes the toss of gravel from the electric vehicle. The promise of an imported treat and a four-hand scratch have left any horn in the dust.

John opens his door toward the porch steps. Greg opens his door to love. Max stays with his mouth open.

"Maxy Waxy! Buddy, buddy. Yes, Daddy knows you like your head scratched. John, he's waiting. I'll give him his treat."

Max opens his jaws and hangs out his tongue, the table set for the exotic dog cookie. A symphony of love plays out with a new-Master-and-old-dog duet.

"Pup and circumstance for my Maxy."

Both hands on the dog's head, Greg nods to John.

"All hands on deck, buddy. Get over here. You two can bond a bit."

Eating and scratching together with the new Masters, it's Paradise found.

"I'm just gonna keep you, Maxy Waxy," Greg says. "Keep you down on the farm."

Greg looks to see that the Kembers are preoccupied. He leans down to blow in Max's ear. One hand holds his head up while the other flops his opposite ear. Ear up and down, ear back and forth.

"You're just a pussy wussy, Maxy Waxy."

Max looks up with those killer brown eyes. A soft groan rises from his deepest heart. *"Master. Daddy and other Daddy, I love you too."*

Barbara can be heard behind the screen door.

"Why did we move on a focking Saturday?"

Max stands still, a porch witness as laughter moves to more love in the old farmhouse. Hugs, kisses and near misses all round the circle of friends.

"They rang us out of bed at seven A.M.," Greg says.

Barbara's bang on to City logistics.

"Focking City traffic, boys."

John protests. "Eight would have been more civilized. I hadn't started my second capp or the *Globe.*"

Barbara looks at the job from the receiving end. "Early start, early finish. They had everything of yours off by two o'clock. Two hours before you guys arrived."

Barbara eyes up the new roommates. "Guys, you need to get into the flow of the local know. This afternoon, the tug-of-war tourney moves from the Kember Farm to the Ilderton Fair."

A partner-shared half-dumb look. "Huh?"

Barbara goes right to the ignition spot. She points at the black circle of turf, front lawn centre. "Remember the focking fat burnt squirrel?"

Greg has told the nutty tale to all the City. "Of course, who wouldn't? Rocky the flying squirrel flames out. That's a nutty tale."

"Chase, Greg. It was a Chase-down. I'm talking about the team at Easy Lift Movers, who moonlight as St. Marys Volunteer Firefighters *and* …" (Pause as she pulls her hands on the large invisible rope. Pause moves to the punch line with no response from either, except a half-dumb look) "… tug-of-war team with a *big* provincial competition. They have a chance to be Ontario champs at Ilderton." She smiles at the two. "That's why there and back by two. The lads have a focking date with destiny at Ilderton's fair."

Max watches the old Master open the leafy-coloured opening that makes things inside easier to smell, hear and see for an old dog. Barbara points to their assorted baggage, then moves the pointer to the floor of the hallway as she passes through the screen door.

"Drop 'er here. Shoes off."

The house tour starts.

"My God, Barbara, the office space is perfect. Thank you for clearing the space."

"Space? Space? John, your space is full of boxes marked John's Office."

Greg gets the point, wondering where he fits into this space. Barbara pirouettes to cross the hallway, twirling her fingers in the air on her march forward.

"Walls bare for your artwork, same as the living room …"

March on.

"Left the sofa set, Greg, as requested, your auction stuff from Mike's, more boxes. The two beds are on the wall."

She points at the area between two doors as she weaves the obstacle course of front room–marked boxes to cross to the other side.

Boys in the hall remain in a slight stage of fright.

"John. They think we share a bedroom?"

"Not with your snoring."

"Well. They think we share?"

"Don't scare the natives, Greg. It's for a few weeks, a day here, day there."

"Ear plugs all 'round, buddy."

Their moment is interrupted from the back of the hallway. "Your coffee machine is back here on the counter. Right where you said it would fit. Otherwise we did *not* touch a thing."

John calls out, "I'll put capps on, Jimmy, easy peasy."

With the first stage of the move complete, and a quick-march tour, the group returns to a quiet, short time on the grand porch. A breather with capps in the comfy wicker chairs before the plans kick into gear. For their Century Farm life, the Kembers have always gone to the boiling kettle for a spot of tea. Sometimes on Saturdays, Jimmy has a caffeine hit at the Sunriser. As new residents of Thomas Street, Jimmy will be able to up the caffeine catch with free-will drop-ins to the coffee klatch. Barbara's range will include Tims and the downtown baristas for a steeped tea. The Kembers, from the Kember Century Farm, will be located in the Andrews House when Ben and Faye Andrews complete the move to a model Bickel Home. Go figure, Town addresses.

Jimmy and Barbara remain gobsmacked by the Italian espresso machine in their ex-kitchen. Out on the front porch, sipping her special treat, Barbara can't cap her surprise.

"Thank God the kitchen was empty. *Bang.*"

Barbara draws her head into line with her left shoulder. She looks out from the porch, out into space, with all heads trying to follow her intent. All eyes follow, trying to mark the point.

"Bang," she says again.

Max wrestles on the mat with the intent lost in human translation. The Missus repeats her head-turn to a different invisible target, then stares at some other damn spot.

"Bang! Incoming."

All eyes move to the new incoming stare-projectile. She has the audience in her hands.

Jimmy turns to the lads. "Ignore Barbara, boys. She sees squirrels. Next time we'll have the gun out on the porch."

Barbara splays her hands down, motioning to a vacant landing spot on the deck. "Voilà. It's focking Cappuccinos on the farm."

Extra voilà with the target revealed: a John Capp.

"I could get used to this," Jimmy says as he sips his John Capp.

"Focking right on."

Barbara savours the flavour of the last few sips. Then she gets up from the comfy front-porch capp. She's up and away for John's second passion in life besides the bean, notwithstanding the Curly Top sommelier. She returns to the right shelf of the fridge for a group offer on wine pulled from the boxes marked Keep Cool.

Her smartphone app review of the bottle choices revealed four-star ratings for most labels. Grabbing a refreshing white, Barbara returns confident to the group. (Greg is heads-up on the label choice. He did the exhaustive research, including a ladder to heaven on multitudes of tastings that poured past the midnight hour.) Day One on the farm and Greg and Barbara already have palates in sync. Barbara pours.

"Focking great drop, Barbara," Jimmy says as he samples. "To the move. To the success of Say Cheese Artisan Goat Cheese."

John audits in reverse. "Remind us. Why did we move on a Saturday? We're all retired."

Greg gets realistic. "Retired? Retired from City to a full-time, overtime, part-time job in the Country."

The Professor speaks. "Well, Aldert will be back next weekend. He's one of our most important assets." The lads step back in slight amazement at the introduction of a new character. They turn over the name together.

"*All-dirt?*"

"Aldert. That's his name. He's the only helping hand you have, lads."

The partners are still scrambling to get a grip on the announcement. "All-dirt, our helping hand?"

Jimmy watches the two as he spells it out in slow motion. "A-L-D-E-R-T." He lets the spelling lesson settle in.

"Aldert is the closest thing you have to survival on the farm. He grew up here as my helping hand. He's still a young lad. He is a natural shepherd."

Barbara smiles. "Jimmy, that young lad's become a mountain man."

Greg and John have been dim, unaware of the possibility of some assistance with the farm chores at hand. They have not heard the word "survival" used to date. "Nightmare" did come up once or twice, of course. John is stuck with a possible miss on the farm balance sheet; Greg is stuck, period. Jimmy points his wine glass off into the setting sun.

"As we speak, he's at a herd-management course. A three-month certificate at the agricultural college in Centralia. Back next weekend. He is *the* Shepherd, lads."

Words stick to the partners' silence: mountain man, natural shepherd, young lad, herd manager, neighbour, grew up. All of this gives them a lot to absorb on the subject of Aldert.

The porch group reach for more crispy B.C. Pinot Gris. Little said, lots understood. The upstairs–downstairs team all have a good sleep.

Greg wakes bright and sunny, pulling his brand-new rubber boots on in the kitchen.

"You do have gloves?"

Jimmy does not wait for an answer; he's off through the back door. Greg drags along after thinking of one thing: shit. John might slide through a nightmare of shit, but Greg, Day Two on the farm, has returned to *slopping* shit.

Greg grabs a shovel but sees no digging prospects in a shit-free barn. "Jimmy, there's not a lot of goat shit. I thought the job would take much longer."

"Goats are just like people. They like a clean house, like their shit outside, and they like a routine. So let's get them milked, and outside."

On his way back to the house, Greg sees the rural-route mail being delivered by a minivan with a red flashing light. He checks Barbara's sideways cheese wedge of a mailbox, then finds John inside in his new office.

"My goodness, John. Your office! Neat, clean. Shiny. My goodness." John keeps head down on the screen while Greg's eyes wander the room, wondering where he'll put his laptop. "Look, our first piece of mail."

"What is it?"

"A congratulatory letter from the mayor. Calls himself Cheeko?"

Greg has John's head up now.

"Cheeko?"

"Maybe he's Mexican or something. Calls us gentlemen, and wants to invite us for a coffee at that castle town hall. By the way, we need to put an ad in the *St. Marys Journal*."

"For what?"

"For some farm labour help. Saving Jimmy. I think start with two for goats, milking and more. Then pick one or none, or keep them both."

"Slopping the barn?" John asks.

"Train them in slopping, and slopping they will doo-doo."

"All-dirt doesn't do the milk shed, as the Shepherd?"

"He'll go over the loading, cooling, unloading, cleaning." (An alas look on John's face.) "But no cheese, please."

"I'll write that ad," John says. "It'll be in this week's paper."

Every morning that week, the two couples have John Capps before starting their chores. Ceramic Barn high-top coffee cups with a goat profile are in the dishwasher. John is on the books. Greg milks the teats and slops the barn, under Jimmy's tutelage.

"We need to order some logo cups," Greg offers, on a mid-morning break in John's office. "Sales point on the web, if no gift shop."

"Greg, relax. Coffee cups with Say Cheese logo are not in the cups at this time."

"We need them for the launch."

"A launch of what? There's no cheese factory."

Greg lightens the duties of a launch. "There's a farm with new owners …" (palms out to John behind his desk). "Ta-dah! Us! And we are tidying things up."

John's already had too much of weekend farming to let this go. "How do you tidy things up on a farm? Do not let the Kembers, a neighbour, or in fact any native hear that. Tidying up, my goodness. Did you slop the barns after school for your father or 'tidy things up?'"

Greg smartens up to defend Gregzdream. "We have sixty-plus goats, a prize-winning group of ladies with big teats. The barn is super organized and spotless. Next door is a good-to-go milk shed. Yes, still a milk shed, but primed for cheese production. Plans on the wall duplicate the results on the floor — a CAD design-build, the schematics on all equipment laid out to a T."

John audits his partner well. "Plans pinned up on the walls don't make cheese."

"Plans that are complete on the ground," Greg argues. "A nice tile job with a perfect drain slope, I might add."

"Okay. But good job, Jimmy."

"We — Jimmy and I — can milk. We, Jimmy and I, can filter the milk. We do have the whey tanks."

"We — Jimmy, you, I and this All-dirt — need to pull it together."

"All-dirt's incoming on Saturday. We'll get him in the interview process."

"Let's meet with him," John agrees. "But let him get back up to speed with Jimmy."

"I get it. They can milk; we — not you but the three of us — can slop. But I need to promote myself off the pitchfork delegation. Yes, we need to interview for more slopping hands."

John does the sum-up. "We can slop and squeeze goat teats till the dust on the 6th disappears. We need to make cheese."

Greg is forward on defence. "Yes. But. We, Jimmy and I, are pulling the process together. While we find the right person to be our cheese-maker, we find two hired hands, for four hands. Get up to speed with this most important All-dirt. It's balance in life, between work on our list of to-do's and neighbour relations for newbies from the City. It's paramount in our rural-routed lives that we introduce ourselves. Show them the Citiots can do things in a proper Country way. Maybe it should be an open house, or a potluck, or just have the neighbours over. But we are launching ourselves into a new life, a new postal code, and we will make the best in goat cheese. But at the same time, the Big Launch in sync, without a hitch. Look …"

John leans in with a squint, almost blinded by this address to the nation. Greg can't be stopped.

"We're great. We *are* hospitality. We've done it all before. We have the hospi-tality gene. It's just a different GPS now."

John pounds out a more grounded view. "Like our City jeans. A very different viewpoint in Transvaal."

Greg pulls the nail out. "John. They don't wear bib overalls. Let's do it up right from the start."

The lawyer and CA, the auditor, is impressed with Greg's enthusiasm. "Well stated, partner." Nonetheless, John reels him into the reality of their situation. "The Big Launch, buddy. Right from the start, there's already just too much on our plates. And no cheese. First things first. Our list …"

Greg's cheeks puff out. He's doing red-face. "No-o-o-o *party?*"

"Bigger, better party later on … after we start making cheese. Think about it. A big party to celebrate cheese. More than an introduction, a cheese presentation."

Greg's eyes water up. John needs to reach, and deep. "Three in one, buddy. Big."

"Big?"

"Do it right, all three. The Big Launch, a Christmas celebration, AND … Wedding Girl."

Greg remains grounded. "By the way, I already have the ad running."

"For the farm help?"

"Yup."

"I thought a partner–partner review would happen on the wording."

"Easy peasy. We have time constraints. Thought I would save you the distraction. You're working so hard."

"Nice. So what did you say?"

"Ten cents a word, you know. Sunday-at-five deadline for a Wednesday afternoon paper. Go figure."

"The ad, Greg."

"Here, I have it on my phone. Ready?"

John smiles. Greg does two eyebrow raises.

"*ROOM FOR TWO: two hard-working, willing hands for full-time help on a prizewinning goat farm. Farm experience welcome. Goat experience an asset. Call for an interview time this Saturday 9 to 5 at Say Cheese Artisan Goat Cheese, 5757 6th Concession, first right south of St. Marys on Water 519-461-0461.*"

Greg stops with a big self-congratulatory smile.

"Good, Greg, but … two willing hands? What are they, amputees? Two one-armed farmhands?"

Big frown. "At least I didn't say RR #3 Thorndale. That's confusing enough without getting out the army survey map for Transvaal. 'First right south on Water' works. Not a Citiot on that, John."

"Then Saturday it will be, Greg. But you answer the phone and make up an appointment list. Ask Barbara or Jimmy or both about the prospects. Barbara could help us with the in and out of the interview."

"And coffee?"

"For the prospects, maybe. Capps for you and me."

Greg right-thumb motions a hitch to the kitchen.

"And Barbara?"

"Of course, if she's not stuck on her steeped tea."

"That's the Tims Town thing for her. She'll be a go for John's Capp."

"You're in, Barbie."

"Maybe we can request some of Barbara's apple cinnamon whole-bran muffins?"

"Yes, sir. Or rather, yes, ma'am."

John can charm. *"Would that be a second Capp, Barbie?"*

Greg returns to slopping the barn with Jimmy and milking the ladies, afternoon shift. Max sees new Master leave without giving him a head-scratch. "Thank God it's this Saturday," Greg says to himself as Max follows him. "Two interviews booked. Can't wait for farmhands. That's two pairs, four hands."

Max gives up on the head-scratch but still stands by for any potential treat.

Jimmy is out in the milk shed with his long checklist of small stuff left to do. Max can hear him mutter a familiar phrase. "Where's the cheese, please? Thank God Aldert is back on Saturday."

The *St. Marys Journal* is still a fresh read when the big day arrives. Early rise and shine on Saturday gives John and Greg a little catch-up time. A hectic week of arranging, organizing and slopping is set aside in the cool morning's dawn. The Gregzdream partners take the opportunity for contemplation well before the first of their interviews, which start at ten. As they head out the screen door to the porch, an interruption from Jimmy:

"Don't forget Aldert."

After the interviews, at two o'clock, the partners are scheduled to meet All-dirt the Shepherd and greet the herd. The second part of a two-part day.

Second head sticks out. "Capps still on, John?"

"Capp coming up, Barbara."

Max is lost in patience, waiting for the usual morning scratch and tasty treat. His dark chocolate eyes are fixated on the screen door action. He senses intensity.

His Masters are off the customary sunrise porch perch.

"We have four interviews," John says.

Greg supports his exacting partner by nodding.

"One per hour," John continues. "Gives us lots of time to move them in, move them out."

Greg nods with a question. "Time overlaps?"

"I've asked Barbara to have them sit on the porch. Give them their coffee there."

"You *are* making Capps."

"No, Barbara has the Tims pot going. Welcome coffee. We're in the office, waiting."

Greg picks up on the flow. "Interview cut short?"

John has a plan. "John Capp time."

Greg continues to ask. "You're hired?"

"Capps all round on the porch, buddy."

Before ten, both men get up off the comfy chairs on the porch, pass through the screen door. Max gets a pass-by scratch.

"O-o-o-o-oh, Maxy Waxy," Greg tells him, "I left your treat on the counter. Let me get it."

Max can understand *O-o-o-o-oh* and *Maxy*, but the rest is lost in translation. Hope might lie behind the swinging screen door.

Before anyone can say "one more capp," a dust plume rises from the canopy on the 6th Concession. John turns back to the wash of sunrise that's crossing the farmyard. "Hurry. Hurry. Our first interview arrives. The Kembers are in the kitchen, expecting another refill. Two more John Capps coming up."

"The Kembers will love you. Johnny on the spot."

"Better than Johnny come late."

Two barks off the porch with steady tail announces the arrival of an unfamiliar vehicle. Barbara, Capp-less, steps out the open door to catch the old dog.

"Maxy Waxy. Mat, Maxy. Mat, old man." Max picks up the Maxy and Mat but nothing more. Double nothing more, when Mommy-Wommy brings no focking treats. The old dog bobs his head under Barbara to gain a few head taps, then moves back to his clean and comfortable mat.

Jimmy grabs his java, off to the barn. Barbara settles in for a welcoming direction. "Okay," she says. "Give 'em coffee. Line 'em up, stack 'em up. In, out, easy peasy." Barbara backs up through the screen door, whispering. "Who's on the list?"

"The *Journal* ad was very successful," John says. "Tons of calls."

"Who?"

"Dozens of calls. But every one asked about the wage. I said the job starts at minimum wage and increases with experience. Everybody moved from wages right on to benefits and vacation time. But most did not ask for an interview appointment."

"Who?"

"Well, of the dozens and dozens of calls, four appointments."

"John." Barbara has her Capp-free hand pointing at the screen. "I'm not a focking owl. Who's on the list?"

"Well, our first interview is with Heber Stadnick and his son Wilber."

"Should have recognized the piece of junk coming up the laneway. Might have to put Max inside the back kitchen. Focking weird world."

"Focking weird what world?"

"Thought the Stadnicks were still doing time."

"Well, their time is ten."

"No, I mean time in the pen for rustling."

"People still rustle?" Greg asks.

"People with an unmarked five-ton stake truck. Ramp and all."

"Well," John says, "it's ten, and look, a beat-up grey stake truck. Real rusty."

"That should have been be a four-bark response from Maxy Waxy," Greg says.

Barbara watches the rust bucket slide to a dusty stop. "Maybe some focking teeth, too."

John is prompted back to the list. "At eleven, two cousins. Ronnie and Donnie —"

"Well, turn the mic off, John. Ronnie and Donnie are twins, not cousins, but their last name is Cousins, and they *are* the product of interbred cousins. There may be a chimpanzee in the family too. No, they're too stupid to be from any monkey or ape. That's how dumb that pair is."

"Barbara, we need helping hands," Greg says. "Can they work?"

"Work under direct supervision. You can't leave dummies like that unsupervised."

"They didn't ask a lot of questions."

"Those cheeseheads!" she says. "No brains means no cheese ahead."

John turns to noon. "At twelve, two men from Thorndale. Eric Goss and Murray Elliott. They say they have farm experience. Have worked together in the past."

"The past?" Barbara says. "I'm a little vague on these two. One's an Elliott. Focking hundreds of Elliotts in Nissouri Township."

Greg adds in his sense of geography. "RR #3 Thorndale is in Nissouri Township. Even though I can see the steeple of St. Marys."

"No matter. Four barks and more for this one. No bites."

"At one, our last interview, are two brothers, Faisal and Ozzy Kuleimann. Must be family day on the farm."

"I know Faisal and Ozzy," Barbara says.

Greg and John almost lose their mouthful of splendid John Capp. How in the rural world does Barbara seem to know *everyone* and rural *everything.* "How?"

"They're two Syrian lads sponsored with their family by the Methodist Church."

"Refugees."

"No. Welcome citizens to our Town. I thought the boys were working at the IGA. Stocking shelves, sweeping, shovelling in winter and doing carry-out for the older people."

"Opinion?"

"Real nice young men who are ready to work."

Pause as the ten o'clock approaches.

"And we're ready here. The coffee pot is on. The muffins are in."

"In?"

"Warming up on low in the oven. Focking amazing with a slab of butter."

Goats' eyes watch the porch gathering from the west paddock. The black ears pick up on the stake truck before Max.

Max stays on his mat in a low growl. The ten o'clock runs quick and short onto the dirty. John allows no slack on the line of thought. "Do either of you gentlemen have a criminal record?"

The men stand frozen with their coffee mugs.

"We need all employees to be bonded. That's a rule when you supply hospitals and clinics with goat milk."

Barbara, back in the kitchen, misses the quick exit. She asks for the dirty. Greg keeps it short.

"You were right on, Barbara. Criminal records. *Adios.*"

John adds it up right. "Opportunity knocks off. Another capp while we wait, folks?"

Over an hour passes before gunfire is heard down the concession. Barbara steps in.

"Not gunfire. It's Ronnie and Donnie in their '83 Bronco II. No muffler, no wheel bearings. If you walk anywhere in Town you can hear the dummy rattle before you see their stupid focking faces."

The dim-wits, however, are polite and thankful and answer all questions.

"So you want to be farmhands."

"Four hands at your service, sirs. We're twins. That's us, right Donnie?"

"Weesies four hands, Ronnie and Donnie."

"Do you have any problem with a sunrise start on the first milk shift?"

"No worries. We'll get Momsie up at the crack of dawn. We loves our Momsie breakfastses."

"Tell 'em." Donnie nods to the partners.

"Weesies do the dishes and be right here at the crack of dawn."

Greg can't help himself. "Momsie is always right. My Momsie used to say —"

John gives him a side kick. "How experienced are you with animals?" he asks the twins.

"Donnie and I have always had a dog. Momsie has two cats."

"I was thinking about farm animals."

"You know. We were thinking the same thing. We should learn a little something about farm animals. Horses. Chickens."

Greg can't help himself. "Alpacas, deer, gerbils …"

"Gerbils?" John says. He's had enough of the nonsense. He turns back to the twins. "Do you have a reference?"

"In the phone book?"

"No, a person we can call up. Someone who knows you. Someone that can recommend you."

"Momsie knows us bestest."

John hurries to sum it up and move on. "Where can we get ahold of you, then?"

"Weekday and Saturday mornings, we're in a back booth at the Sunriser."

That's it. Barbara shows the guests the screen door. John runs to the espresso machine. Never enough John Capp.

The shelf-clock on the fireplace mantel chimes high noon with twelve clear bells — more importantly, with warm muffins enjoyed all round. No chime at twelve-fifteen for another muffin round.

"I feel like Martha and the Muffins," John says. "Barbara, they are so good. Count me in for thirdsies."

By the time one o'clock hits the single chime, the three on house and interview duty are muffin-stuffed and Capp-satiated.

But, it's time for the next round. Barbara welcomes the young brothers with a steamy coffee, a hot buttered muffin and a warm introduction, then leads them into the office.

"Faisal. Ozzy. You guys look more like twins than brothers."

"Many people make that remark. We are just one year apart. Ozzy is the younger."

Faisal flashes a full smile. "I have a unibrow, just like Frida Kahlo, eh."

Barbara marvels at the English syntaxing by a young man who spoke minimal English two years ago. She restates the local conclusion. "Twins."

The label will stick on the Syrian Twins.

"Tell us why you're applying to work as farmhands," John asks.

"Both of us work at the IGA. It's nice job but we want to work outside. Learn something else. Maybe how to make cheese. We are willing to work hard and learn what is taught to us."

"How about goats? Any experience from Syria with goats?"

"My father was a business professor in Damascus," Ozzy continues. "Now he faces shelves at the IGA, with his sons." Both lean on John's desk. "We had never seen a goat other than in photos and TV until we moved to southwestern Ontario."

Greg leans in for no reason. "How about camels?"

"Well sirs, camels, like Christian infidels, are something in your Bible."

John moves past Greg's review of Noah's ark. "No farm experience?"

"We are sorry, sirs. But no. Just a desire to work hard. Learn. Appreciate."

"Okay," John says. "We have your contact information. We will get back to you."

Brothers stand and turn to the hallway. Faisal stops, reaching into his pants pocket.

"Our contact at Federal Employment told me that I should give you this brochure at the end of our interview."

"A brochure?" Greg smiles. "For us?"

"It explains the grant program for refugee employment."

"And?" John asks. "Have you read it?"

"Of course. I wouldn't give you anything that I didn't read and understand, sir."

"Give the summary, Faisal."

"Mr. Greg and Mr. John, you will be eligible for minimum ten dollars an hour up to the maximum of full hour's wage subsidized by the government."

John and Greg pause, allowing Faisal to continue adding value.

"For up to a year. For both Ozzy and myself."

John takes over the quick audit review. "You're hired. When can you start?"

John is extra polite to the nice lads, finalizing simple forms and contact information. He makes small talk. "Faisal. Is that a common Syrian name?"

"Yes it is. More important, it is my father's, and my father's father's. And on."

Greg steps into the circle. "And Ozzy. Is that Syrian?"

"No. Not even close. My father loves Ozzy Osbourne."

That stand-up revelation brings the four to their feet. John has one hand out to shake. Greg has both up for high fives all round the four hands. "Way cool. Ozzy Osbourne, wow."

"See you Monday, eight o'clock sharp," John says. "Report to All-dirt."

"Aldert." Ozzy lights up. "Sure, we know him. He was two years ahead of us at St. Marys High School. He dates our friend Ian's older sister, Mary Beth Johnson. Sure makes a mean crème brûlée."

The brothers are waved off the front porch across the front yard to catch their volunteer driver.

They pass the full ladies' court, way out to pasture. A set of grey eyes, front row, west paddock, watch the Syrian lads hitch a ride to Town from the end of the double pathway.

John retreats to the bathroom.

"I have muffin mouth and caffeine breath. I need to brush my teeth. Mouthwash …"

Greg is off across the hallway.

"Me first — my pee meter is on overflow after all those Capps."

Chapter 10

"Come meet the herd."

Aldert comes out of the barn right on time, with an engaging smile. He moves in on Greg and John, shakes both owners' hands. The partners signal a quiet marvel at his hand size. Aldert heads off to the front east paddock, the partners lip-syncing behind at the size of him.

"All-dirt," Greg shouts out. "Excuse me. We've already met the herd."

The partners tail up behind the hunk of a human specimen. Aldert turns without stopping as two goofy smiles nod back at him. "You have *not* met the herd."

A tiny protest from wilting flowers in doubt. "Jimmy gave us the big tour. Did he not, Greg?"

Greg is frozen in response to the towering man-boy directing them on a forced march.

"I am the Shepherd," Aldert says. "No one meets *my* herd without an introduction from the Shepherd."

Marching along, he turns again with his huge smile. Aldert takes up any slack on the perception of owner and employee. "You are the owners, and you are my bosses. I'm the boss of the herd. You boss me, I boss the herd."

What a nice smile. Neither partner has read this information on an internet search. The man-boy smile keeps talking.

"The herd only listens to one boss."

The students repeat. "You are the boss. The Shepherd."

He stops and turns again. That big smile. "Wrong."

Greg and John are limited to a half-smile back, stuck in the tracks of ignorance. Is this a trick question?

"No," Aldert says. "Queenie is the boss."

"Queenie?"

"The queen of the Nubian goats is the boss female. Hence, Queenie. She runs the does, and I run her. With a little help. Now" — he's talking in a quick stride toward the wood-slat fence — "are you ready to meet Queenie and the home farm team?"

The fools nod their heads. Back on the march, they echo in agreement. "Yes."

The Shepherd stops — he isn't listening; the hunk of a man-boy is whistling. Through pursed lips, he lets out three high-pitched calls to no one in particular. That's how it seems. A call-out in the crisp fall air. In an instant, it's a rush — from the west side back of the farmhouse, a dog pack is coming straight at them. Greg thinks they look furry and fierce. John sees teeth and hunger for meat, for Citiot blood. Aldert sees the surprise in both partners' faces. Greg quickly thanks everybody for whom he might owe gratitude, while John reviews farm-touring protocol under D for dogs. Both are bewildered.

Aldert shouts, with that wide-as-Niagara-Falls smile. "A little help from our friends."

The owner bosses are about to observe the real bosses in action. Aldert sifts and syncs the information for the farm couple.

"Think of me as the team coach." The pack of three collies is on the boys, flashing shiny teeth and wet lips. "These are my assistants."

The lads start to back up, even Curly Top, the former hobby horse farm boy.

"No, gentlemen." Aldert makes a circular motion with his hands. "Step up, gentlemen. Meet my assistants. Sit!"

The gentlemen hesitate at the command. The dog pack forms a half-shell, seated in front, close in. They're corralled, still standing. Greg and John cannot help but feel faint in the knees. Later, much later, there will be laughs at their very real inclination to sit in this terrifying moment. Greg and John look down at the assistants being introduced. Happy faces, hanging tongues, wet eyes looking up at the owners. They seal the deal. The dogs line up with sharp smiles in front of their head coach. The Shepherd motions.

"Hold your palms out. Up, gentlemen. Move a little closer."

Greg has flashbacks to Ina Stewart's Grade 1 class. The prospect, the anxious possibility, of facing the strap. Years later the palms are up again, waiting in anxious fear.

"I swear to you," John says, frozen in confession. "As a boy, the neighbours' dog Ripper terrorized me behind their fence." He can't find a finish as the dogs begin a session of energetic boss-licking.

"They like you. Now for introductions."

One very short whistle and the trio line back up. Their heads are directed left to the Shepherd.

"Ladies. Meet your new bosses. Gracie."

The first collie acknowledges with a smile, her tongue hanging out.

The second nuzzles up beside Gracie. "Lizzie," Aldert says. She duplicates the actions of the first, her upward gaze following the slightest indication in her Master's moves.

The Citiots look to their Shepherd without a question. He has the answer they need to understand.

"They are sisters," Aldert says.

The pair reply. "Nice."

Aldert gives a short whistle. The third dog gets the message.

"Coca."

The last collie is darker and a tad smaller than the sisters. A look back to Aldert. The partners laugh.

"Coca collie, eh?" John says.

Aldert points to his assistants, all rowed up in front for the human trio. "Now give their heads a rub, their ears a flop. Go for it."

It's a group grope of heads, fur and slobber. Love at first sight is doing the rounds.

"Gracie is the older sister of Lizzie. Different litters."

The lads fall in. The hunk's doing eyebrow raises.

"Coca is a niece. The youngest of my ladies and the smartest."

Max is up from the mat in response to the other dogs on the property. He clocks the Masters with a natural sense of time. *They sure are taking a long time with those skittish yapping bitches.* On edge at the porch steps, Max grumbles in a low growl at the group of ladies taking up his head-scratch and ear-flop time.

Out back of the barn, Frankie and his pig family are still living high on the hog. The tin canisters pour an unlimited supply of goat milk from heaven above. The goats chewing in the front east paddock listen to their instincts. There's a foreign mix rising with the rising sun this morning, of Citiots walking beside the Shepherd and his beasts. Queenie feels the official introduction coming. The team pay no mind to the human trespassers. All eyes face the ground, ears pointed to the queen of the team. The dream team of Nubians is led by the largest, a Lyle's-corn-syrup-coloured goat with a snow-white face set with icy blue baubles. Blue eyes that don't just see for miles and miles, they see through all. The Queen has royal pride in the udder subject of milk production. The Kembers aren't kidding when they say she's an amazing birther.

"Barbara, Queenie's birthed another set of triplets."

"Got to be the fourth season in a row."

"I can't remember her birthing anything but three."

"Sex?"

"Two does and a billy. All jet black with snowy faces."

"The eyes?"

"The does have the mother's. The billy is one ice blue, and one —"

"Two different colours?"

"The other is one weird psycho-looking marble."

No matter how the acorn falls from the old oak tree out back, she's exotic, the Queen of Nubia. Aldert coined her Queenie, Jimmy told them. The real introduction continues.

"The ladies are in fact ladies. Remember I said that I would explain the absence of Max? Well, it's the same for any male dog. It's the same for any four-legged male, including our one farm goat male."

Greg's in. "The house stud."

Aldert smiles a mile. "You'll understand in a minute. First things first."

John likes the organization of the Shepherd's thinking. Aldert repeats that short whistle and the collies come to sit up to his attention. The Shepherd turns to his bosses with reference to an unfamiliar local rite.

"You'd think they were in the Methodist Hall. Listening to Pastor Harlton." He stops, looks to the happy faces, motions with his hands to his right. "Crush."

The three dogs go right, the humans go left. The Shepherd calls in reverse.

"Crush, Gracie, crush. Crush, girl."

That's it. Gracie takes off stage right with sister and niece in tow.

"Gracie leads. The others follow."

John cannot help himself being stupid. He has Citiot jeans on. "Leads? Follows? Leads and follows to where?"

"Gentlemen. The ladies are all naturals. Just watch this."

"The dogs are rounding up the goats?"

"It's a natural thing. They round up one goat. Queenie is the boss goat here on the farm."

The humans head left to the paddock facing the 6th Concession. The dogs are right out of sight. Aldert answers without questions.

"The goats do the opposite of what humans want them to do. The dogs give the Shepherd his edge."

John's turn to ask for a definition. "Edge?"

"Go." Three short whistles. "Get Queenie. Good girls." Aldert turns back. "The Shepherd needs the edge."

The herd appears stage right, moving stage left with two collies pressing on the wings.

"Look," Aldert says. "Behind the herd."

Gracie is pushing the rear of one huge black goat, three times her size. The collie nips the giant's heels.

"*Na-a-a-ah ni-i-ice, Gracie. Na-a-a-ah. Be-e-e ni-i-ice.*"

Aldert boasts a supersize smile. "Gentlemen. Meet the Queen herself."

"Queenie?"

"The real boss goat."

"We need a boss goat?"

The community-raised lad is patient and polite to a fault.

"Yes, it's the natural order of things in a goat herd. Dominant alpha female is the boss. In charge of every detail in the field, the barn or the milking shed. The dogs can give herd direction, but Queenie holds the ultimate control."

Aldert motions to the partners to step up on the bottom slat of the fence. Aldert's height allows him to peer over the top slat. Aldert reaches for his pocket. Queenie signals royal assent as she lowers her beard to graze the lower slat of the upper section. Palm flat up for the Shepherd, who feeds his Queen a green apple.

"This is the boss, the Queen of Nubia, and here's the herd. We have up to sixty females scheduled for breeding in about three months. It will be a busy winter and spring. Lots of milking."

"Why is it busier then?" John asks.

"Pregnant Nubians produce the best of their best-of-class cream in pregnancy. Even more when the kids come."

"Kids?"

"Goats produce twins and sometimes triplets. Our herd could be 120-plus in the spring. In the next year there will be tons of milk."

The partners contemplate the numbers in silence.

"All hundred-plus females under one queen," Aldert continues. "Tons of milk. No quota. The richest cream."

The partners catch themselves in one thought: *Brie.*

Aldert gives three short whistles. "Watch nature take its course."

The collies circle back in a storm, lowering their bodies down to army-crawl under the slat fence. This gets herd attention as all beards lift off the afternoon chew. The dogs have to press, to force movement from the frozen group. The ladies are pushed, without cooperation, into a lineup three to four goats deep. Dead centre, head above the crowd, is a gilded bronze giant.

"Watch Queenie. Her team will resist and resist. Not one goat dares to move until Queenie leads them off."

Two long whistles and the bitches back off the ladies' group. Back under the fence for scratches and ear-flops. Unplugged, the whole team moves off under the magnificent bronze queen's lead.

John's Citiot brain is still connected to his Citiot mouth. "Where they off to?"

"Either the front or back paddock. Both gates are open." A big gander up at the sky. "Not too hot. I think it'll be along the far fence line."

Both bosses echo, "Why?"

"Goats love a good chew. Nothing better than the hawthorn grove on the property line."

Greg had those same thorny bushes on the 150-acre Kingston homestead. "Kind of a lot of pricks?"

Aldert has eyes on the herding. John is watching his partner. Sure enough, Greg can't help himself.

"They love the taste." The eyebrow lifts raise no reaction from John, who narrows the conversation back to smart.

"What brings them back to the barn?"

"Sometimes Queenie. Sometimes the collies. I let the dogs loose more as an exercise than anything. Sometimes it's crappy weather — goats don't like getting too wet or too hot. On a bluebird day, if I leave them long enough, by the end their teats are swollen and they're ready to march themselves to the milking stalls."

Goats know that suction cups spell relief, with a bag of feed supplement that covers all beards. The mountain of a Shepherd rubs his belly. That mile-wide smile. "Goat yum-yum. They live to eat."

"And sometimes the collies?" Greg asks.

"Not often I go to the dogs. Queenie likes her supplement. She's used to the milking-machine routine. The queen leads the way."

The partners nod with a that's-kinda-easy understanding.

The Shepherd continues. "Every one of them hits the hay in the barn, every night. Sweet dreams all."

Stupid auditor question: "How do you know if one is missing?"

Greg speaks out of experience. "Always a count."

"Correct, Boss. The #1 rule from my herd management course is always keep proper records. Number-one rule for Jimmy from my first day on the farm. He wrote an incredible piece of software for our Say Cheese herd management. That's one computer in the barn, another by the office in the milk shed, all for record and reference. My most important job is data entry."

Greg speaks up from known experience with Jimmy. "It will be *our* job."

John the Auditor is so impressed. Aldert gets more technical.

"Jimmy has included algorithms that track milking times, the amount of product, fat levels and on. The software grinds at the recorded history. Jimmy tracks the order in the goat lineup."

"Can I look at the records?"

"Better, John. With technology, everything is online. All data backed up."

Aldert continues. "And the algorithms deal with excess time, less product, reduced fat. And the blend of the line may suggest something different. So we can anticipate infection and such before calling a vet. We adjust feed supplements to complement output."

"Vet could be a big expense."

"Big enough for me to shove the thermometer in their butts myself," Aldert says.

Big-butt looks on the Citiots.

"All part of being the Shepherd."

John the Auditor is no stranger to the expense of outside professional help. That's where the big City money came from — offsite work. John goes analytical all the way to input. "So, for example, if goat #39 is consistent in the lineup and her output of milk drops, it's likely a health issue?"

"Good one, and yes! We would pull 39 out of the line for a checkup. Could be lots of things, but we're onto it. Might mean a parasite. Those can swell the joints. Might be the teats. Swelling, rash affect the suction. Lots of things to deal with." Aldert winks. "Maybe thermometer time."

John ignores the potential butt jokes. "What do you do if you have an idea of a problem?"

"I get take-out."

The Citiots stop in confusion, look around for an answer. "Take-out?"

"I get take-out. I take something out of the refrigerated medicine cabinet in the office. We're all state-of-the-art technology on the herd health here. You can thank Professor Jimmy for another home run on the farm."

The partners smile and nod to their few weeks of Citiot success, or at least their forward motion in Gregzdream.

"We'll move the tour along now. The barn and milk shed will come later."

"I've had a long tour of both," Greg says.

"A little slopping, Greg?"

Greg is caught in the spotlight. He realizes that Aldert has been given all the slop and dirt by the Kembers. Aldert continues to milk the slop for fun.

"We can meet in the milk shed if you're around at four o'clock. Get into some of the teat action?"

"Lots to do," Greg says. "Lots to do, All-dirt. Finish furnishing the house, social media presence, feed our first dog, lots on our plate."

"Remember the milking tour — just listen for the goat bells getting closer around four. The collies will be out. They need the exercise."

The Shepherd is not letting go of the goat tour. He turns to the opposite side of the farm. A dark, solitary figure from the west with black eyes is onto their change of direction. Aldert directs things forward. "Let's head over and meet the King."

"The King?"

"More of a general, actually, but I like to think in the terms of Queenie and the King. You met the herd boss. Now we meet the queen's sequestered consort, Napoleon."

A forced march to the front west paddock on the other side of the double driveway. The three ladies follow. Max follows the action, sitting up for a view from his porch mat. If the old dog could roll his eyes he would at those yappy bitches. *Still with the Masters.* Max can hear his stomach growl.

Aldert looks back over his shoulder. "What did Jimmy tell you about this paddock, Greg?"

"Me. Tell me?" A blind man could see a whole paddock dedicated to one goat. But not the Citiots, until now.

As the group of six approach the fence, Aldert moves his room-wide arms to hold up his bosses. "Not too close."

The collies stay back, knowing the drill.

Greg and John are ready for hug support as they look into those polished pieces of coal, dug deep into a bulbous bearded head. No light in these caverns. Awesome sight. "Is the goat dangerous?"

Greg can't help himself. "It's a freaking pony."

John shakes his head. "No, a focking horse, Greg."

"Let's not talk about horses," Greg says. "It's a focking pony."

Aldert pulls on the reins of alarm. "Semi concern on the goat. Major concern is those electric wires there, waist high."

He points at the second and third slats.

"Let me throw the switch off. See it?"

The Shepherd's vast reach allows him to pull a lever attached to a wood post that anchors the galvanized gate. "We need the gate to be that wide for tractor access."

He sees more questions before either partner speaks. "We'll just have to get Greg on the tractor. Disking. Posthole digging with the auger. And manure spreading. All in a day's work for a farmer."

The two stand back with eyes forward. Roving inspection reveals a string of porcelain insulators on two slats around the entire fence line.

"Is it really necessary to have an electric fence with two wires?" John wonders aloud.

"Whoa, yes," Aldert says. "That Napoleon has been … uh, can be hard on the fencing. A little charge just backs him off. Watch as he comes closer."

"He comes closer?" John says.

"Not without help from the assistants. Or treat persuasion. We have both today. Perfect for a General introduction."

Aldert motions his hips back and forth, back and forth with that smile.

Greg and John half smile at the hunk doing the dirty, even in jest.

"Think of him as our team quarterback," Aldert says. "He's an all-star, gentlemen."

The big-as-a-king goat pays no heed, backed off from the paddock fence. Aldert gives two whistles.

"Gracie. Come, girl."

Without a book of instructions, Gracie and the ladies crawl under the bottom slat. They get right to it. The collies move Napoleon closer to his Master. Aldert surprises his bosses with a handful of fat green apples from his shoulder bag. Napoleon comes in closer, easy peasy, with a green apple in his coal eyes.

Aldert holds four apples in his baseball glove of a right hand. First he passes two each to Greg and John. He motions his left hand upward, waving a come-hither to the fence.

"Down. The arm must be down. Look for the porcelain handle down." He repeats all for caution's sake, staring at the post. "Do not touch that wire. It'll knock you off your feet. Napoleon never did stop on a yellow light."

Greg interrupts. "A yellow light?"

"One wire doesn't hold him back. It takes a full current of red with two wires to hold his attention."

The partners are in rapture. Aldert turns back to the now-safe fence.

"Napoleon."

The huge goat knows the reward drill. He's ready to show himself off. He plays the all-star in his private kingdom.

"Napoleon, up!"

The King stretches upward with his front haunches. His hooves reach over the top slat. Napoleon's hoof reach allows him to rest his hooves on Aldert's broad shoulders. The Shepherd's right hand pops both apples into the open side of Napoleon's mouth. His left hand pulls out four more.

John leans close to Greg. "He just reaches in his pocket with one hand. Presto for four apples."

"He's a hunk."

Aldert smiles at the whisperers beside him. "I think the old goat stretches out at about ten feet. Amazing, eh?"

Jumbo silence and stare back.

"The fence tops six feet," he continues. "He's too big to jump. But could he do damage! Without that charge on the third slat, we'd be chasing him up the 6th Concession."

He laughs. Still nothing from the partners.

"Not before he has mounted most of the does, though. He's a breeding machine. Aren't you the big stud?" Aldert can't reach his head or ears so Napoleon gets a collar rub. "Napoleon. You big suck."

Nothing until now has prepared the City lads for the full exposure of a humon-gous goat stud. The tools of an all-star team quarterback are hall-of-fame stuff in Town and Country. Greg can't help himself on a famous standing monument.

"My God. Look at the size of those nuts."

(See how our cheesy story turns back to nuts in a spin of a shell.)

Aldert adds the Town vernacular. "Real set of arnies, no?"

John is clinical and exact. "His flaccid state looks like it's over two feet."

Greg gets technical. "What does Jimmy's algorithm tell you about Napoleon?"

"Size matters." Aldert gives up some dirt with Shepherd pride. Nothing left under the carpet. "I'm telling you, he's *the* man. General Commander Stud. You should see him in action. A team player, our Napoleon. Wait, it's coming up soon. Three months."

The hunk winks at them. "It's in the software. Jimmy will have it booked. The most advantageous day. It's a breeding rodeo."

Greg asks the obvious stupid question. "But those horns. They could kill someone."

Aldert's smile disappears. "Listen, Boss Greg and Boss John. No one enters the paddock without the Shepherd. If for some unexplainable reason …" The hunk is not smiling. "If you are confronted by Napoleon —"

Audit the advice. "You mean … if he gets out."

"Yes. You guys are not stupid enough to enter the paddock. Right?"

A chorus of agreement. "Right."

"Do not approach Napoleon. Do not stare at him. Turn away. Move away, all in slow, deliberate motions."

Aldert takes three crouching steps backwards. Greg can only think about saving his ass.

"What happens if my ass is between me and the fence?" he asks.

"Run."

"But if he catches up?"

"Run faster. And do not touch the electric fence. Jump for the top slat."

Greg looks up to the six-foot-high top slat.

"Jump!" Aldert says. "Like you're in a high jump competition."

Greg's still looking at the tall fence. Greg hated all that jumping shit in high school. He's looking for a pole to vault with. "Jump over the fence?"

John audits the jump possibilities. "What happens if Napoleon jumps too?"

Aldert tilts his head. Pursed lips sideways, squinting eyes in the imaginary pain of it all. "All goes back to one time." The Shepherd seems lost on the event horizon. A memory switch goes on. "One time. Napoleon tried that once."

A pause and breath.

"Big buddy here knocked the top six-foot slat clean off. Sheared it with his hooves. We were picking up pieces sixteen feet away on the farm lawn. But …"

Greg and John are sheep flocking to the Shepherd in quiet rapture.

"Get this. His equipment." Aldert's palm mittens widen out, turn up for a silent metaphor on size. "Those arnies hit the third slat. No passing here. They drag over, catching on the top electric wire."

He points at the third slat. "That. That wire wrapped around his bag."

Leaving no doubt, Aldert squeezes his face in pain, grabbing at his crotch. It's male instinct as the partners face the pain with both hands in zipper sympathy. Aldert gives a blow-by-blow.

"You know that blue-ball, burning sensation?"

Partners are wide-eyed to the possibility. But hold on.

"Worse. Thanks to his apparatus."

The partners are lost in rural translation. "His apparatus?"

"His big tool. Huge. His ding-dong pushed past the fence."

The Shepherd inches his hips forward while looking back at something lost, left behind.

"The tool bag is hung out on the line. The wire got a stranglehold on the swinging bag. In fishing terms, it was a snag."

Greg backs in. "Snag of the bag."

"Right across the wire. The shock of it all blew the circuit on the panel. Blew out the whole 6th Concession."

(Indeed, the *Journal* reported a "domestic agricultural incident of unintended results." Powerless neighbours, the South Western Hydro response team, even Big Bob, who drove over to cover fire concerns — all were mentioned with a quote or two:

"The Missus and I were watching Money Bowling. *Asked her if our Country Cable bill was a problem."*

"I told him we paid the ZIT bill."

"Never noticed a thing. Had the chainsaw buzzing back in the apple orchard."

Typical of the small-newspaper story is the opportunistic advertising; the chainsaw operator adds some value:

"Looks like a great apple crop this year. We're offering, for the first time, the Crispy Crunch variety.")

"Otherwise there would have been a search — search for a new stud."

Aldert fills their Citiot heads with a bit of Nissouri Township leg-pulling nonsense:

"No balls. That would be one big barbecued goat." A moment of contemplation on the barbecue. "Wouldn't that be a full-on group party!"

Greg and John are in a vegetative state of horror. How could you eat your studfast team King?

"Just kidding, guys. Napoleon is my goat. Furever and furever. Eh, Your Highness?" A man and his goat, in for a buddy neck rub. "Napoleon will never think to leave his paddock. Not unless there's fertile female goats smelling thereabouts. He's only an escape artist when it comes to breeding space."

John is pragmatic. "Big ouch for the poor guy."

Shepherd correction. "The guy's a billy."

John does not connect the wire. "Billie, then. I guess, if … Billie still has his balls in place. That's good?"

Greg understands but does not address John's homophonic confusion. Instead he pauses in disbelief at the thought of Billie the appraiser, a hay-topped Gollum, morphed into a General goat. But Aldert keeps it moving:

"Still, he could have lost everything. His arnies knocked the complete electric service out. It was the day all lights went out in Transvaal. That was good as an alarm. The compressor went off in the milk shed, electricity out, so it's dixie-doo out the door — something's wrong on the farm."

The partners coddle their parts in synchronized support.

"What happened …?" Greg attempts. "What happened to his … parts?"

This time round, Aldert cannot help himself with some direct Nissouri Township humour.

Aldert puffs out his cheeks. Father Wind extends those baseball-mitt palms. "Those arnies went from honeydew-melon-size swollen" — the arms go for full extension — "up to watermelons."

His head turns side to side for a pause in reflection.

"Kinda the same shape too."

Head-shakes with arms extended.

"But black as an inkwell."

Greg and John look at each other with a shrug — how black is an inkwell?

Aldert paints a more practical picture:

"No good being the team quarterback if the equipment is damaged. If the quarterback can't throw it into a few Hail Marys. You don't want testosterone over-cured stud on any barbecue."

Greg can't help himself at the horror, the fascination of the huge stud on the spit. John is fascinated, horrified by the idea of honeydew melons swelling into watermelons. Black watermelons. Of course, his real fear is having his own apricots turn into grapefruits. Getting caught anywheres is a shocking vision.

"But All-dirt," he asks, "how does Napoleon know when to approach the fence?"

"My general theory is that he senses the hum of the current. Real smart aren't you, General?"

The liquid coal eyes look back, deep puddles of concentration. Even the Shepherd fails to hear his royal charge:

"*Na-a-a-ah. Tha-a-a-at was a ba-a-a-ad da-a-a-ay. Na-a-a-ah again. Na-a-a-ah for Napoleon.*"

"My God, Greg, *look* at the *size* of his tongue," John says. "He doesn't even chew the apples. He lassos them, inhales them whole!"

"Yippy yahoo, he's a cowboy."

Aldert turns on Greg with his smile.

"Your turn."

Greg blurts it out. "Our turn? My turn? No way, my turn."

Aldert's turn to buck up his bosses. "Look, Napoleon will never stand up like that for anyone, anyone but the Shepherd. Just hold your one apple out. One at a time, palm face-up. He'll stick his beard through the slats and just hoover it up. Remember how Queenie took it."

Queenie taking it was hooves-down an easier experience. And it behooves Greg to simply bring it up. "We did feed Queenie," Greg remembers.

One hand each, they reach out, one time each.

Napoleon in turn slobbers away at both offerings. Huge nose in, he repeats the tongue hoover for the second set of two apples. Aldert never leaves his audience without a taste of humour.

"My big stud loves his tart treat."

Curly Top is still fascinated by that tongue. "Nice wet tongue job."

John breaks a smile and stops. Both he and Greg have more stupid questions.

"What is that *goo* on his horns?" Greg says. "It … smells!"

John qualifies the smell. "It focking stinks."

Aldert gets a laugh at the direct connection to Mrs. Kember.

"Napoleon secretes his very own secret sauce from the horns. You should see the horns in breeding season. It's messy." The hunk pinches his nostrils. "It's sinus-clearing stuff."

John sees a few more monogrammed hankies on his shopping list. He whispers to Greg: "Stinky yucky yuck." He leans in on the stinky thought. "Breeding season would be a great time for our road tour in Sicily."

Greg is fixated on the arnies squeezing out toward the ground behind the hindquarters of the King. Distracted, he comes back too loud. "They do have lots of goats in Sicily."

John audits his own embarrassment. "Shut your gob, Greg."

Aldert is still looking at his pride and joy, the General. It's time to breed the common background information on the male situation.

"That's why Max is never allowed in this paddock. It's a male thing. One stinky four-legged stud in the paddock is more than enough." Greg and John look back toward the mat on the porch. Let a comfortable dog lie. "The porch is his Max spot, his paddock. Good spot for a smart old dog."

The partners can't help but imagine a Friday fight night on pay TV, a fright of imagination between one mean dog and one big goat.

Aldert pounds a nail into that silent TGIF idea. "Max *would* back down from Napoleon."

Both Greg and John are fixated on the horns. The Shepherd appraises his quarterback's performance.

"That equipment below." Aldert's eyes dart to his left, fence side. "That takes care of the whole harem. Napoleon is an amazing stud. He can mow over the entire doe team in heat. He waits, watches and wonders from dusk to dawn on his escape rut. When he's loose, this big buddy can ride the range all night."

The lads look puzzled.

"It's all about the sauce. That ooze is a combo of K-Y lubricant and Chanel for Men, slathered on his horns. Gets the ladies fiesta ready."

His mile smile widens with two eyebrow raises.

"The ladies line up like it's Friday night at Bobby's Soft Ice Cream."

Greg wonders if Aldert plucks his bushy eyebrows. John thinks this huge goat must have some kind of heterosexual dysfunction. He waits all year for twenty-four hours of rutting. The Shepherd starts to move on without his small human flock.

"The horns," he says with a look back. "Step on his patch, you are fair game for those horns."

Aldert whistles to the collie lineup. Off they march.

"Hope you enjoyed meeting the herd." He focuses on Greg, pointing at his watch. "Almost four o'clock, Greg." A pause on Curly Top moves to both partners. "I have chores to do. It's milking time. Queenie will be lining the team up. Can't keep them waiting."

John and Greg step up onto the porch in silence. John wants to get online and look at the production figures … but his mind is stuck on watermelons. He'll never ever look at a watermelon the same way again. Greg is happy to join Barbara in the kitchen, maybe a glass of Pinot Gris, maybe a shot of that watermelon vodka Barbie has hidden under the floorboard.

Later that evening, over dinner on the porch, Greg asks Jimmy and Barbara how Aldert came to be part of their lives.

"What is it that makes him *the* Shepherd?" John adds.

Pause. Jimmy and Barbara regard each other. "You want to go first?" Jimmy asks her.

Chapter 11

It didn't start off so bad for the miracle lad of Transvaal and Town.

The name Aldert originates in Holland. Some distant relative was an admiral in the Dutch East Indies navy. His mother, Linda, is a local yokel. His father was second-generation Dutch. No comfort that Aldert is a major name in Holland, when it doesn't translate well into English.

His natural father dies in a car accident before Aldert can remember. Memories are built from a photo album his mother hides under her sofa sewing chair. Aldert learns to seek out these small memories on his own when no one is home. This helps him build a better picture of what could be.

He has a good picture of what his father looked like. Linda refers to him as bigger than life. The young boy has no living Dutch connection. Grandparents are long gone and forgotten. The rest of the family is a tiny group of distant cousins over the great pond in an unknown and unfamiliar homeland.

He does remember the start of Hell, the arrival of the stepfather.

Fat Al Stollery.

The young boy grows up never ever to refer to this intruder as his father or even his stepfather. Always Al to his face, Fat Al when out of earshot. Fat Al holds their small farm home in a reign of terror. The boy bides his time to gain his voice.

Al sometimes tries to turn him into his namesake, but at twelve Aldert makes it clear.

"I am All-Dirt." Phonetics for the fat dummy. "Named for my grandfather. I am not Al or Little Al."

It's a standoff at the right, chosen moment. Al is too fat and drunk to react, to do anything. Through black and blue his mother defends her second husband.

"It's the Army injury. Blew an ignition cap from a hand grenade … went right off in his hand. It gives him pain all the time. Can't sleep. Makes it hard to work at the Plant."

Aldert nods in sympathy to Linda; he could never give his other further grief. He despises the fact that anyone would choose to hit any woman, child, man or beast.

Fat Al Stollery has not escaped the notice of the coffee klatch along the S-shaped counter at the Sunriser. A complete asshole drunk and loudmouth like Fat Al Stollery is hard to miss.

"He was a fatty as a kid. Where's the self-esteem? That's what I ask."

"I remember him in Cub Scouts. He was a tub right from the start."

There's always a neighbour. "The one place he could get a job was the Army. They made him lose eighty pounds before enlisting him. Fat Al thinned down, but not for long. He packed it in after packing it all back on within a year."

"Always fat. Always stupid."

"Look what happened on the range. That was real dumb. It's a fucking army practice range. Never ever pick up undetonated ordinance. That's how stupid he is."

Someone disagrees in the back. "Maybe not so dumb. He counted on a disability pension."

"Never could count, no matter how many fingers."

Ouch.

Another coffee-slurper comes out as a cartoon bear in a dumb comic voice. "*Doh dee, doh dee, doh doh, doh doh dee. Dum dee dum dee doh doh. Dum dee dee.* What do we have here? *Dum dee dee … BAM!*"

The whole room wakes up in laughter at the sad display of stupidity. The slurper is looking down and dumb at his hands. "Only lost a three fingers. *Dum dee dee.*"

Someone in the back is up to establish his in-the-know credit. "Two and a half to be exact."

No matter the facts, it's bad for the lad and his mother.

"Fat, stupid and worse for those poor folks. Fat Al's a nasty drunk."

"Can't face your stupidity when you're too fucking dumb."

That stops the room in thought for a moment.

"Coward, if you ask me. Laying a beating on the wife and the lad."

"Don't think he touches the lad. Have you seen the size of Aldert? He just had his twelfth birthday."

An in-the-know with conscience wades in on the skinning and flaying of Fat Al. He looks at the slurper and the last speaker.

"We need to look in the mirror. Ask ourselves who's the coward, us or Fat Al. If we're not cowards then we should have a talk with Fat Al. Introduce him to civil boundaries. That's what we should do. Instead of talking about the fat piece of shit all the time."

Both reply back, a duet in reversal. "Not my business."

What does Stormin' Norman advise? "Life is too short for assholes."

Transvaal neighbour Lochlin Austin sets the scene. "Our lad Aldert is the unofficial stepson, but he's the official farm hand. He's the one doing the chores. She cooks, cleans and feeds the chickens and such. Aldert carries a heavier load with feed bags, slopping, water and much more."

The Kembers, Transvaal and Town natives, the coffee klatches from the downtown cafes, Tims and of course the source of all sources, the Sunriser, *all* are in accord:

"Thank God it's the one boy. More children? Hm-m-m-m."

"Thank God it's a small herd. Less than twenty beef."

Township humour. "Maybe someday Al will get all twenty in the same colour range."

The reverse S, the back booths, the three helpers in the kitchen and Braedon with two customers at cash all mutter the same thing.

"Fucking fat hunk of shit."

Exception is the one dim light in attendance, Ronnie.

"Women have their beguiling ways too."

One of the in-the-know patrons strikes that light out.

"That's a big word, Ronnie." Ronnie has a goofy smile. The room turns. "You're as *stupid* as Fat Al."

The whole line along the S-shaped counter twist on their stools. The in-the-know shines a bright light, exposing the dim-wit in his tracks. He freezes with a full-dumb look of terror. The in-the-know pours it on.

"No woman, no child, no person should have to put up with that alcohol-fuelled abuser. *You* need to get a neck-up check-up." All stares stick on the frozen head of Ronnie. "You are a *fucking* moron too."

Neither Ronnie nor his brother Donnie show up again in the back corner booth for months after that day.

Braedon heads out from the pass-through kitchen window. He waits for the stools and bench heads to focus forward to him. "Someone should call someone. The police, eh?"

"Who do we call, the Provincials or the Chief?"

"Ask him when he comes in."

The in-the-know. "No matter whose jurisdiction, police intervention could cause more violence. Social Services may be the approach. A professional approach, no doubt."

"Don't spark a fire at home unless it has a place. *Aargh. Aargh. Aargh.*"

"Someone, no doubt, will call on Fat Al. I guarantee that."

The room agrees.

The room does nothing.

The closest neighbours in geographic terms are the Kembers, Jimmy and Barbara. She is the first to tune into the problem. Even without any children of her own she's a natural.

"She cowers. The boy hovers. Not right."

"Barbie, I hear you. And I can hear them." He points to the west wall of the kitchen. "All the way over there."

Barbara doubles down. "Real focking arsehole that turd is."

The months go by and no priest, no police officer, no one from the social service system steps in, nor any of the over-opinionated coffee slurpers. Barbara is the first. She turns the heat on the cause. "We need to step in on Al."

Jimmy's face turns red in alarm.

She continues. "Careful, Jimmy, tactical like. No need firing up that fat focking ass with control issues."

Jimmy has thought long and hard about this. The commute to Western gives him thirty-five minutes of contemplation (if he turns off CBC). The Nissouri-born professor is the renowned consultant and guide to some of Canada's largest businesses. He mixes well, the Professor, with his generous dash of rural roots. Jimmy has mapped out his approach, a business deal with the fat focking ass.

"Make it monetary," he says. "Money talks. Ask Al if we can hire Aldert after school."

Barbara plays a mother card. "He's only twelve."

"He's smart. And look at the size of his hands and feet. He's a big kid. He'll work like a man. It's in him, I can tell."

Barbara is a little surprised at her husband. He has an Al-plan, and well thought out.

"Remember," she says, "focking life comes after you make the plans."

"Barb, I think that the both of us can do some good. Work like a team."

"I am on the team. But listen to me, Jimmy. He's abusive, and I will never ask that focking piece of shit anything, ever!"

He touches her shoulder. "I think that *I* can make this work. Put the squeeze on that fat hunk of focking shit."

They smile, then laugh together.

Jimmy has heard the wrongs, while working around the barn and the yard, from Fat Al Stollery over the fence. Jimmy could feel the bad vibe. He could sense trouble during all his encounters with Al, Linda, or the lad.

Barbara reminds him of the family order. "They are *not* married. The focking fat turd just showed up one day."

Both remark that mother and son both avoid eye contact while Al's in the picture. Mother sticks at Fat Al's side. Aldert stands off in the shadow thrown by the hunk of shit. Fat Al shuffles through false nods and fake smiles. Jimmy and Barbara soon recognize this as his routine. The see-you-on-Sunday priest or the eight-to-four social services worker are both useless. If the so-called authorities would show up after five any day of the week, the fat turd holding court would open their eyes to how drunk he gets by dinner.

Barbara has been onto the boy's potential as a farm helper since well before his twelfth birthday. While Jimmy was off commuting to Western University, Barbara was an observer at home. She took her cue from the rattly diesel of the school bus followed by four woofs from Max.

"Jimmy, I can see him walking along the fence line."

Barbara at first assumed it was a detour under their front-yard canopy from the Stollery barn. One afternoon, though, when she's out in the squirrel-depleted tulip garden, she picks up on his complete route. Aldert is not detouring. He's not short-cutting either. He follows a direct path to the west paddock.

Aldert is on a personal path that leads to learning. When the school bus drops him on the day Jimmy is home, both Kembers can see him follow the fence line past the house.

"Listen," she says. "He's calling to the General."

The Kembers peer around the porch corner.

"He's even got nicknames for him, too. Listen."

The boy is calling out. Max watches, too, through the side balustrades of the porch. The firm voice of a young boy in full command. A sweet voice that carries back to the porch.

"*General. General. General.*" Aldert blows out a short high whistle. "Here, Boss Goat. Here Boss Goat."

Aldert thinks the General has beautiful colours, all two of them — he's all black with a white face over shiny coal eyes. The General waits for a beard scratch. The boy shares a saved piece of his lunch carrot. Boss Goat has a general liking for the young Aldert.

Barbara keeps watching, pulls her husband closer. "Wait. It gets better."

Boss Goat sidles up to the fence, not close enough for electric-wire concern. The young man reaches into his side pocket. The shiny coal eyes follow the apple hidden in Aldert's hands. Napoleon opens up. Teeth separate to free a python-sized tongue which hoovers up the apple. Aldert gives Boss Goat a head rub. Jimmy is stunned.

"He's a natural. Number one, he has a treat. Then" — he squeezes the back of Barbie's neck — "he gives him a head rub. Amazing."

Barbara agrees. "The kid's a natural shepherd."

"He has a nickname for the General too!"

"And what is that?"

"Napoleon."

"Napoleon? Where does that come from?"

"Think, Jimmy. You're the focking academic."

"I'm beat on that one."

"No wonder you're the lost genius at Quiz Nights. You call him the General. The boy's picked this up to name him Napoleon."

"How do you know that?"

"I won't focking play Quiz Night on your team anymore, dear. Listen."

Jimmy watches her cup her right hand to her ear.

"I can hear the boy."

She lowers her voice to echo Aldert's calling. *"Napoleon. Napoleon. You're the boss of all. The General of all. Napoleon."*

"Wow," Jimmy says. "Smart boy."

"Smart is not the full point here. The point is, Jimmy, *you* need some focking help. You'll die slopping those stalls before goat cheese gets to the IGA. I'm helping you with forty-plus milkers. Spring will double that up." She pretend-calls over to the west paddock. "Right. Napoleon. We're not worried about your help with the ladies." Her eyes turn on her husband. "Jimmy needs the help."

Jimmy thinks of all the time he spends milking, slopping, and feeding Frankie. "Both of us, and the kid, Barbara. We *all* need the focking help."

The couple laughs all round.

Help it is. Jimmy plans to knock on the Stollery door the next day.

"I'll do it before the school bus comes. Get Al right after work. He can't finish two beers on the short commute. Primed and ready."

Good strategy, as Al works an eight-to-four-o'clock shift, so he would be somewhat sober after a short drink-and-drive home. Not ready to sleep yet; ready instead to wet a dry throat, and therefore primed to listen. Say anything that moves the speech along to Happy Hour.

Jimmy follows Al's rust-bucket up the laneway. Catches him at the front door. He keeps his course direct, straightforward, all true to the point.

"Hey, Al. Thought I'd catch you for a heads up. On the boy."

The pea in Al's brain rolls. The boy? He means the kid, don't he?

"I need the help," Jimmy says. "Can I hire the boy for some chores when he gets home from school? Of course … after he finishes his chores."

Al offers some sober bullshit. "Family responsibilities come first. His chores have to be done. Kid needs his own money."

Jimmy is thankful there's no Barbara in a background chorus. He could just hear her on Al. (*"You fat focking slob! Why aren't you helping around the farm?"*)

Jimmy picks up the slack. All true to the point. "Minimum wage to start. Expanding the herd to make cheese. So there will be incentives."

Fat Al registers the notion of money coming into the house because of someone else's farm work. He hangs on to the new and last word. That's a big one. "In-cent-ives?"

As Al tries for sober focus his fat eyes bobble like fried eggs. Jimmy beats him to the next idea.

"Have some rewards figured out to make it worthwhile. Bigger business along the way. The boy can be a part of it."

"Make it worthwhile, yes. How 'along the way'?"

Jimmy moves a little closer. "If he continues working, I will need him happy happy going down the road."

"The road? Happy happy?"

All true. "Expanding the herd. Finishing my milking shed. Big stuff where I need the help. The boy can work along with me as much as he wants."

Jimmy senses the conversation going off track. He needs to get the boy to first base. Jimmy goes for some heat on the full count. He fires a strike. "Ten bucks an hour to start. But I will work him hard."

Al knows his dim-wit nephew pumping gas at Dobson Ford makes eight dollars an hour. All the fart-face does is read — sorry, look at comics. "Sold, one boy. When can I send Little Al over?"

The next day Aldert shows up on the Kember porch. For the first time he follows the wrong side of the electric fence. The General shadows his friend for a sunrise scratch.

Jimmy give his first instruction. "The on-off switch for the wires. Left, there on the post."

"I can spend some time with Napoleon after work."

"Let's go meet Queenie and the girl's team. Have you met them yet?"

"I've seen them on the front fence line. Seem to stick together. Beards always down in the grass. She's the Queen. Leads all. Speaks for them all." The boy, soon to be a young man, soaks up the farm food chain.

"We'll start today with some slopping," Jimmy says.

"I know all about that, Mr. Kember. And I do realize, Mr. Kember, that I have to be friends with Queenie to meet her needs."

"Aldert. Mr. Kember was my father. Jimmy please."

"Yes sir. Jimmy."

"Have you worked with a Bobcat?"

"Not in our barn. All by hand. My hands. But my mom lets me drive her car. It's a standard shift. No problems for me … Jimmy. I would love the opportunity."

"There will be more cleaning, sanitizing stuff. Then eventual milking in that building." He points to the left, then to the drive shed on the right. "Let's look at the Bobcat and MotoMotion tractor. Then the milk shed."

"Yes sir … Jimmy."

"After, we'll sneak around back of the barn to meet Frankie."

"Frankie?"

"My buddy the pig."

"We've never had pigs."

"Start Monday after school, Aldert? Have to keep in mind I promised Al that you would not skip your home chores."

"Yes sir, Jimmy. My plan is to come here right off the bus. Work till dinner. Then I'll do my home chores and homework later."

The boy is most efficient on school days in order to make it by four o'clock. A hop and skip from the bus stop and he pushes the start button.

Every weekday off the bus, Saturday and Sunday mornings across the fence, Aldert shows up to work. Always on time, ripe ready to get on with the job no matter how little sleep or nourishment.

On Saturdays, Barbara makes sure to detour him through the back kitchen door for a heaping breakfast. Sunday she leaves a sandwich on thick fresh bread on a comfy, shady porch chair. After school there's a brown paper bag with a treat, left in a secret spot. Barbara can see him out the side window.

"Aldert never peeks in the bag. Always smiles."

The boy becomes a man alongside the Professor. Books, some courses, and visits to other farms transform the all-round goat-keeper into the future Shepherd. Every November Jimmy and the lad load up the best and head off to Toronto. Aldert looks back at the City through the alleys, stalls and loading ramps of the Royal Winter Fair. The student loves the Professor's instructions.

"It's in the grooming," Jimmy says. "Breeding by #1, the General."

"Napoleon, Jimmy."

"Napoleon's service and #33's birthing have given us this fine goat."

"Buttercup has given us Luna," Aldert says.

Jimmy learns not to ask. "Luna's the goat she is because of #1 giving it to #33. At this time, it's our grooming that will take her — sorry, Luna — up to the prize ring."

By Jimmy's side, Aldert spends hours brushing, currying and priming Luna. "Luna's a showgirl. Aren't you, Luna. Show me your smile?"

The older man swears Luna understands every word the lad says.

After two years helping the Kembers, the boy moves off on the same bus to a different school. He heads to grade nine at St. Marys High School. As a secondary school teenager he has an immediate revelation.

"Jimmy, I do not want to be a goat-keeper."

That stops the Professor in his tracks. The lad moves past his panic face.

"No, no, no. Jimmy, I love the farm and the goats. Even Frankie. Max, of course. In high school people will ask me about my interests, my after-school job. I do *not* want to tell them that I am a goat-keeper."

Jimmy listens with his heart. Aldert is a quiet lad, but right now he is passionate and breathless.

"Hockey or soccer," Aldert says. "A *goal*-keeper is okay. But a goat-keeper …" There is no mile smile reaching across his face. "It will be murder at school."

Jimmy is touched. The Professor and Barbara do not have children. This is unfamiliar territory never crossed with young cousins, nieces or nephews. The esteemed consultant on what to do is stuck on what to do. Country logic prevails.

"Aldert, what would you like to be called?"

The young man commands his title. "The Shepherd. I want to be called *The Shepherd.*"

"Kinda biblical, eh?" Jimmy smiles.

"So be it," Aldert says. "Maybe a better name will help the position get the respect it deserves."

Jimmy tips his cap. "So be it. The Shepherd."

He later recounts the discussion later to his wife.

"Focking wow." She wipes her soggy eyes. "Angels come from Heaven; now we have the Shepherd who came from Hell."

Back from the Winter Fair in short order Luna gives birth to one big kid, a billy. A difficult birth, with all six hands and an extra pair of rubber elbow-high latex gloves from Veterinarian Jon Heidel.

Citiots hearing the soggy story now find the subject of rubber and latex an inspiration. Greg winks. "I see a latex slash rubberwear party, eh?"

"Call it Vet Night," John laughs.

"Animal Farm."

Greg pretends he's snapping gloves. *Snap. Snap.*

"Are you making innuendos?" Barbara frowns.

The partners speak in sync. "Don't scare the natives."

They leave another theme-party idea in laughter as Barbara and Jimmy return to the story. The white star-faced kid is about to be abandoned by the moon princess.

The new billy is a slippery black seal with feet, a handsome billy bundle welcomed into the hands of Barbara.

Barbara notices right away that Luna does not take to being milked by a raw set of teeth. "Jimmy, focking warning. Mother is in stress. She is *not* responding to her kid. Look, the wee billy will die."

All eyes are on the surprise kid and worn-away mother. Action is needed.

Jimmy cuts the cord. Barbara cleans the kid. Rubber gloves and antiseptics all round with teamwork. Dr. John deals with leftover yucky birth stuff.

The young Shepherd will take seasons to learn to keep a still stomach during kid birthing. The Professor, though, is an automatic farmer in action. He comes up with the executive decision. "Shepherd."

Aldert looks up from his turn with the kid in arms.

"Shepherd. Congratulations."

The young Shepherd is silent, questioning with a half-mile smile.

"You have the first member of your flock," Jimmy says. "It's yours. You just have to keep it living."

Barbara teams up with her favourite boy. "I've done it a few times. Momma milk, nutrients, a few needles and lots of focking love, Aldert."

Aldert has new tears of ownership pride. "Thank you, Barbara. Thank you, Professor … Jimmy."

"Your goat will always have pasture at the Kembers," Jimmy says. "Maybe sequestered space as a male with Napoleon for a year."

"I'd have to keep tabs on that relationship," Aldert says.

"Never mind. We'll work it out. The Shepherd will always have some pasture on the Kember Farm."

No more questions at that moment, but one answer pops up.

"Hector."

"Hector?" The Kembers give a puzzled look.

"It's Greek."

"Aldert," Jimmy says. "I know who Hector is. Why the name?"

"He's a warrior on his own. A Trojan prince dressed in black. He will be a fighter. See the star on his face? A leader that inspires all." Aldert looks to the Kembers. "Of course, with all of your help."

"Teamwork, Aldert."

Big hugs all round to more direction in the community-raised lad's life.

"Careful, don't crush your future focking herd there."

Aldert soaks up everything Jimmy pours out. He buys into the goat herd with heart and soul. The young Shepherd tells Jimmy *all* his dreams on their drive back from the Winter Fair the next November. The twin-axle goat trailer marked *Kember Farms* tugs along behind the F-350 with its chilly cabin. The double cab goes quiet.

"I have two thousand dollars saved from these past four years."

Jimmy is impressed. Acts surprised. "What are you saving for?"

No surprise. "My own herd someday, Jimmy."

"What better way to start off? Your first goat is one fine stud."

"Hector's a warrior."

"Royal bloodline. You can develop great stock."

"My herd will be one-hundred-percent Nubian. Like yours, Jimmy."

"We may need a little help from the General in both herds. Expand your prize-winning DNA."

Farm humour on the betterment of a new herd puts big smiles on their faces on the return to Transvaal. The professor shepherds his student.

"Lad, why don't we check out the Cliptown auction? I'll show you the buy-and-sell routine. You don't need a farm to do that."

"We've done a drop there. But I've never been to the auction. Any auction."

"We have a cull coming up before birthing. So let's get organizing."

"Super, thanks."

"Day off school, too," Jimmy says. "Wednesday is auction day. I can send you a note."

It's the last year of Aldert's bus tour to and from secondary school in Town. He has refined his identity as the Shepherd. No more vomiting during spring birthing. And man, look at the size of him. At sixteen, he fits a big seat beside Jimmy on the road; big hands for barn slopping and milking at the farm.

The Shepherd displays a soft deference to his wise teacher. "I need pasture to make it work."

His teacher is smart and generous. He knows the lad is a big thinker. "Cut your does in with the home team. Pasture and feed for the visitors will be free. Plus, Napoleon can throw a few in for you" — the big hand is always surprised by the helpful nature of his boss — "compliments of the house."

Aldert concentrates on the Professor. "Throw a few in, compliments of the house. That's dirty business to promise."

(That's real Nissouri-Zorra Township humour. Across the dirt fields, the dusty concessions north along the Thames Valley towards Town, the perspective changes. The in-the-know, even some of the dim lights around the reverse S, call it different: "That's Blanshard humour.")

No matter the geography, Jimmy adds on more business. "All the kids will be on your ticket. Yours to ride."

Aldert lights up in a vision of his own herd. He's in a storm of names. *Sugar Plum, Flossie, Gum Drop, Jube-Jube, Black Molly ...*

Jimmy comes in with more additions. "I'll pay you thirty percent of the market price for your milk."

Jimmy tunes the young man in with a deep inhale. "Transportation is free as long as *you* do the planning. *Both* herds are able to head in the same direction. That means yours will have to be on the path from your pasture each day."

The professor pauses, nods. "Teamwork. It will cut down the hard work. We'll track it on the app. I'll write a complete subprogram on your herd ..."

The lad does not need to be a math professor to count up to a great win-win deal with his mentor. Aldert picks up quick. He sucks up the coloured graphs in his file that follow his herd health.

Fat Al has no idea the amount of money Aldert has hidden somewhere in the house. The stash will combine with Jimmy's free benefits to facilitate Aldert's plan to get out of Hell. Fat Al never walks back of the barn paddock west of the miscoloured heifers. No idea the count back there.

Back behind the Kember barn, Frankie can't count anything. Frankie, like Fat Al, never thinks about anything more complicated than jamming something down his throat. They are both porky reactors. Frankie is comforted with the high level of goat milk in the pig trough. Fat Al sucks back another Red Label from today's fresh case of beer.

The mountain of dust that day has a strange shape as it grabs at the rattling school bus, following it down the 6th Concession to stop just past the Kember farm. Off the bus, the Shepherd always heads to his number one, Hector, on the east property line of hawthorn trees along the double-wired fence on the far side. The lad has taken Linda's scrub land, a cover of embarrassment, from dark to light. Napoleon and Hector love the fence lined with chewy treats. The branches reach far enough into the goats' private paddocks to avoid any shock from the double wire on either side.

"Na-a-a-ah. Be car-r-r-r-re-ful. Na-a-a-ah go-o-o-od."

Hector can hear the school bus as he pulls over against the southern corner of the fence line. Easy access to the returning student; no treat left from lunch.

Today, though, no visiting hours.

Aldert drops from the bus steps. He stops while the ride moves off. He's not hearing anything strange over the rattling, but he waits and listens for something. An immediate recognition, even above that diesel engine.

He hears a shriek from Linda. He moves up the yard towards the house.

At sixteen he is no match for Al's weight, three hundred pounds plus. But the lad is a mountain of power, topping the scales at two-twenty plus on six feet four inches of muscle. More than a silent boy who watches at the end of the kitchen table. More strength than a beer-soaked brain could absorb.

Successful business people call it "sharpening the saw." Time out to read, educate, learn and contemplate. When it comes to the wood pile, Aldert and Fat Al have different approaches to life skills. For Fat Al, working the wood pile means heating the house. Unbeknownst to Fat Al, Aldert's labours on the wood pile have turned him into an axe-wielding machine. Linda has watched her son in silence as he grabs the block with one hand, wields the axe with the other.

Chop. Chop. Chopping machine. A Viking.

More time chopping piles on the rage. Aldert takes the semi-useless work as a full-on exercise. Shaping the body and sharpening the mind. Aldert has had many walkthroughs on this trail of retribution with many days on the wood pile. Days chopping the stacks of maple, oak and walnut, he's rehearsed scenarios, actions and reactions. Fat Al never buys a chipper.

"Why would I pay for a machine and the gas to use it? I have you, Little Al."

This late afternoon off the bus, Fat Al is tuning up Linda before he heads off to a four-o'clock shift at the cement plant. Aldert moves with purpose. First stop is that wood pile for a broken axe handle.

Hector has followed Aldert's path to the southwest corner of the paddock. He is all aware that something is different, the walk, the urgency and the direction. No Master. No treat. No head scratch.

"Na-a-a-ah goo-o-o-od. Na-a-a-ah goo-o-o-od."

Aldert does not break stride, grabbing his well thought-out weapon of choice. A symbol, an icon he carries forward towards the porch. Aldert is so committed to the plan that the collies hold back in anticipation. No stir from inside the house, no curtain parted, not a motion to the commotion that approaches. Such is the current of his concentrated rage. He strides over the three front steps, bounding up to the tattered screen door. Aldert is quick on the pick-up and cool-down with years of pretending how. The rage meter drops to zero.

Tap, tap on the front door.

"Fuck off Aldert." The turd grunts it out without hesitation. He has heard the rattling bus. He has not registered that the collies are not barking. "Fuck you 'dirt. Not your fucking business. Just FUCK OFF!"

The son zeroes in, more Zen monk than Samurai or Kamikaze pilot.

Tap. Tap.

Fat Al thinks he's Steven Seagal. "Fuck off boy, or I'll straighten you out next."

Aldert keeps it low on intensity.

Tap. Tap. Soft but firm. "Need to talk to you, Al."

"Fuck off, boy! I'm giving your Ma a talking to. You're asking to get a fuckin' beating."

Aldert needs a sure way to get through to the dangerous shit-brain. "It's about school."

Fat Al, with nothing positive to offer Aldert, nonetheless takes school seriously.

Breathe in, breathe out, be steady. Breathe. Be ready to chop.

Aldert imagines the free flow of his axe splitting a wood fence post.

"What's the problem with fucking school, boy?"

Calm. Calm, and breathe. Ready. Steady. He's calm and ready to breathe the words out. "I have a letter from school."

"A letter …?"

Another breath of words. "Addressed to you, Al."

With eyes closed, Aldert stays tuned in to the quiet behind the screen door. "It's sealed, Al."

Aldert said it. Al. Aldert addresses the piece of shit by name for the first and last time. A well thought-out maneuver in his wood-pile plan.

Breathe. Wait. Breathe.

Aldert can hear feet shuffling. The fat fuck's mind would be shuffling back and forth on a sealed envelope, from school.

Aldert stops breathing. No more practice thoughts, the game is on, a sealed deal. The bait waits on a hook for a fat fuck.

The soft whimpers of Aldert's mother can be heard from inside. Aldert's axe-free hand pulls on the handle. The fish is hooked onto the inside handle. Fat Al never did catch up to the idea that the boy has become a man. He looks up to a stranger at the door. The strange man uses a left hand pull on the door handle, to bring the pineapple head into axe-radius range. The turd scans the man's face.

The stranger's right hand swings up to strike down from heaven above. The pineapple splits open. A gash slice above Al's eyebrows with the counter-clock-wise windmill hit. A mark to remember forever in reflection.

The wood-pile training makes it a natural hit. Smooth, precise to the exact contact point. The handle slices to the core of that fucking pineapple. The language response was never scripted or rehearsed, total improv. Words never heard from the community-raised and -loved young man, the pride of Town and Country. "Fuck you. You fucking …"

Before a third f-bomb the sixteen-year-old retracts the handle, ready to cue up the stunned lump for another strike. Aldert reverses his hand position to allow a forward thrust to Al's mammoth gut muscle.

Fat Al's carp mouth opens up, exhausting air that sounds more fart than exhale. *"Pff-f-f-f-f-ph-i-i-i-if."* Al crumples to his knees.

The axe master clocks the handle righty-tighty for pivoting power. He swings in again.

Another mouth fart of terrible pain. *"Pff-f-f-f-f-ph-i-i-i-if."*

A little karate from St. Marys High School phys-ed merges with eight years on the woodpile. As Fat Al fades to the porch deck, Aldert reverses for a single. He hacks at the back of his flabby knees. Al rests in a prayer on the floor.

"Never ever touch my mother again."

Knock on the back of his head.

"Never come on this property again."

KNOCK. KNOCK.

"And further. Never approach us. Never talk to us. No contact!"

KNOCK. KNOCK. KNOCK.

"Do not *ever* refer to me *again* as Little Al. You fucking loser!"

An all-new Aldert drops his third f-bomb. All Fat Al can do is lie, lie in fetal moaning on the ratty porch deck.

From next door: "Jimmy. Call 911." Maybe it's the calm focus brought on by her primrose tea or maybe it's her would-be mother's intuition, but Barbara's been glued to her living room window. "Something's wrong next door."

Jimmy knows what something next door means.

As the ruckus slows down to retribution, calls have been made. Next-door distress brings in the neighbours. Aldert's status as the community-raised lad doubles the concern. With him and Linda in Hell, who gives a shit about the fat turd?

First come the Kembers, at a full run. Second come the Austins across the 6th. Third call, three properties over, are the Havmores. Dispatch records five calls altogether. Three neighbours get a follow-up from a passerby on the concession.

"Seems to be some sort of fit. I can see people running across the lawn. It's the Kembers. The dogs are barking too. Somebody's on the porch."

Linda dials in last, fearing an axe murder on the front porch.

The saviour comes from the 911 crew. Eight-minute response for Lorne Albert and the ambulance crew on shift. They have the fat lump strapped and bagged in three minutes. Fat Al is off to St. Marys emergency before the Chief himself arrives.

The Chief knows enough to skip the lights and siren. He can follow a plot line. "Sad, sad, ad. I dreaded this day."

Fat Al will never come through that screen door again.

The Town and Country community follow with pride Aldert's graduation from St. Marys High School. After school, a drive to graduation in Herd Management. Never did young Aldert have to worry about a lift from here or there. There would always be the return ride back on weekends waiting for him. An anonymous pool of drivers puts the pedal down, drawn from a diverse group of Moose Lodge and Methodist Hall Senior Choir members. Thank you, Barbara. The list goes on to two book clubs, the CWL and the Horticultural Society. Thank you again, Barbara. Braedon, with Jimmy direction, covers Sunriser participation. Three months of daily drives by group oral support.

"I'm coming back from the Lake on Friday. I'll pick him up."

"He's on my way to Goderich."

"The wife likes a drive to the lake."

"The lake? That's twenty-five more kilometres."

"Hey, the lad deserves an order of Cheryl Ann fries."

Cash flow comes too, courtesy of a teddy-bear cookie jar beside the cash register.

On a Stormin' morning, Norman drops a twenty into the pool.

"Aargh. Aargh. Aargh."

Pirate Captain leadership chock-fills the teddy with twenties and — look close — a few pink fifties. The coloured paper piles up behind a message out front on the label:

"Let's HELP Aldert Off to College."

Al lives with the demons of a ruined life. He shuffles slower, with a wandering left eye. Cane or walker depends on the day, for his long-term stay. A stay far, far away in the disability ward of the Inverton Psychiatric Centre. Irony moves north to roost, hundreds of kilometres from Transvaal and the comforts of civilization.

Nothing will ever douse the flames of hate from the young man. Nothing will ever stop the flapping tongues. Fat Al stays on the fires of retribution, a skillet for gossip refinement.

"Fat Al faces a dose of Hell up there. Served up day and night."

"Frozen hell in winter, that place. Problems with heating."

"Could be some ass adjustment too."

A wag lifts his butt from the stool for the locomotion. "Gets real hot having a shower." Obvious motion of intent gets snickers. "Squeal like pig. *Oink. Oink.*"

"His fat ass will finally get the workout he deserves."

Among the coffee slurpers, not much is mentioned on legal consequences. Local justice serves the community well. A lost case of an unidentified young man never to be opened.

What about the police? Charges?

The St. Marys Constabulary under the Chief takes care of all the loose ends. Aldert has just turned sixteen. The Chief keeps it to a juvenile report. The Kembers, along with two other neighbours, back up the Chief. All speak to that day backed up by the horrors of previous days and months. Linda and Aldert huddle in a daze from the fateful step off the school bus.

Aldert remains firm. "Do not call that piece of shit my stepfather. He was never, ever married to my mother."

The Chief is known, in candid moments, to weigh in on the incident and what it shows about the duplicity and hypocrisy of his community. "It took a boy — just sixteen years old; he's still a boy — it took a boy to put the end to Hell on that farm. The community at large should be ashamed to allow this to continue for *eight* years. I am ashamed. You should be, too."

Chapter 12

The Syrian boys find Aldert funny, with new words and new experiences from the milk shed.

"Faisal, wipe the suction cups. Ozzy, bring 'em in on stage. Let's rock."

The polite lads whisper in their mother tongue to help clarify anything lost in translation.

"Are cups not for tea, or measuring?"

"The syntaxing in English is so vast."

"Rock? Do we turn into stone or put on music channel?"

"Lads," Aldert calls out. "I said let's rock."

Faisal and Ozzy rock hard every day, sometimes with Jimmy, most times with Aldert.

And the Big Launch? All good but now simmering on the back burner. Wayyy back, as the big question continues.

Where's the cheese?

And where's the cheese-maker?

Out in the milk shed, Greg has graduated from slopping to sanitizing. He sprays, brushes and rinses. Greg is thankful to have no mirror to reflect on his red rubber boots, blue latex gloves and white synthetic hair beanie. His red, white and blue is the dress-up for living the dream. The step by small step, over years and years, to his Gregzdream now has a uniform. Up there on the wall is Jimmy's dream in measured plans, and Jimmy can show the imaginary expansion on his laptop with CAD. Listen well to the source.

"If things go well, there's room for expansion on the west side." Jimmy can milk, talk and point at the same time during the milking parade. "I'll show you on the office terminal. Our advantage is big capacity for cheese production. Our need will be more cooling, long-term storage. That's why the two-twenty board comes in on the corner. That's why there's a concrete pad with rebar on the other side of the cold-room wall."

"You can sanitize the tanks, wash down the floors," Jimmy tells Greg, picking up two pails of fresh milk. "Aldert and the twins will settle the herd in. I'll take this for Barbie. Her and Aldert have something creative in mind."

John organizes Jimmy's advice inside the house. His office desk has a second set of all Jimmy's dream plans in exact measurements, on paper pinned to the wall.

"I have it in CAD," Jimmy told him, "if you wish to get … exact."

All measured, everything costed out in graphs, charts and notes with asterisks. John audits further than CAD. He pops his head into the back kitchen.

"Jimmy, that app of yours is amazing. You could sell it."

"Thank you. First things first. Let's build up production for some cheese, eh?"

"Before building up anything, I'm building up a big appetite. Barbara, I'm starving to sample some of these Aldert creations."

Barbara lifts her head from the vast work counter. "Give me some focking credit in the mix, John."

John lists in troubled waters. "Sorry, Barbara. Barbara-and-Aldert focking creations."

Say Cheese has gone stove-top delicious after work. Barbara's tiny homebrew batch gets used up in creative ways to be hoovered up in no time. Aldert has wonderful experiments for all to sample. The afternoon becomes a gathering for little cheese and lots of talk, including the Shepherd, the partners, and the Kembers, who slurp up John's special Capps.

"Secondsies, people." On a mid-September Saturday afternoon, before milking, after the lift on the front porch, refreshed palates all round, spur John to action. With full attendance, he pulls from his head a checklist on his master plan, an umbrella of research and support backed by years of Jimmy homework. Barbara is already rolling her eyes, long past more focking details. More focking talk. She's warmed herself up with the first capp, heated up on secondsies, and now she's changing to cool refreshments.

"Focking great drop, boys."

Greg the sommelier smiles.

John smiles at the professor, sticking to the list. "What do we know about a cheese assembly line?"

Jimmy lowers his wine glass.

"Examples galore on that CAD package prepared by the Swiss manufacturer, Allmer. Step by step. We can bring it up on the terminals or watch and learn on your iPhones."

Jimmy takes a sip, puts down the glass, extending both arms toward the partners.

"My software app integrates with their software platform. I can read the graphs, then adjust the whole process as slick as yogurt."

Greg and John are stuck on yogurt. Their look forces another sip of wine and a reboot on the point.

"Integration. Fine-tune, tinker to get the best from the herd, the best from the Swiss equipment *and* the best cheese."

"Like the Cappuccino machine," Greg says. "Espresso cheese. Brie, anyone? Triple cream? Press the button."

The goat-herd management software app is world calibre, thanks to this renowned business consultant right here on the Century Farm in Transvaal.

Greg and John charge glasses in appreciation. Aldert keeps to coffee while John toasts.

"Thank you, Jimmy. Greg and I would have been years behind before we even got started."

Bang! Jimmy comes back. "We'll be sitting here a year from now with only more wine to show for ourselves" — all attention is on the professor — "unless we get a cheese-maker."

Greg is ready with more wine toasts. "Cheese-maker!"

Why not toast on a great drop, and onward, with a yummy Great North Pinot Gris.

"To Monday's *Globe*."

Sip. Sip.

Jimmy slows it down. "Word deadline for the ad is five PM today. No ad, no cheese-maker, and the cheese stays in the kitchen."

"We'll drink to that," Greg says.

John sets his wine down, pulls the wicker chair up to the matching table, setting up his laptop. He starts off, the ringmaster for the opportunity.

"*CHEESE-MAKER for Say Cheese Artisanal Goat Cheese.*"

Stop from Jimmy. "Artisan."

Pause with sips around.

"Your call," John says.

"*Artisan Goat Cheese*, then."

Pause, start.

"*Sixty-plus, prizewinning milk herd, goat-keeper —*"

Stop from Aldert. "Shepherd, please. And the team is more like seventy-plus."

John acknowledges the sensitivity of name labels. He's had a lifetime of it: Over-Auditor, Under-Tolerant, Over-Under Advocate, and The Straightest Gay on Bay.

"Okay," John says. "*Shepherd-managed herd, 150 acres, prime paddocks. We need you. Make prizewinning cheese with us. State of the art facility, computerized —*"

Greg is feeling technical. "What about the cameras and Jimmy's software and app?"

Barbara looks over her glass, up from her readers. "Way too focking detailed."

Even the auditor agrees. "Southwestern Ontario near St. Marys. Forget any Transvaal."

Greg can't help himself. "Don't let the Transvaalians scare you."

John looks up from his MacBook Air. "Sound good?"

"Great," Greg says.

"Let's focking do it, boys."

John stays on track. "Direct phone call, email or application …?"

"Phone or text can work for quick response," Greg says.

Thinking. Thinking. John lays it out. "*Both* our cellphones."

Partner inspection. "With message instructions."

"Let's focking do it, boys."

L'ESTRIE, QUEBEC

The Knowlton village IGA's long cheese counter features a flourish of nutty hard or oozing creamy whites, off-whites with flush flowery rinds, and the in-between tastes of heaven and forest floor, in exotic local cheeses.

"Serge." The cheesemonger catches Serge on a pass-by. "*Un petit gout de ce fromage magnifique? De Farnham, La Grange de Sergi?*"

Serge Lamontagne, the father of four adult sons, farms a vast tract of land with roots in Quebec history from the times of Champlain and Radisson. The Lamontagnes come from the Brest region of France — famous for making chèvre from sheep and goat, a skill brought to the New World but scarcely used in the two hundred years since.

"Certainement, Lucie, magnifique."

"*Certainement, Lucie, magnifique.*"

Serge reaches into the plastic cone with a drawbridge lift opening to pick his morning sample. Lucie always says that a cheese has its day.

With skiers from Ontario and New England flocking to l'Estrie in winter, and hordes of visiting cyclists and hikers in summer, the word gets around. Out-of-province people make a point of stopping in the l'Estrie region for raw milk cheese, *Le Diable* beer, *foie gras*, and duck sausages from the Knowlton Duck Farm.

La madame de fromage at IGA has infinite patience with *les Anglais*. She relieves their brain freeze in this review of Grade 10 French.

"*Bienvenue.* Would you like to sample *le fromage*?"

Serge watches an anglophone couple caught in their tracks at the long cheese counter.

"*Monsieur, Madame,*" Lucie continues. "We have seventeen *fromages au lait crus du Québec.*"

The *Anglais* suck up the direction but lean back on the raw pronunciation. The cheesemonger blows it out, the word for "unpasteurized" *en français*: "ka-ruhhh."

An automatic Grade 10 response from the husband. "*Comment?*"

"Harvey. It's '*qui.*' Qui?"

Lucie sees that the word for raw is already lost in translation. She blows it back, her lips moving in slo-mo. "*Le frow-magge ka-ruh-h-h.*"

The cheeseheads remain in awe at the selection. "What a selection. Do you have recommendations for a suave *le fromage Québec*?"

The cheesemonger passes a binder to the *Anglais*, full of tasting notes the like of which are scarce as raw milk cheese, almost never seen or heard of in the rest of Canada.

"This is a dark-beer aged cheddar from Ayer's Cliff. The triple Brie is from Charlevoix." An inviting smile. "*Le Bri-i-e ka-ruh-h-h.*"

All with tastes off a hand slicer.

Serge is off to grab his reserved copy of the *Globe* and touch base with Robert, the store owner.

Serge's oldest two sons work with their father on the rich, 300-acre, 120-Holstein operation. The family counts up their success with two huge blue silos for corn.

The endless labour of clearing land to produce cereal grains for livestock and fresh bread! The need for beef to feed, to trade and to eat has dominated many Lamontagne generations. Survival first. The family developed an integrated approach with added cash flow, using Holsteins. Great-grandfather began to concentrate on vast volumes of cow milk. As transportation infrastructure improved, the product was exported for the consumer. And not to leave any spilt milk, leftovers were used to make farm-gate raw cheese for family, friends and then more friends. Let's not forget cottage cheese, chewy fresh curds and homemade *poutine maison*. The grandfather became a recognized leader in the

Quebec industry — also a familiar face to *les Anglais,* on the prize podium at Toronto's Royal Winter Fair.

In Grandfather's time, cheese-making was limited to unpasteurized cheese on the farm kitchen stove. With the current generations, though — the eleventh and twelfth away from Brest — Serge Lamontagne has introduced and instructed his sons on serious cheese-making. Their new brand is exploratory, with the name *l'Estrie Fâche.*

(Does that name not mean "the mean east"? *"C'est une blague avec double entendre."* The cartoon logo features a Holstein with Ray-Bans. A funny little character — calf doggie with a fat cigar stogie in his mouth. "T-shirts and hats with the cool cow sell well.")

The overall direction of farm production is west to Ontario. The bulk of the milk product is shipped to Northwood Dairy in Trenton, Ontario. The farm provides plenty of milk, enough to support grandparents, parents, two sons and their families. Enough for Serge to lead an investment in a co-operative cheese factory in town. The mean-cow logo will be part of another sideline at the co-op, which has thirty local milk-farmer members.

Le Cooperatif Lait et Fromage de l'Estrie, S.A. has gained immediate ground at the Quebec cheese counters and at Kensington Market in the City.

The Lamontagnes are number one in quota, production and prize haul. The family has the biggest slice of the new cheese factory. Serge holds tight to his home farm card with his two sons, while letting the tethers out on the big invest-ment. With thirty bosses, Serge makes sure that well enough is well left alone. Louis Veuille, the prizewinning cheese-maker hired from Switzerland, is the big cheese, second to none — even if Serge's associates at the co-op sometimes don't understand. *("Serge, c'est Louis." He speaks with an accent. He does not understand the Québec French. He thinks he's some sort of big cheese.")*

The co-op's hundred-thousand–square-foot factory *is* big-time equity into unknown territory. Serge has had it all thought out with top consulting and the support of the province. A cheese factory in town was an easy sell. ("Knowlton has good municipal water. Upgraded sewage system two years ago. Central prox-imity to the farmer and the highway.") From Highway 10, it's west all the way to Ontario, south on 15 to New York.

A third, unmarried, Lamontagne son can't cut any more of the pie, so he's a large-animal veterinarian in town.

Father is steering the course for his fourth and youngest son, at twenty-four years old his namesake, the fourteenth Serge Lamontagne, *le Petit.* His Papa, *le Grand,* has thought and planned for the last child for years and years. Over baling, milking and slopping, on the drive to Tims in Knowlton and while savouring his favourite dark brew through and through.

"Chérie," le Grand called out to his wife on his way out the door one morning a few months ago, "I'm off to make the cheese."

Madame Lamontagne, sitting with *le Petit* in the kitchen, leaned toward her son. "Papa. *Pf-f-f-f-ff.*" Maman can be so funny. *"Papa va à Tims."*

Almost as if *le Grand* could hear through walls: *"Le Petit,"* he said. *"Nous allons à Tims."*

Boots off the floor of the mud room, into the pickup, for the routine trip to Town that always includes a coffee stop. On that day, those thoughts through and through came to a conclusion in presentation to his son.

"Serge, you will always have ownership in your family's farm."

His father maintained direct eye contact, coffee down, a supportive hand on *le Petit*'s shoulder. "The cheese plant will need a few years up and running to stabilize in the market. You *will* have a role there. But you need the experience now. Your family can use a future *fromager*, not just kitchen experiments."

Le Grand paused for a moment to give *le Petit* the chance to get used to this new vision of his future.

"You know the process," he said. "Not just for you, your love of *poutine maison*. But your assistance has graduated to independence."

Serge lowered his hand from the shoulder to touch his son's forearm.

"*Mon fils*, your curds are the best that I have ever tasted."

Father tapped his smiling son's hands.

"A few years, *mon fils. Donnez-moi, ta famille, quelques ans.*"

Father turned off the tap for a squeeze on the hand.

"The fourth needs to find his opportunity elsewhere. After these next few years, our family will be even more successful. The experience must come from our biggest market."

Le Petit knew the answer before he asked the question. "Not here in *les Cantons?*"

"Here, you would bring little forth. You'd be playing second fiddle to our Swiss cheese-maker."

Le Petit frowned, struggling with the fiddle metaphor.

"You know," *le Grand* clarified. "The backup goalie."

Papa backed up *le grand plan*. "Not here on the farm. Stay working in our industry. Bring back new knowledge. This will always be your family farm. First, school."

Le Petit had heard the talk. He was ready. "I have the college brochure, Papa."

Papa had confidence in his namesake. "*Mais oui!* The brochure starts the process. Serge, my son, remember it is all about the paper. Without a certificate as a cheese-maker, there is no credibility outside of your family and l'Estrie. No second fiddle."

"No backup goalie here, Papa."

Serge *le Grand* laughed, then slipped back from fiddling to figuring.

"You already have the background and knowledge with livestock. It's in your heritage. Cheese is the future: prizewinning product."

Le Grand reached across the small table, his hands covering his son's shoulders. It's easier said than done, as *le Petit*'s shoulders are hard to cover — the son is a big man. Parents see him as the smartest of their four. Still, Papa read the milk mantra to the very able boy.

"*Le Petit, c'est toi, le grand avenir avec le fromage.* We need to process more of our product. Quotas are restrictive and expensive. Someday we will want to process our product out of our barn into our tanks. We can push the business up a notch or two with craft cheese. No restrictions if the manufacturing is on the same property as the product. Your success will support our success — the family future."

Le Petit saluted with his college brochure to his forehead. "Cheese!"

"Yes, with cheese, *mon garçon*, we'll be off the quota restrictions."

The son brochure-saluted again.

"Maman and I, with your brothers, support your choice of cheese-making school. Your family wants you to be our Certified Cheese-maker. Serge, after graduation, go from here. Opportunity lies farther away."

Le Petit wavered, testing parental waters. "Away?"

"Ontario."

"Why Ontario, Papa? Why not in *la belle province? C'est très grand.* Or why not New Brunswick? There are more francophones there."

Le Grand served grilled cheese plain and simple.

"*Mon petit*, I can hire a cheese-maker in Quebec for not much over minimum wage. Our market has too many chefs in the cheese process. We've had discussions about adding Ron Cloutier as our assistant cheese-maker. If Louis can expand our production."

"Ron? If …?"

"Sorry son, not at the Co-op, not now. If — I should say when — we start *la fromagerie.*"

"*Mais Papa*, would I … could I not be the assistant *fromager*? Work for Louis? Who better to learn from, Papa?"

"Sorry, son. Go to Ontario and come back to us *le chef, le grand chef fromager.*" Father knows best. "Or would you rather be the backup goalie, *le petit fromager*?"

Serge *le Petit*, overwhelmed at first but now warming up to a grand new life, had some second thoughts. "*Pardon, Papa*, but my English? It sucks."

Papa laughed. "That's why we practise. My bad English and your bad English might add up to something good. And what about hockey on Saturday nights? We do watch the English version."

Son had *le petit dumb* look. Papa polished up his best announcer English. He puffed and huffed. "'He shoots. Holy Mackinaw. He scores. The game is tied. We may see overtime yet.'"

"That is *le hockey de Bob Cole.* What does that have to do with *le fromage*?"

Papa had a game plan tucked in his side coat pocket. Something to share over two dark brews. "Here is the *Globe*. Read and learn. I suggest, before you put the newspaper down, you look under the Employment and Investment word ads. There, in the Opportunities section of the *Report on Business*. Interesting reading."

Le Petit looked down, puzzled, at the copy of the *Globe* his father had passed on to him. Father motioned with a look across the street.

"Easy purchase from the IGA. Reserved every day, paid for with a business cheque."

The dark brews were memories as the Lamontagnes returned home that day.

"*Papa*."

Le Petit waved the college brochure.

"May I borrow your truck?"

Le Grand was impressed at his reasonable ask.

"I want to go right over to *Le College Agricole de Knowlton* with an application."

Every weekday and Saturday morning, for the four months since that day, *le Grand* has driven to the village IGA for the *Globe*.

"*Cherie*," Serge *le Grand* tells his wife each morning, "*je vais à la fromagerie.*"

"*Oui. Oui. Prendre n'importe quoi.*"

Robert Côte, the IGA owner, loves seeing his old schoolmate march up to his service counter in the mornings. Robert knows Serge is off to Tims.

"Off to the factory to make the cheese, Serge?"

"*Oui, monsieur.*"

Robert smiles. "*Serge. Le* Globe, *monsieur. C'est très cher.*"

Robert has never asked his friend why the expense of this *journal en anglais*. Money is a personal thing, and business is business; don't question a sure cheque. But …

"Serge. Are you planning a trip to Toronto, *mon ami*?"

"Maybe if the price of milk goes up. Otherwise, Orford for hiking."

Robert towels the counter with his right hand, uses a feather duster for what's left.

"That *Globe*. They say it is the most read of the *anglais* dailies."

Serge mutters under his breath. "Just a dream journal for me."

Robert wipes the counter, slow and deliberate; adds some contemplation.

"Dream Journal? *C'est quoi?*"

"Do you ever check out the Opportunities for Investment, or in fact the employment word ads in it?"

Serge would have guessed Robert's lack of English may be the problem. But no — it's geographic:

"My mother was *Anglaise* from Montreal. Just no interest in Ontario. Even the few cousins in Ottawa and Cornwall."

Serge does not give in. "Super inspiring. Super fun reads."

Neither does Robert give in on giving up. "Not interested in Ontario."

Serge moves in closer. "You like camping at the Sandbanks."

"*Mais oui.* And I would like to visit *les grand chutes Niagara,*" Robert insists. "But I will not read the *Globe.*" He's hissing out the insistence. "*Pas de truc d'Ontario.* No puck luck for those Maple Leafs, *specialement.*"

Serge parallels the thought. *"D'accord pour les Leafs."*

Two people are at the next checkout, one checking lottery tickets on the scanner, one pulling skin magazines off the top rack. Everyone pretending not to listen to other conversations perk up at the mention of *les Leafs.* Serge and Robert are up front at service when *all* goes sour on the topic of *les Leafs de Toronto.* A series of spits cascade off behind the two old school friends.

Pf-f-f-ff. Pf-f-f-ff. Pf-f-f-ff.

Spit flies to two wastebaskets; one hits behind the soda machine, another rolls into the dusty corner at the far end. Two horks fly into open and closed handbags, while one desperate gob lands on an overcoat cuff.

Pf-f-f-ff. "Les Leafs."

While *le Grand* continues to turn the pages of the *Globe* for his Opportunities review with a dark brew, *le Petit* has landed his certificate in no time. The *Globe* is read through and through each day, but it's not until the second Monday in September that Opportunity rears up. The late-summer foliage has a hint of autumn in cider yellows and serviceberry reds. And by chance, father and son are together for a coffee for the first time in some weeks.

Le Grand demonstrates a well-read morning routine by ignoring his cup, turning his mug to the back pages for the small, white-on-black title bar that spells out Agricultural Opportunities. The *Globe* is not above pretty words for farm labourers: elbow-length latex, seasonal operators of complex equipment, or plain old slopping shit-shovellers. It's just that this genre of farmhand language is more likely to appear under "Help Wanted — Agriculture" in the *St. Marys Journal.* The *Globe* advertises opportunities that need to feed off investment and may include employment in a management way. Something agricultural, outside the City zoo perspective of the wild world of keeping lizards, Pinocchio-nosed lemurs, Elvis-topped alpacas, translucent toads, chippy cockatoos, hammy hamsters and those off-green turtles under plastic palms. And as for the investment, the opportunities lie in worm farms for bait, trout farms for the catch, mussel poles for steaming pots, and vacuum-packed precooked lobster for export. Investment opportunities have listed a lot of beefy operations and some milk quotas in Interior B.C. And three months ago, there was a sheep ranch for sale in Canmore. But almost never cheese-making — never here in Quebec — and never ever goats.

Le Grand sees it before *le Petit.*

"*Garçon.* It jumps right off the page. *Et voilà, c'est l'opportunité.* Get ready."

Father passes over the single-page section of the *Report on Business.* Yes, that word ad that was tweaked a dozen times by the Kembers, Greg and John after the household switchover. Nothing is lost in translation on the point of opportunity.

> ***Cheese-maker, goat cheese factory start-up:*** *Seventy-plus prizewinning milkers. Help us make winning cheese. 150 acres, state-of-art factory ready to go. Canadian Cheese-maker Certificate required. Super opportunity to grow with us in Transvaal Ontario.* <u>*www.saycheese.com*</u> *Please download the application attachment for full instructions.*

Le Petit repeats the ad, word for word, in English.

"C'est très bon, Papa. Mais fromage de chèvre?"

"Le fromage, c'est le fromage, mon fils. An opportunity is an opportunity."

At home, *le Petit* makes the next big move, off to his bedroom computer. He says to himself in English:

"I am a certified cheese-maker. Fourteenth generation on the Lamontagne Holstein farm. I can milk. I can make my whey, curds and cheese for the best in flavour. Goats? They are smaller cows with just as big teats. I will make the best-tasting goat cheese for all to see."

Serge smiles to himself.

"Say cheese … please. *C'est le grand prix.*"

He pulls the application off the printer and heads back to the kitchen with pen in hand. His father is boots to the floor heading out for chores, but he pulls a postal tip from his upper jacket pocket. "I still have those fiftieth-anniversary Habs postal stamps. That'll show them who we are."

"Save the Go Habs Go, Papa. The application will be done online. I am doing a rough copy to make it perfect."

Six hundred kilometres away in southwestern Ontario, an echo of response. One echo.

"The one and only," John says. His manner has turned to frustration. He counts time.

"It's forty-eight hours since the ad. One reply. A French-Canadian kid from the Eastern Townships."

Greg turns logical. No point poking his very hairy bear on the short schedule of things. "Aldert is his same age, isn't he? Can't discount a farm rearing."

John leaves the Cary Grant reference alone. "I told him in my email ten this morning. Let's make the call."

"How about another John Capp, John?"

Greg is still in fun mode. Showing off his Grade 12 Ontario *français*, he blows it out his nose. *"Bonjour monsieur …"*

John finds a nail to pound in to the translation. "Okay then, *mon ami*, you make the call. I will give you a list of questions for the young lad. On the speaker, please."

Greg dials up the 450 exchange. "Let's not put him on speakerphone — a little overwhelming for the young lad to start off with an audience. We can listen with our heads up together."

Greg drops the phone to make a point at it. "He's on!"

John points to his right ear. Phone goes up to the curly top.

"*Bonjour, je demande le Serge est* home."

Silence on the other end. Everyone in Knowlton is waiting for the call on young Serge. Less than twenty-four hours after the word ad was published, the oral word had flowed all over the village, from the Knowlton IGA checkout staff, including Robert and Lucie, to the stragglers at Tims who dark-brewed around the news, to Swiss cheese-maker Louis and the staff at *la fromagerie*. All before Maman answers the phone and passes it off to her youngest boy.

"*C'est Serge,*" comes the voice over the phone.

Greg clears his throat. "*Bonjour Serge, c'est Greg et Jean de Transvaal.*"

"*Mais oui. C'vrai. Les* goat farmers *d'Ontario. Bonjour messieurs.* I speak English."

Greg speaks up. "*C'est, c'est* marvellous. First, Serge, you are an Agriculture Canada–certified cheese-maker?"

"*Oui, monsieur.* I have completed *le dernier stage.*"

Greg puts the phone on his red-checked flannel shirt. "He's an actor. He's finishing on stage?"

Half-dumb looks all round the porch. Greg raises his hands and shoulders to John.

"Congratulations," he says to Serge. "But are you licensed to make cheese? Not acting."

Le Petit puts the phone on his blue-checked flannel shirt. "*Maman. Papa.* They think I am in theatre. I told them my certificate stage *c'est complet.* They asked me if my acting was over?"

Maman and *Papa* motion to the phone, both with a look *demi-stupide.*

"No more acting, *monsieur.*" Shoulders and hands up to his parents. "Licensed cheese-making. *C'est le meilleur.*"

Phone back to Greg's red flannelled chest. "He's finished with Molière. Licensed to make cheese."

John motions to the phone. Greg coughs it out. "*Serge, mon ami, vous êtes très joli.*"

Serge back on blue flannel. "*Maman. Papa. Je pense que les hommes son gais.* Greg just called me … cute."

"*Serge, restes au fromage.*" Le Grand's advice. "*Conservez le fromage.*"

Both motion to the chest phone. Serge hesitates.

"*Ton cousin, Gaetan. Il est gai. Pas de problème.*"

Parents lift their shoulders in support, pointing to their ears. Serge lifts the phone up.

"*Merci, monsieur* Greg. You speak well French."

Greg's back on red flannel. "He says I am a well on *le français.*"

Bing, bong, bang. In minutes, the deal is sealed. *Le nouveau fromager de Québec* is so excited, sticking with the cheese.

His phone is back on the blue flannel. *"Les gais adorent le fromage."*

Un des gais, that's John, grabs the phone.

"*C'est Jean, Serge. S'il vous plaît, monsieur.* You need to pack up now. Get on the train in Montreal tomorrow. Come and make cheese."

Phones are off the flannel shirts, everyone has a list of to-dos.

Le Petit with his mother's help is packed *rapidement.* Maman has worked it out with wallet and laptop.

"You have enough to get by. I googled *Le Tigre Géant.* There's one in the small city close by. I will send you the link."

"Nothing, *Maman*, in the small town? St. Marys?"

"They have a dollar store and some small stores that I do not know. There's The Source, which could be like *La Source du Sports* in Cowansville. *Le Tigre Géant,* I know. I know that you can buy all the clothes you need there."

She pinches his blue flannel shirt with love.

Serge could overnight in Montreal, close to the train terminal, with one of their many relatives, but instead Papa and Maman will do the dark morning drive, with some drive-through dark brews first, to send him off in person. On the opposite side of Ontario, after *le petit joli* phone call, John has moved ahead in anticipation, making the arrangements.

"I'm calling Joyce at the travel agency, Barbara's quilting friend. She can book the tickets for pickup in Montreal. I will ask her to book in the name of Serge Lamontagne, Cheese-maker."

Chapter 13

In Maman's loaded Town & Country van, they were off for goodbyes in Montreal, for a changeover in Toronto that would reach the small Town of St. Marys. No sleep all night in anticipation, but in the van, Serge couldn't keep his eyes shut hearing all the Morse code of instructions from Maman. They travelled from Knowlton with a four-o'clock wake-up to a first stop for gas and the dark brews. He savoured each sip as he walked through it all in his mind: the Lamontagne generational farm property, his graduation in cheese-making, and now off to a place where everyone would speak English, a place called Transvaal. The day before, Serge had explored the farm through the Say Cheese website and internet satellite views. Le Grand approved the lay of the land. "The land is naturally drained to the small creek," Papa said. "It has a big barn, and … and new roofs on sheds. Looks like a composite." Both put their Gallic noses to the screen. "Roof seamless. New technology. *Pas de bavure. Très intéressant.*"

Papa noticed the best of the designated Century Farm. "Nice canopy fronting the century home. A double laneway to the concession road."

Closer examination verified their sixth sense on the roads' surface materials. *"Mon Dieu,"* le Petit said. *"C'est le gravier! La poussièrre."*

Serge's train trip from Montreal does not feature dust, but his mind is fogged up, tied up in sleep, interrupted by the switchover in the City.

On his way again, passing through the vast countryside after stops in Guelph and Kitchener, Serge soaks up the richest agricultural landscape he has ever witnessed. Remember, *la ferme de Lamontagne* is a steady star in the Townships. Smart generational farmers with a nationally recognized herd and a substantial quota. Le Petit calls his father from the Via car.

"Papa, c'est magnifique!"

"In English, my son."

"The farms here. They are big, even bigger than ours, Papa. But, there are so many. So flat, Papa."

Their Knowlton farm is hilly compared to flatter southwestern Ontario. Any person to handle a pull plow or scuffle the hay can feel the grade. Hilly means harder work. But le Petit will learn that flat can also have a lot of roll, a lot of rock.

"This farm I can see *maintenant*. Three Harvestore silos, Papa. Three, like ours." One, two, three, holy cow. "And there's another triple!"

The home farm's three gigantic, navy-blue storage towers are three more than at most *l'Estrie* farms. A flag post of farm production. He's seeing doubles and triples up time and time again alongside the tracks, into southwestern Ontario.

Et voilà.

Serge is taken by surprise by hilly St. Marys.

The conductor, who is from Quebec, invites him to the connecting platform between rail cars to introduce Serge to the Town.

"C'est très joli, le meilleur de toutes les petites villes d'Ontario. La vue. Tellement bucolique, monsieur."

Whatever *bucolique* is, Serge sees beauty.

The train creeps across the 1857 stone trestles pulled together by steel and iron, covering the gap over the creek — a narrow ribbon down below with a curious name the fishing fan will puzzle over. *La Crique* is named after a fish that does not exist. Serge closes his eyes and tastes the air as he stands in the doorway between cars. That Country smell, fresh with a bouquet. The slow roll with its *clack, clack* does not distract from a panoramic soak-up of the bird's-eye view up the creek. Serge has seen the map, where a small blue line runs off into the larger blue ribbon, the Thames River. Here at the Thames River confluence, a driver turns left, south, to the red dot stamped Transvaal. The Google satellite search gave him lots of heads-up on the layout of the land. Maman has shadowed much of the research with parental approval, in the form of sidebar links that she sends to her son. With her help, Serge read about the history of his destination before his departure.

"Papa, our family already counted up five generations before *la ville de St. Marys* was incorporated."

"You will learn from their way, starting today. On to *our* tomorrow, *mon fils*." Le Grand's hands on le Petit's shoulders. "*Pour maintenant*. Forget yesterday."

Father knows best, but good local research might improve the vision. So he researches St. Marys historian, Larry Rhodes, who situates the Town "in the confluence of the Thames River."

Now, Serge looks up "confluence" on his smartphone translator app:

"*When two bodies of water meet in …*"

Serge cuts to the chase of meaning: it's hilly.

From the flat-screen vision of a cell and a laptop, his arrival switches to a panoramic that's as good as the out-of-this world black-and-white movie switch to a technicolour Oz. The only witch for Serge has been "which" path the cheese-making certificate will take him down. In a whirlwind of change, he moves from the golden corn fields of l'Estrie to corn crops out of province, as striking as an alien world. *Les Serges, Papa et le fils,* have never seen or experienced the English show *Green Acres*, but every family knows the wizard and the good witch.

The big-as-Kansas vista from the high viaduct carries Serge to the heart of St. Marys.

"*Ce n'est pas une confluence,*" he says to himself. "*C'est* … a pumping, healthy heart."

Many on the Via train sit up in response to the splay of splendour from a train that traverses a civilization of dumpy backyards and grimy industrial areas, in between patches of farmland. Citizens in St. Marys are never surprised by people's surprise at the wonderful world of St. Marys:

"*Best kept secret in Ontario. Our Town's the prettiest.*"

"*Don't need all that Niagara-on-the-Lake bus traffic.*"

(Big group head nod all round.)

No surprise here until you dig deeper into local conversation in order to gain an understanding of the vernacular, the syntax, the wordy wisdom of rural talk.

This is humour and wisdom from the Townships of Blanshard, Nissouri, Fullarton, Hibbert, and never forget Zorra.

"Drive *to* the City, and the highway traffic reports radio out your way," goes the familiar complaint. "Drive *from* the City to St. Marys, nothing to hear in your way."

One wag adds it on. (God help us on this subject, making fun of Citiots.)

"Tell 'em you're from St. Marys …" (shoulder shrugs with half-dumb looks) "… and you get the stupid questions: *How far is that? That's how long of a drive? Is it near the Theatre Town? Smiths Falls? Are the electric car plug-ins free? Do they have hot yoga?*"

Another wag has the response.

"Hot yoga? Goat yoga, more like it."

"See focking Jimmy."

"Who's-the-husband goat yoga."

"*That's* hot."

Today as lunch rush at the Sunriser winds down, Braedon has one eye out the window, the other on fresh coffee coming up.

Since the fire on the Kember farm, it's been a month and more of confessing import witnesses, never-seen-before experts, the usual dummies, and a ton of wannabes, all loading up the S-counter.

Months and months before that, there was a long list of contractors, carpenters, plumbers, electricians, welders, tilers and fitters heading out to the Kember farm — and that was after the Swiss installers who joined Jimmy back in the spring. And the roofers, who were Amish from Zorra Township — men without cars and one cellphone. (God permits phone calls to Doug's Pro Lumber all day, and at the end of the day for the white transportation van.) Not to mention one complete-surprise witness. A recent engineering report came by accident, when a Citiot from the nearby City with *Le Tigre Géant* stopped for directions and stayed for coffee. Ends up he's a nephew of Rick Mustard. Started off with proof on paper.

"Measured drawings."

The young engineer fit right in, knows a coffee klatch, had heard about the Sunriser.

"Engineer-approved, made to order, but ordered and designed by the Professor himself. Real high-tech stuff."

The young professional canvassed the room's attention.

"Approved by my engineering firm."

The new witness to events, a new friend to the morning's gathering, was far ahead of the usual Citiot.

The room nodded, waited for more information from Young Einstein. "Jimmy has it all on CAD," he continued. "The equipment imported from Switzerland *and* installed by a team, right official-like from the company. I can study the whole thing remote, over ZIT."

Whether they'd actually met the Swiss team or just heard about the visit after the fact, everyone in the room paused for further leftovers to gobble down. A dim-wit interrupted the company's vicarious installation. "Jimmy took them on tour. Niagara Falls."

Donnie was comfortable enough to step up second to the dummy brother, Ronnie. "Didn't do the Maid of the Mist."

An in-the-know settled things down with reason. "So, when will there be cheese?"

The professional, political response: "I'm plan approval and installation. Nothing on makings," the engineer clarified. "What can I tell you?"

Even weeks later, a fade past the shining light of Young Einstein, the wannabes desperate to be in the know fire up the story with their myopic embellishment. These are the tradespeople who have never done the job or seen the job done except at some relative's home. The floodgates open to hobby opinions on grout application, coats of paint and mucking drywall.

"Not much in drywall. A fiberboard with pre-installation colours. They can power-wash everything."

A smart arse. "Don't wash off the measured plans plastered on the wall."

"No worries. Jimmy has them on focking CAD."

The wannabe on the floor ignores the chuckling from the counter. "Still, they sprayed a final coat. Industrial stuff from Doug's."

"Nicole told me that the paint is twice the price of their best indoor-outdoor."

A group thought.

"Hm-m-m-m."

All in Town and Country take good intentions and limited plans on home projects to Doug's, with mixed results. These are the self-called experts, these contractor poseurs talking the subject of construction; no keeping this bunch on the ground. The group move up on roof expertise, with no tea-drinking Amish roofer witnesses in the coffee court. The wannabes can cover a lot of roofing with no expert challenger in the room.

"The milk shed, the drive shed both been roofed with new plywood."

"Should have been steel." Someone has been to Arizona. "Those red fabricated tiles look pretty pretty."

Someone has read the latest issue of *Home Builder Magazine.* "That rubber, seamless system seems popular."

"Comes in ten-by-eight sheets. A blow torch makes it seamless."

The irony of Amish flashing blowtorches on a high-tech roof is lost on the morning group.

"Stop Leak, in a spray can. Doug's has it in stock. Squirt and seal; it's the real deal."

Back on top of the roof with the ten-by-eight sheets, the image is covered with humour. "Just a big plastic condom, right?" The speaker pulls at his hooded jacket.

Yuck, yuck.

All possibilities under the new roof of the milk shed have been dissected.

"Interior insulated, heated tile floors with drainage."

"Computer terminals everywhere, tracking everything. And have you seen their office?"

No one has, so no one answers.

The sewage guy comes out from a rear booth to ask about the elephant under the front yard.

"How's the weeping system? If there's cheese, there's whey. And lots of whey to dump out through their weeping bed."

"No point. They tank it up. Truck it out."

"Not all. They haul it back of the barn with the four-wheeler."

"Back of the barn?"

A stupid question with an obvious answer:

"Frankie."

"Hm-m-m-m."

The drywall wannabe who has finished a rec room repeats the unessential. "Yup. Not much drywall, all walls are prefabricated. A synthetic product that can be power-washed. No fading colours."

"Hm-m-m-m."

The room's conversation fades to practicality, with a healthy touch.

"Easier for sterilization."

Many have a past on a dairy farm. Same but different.

"Fiberboard passes inspection?"

"No problem there. As for the equipment, it's all stainless steel." The look for emphasis. "*All* equipment shiny, shiny."

The imagined cost gets a whistle.

"It was shipped all the way from Switzerland."

Whistle again. Ronnie shines up his stupidity.

"Swiss cheese?"

The in-the-know carries on, oblivious to the dim-wit out back. "They're ready to go, to make cheese."

"What about making *focking* cheese?"

Chuckles from all around.

"Can't say 'Cheese please.' Not yet."

The reverse S-counter shakes with cheesy snickers. Braedon's neck stretches out the kitchen pass-through. Here's fresh information from the opening:

"Jimmy told me they hired a cheese-maker."

The room stops in their thought tracks.

"A cheese-maker?" An echo of amazement. "In less than two weeks?"

A booth in-the-know backs up the master cookie. "Licensed and ready to make the goat cheese."

"*Goat* cheese?" Another dim-wit member gets a silent groan from the attendees.

A group grope of half-dumb looks is broken with one big word.

"Feta."

The dummies are best left alone in their inherent ignorance of said goat product. The topic runs off on the GPS possibilities of the next-door province. "He's French-Canadian," says so-and-so.

"From Quebec?"

"No, dummy. He's off a Holstein farm in Cochrane, Ontario."

Although no one in the room is exactly GPS-clear on l'Estrie, only the two dummies are sitting blind to the silliness of milk and cheese in Cochrane, in the Nickel Belt.

"He's fully licensed. Family has a generational milk farm in the Eastern Townships."

"Licensed cow milker?"

"Licensed cheese-maker."

A fresh backbench informer has been saving the big one. He unloads:

"Three hundred quota."

The silence, from both farmers and non-farmers, rebounds back and forth in the room. Add a whistle or two, with all heads nodding.

Even a Town person knows a quota above fifty is more than a handful for the automatic milkers. But holy cow, three hundred.

Another set of whistles rounds the morning gathering. A herd unheard of in the Transvaal and Town areas.

"Wow."

Another cow wow.

"Family owns a cheese factory too."

If that's not big cheese, add something nutty.

"Use a cartoon on the label. A cigar-smoking moose with Ray-Bans."

Reason pulls the group back from the wild frontier of Quebec. "That may be a moose on the label, but the milk comes from cows," says a back-booth voice. "These are … goats."

An in-the-know farmer is present and clear. "Goats are four-legged. Teats as big as any Holstein. Think of them as dwarf cows."

Silence across the room as all imagine what a dwarf cow would look like.

"My cousins have dwarf goats. Not for milking."

"Are they yoga goats?"

"No, midget-mind."

Most agree goats are a milking creature. But enough on agriculture, a subject down a notch in interest from barbecue, secret sauces, any recommended food to eat, feta, and who's-the-husband. Another subject cranks up the tempo. Bobby Bynck pipes up.

"Bet you … bet you he's a Canadiens fan."

Quebecers all agree that Montreal fans are the greatest of all hockey fans. The lustre fades, though, west of Cornwall and east of Moncton. Southwestern

Ontario shows a hint of Wings red but remains otherwise true blue with the Leafs.

"They call them the Habs or the Canadiens."

The mere mention of hockey anything brings up automatic optimism, an illusion flaring up like a common cold, for most of Ontario, much of English Canada. The Maple Leafs City lies by the Great Lake in a famous pose of hockey hopelessness.

"Leafs are looking good."

"It's pre-season, dummy."

Six blocks away, Serge bounds off the rail car, stepping onto the St. Marys platform and into his new life. He spots the three greeters right away. Greg has the lead hand. *"Bonjour. Ah. Bienvenue. Ah. À Sainte Marie."*

Serge looks up in surprise, trying to sort the heads, eyes and faces of the trio. *(Ce sont les deux; qui est l'autre homme?) Et voilà, la voix en français*:

"Bonjour. C'est bonne, la voyage?"

Serge has to wonder why he's been doing all that *Globe* reading when they speak French.

"Merci, messieurs. Je suis très bien. C'est mon plaisir. C'est régal. Salutations ..."

The three greeters stand stunned. Serge picks up the cue.

"Gentlemen. I do speak English. Slow and steady, that is. I am Serge Lamontagne. *Salut.*"

Les trois, wow. *Les trois ne répondent pas.* Serge answers their faces with his mile smile.

"I learn English from the *Globe.*"

That answers a lot about how come he speaks English. And the lad reads the same newspaper as us, the partners both think — another *et voilà* moment.

Les trois are impressed with a world traveller on his *première* trip from *chez maison.* Greg is left with an empty well as he quickly uses up his limited vocabulary from high school in Kingston. Curly Top's in a sweat but stays on top of the official greeting. He reaches out for a shake, then moves Serge's hand along.

"I'm Greg. My partner, John. The Shepherd, Aldert."

Hands a-shakin' all around.

Serge focuses on *l'autre.* His one-word response hints at an impression. "Incredible."

The Shepherd has palms like a goalie glove. He's even younger than himself. Serge steps back in thought, a pause. *Il est gai aussi?*

No matter, Serge's laissez-faire is backed by family familiarity, his queer cousin. Michel came out with support from family and neighbours, years ago. They shared a bus ride to high school in Knowlton, shared chores on Saturdays, church on Sundays. Family fabric that is backed and covered by the entire l'Estrie community. Time to step out, step up to his new bosses. Serge surges into a full greeting. This is it, the breakthrough moment of this new life. Le Petit opens his arms to soccer net width. He grabs on to each man with a bear hug. Serge hangs on to plant three side-by-cheek kisses on *les trois*. After the right, left, right approach, he returns to attention with his mile smile.

"I feel already St. Marys my second home," he says.

Les Trois are overwhelmed by the *joie de vivre*. Still, a GPS correction from the accountant who's been auditing his partner's bad French and the young man's reactions.

"Actually, Transvaal is the location."

Serge motions to the Victorian train station, the Victorian water tower, the Victorian homes and the Victorian church steeples popping out of the maple canopy.

"All this will be my home."

(Another cell call in the first free moment after he arrives at Aldert's that night: "Papa, there are more old buildings here than Knowlton." "*Les Anglais,* le Petit, can build and build. *Mais c'est dommage,* they cannot build a winning hockey team. *C'est l'histoire.* We have the Cup champions.")

Aldert manhandles off Serge's two large suitcases. Greg grabs two small boxes. John leads Serge, with his massive backpack, to the car. Young Serge knows cows and cow cheese. He's certified. These goats, though, will be an experience. *Mantra, Serge.* He repeats to himself, *Dwarf cows with same-size teats.*

As Aldert loads, Serge walks a circle around John's car.

"Wow. I have only seen a few of these before. In the parking lot of The Glen ski resort."

An Austrian group would stick to the topic of skiing. Quebecois, likewise, need only to hear the name The Glen to get emotional on the subject. People in Ontario are more apt to water-ski than snow-ski, with a *That's nice* look for those who choose to embrace winter. A March snowfall has Quebecers pulling their skis off the garage wall and heading to the hill, while people in Ontario look out the window, asking how many more days of this crap. They stay inside or go to the mall.

For Serge, his twenty-four years, notwithstanding cows and *les Canadiens,* have been focused on making cheese by day and dreaming of cars at night. He stands and soaks up the exotic car.

"I have never rode in this one. Except maybe a golf cart."

His smile is bigger than a mile. Aldert finishes loading up the trunk as John swells in silent pride at car recognition.

Greg looks up for an injection of silly. He backs up, slapping his hips. *"Ride 'em, ride 'em, Rawhide ..."*

Serge's smile disappears as he's taken right off the dream of an exotic ride. He comes to, staring at Greg. This will be his first taste of a Velveeta trail of cheesy humour. Greg is an urban cheeky monkey unlike anything he has ever seen in rural Quebec.

(Another cell call later to put words to thoughts. "Papa. Michel does not make the humour … like that?")

As Serge stares at Greg, then back at the car, Greg stares into space. John smiles at the recognition for his car, lost in a moment of vanity. Pride in ownership makes him forgetful of Jimmy's advice: *Dump the pumpkin-coloured exotic in exchange for a pickup.*

Aldert picks up on the awkward silence as they all get into the car. "Serge," he says. "First a short tour of Town. Then we'll go to my place so you can get settled in. The Kembers told you you'd be staying with me till they get settled in on Thomas Street, right?"

Aldert's mind is still adjusting to the idea of the Kembers living in Town. He kills himself thinking of the urban peasants, Jimmy and Barbara. *You've done gone. Done gone suburban, folks.*

Serge has already met the Kembers over the net. On the opposite side of the Ottawa River, le Petit looked up their former farmhouse and their new Thomas Street house: "Papa. This Jimmy is a full professor at the Western business school. Look, he even consults with the Desmorneau family."

All Quebecois have pride in the Desmorneaus' worldwide conglomerate, MORNO Inc. No one mentions, though, that the French-Canadian family comes from Mono, in Ontario. The billionaire family has a sense of humour in company naming, combining place and surname. These are not dairy farmers.

Barbara, meanwhile, is excited to jump from three adopted sons to four: a long-term Shepherd, the new owners who start as boarders, and now Serge. It's even better than her favourite TV show growing up.

"*My Four Sons*," she joked to Jimmy the night before the big arrival.

Jimmy tries a rein-pull. "Barbie. You're adding too much into this. He's just boarding until he finds his place."

Barbara translates for her husband. "*Bonjour, Serge, comment t'allez-vous?*"

Pull again. "Don't get ahead of yourself … with that high school French."

"Mr. Kember, how many times do I have to remind you — I *taught* high school French, not just English!"

Jimmy has crossed the invisible line of two 6th Concession solitudes. Barb rolls it out over any opposition.

"I'll show you," she told him. "I'm giving the kid a call. *En focking français.*"

Jimmy knows after enough pulls, it's silent running. Barb rolls it on.

"I'll focking show you. Jimmy, you know what 'teacher' is *en français*, eh? *C'est 'professeur.' Je suis la Professeur, monsieur.*"

And that's how le Petit Serge first met the Kembers.

"*Bonjour,*" she said on the phone. "*C'est Barbara d'Ontario. Et Jimmy. Les Kembers.*"

"*Bonjour, Madame. C'est Monique, la mère de Serge. Pardon, Madame Barbara. Je donne le cell à mon fils.*"

"Pardon, Madame. D'abord, c'est Serge, le grand Serge." Papa adds on the l'Estrie charm. *"Enchanté."*

Barbara is on; maybe it was the two glasses of wine, but she's on. *"Quelle dommage pour vous, mais, pour nous à St. Marys, nous gagnons un nouveau fils."*

Afterwards, Serge *le Grand* will tell his wife how lucky they are to have *le Petit* staying with a host English family that speaks *le bon français. Le Grand* adds more for Barbara and Jimmy in Transvaal.

"C'est un grand surpris. We are honoured. *Mon garçon a du talent."*

He covers the phone with his large hand. Barbara hears *tout. "Serge. C'est la Madame Barbara au téléphone … de l'Ontario. Elle parle français."*

Each and every retired French teacher in the rest of English Canada would swell in pride at Barbara's courage in telephoning l'Estrie. Barbara talks long — *plus de questions* on likes, dislikes, dishes, disses and misses. Familiarity, she knows, will help her prepare the perfect *bienvenue à la village de St. Marys.*

From the southwest of Ontario, Jimmy gets an invitation to interrupt just once after introducing himself. Teacher in command, Barbara rolls down her checklist of notes *en français.*

"Il n'y a pas Saint comme Catholique," she told him, explaining the Town's spelling. *"c'est Protestant, moins l'apostrophe."*

Serge would research that peculiarity later.

After the cheese-maker's arrival, the quick tour of the Town weaves past the highlights.

"And the library," Greg says, *"la librairie,* is a Carnegie."

Serge has never heard of the Carnegie bookstore chain. Chapters, *oui.* But the stone-faced Greek-style classical building looks, looks like … looks like *une bibliothèque* in one funky building.

"Here's the 1868 *le pont d'église."*

"Et la crique qui n'il ya pas de poison avec son nom."

Something here about the creek not being polluted. So it must be great *pour la pêche à la ligne.* The three on the greet could hear the visitor.

"C'est bon."

Greg points up twice, once to the City train viaduct, then off into the trees on the hill straight ahead.

"Two rail stone *les points construis pour la compagnie* Grand Trunk."

Stone points. The bridges must be monuments to this big suitcase company.

Architecture was never a strong point with Serge, no matter how Maman tried to interest him.

The other bridge appears to their right while Greg points ahead. "This is the three-arch pre-confederation *Pont* Victoria."

"C'est un pont magnifique, glorieux, messieurs."

Serge could see Greg's eyes roll back into his head, the memory-search look, browsing through his high school French dictionary. Curly Top is so happy as a self-described success with *le grand blah blah en français* that he has no mind. The Big Launch is on the back burner. John and Greg have been on a tour treadmill in the last four weeks, giving tours for necessary friends and a few unannounced relatives. Always a welcome to former neighbours. With all, there's a where's-it-all tour. The good, the bad and the weird.

City visitor humour.

"Where's the gay chapel?"

"We'll get Billie on that."

"What?"

John picked up with a spin on some local humour.

"No, who. He'll have the Balls on that."

Greg added to the confusion.

"The Arnies."

"What?"

Incoming unknown visitors were no longer a surprise.

"They say they're friends of Agent Stevie?"

"He dates my sister's brother-in-law's brother."

The questions kept surprising, though.

"Where's the Nazarene Shrine?"

"I'll call the good Catholic boy, Aldert."

"How about the spa?"

"The what spa?"

"Where's Starbucks?"

"Three blocks from your condo!"

Sometimes Greg just couldn't help himself with a dumb answer for a dumb question.

"Agent Stevie gave you our number."

"Who's Agent Stevie?"

Known relatives were a surprise.

"Aunt Alice, Uncle Arthur! What a surprise."

"Checking up on my favourite nephews."

"There's just one nephew."

"Well, one nephew could take his favourite Aunt and Uncle out to lunch."

John was quick to suggest The Bucket for its buffet — cheap and … cheap. Greg grabbed him off to the back kitchen. "We'll just get our jackets, Auntie Alice, Uncle Art."

Alice and Art were too deaf to hear.

"Alice Malice. Art the Fart." Art of useless fame, less than gas without high-octane Alice. Alice was great at everything except pumping a meal on the table. Correction — she thought she could cook. The overconfidence and complete lack of talent in the kitchen created the malice in Alice. Greg pushed John out of sight.

"John. You threw up all night the one time we ate there. You said never again?"

"Maybe they'll never come back."

"What will we eat?"

"I'll get a Western," John said. "Can't ruin that."

"I'll order wings. Can't ruin them."

John previewed another freaky oddity about his relatives.

"Watch — they won't miss a free fill-up on the feed bag at the all-you-can-eat buffet. They'll slide a few extra in her side bag. Watch, it's the size of a gym duffle bag."

That was their one last kick at The Bucket, unless another future audience changed the direction of the tour. The local parts of the tour have been gleaned from the Kembers, Stormin' Norman and Billie Ball. Cheeko the mayor gave His Worship's tour during their first week in Town.

"What can I say?" Cheeko had pulled up beside an East Berlin knock-off cement complex blocking a river view. "My biggest infrastructure project. What can you do, I ask you, but build the best sewage treatment plant in the great Town of St. Marys in the richest County of Perth, nestled dead centre in the fertile hills of southwestern Ontario. What can I say? Maybe the best sewage treatment in our great province."

The partners gave each other a silent no-shit look. John did *not* need to ask what was percolating under that Curly Top. Cheeko fit in as another character in their parallel *Green Acres* world.

Now, John steers the streets while Greg frames the great Town vistas, one by one.

"This is the view that the locals love," Greg says as the occupants look up the river. "Turn right, John."

Serge looks right.

"Another view locals love. The Opera House."

Serge looks confused. Opera?

Greg points ahead to the steeples lining up along the view from Roger Park. Serge looks left. Aldert and Serge are rubbing shoulders on the turns.

"John, slow down please." Greg taps John's accelerator quad. "You know our tour. Look, you can see the four steeples in this view."

Aldert nudges Serge with a wink. "The tallest steeple, if you need to confess, is Holy Saint Mary."

Two mile-wide smiles.

John is off to the tour finale. He slows down on the newer expansion bridge over the Thames River, on Park Street. A marvel in stone appears upstream with the three-arched bridge, the steeples, and the bell tower in panorama. The falls appear as a curtain of water through the arches. Above the falls, the outline of the 1865 Grand Trunk viaduct flies across the sky. John turns right on the green light as they pass the Opera House, which stands next to the river. Serge can see why the building is described as an eye-puller, the way it highlights the expanse of the stone downtown.

Greg slides into the flow of the Kodachrome vista on show. "Better than the prettiest Irish village. No offence, Aldert."

"None taken, Boss. I am a Transvaalite."

The three laugh, leaving Serge caught in the middle. Serge has never lived anywhere but four kilometres southeast of Knowlton, Quebec. At this moment, eight-hundred-plus kilometres from there, far away in so many ways, and on a tour of the sites with his bosses and a Shepherd.

Of course, Town and Country people, knowing all the sites in the local way, concentrate on recent changes in their well-rehearsed roll about the Town. It's a different sort of roll-around with husband and wife:

"Now Dear, whose car is that in Betty's driveway?"

"Go by the Smiths. Tony's out of jail. See who's home there."

"Why are the curtains drawn?"

"How can they afford that car?"

It's another kind of special run for buddies who need a smoke or a nip to see some stray tit with the well-travelled escape clause, *"Honey, going to Dick's Variety … back in a bit."*

"Aren't I your buddy? Same time each week, she washes her car with no bra. Don't you love her cut-offs? But the wet T-shirt show is amazing."

"I told you she puts her skimpy undies on the clotheslines."

Unless the town hall burns down, there's nothing for locals to see but the changes.

On his first time in Town, Serge soaks up the sights.

"Look there," John says. "That's … Doug's Hardware. *C'est même que magasin général.*"

Greg, out of Kingston High School, translates. "Home Hardware."

Serge reconfirms with head nods. "In Knowlton."

The tour passes through the downtown, lost in translation. The town hall passes by again.

"Looks like a castle," Serge says.

They pass the Bucket Bar in the old post office.

"Looks like a jail. *Trop de pierre* — sorry, there's lots of stone building here."

"St. Marys has a nickname," Aldert says. "The Stonetown."

They move on, pausing at a hover point around the confluence of the Thames and *la crique*, named after a nonexistent sport fish. Serge had drone-scoped with his father all the potential fishing spots, from here to Transvaal and back. Seeing the creek now, he talks to himself. *"Je ne comprends pas.* Sport fishing in this village?"

Aldert's love of fishing and marginal high school French allow him to step in. "Serge." Shakes his finger. "*La crique, c'est* dirty."

No big smile.

Greg translates. *"La crique, c'est sale pour de pêche."*

Aldert again; he has the experience. "Carp, suckers, sunfish, bass and lots of snapping turtles. Not many frogs."

Serge marvels at the abundance *de vie de la crique*, yet nothing for the grill. Greg picks up the theme of catch quality for some fun.

"Unless carp is the French-Canadian thing?"

Serge gives him the French-Canadian thing back. *"Pas de ce poisson. La carpe est terrible."*

No need for translation from the look on his face.

(Le Petit's phone call later describes *les Anglais* as a people who know nothing about *le poisson-gibier*.

"Papa, they catch *la carpe*. I ask *pourquoi*. They tell me it's the fight of the fish. They release the ugly *poisson*. It's for the fight, Papa?"

Le Grand calms his son. *"Plus le jeu pour vous, mon fils*. Let *les Anglaises chercher* the ugly fat *poisson*. More for you in the game fish.")

Greg points out the gas station, even though Serge doesn't own a car, and then its important neighbour. *"Auprès le gaz, il y a le Supermarché McTavish."*

Essential survival interest in the big grocery store when the arriving roommate has little notion of his host's devotion to *nouvelle cuisine*. Nor is he aware that all fare is backed up by on-demand Barbara. Serge will seldom pass the automatic door of McTavish's. But he does have directional sense. They are taking him in the wrong direction. He would rather see the farm.

The exotic electric hovers back from the eastern edge. A packed parking lot that was on Serge's right before is on his left this time. Serge can see the filthy neon sign's two words:

The Sunriser.

Underneath is harder to see:

What you need rises in the East.

Serge finds himself quietly laughing at the sign. The bright letters with a big and loaded hot dog under a partial sun. Wow. He thinks it should skip the dog show: change the wienie to a black flashing silhouette of a *danseuse*, with new neon-red letters: *Le Ballet de Sunset*. He further notes that there is no comment, not a whisper, in the already quiet car.

Not a peep on the Sunriser.

Serge counts the vehicles surrounding the diner. There's an equal number of cars and pickups, plus a few vans and four motorcycles in one group. Even busier than Tims in Knowlton but fewer pickups. Maman always recommends breakfast first; she had sourced the Sunriser Diner.

"Le dîneur, ç'est pareil en anglais, mon fils. It is a restaurant that opens before dawn. For the working man. Son, do not skip a good breakfast." *Sa maman comprend la meilleur*. "Son, even if you must pay for it. Pay and eat well."

The tour continues all the way out west. The path is clear toward one essential detail of Town geography. Greg sums up.

"Beer store at the west end, groceries and gas at the east end. Now we're off to the farm. Off to meet the wizard and his wife, the Kembers." Serge welcomes his final destination, Say Cheese Artisan Goat Cheese, and looks forward to resting at Aldert's house.

Serge's introduction to the herd will be a goat volunteer basking on the barbecue. A young billy takes one for the exclusively ladies' team.

"*Na-a-a-ah. Na-a-a-ah ba-a-a-ad. One for the tee-ee-am.*"

As all leaders do, Queenie grabs full credit where credit is not due. "*Na-a-a-ah. Na-a-a-ah the lay-lay-dees. Queenie takes care of the lay-y-dees. Billy, bye-bye.*"

Quiet on the sidelines as they head back toward the farm, Greg has big thoughts about a three-in-one party.

"A full Wedding Girl cast," he says to himself. "It will be a complete blast."

Chapter 14

Weeks wind down to the big move from the old kitchen on the farm as Barbara anticipates her high-tech renovated kitchen on Thomas Street. Her dream is about to come true, with a gas stove, hand-beaten copper hood, and German-built wall oven. A sliding garbage compactor and built-in glass-door wine refrigerator. Gas is a turn-on for Barbara's happiness.

"Focking pours out the BTUs. Hot, hot. I'll have to be careful on the gas. Gas loves my cast-iron pans."

She sighs up to the heavens. "Thank you, Benny and Faye."

Now, hours before her fourth son's arrival from Quebec, she winds down with the tools that the Century Farm has given her for all these years. She's perfecting her cheese soufflé, so conversation is kept low on the volume.

"Have to step it up, Jimmy. Aldert's focking brûlées have changed the game."

A little in-kitchen competition for the pair.

"You'll show him, Barbie. Experience counts."

"Sh-h-h-h-h, the soufflés need to rise. Jimmy, the lad's making brilliant brûlées from scraps of goat milk."

Indeed, Jimmy has tasted the success and helped spread the fame of the flamed dessert from friends to neighbours to his more-and-more frequent visits to the Sunriser. Now, his eyes come down from sweet, dreamy heaven to the cold stare of his wife.

"Meanwhile, look at you, Jimmy!" (It's a set-up: in an odd sing-song voice, she's a mockingbird.) "Jimmy, out in the milk shed feeding his garbage whey to focking Frankie and his pig gang."

Outside the fences of the Century Farm, Aldert does get the attention, it's true. Loose lips give his brilliant dessert legs.

All agree.

"That lad is our miracle."

"Born into hell. Delivered to heaven."

Greg avoids the madness of the two experimenting in the kitchen, working up their goat-milk creations for the introductory barbecue. Instead he hovers off to the IGA across the river to buy some feta.

Picky, pokey and pointy fingers sum up the selection of cheeses.

"Hm-m-m. Nothing Canadian here. Here's Pine River, a local product. But I don't want a cheddar."

He buys American feta to mix into his famous red-skin potato salad. Curly Top talks his way through the IGA vegetable aisles next.

"Wow. Bags and bags of potatoes. These people love their potatoes. New Brunswick, PEI, Tilbury and get this, l'Estrie in Quebec. That's where Serge is from … and potatoes are on sale."

(Brad, the produce manager, would tell the staff at break:

"This guy. With curly-top blond hair."

Slurp. Slurp. He talks through his coffee. Brad tweaks his free hand. "He's squeezing the potatoes."

The tweak turns to a closed fist. "I'm talking *squeezing.*"

Slurp. Brad's slobbering out the words, hence a dribble. Dibble-dabble on the dribble with a handy-wipe. "I've seen tomato, watermelon, grapes, oranges … even cheese-squeezing. When I worked the aisles, there would be people squeezing tissues, toilet paper and paper towels. But I have never seen anyone squeeze potatoes. Like, this guy loves his potatoes."

Brad leans in to the small group. "He was talking to the potatoes. Talking to the potatoes!")

Back in the kitchen, boiling up the Ontario-grown potatoes, Greg's working up a question for Barbara and Jimmy beside him. Everyone is working up a storm for this afternoon's barbecue to welcome the *fromager de Québec.* Aldert will be walking him over from his place in a couple of hours, once Serge has had some time to settle in.

"Who's the nice gentleman in the produce department?" Greg asks. "With the horn-rimmed glasses?"

Jimmy is first. "Brad Knight, I'd say. Why?"

"I swear that he was giving me the queer eye."

Barbara gives a second view, a better look.

"That's no focking queer eye, Greg. Brad's walleyed, with four sons and a cross-eyed wife who needs the glasses even more than him. But Greg, I do have to admit that old Brad is kinda … queer-*eyed*."

Red-skin potato salad with imported feta — check.

Aldert's masterpieces with the caramelized top — check.

John the Auditor fires up the master Italian espresso machine. Wake-up cappuccinos are necessary after a full-steam-ahead morning on the farm and touring the Town with Serge.

Out of left field, Jimmy offers a surprising finish on the day. "What would be better after an excellent John Capp …"

Barbara is in husband shock as she wonders where this is going. The room goes silent for the Professor's pronouncement. He holds up an empty hand like the Statue of Liberty.

"… than my personal boutique Mezcal to celebrate the unusual circumstances."

There's no question that recent circumstances have been most unusual.

John tips his Capp to Greg. "Unusual changes."

Barbara comes back to Barbara, jarred to the reality of a dank stain on her front lawn. Natural gas in Town, whoa. "Unusual focking incident."

Greg returns the tip of the Capp to John, then turns to Jimmy. "Unusual brilliant choice. It would be unusual not to begin."

John audits this path for a redirect. "Later, partner. Later."

Barbara backs him up. "Slow down, Jimmy. Let's wait till after we eat. Successful, sumptuous soufflé out of the …"

The soufflé slides from the oven, puffs with airy pride, stopping Jimmy in a stand-still stare. Easy-does-it guards the sweet expansion as the bake pan swings to the kitchen counter. Jimmy's held in stride as Barbara beams in pride.

"… vintage electric oven."

Jimmy goes to the counter next to the soufflé, holds up the bottle of golden throat-charmer for inspection. "John, check this out. Hardcore — *verdad, amigo*?"

Jimmy, as part of his consulting sideline, has seen the Latino world, *mucho de México*. The Professor has trip-summary bullet points after repeated visits.

"Same time zone," Jimmy says. "No jet lag. Easy calls back to the farm. I love working on my Spanish. What can you do? What can you say?"

John looks deep into recent memory. Who is Jimmy pantomiming? He's heard that phrase before. Nevertheless John finds a new *compadre* in the worship of Agave. John holds the bottle up to the passing sun, whose light bends through a prism the colour of first-boil maple syrup.

Greg looks up into the glory. "Can't wait for dinner. A real golden throat-charmer."

Jimmy can't stop playing the Statue of Liberty, rotating the bottle in the glow. "This is the real deal. I guarantee the quality. A total boutique purchase through Mexican friends."

He stops rotating at the maize-coloured label showing a rectangle of weathered wood bearing two words.

EL MISTICO.

Jimmy can't make out the small print. "Can you guys read that for me?"

"Mezcal de Moda, Oaxaca del Estado de Oaxaca México," John says. "Label does look like a wooden sign."

"It is the sign." Jimmy has first-hand vision on a replay of misspent yesteryears at a vintage *mezcaleria,* an early bad choice that has become a boutique choice of late. "The sign over a pair of rubbly gate stanchions. The glass-topped walls hide a poor horse behind them. The nag pulls their maize grinder in an infinite circle."

John struggles to pull along with the connection to a golden throat-charmer. "Real horsepower, wow!"

Jimmy pulls away on the memory, rides on *en español.* "Get this." Jimmy has John, who gets little on Spanish and nothing on horses, in his sights. *"Les pregunta. Como se llama el caballo?"*

Jimmy is enthralling himself, mindless of John's confusion, with the question of what the *Mezcalleros* would call their horse.

John is not mindless but stuck on a what's-that-line. *"A Horse With No Name"— is that what that song is called?*

Jimmy arrives at his own punch line. *"El caballo, señor.* The horse. They call him the horse."

(On a different line, a long-distance call to a different world — the small world behind the broken-glass-topped adobe brick wall of *El Mistico, Mezcal Original* — the *Mexicanos* are still laughing about *los Gringos muy estupidos* and their fascination with *el caballo.*)

As the September light starts to fade, the waft of burnt sugars sealing saucy billy on the spit back beside the milk shed spreads to the back kitchen. Here, a wall of unusual noises and sweet aromas mix and mash to complement the night's barbecue. The crème brûlées wait in the partners' wine cooler for later glazing. Faisal and Ozzy are putting the finish on chores, in Aldert's absence. The picnic table is already set up on the porch, covered with a gingham vinyl cover. Jimmy gives billy the kid a once-over, then he's back to the kitchen. Greg puts a finish on dirty dishes and counter surfaces with the dish rag.

Next door, Serge is taking his first steps in a different direction, leaving Aldert's yard on a new work path for the 6th Concession. From the first step off the property line with Aldert, he recognizes the first of many set routines in the life of the Say Cheese Artisan Goat Cheese farm.

"Porch, ladies." Aldert points to his house. "Not today, ladies. Porch."

The collies go from a slobbering sit with a drippy pant to a stand with a tongue rewind, and turn their heads toward home. Aldert walks on without looking back, pointing out the fence line to Serge. "Double electric wires."

Serge has familiarized himself by smartphone with the topography of the farm, including the large empty paddock.

"Napoleon," Aldert says.

The massive dark shape stands centred in the empty field. Ears perked, chin whiskers up to catch the mixed aromas of the stranger and the familiar. A General always watches from afar to get his introduction before he makes his move.

"We'll get a proper introduction to the General tomorrow. Barbecue tonight. Jimmy's been all day on the spit."

Aldert translates "spit" as the rotisserie. His mind wanders back home, to the wonder of St. Hubert rotisserie chicken. Two barks from under the canopy take him from the savoury thoughts of barbecue. He smiles before his guide speaks.

"Max," Serge says.

Aldert nods. "Max smells us, but more important, Max sees all, has seen it all. And Max remembers it all. If that dog could talk …"

Aldert shuts down for a moment in total recall of recent incidents. Serge continues with a point from his website and satellite research, with his finger toward the far paddock. Points out his website and GPS satellite homework. "Are those the ladies over there?"

The mention of goats brings the Shepherd back.

"Most days. Faisal and Ozzy put them down in the barn early today. We'll meet them tomorrow during the milk shed tour."

The young Shepherd gives the young *fromager* a wink and a nudge.

"After breakfast, eh?"

Serge is most excited about getting hands on, shoulders down, in the milk shed, making his whey into cheese. His impatience to get started is softened by two consolation rewards: barbecue tonight and a big breakfast tomorrow. Jimmy explained in advance that September nights are cooler and the barbecue, if outside, has to be earlier. Serge is completely familiar with wet, cold and freezing from the three seasons of l'Estrie. On his four-wheeler, his Ski-Doo or Grandfather's hand-crafted wood and sinew snowshoes, he has faced all conditions — and all conditions always included barbecuing. As Grandfather would say, "A full stomach is the foundation for the full experience."

Grandfather would repeat the same recipe to his outdoor barbecuing audience:

"Cast-iron pan, aluminum lid …" (Holds up the tarnished lid) "… with wood handle. *And,* insulated dishcloth …"

Grandfather's list always included bacon fat, sweet onions, green peppers and a clove of garlic. Grandfather used the term "catch of the day" to refer to a Noah's ark of game cuts. Turkey, duck, goose, pheasant, grouse and pigeon were among the avian choices. Furry creatures could be rabbit, bear, deer, elk or, on special occasions, moose. On very rare occasions was what he called "surprise meat." Never ask what the surprise meat is. Could be squirrel or raccoon, even porcupine. Just never ask. The meat would be smothered in a dried parsley and garlic garnish with rock salt and pepper. A list that all children and grandchildren would later recite by heart over their own open fires.

"Serge," Jimmy told him over the phone earlier, "we want a proper welcome for you, and barbecue says it best. And not just the Say Cheese team. The neighbours, the Town folk are all excited about the prospects of new cheeses from the farm. We need to do a public introduction at the Sunriser Diner … breakfast with locals. That's the way we do it."

Bang. Suddenly Max has his jowls stuck into Serge's lower bowels.

Serge can check off another introduction.

"*Bonjour, mon ami,*" Serge says, laughing.

"Max likes you. Otherwise …"

Aldert's wink and nudge go hands out for a chopping motion. Serge nods at the idea of such unfortunate introductions, then gives both the old dog's ears a good flap. "Maybe he smells our German shepherd, P.K."

Max escorts the new guest across the rather brown lawn and onto the porch, where the new and old owners welcome him with hugs, double kisses and a chorus of "*Bienvenue.*"

Barbara is quick to round the group with a tray of stemware, while Greg follows up with the pour. Jimmy raises up his glass, lining up a group *ting.*

"*Salut. Bienvenue à Serge.*"

Easy up. Greg is easy up with another pour. Easy up for another toast all round.

Jimmy continues. "*À vous, Serge, nonobstant le certificate de fromager, vous êtes notre futur.*"

Click, click, click, and so on.

Barbara is very impressed with her husband's French; he must have been practising to get that toast down. But now it's time to eat. Salads are on the picnic table on the porch, as evening descends.

Jimmy has another toast already on the table — the focaccia buns in a basket beside the platter of tasty billy. Serge meets the famous Billy on a Bun. Barbara complements the meat-and-greet, the tossed salad and Greg's potato salad with her successful soufflés out of the electric oven. Don't forget the not-so-secret sauces. Tonight's special guest is welcomed by two choices, Heady Honey or Ghost Hot.

The group finishes the Pinot Gris. Greg has the wheel on another vintage wine deal, matching the dinner course with a bingo for the barbecue.

"This is a big-boy Malbec. Imported by my private broker in the City."

To accommodate the vast complications of bouquet from a single-varietal Argentinian, glasses change to wide-mouth crystal. No one has the guts to get into sophisticated wine talk, to approach the topic of the arresting aromas and fruitful flavours. Instead of any talk on the current pour, the company grasses on about the glassware. Somehow copious wine loosens lips, whereby everyone feels entitled to an opinion on stemware.

John comes to the table. "Nice stemware, Jimmy."

Jimmy goes to the source. "It was an easy excuse to detour over from Switzerland after I confirmed the order for the cheese-making equipment with the Allmer family."

"Jimmy had all the plans right there on CAD," Barbara boasts. "Any adjustments, changes, specialization, tweaks …"

"Thank you, dear."

Jimmy moves back in on his story while his wife reaches for another sip.

"The Allmers arranged the whole trip with a private driver, guide, and hotel reservations close to the Reisel factory. Met Hans Reisel at a conference where I was a guest speaker. Contacted him with dates, but everything, everything was arranged for me on my arrival."

Retelling the crystal story loses legs on group interest. Refills bring the picnic table to attention as seconds go round, with Serge passing. *"Lentement pour la rouge."*

Serge is slow on the glass, with plenty of the red to go. He toasts, nonetheless. *"Salut."*

Happy table picnickers find it easy up one for more rounds of toasts. Easy up for *parlez le français des Anglais, aussi.*

Serge would tell his father later, *"Papa. La salade de pommes de terre rouges de Greg.* Delicious, Papa. We need to get Maman to try it. Greg has it on Facebook."

And Billy on the Bun with two not-so-secret sauces — he licked the plate clean. Of course, he would never confess that Barbara's concoctions are as good as St. Hubert's signature sauce. Maman browns her asparagus and shallots on her propane stovetop, covered with an aluminum lid to soften them up. Same *chez nous,* same good *chez Kember.*

"Serge," Barbara says, holding up her glass, *"trouves-moi un nouveau focking garçon."*

Lentement, Barbara.

Serge's face turns red with more than the reflected glow of the sunset and the full-bodied red in his hand. While Serge basks briefly in the moment, the rest remain expectant about what's next. Time to get cracking.

Aldert is off with pardons and a stack of licked-clean plates, followed by Barbara. In sixty seconds Aldert swings back out through the screen door with a butane blowtorch. In a moment of synergy, Barbara sets down six enamelled ramekins, white inside, black outside, along with little spoons, on the red-and-white check tablecloth.

The smell of burnt lavender honey is intoxicating as Aldert moves around the table, repeating the windmill routine of snatch-and-burn for each the six ramekins. Serge joins the group with spoons up as they wait for Aldert to take his place. He lifts a spoon in a sweet ready-to-go toast.

"Let's get cracking."

The spoons dig into the crusty part, cracked and crunched up with a creamy tad of goat milk goo through pursed lips that guard against any loss.

Slurp. Slurp.

The small, deep bowls eat up the short spoons. Six crispy golden-topped black bowls go white-enamel clean on the insides. *("Papa, le dessert du grand berger, Aldert. Wow.")* Aldert's clever creation is a soft cream landing for the evening. But the group is still flying from lavender and *rouge*, and there are more flights yet to come.

Jimmy sees an eventful opportunity. This is his chance for a flight of shots with the golden throat-charmer. He sticks his neck out across the table, with his finger pointing to John and then to the kitchen. John can still see that road-sign label in his mind. He and Jimmy are through the screen door and back in a flash. "Let's have a toast," John says.

John sets the places with shot glasses and limes, two bowls of *gusano* salt. Jimmy tags the thimbles with Mezcal, filled to the caution line. Jimmy nods toward John as they both take their seats. The whole group waits, watches the process, all nodding in agreement to Jimmy and John. Jimmy nods back.

"Yes, a toast."

With a chorus: "A toast."

John tunes in, *en español.*

"Mezcal? Si, el tiempo para disfrutar el Mistico. Andele."

All the group understands is giddy up and enjoy. Palms are up in the shake position to greet a line of *gusano* salt, opposite hands on the thimbles, ready next for the limes, all sublime. Let's get licking, don't be chicken. Greg's looking at the glass, he knows nothing, *poco,* about the agave-based spirits. He holds his empty glass up. "This is something we did bring from the condo. What can I say? Where can you find good shot glasses that don't say Niagara Falls?"

From the beginnings of new routes in rural knowledge, Greg can top it up with naming additions for local consumption. "Or Bo-Peep Gardens, Gumbo's Memorial or Mini Stonehenge, the odd rock haven near Bayfield."

No one's listening. It's a comic grab. Gone in a flash. Everyone is focused in on the small capital letters printed on the empty shot. Glass inspection reveals two words, *POCO* above the caution line and *LOCO* below it. Caution has passed into the warm winds of the late summer's night as they go all-out *LOCO*; life is too *POCO.*

"Salud y succes!" John calls out. "To our cheese-maker. Serge Lamontagne."

The shots go up. The Mezcal, salt and lime juice slide down together.

Greg wipes his lips, motions to his partner. John's concentration on tasting the road sign labelled Mistico has *el gato* caught on his tongue, for a savoury silence. Greg's stare gets John's glass hand up in the air. A response of lime and salt licking all round.

Greg's turn to toast. "To an … *award*-winning cheese."

Self-congratulations, high fives, kisses and *LOCO* hoots follow the "Award" word.

"*Salut*," Serge says to the group.

Easy up for another round of boutique Mistico, salt and limes in a Country party line.

Barbara stops in her tracks, after the lick. "What focking salt is this?"

John has left the jar of ground *gusano*, worm larvae from the agave, off the table. "Mexican salt from the beaches in Playa del Carmen," he says.

Barbara's heard about the nude beaches down there.

"Hope there's no gringo ass-sweat in my beach salt."

As the party line get ready for the fifth shot, the pink zombie elephants are on the scene, with the group almost tail-to-trunk in mutual support. Aldert and Serge are neophytes when it comes to the chemistry of Mezcal. They're young, and *la Mezcal* is young too, all of which creates the possibility of an uncertain reaction to the fermented agave liquor.

Jimmy has that chemical feeling; now he's Jimenez, lost in nostalgia for Oaxaca. John Juan Tito is just a downhill passenger following the road-sign Mezcal, a sleepy, smoky, seductive spirit. Jimenez is pulled back to the reality of the front porch by an unfamiliar voice. *C'est Serge.*

Serge has the floor, towering above the picnic table, speaking in English. He thanks each and every one present with individual words and a vigorous hand-shake. Jimmy marvels at the turn, as the well-behaved lad has barely spoken since the evening's first handshakes and Serge's first, shy *merci beaucoup*.

Serge salutes to Jimmy, careful to avoid any suggestion of another shot round, not saying *Salut*. John misunderstands the hand signals to mean one more pour to celebrate Serge up on stage. The party line rings up another round of fresh limes and *gusano* salt.

Glasses lift. All eyes turn to the young cheese-maker on the bench seat. Serge aligns his shot glass.

"*Mes amis*. To award-winning goat cheese."

Glasses align to the heavens on a cool night as starry eyes are up, lost in space until the blast-off announcement. "*Le Rocket. Boom Boom … et Lapointe.*"

Shots down, the other five at the table all fall to earth while Serge watches the crash in conversation, searching for more words. The group is frozen toast. Serge is the last at the supper table, last man standing, last to lower his empty shot glass.

John and Greg, having reached the end of their high-school French, are first to whimper it out. "*Le Rocket? Boom Boom?*"

C'était une whoopsie, Serge thinks, but how? And what? What possible gaffe could have occurred on this warm night of hospitality? *Whoopsie, maybe they are Leafs fans?* Greg shoots the puck over the boards on that idea. *"What is a rocket? What is a … boom boom?"*

Each letter of L-E-A-F-S flames away in his mind as he lets the puck drop. *"Je m'excuse, messieurs … Henri Richard. Bernie Geoffrion."*

Serge is frozen under the false assumption that *les Anglais* know something about hockey. Greg can't wise up or shut up. "Who?"

Serge has a permanent shoulder-shrug of shock. *"Bien entendu, mes amis,* don't you know *les Canadiens?"*

(He will tell his Papa later under the low ceiling of his guest bedroom: "We say *les Anglais* do not understand our champion *Canadiens.* We say *les Anglais* cannot succeed with *les Leafs.* Papa, no wonder. These people know nothing about hockey. How can they make *le fromage chèvre? Un fromage de grand prix?* With no knowledge of good cheese?"

"Le Petit. It's not them, it's you who is important when it comes to making good cheese. Get going, son. *Tu es le fromager."*

"Merci, Papa.")

Jimmy feels the lad's pain on a hockey cross-check. He's surprised at John and Greg's ignorance of *les Habitants.* This is the true north, where inhabitants from sea to sea stand on guard for the fifth season in Canada — hockey season. Jimmy keeps to himself a point shot on super local hockey history. He leaves for another day a historic mention of the Habs' great Howie Morenz. Howie grew up about twenty-five kilometres from their current location on the front porch, due north.

Up on the picnic bench, Serge still has the floor. He swallows his indignity and speaks from the pulpit of hockey and cheese. All through the life of a Quebec farm boy, Habs hockey hopes and cheesy dreams have complemented each other. A call to overtime now, to detail his game plan.

"C'est le même avec le miel de lavande. *Pardon* — same with honey of the lavender in cheese. This name calls to itself. Calls to us?"

He holds his hand up to his ear, but this party line is a dead end. He plays on for an overtime win. "It calls to be *La Fleur.* Eh?"

Jimmy and Barbara recognize the name of the former Habs captain, the great Guy Lafleur. With the mention of lavender honey, John and Greg's heads are Hab-less but full of crème brûlée. As for the Shepherd, Aldert gets hockey, gets the connection to lavender honey, gets *la fleur* from his high school French, *and* he has heard about Guy Lafleur. Serge is switched on to overtime now; he plays on.

"A cream cheese might be *St. Jean Belle Vue.* Eh?"

Group *huh, eh?* Jimmy picks up the reference to Montreal star Jean Béliveau, but the rest of the party line is dead, again.

Here in the backyard off the 6th Concession, mindsets couldn't be farther away from an ice hockey arena. For the new owners, puckering up on hockey names for cheese is a dark passage up an unknown creek. The horror of it all for John and Greg — their new *fromager*, before even finishing one day on the job, is calling out the names of cheeses without asking. Worse, without first asking: Where's the cheese?

Butt to butt, side by side on the picnic bench, Greg can feel John's anxiety through the pine of the picnic table. Greg can't help himself or John as he rocks himself into the equivalent of an uncontrollable fetal state. Serge is about to fan the flames in a shootout.

Le Grand always advised that the shots you never take are the goals you never make. Le Petit shoots on net now with the greatest saver in Habs history, Patrick Roy. "Triple-cream cheese calls for one name, *Le Roy* …"

Butts off Greg's rocky response, John shakes himself into action. He gains a state of control, interrupting the slippery slide down the ice to *les Habitants*. He reinvents himself as a gentleman coach.

"Serge. *Mon ami.* You *will* be an award-winning cheese-maker. I guarantee it. All the ingredients are here for the best in teams. Look before you at all the best — for starters, the Shepherd."

Aldert tips his cap with his bigger-than-a-mile smile on the evening's compliment. "And the best in business advice. Both Kembers, that is."

John winks at the couple. "Barbara, your secret sauces. Your help with Aldert. Your welcome for Serge. *Merci, Madame.*"

John turns to *le fromager*.

"Best, Serge? The goat team, of course. All bedded down for the night in the big barn. Just over there." He points off into the darkness behind him, toward a softly shining yard light.

Aldert, as a Shepherd would, comes out on the service side. "The Napoleon contribution."

Big smiles. Serge has seen the massive goat on the Say Cheese website.

John keeps going. "The Allmer equipment is the best in the world. All set to go."

Greg, an expert on the grape, then glassware and now software, tips his curly top. "Jimmy, your software, your apps married with our terminal system, the lab … you are a genius."

Barbie steps on it with some marital support. "Focking right on, Greg."

Interrupted partner is back on, tipsy in John's favour. "John is a CA *and* a top contract lawyer."

John, still calm, continues after Greg's re-introduction interruption.

"Serge, *mon ami.*" John waits for Aldert to return to the bench seat. "Serge, what do we know about hockey? As you see, not much. Then there's your Canadiens. We do not mean to insult you, but we know nothing about your Habs. *Pardon.*"

Serge gives a quarter-mile smile. It's okay, because Papa, along with his older brothers and all his uncles and cousins, along with the IGA check-out crew and the coffee klatch at Tims, *all* drilled home the same important fact. *Les Anglais ne savent pas le hockey. Regardez.* They stick to that dead tree with no future leaf growth. They call it hope. They hope to be losers, for hockey eternity. *Incroyable.*

John steps up as arbitrator on a superfan's mindset. He evaluates his accounting experience into the ultimate Canadiens question. "Serge. How much do you think your Habs are worth?"

"Worth?"

"What could you sell them for?"

Every single fan of *les Canadiens* thinks they are priceless, with or without Carey Price. Across all the Tims in Ontario, Leafs fans throw back their evaluation of *les Canadiens*.

"If that goalie is hurt, they are Price-less."

Serge will never be surprised that *tous les Anglais* see Carey Price as the world's greatest goalie, because, *certainement,* he is ...

Serge hesitates to answer as he winds back through his off-ice database. He has read the sports business rankings in *Ice Canada* magazine, month after month.

"Oooh, très cher! My guess would be *un, deux milliards de dollars.* I do not guess, but *peut-être* the most valuable sport franchise *au Canada.*"

(As it happens, Serge is correct up to the last two years: *peut-être un milliard et plus.*)

John drafts up a play that exploits his talents as both CA and lawyer.

"Serge. If we name a cheese after a Canadiens great, what an honour! But it's an honour that we would have to pay for." John rubs his thumb and forefinger together, a money-grubbing rub. "We will pay huge royalties."

Greg translates into small change. *"Trop, trop de monnaie."*

John, outed by his Mezcal-induced state of address, has enough fuel for a giddy-up, a push-pull of his hips, back and forth, back and forth. "O-o-o-o-rrrr."

Serge needs no explanation on any action that moves back and forth at the hips. Barbara translates in simple English nonetheless.

"They sue our focking pants off. Or it will be boom boom, off to jail."

Serge widens his eyes with no smile. John continues on calmly, narrowing his eyes with an easy smile.

"Je suis très désolé, mon ami. Maybe when we get rich, paying the trademark royalties."

In between Greg's ears, he's out in space. "Maybe we fly to the moon."

John ignores the off-course reference to future possibilities, as do the remaining table participants. He plays on a winning future with present pride on display. "More important is to win all those awards."

Yes, John the geek can play a classic hockey deke.

"I promise you, Serge. We will go and meet *les Canadiens.* Make *Lapointe* visit. Have *Boom Boom* good time. *Nous se repartons à Québec quelques fromages de l'Ontario.* And all prizewinners, too."

Serge is lost in the translation of the funny point lost in hero worship of Canadiens legends. Greg hangs on to the fun. "Count me in for some boom boom too."

John turns to motion the next pour. Limes and salt go round.

"À vous, Serge, notre fromager. Les Canadiens. Le futur."

Heads up from John to the young transplant on his first night *en Ontario.* John stands behind Serge, hands down on both shoulders.

"Serge. Not now. It's not the time for us cheeseheads to adopt hockey names, *mon ami."*

Le fromager is not ready for a cold shower. He holds his head up with one hand held high, with a question for the table. He hesitates for a moment as he is reminded of what Papa told him: *"Listen to the English. They are the bosses. The managers of the farm. Listen, my son, listen."* He has one question he must ask before he'll be able to sleep in the low-ceilinged bedroom next door. *"Pardon, le Chef Greg* and *le Chef John."* He nods to each partner in turn, with a look around the picnic table. "What will we call our cheese?"

Greg likes being called *le Chef.* He thinks about putting *le Chef Greg* on his Say Cheese full-colour business cards. *Le Chef Jean* picks up the question.

"After cars."

Serge is automatic-shifting from disappointment to astonishment.

"Cars?"

Greg is off, as he just can't help himself when it's time for show and tell. *"Les voitures, exactement.* And to be precise, auto terminology that includes nicknames and odd names, even mechanical terms."

Greg is in the flow, rubbing his hands together, ready to go. Serge stares around the smiling table, lost in the direction of Greg's forward drive. The ultimate showman doubles down, picking up two tools of delight off the checkered vinyl table cover, for a ta-dah moment.

"Our double-cream cheese will be …"

Greg lowers his hands for little drummer boy, tapping the picnic table with two licked-clean *crème brûlée* spoons. *Tap. Dap. Dap. Tap, tap, tap.* He looks up at all smiles but one.

"Little Deuce Chèvre."

Serge syntaxes the auto term *en français,* then begins to laugh. He's quick, speeding past the translation of two little goats.

"Papa is a nut for Jan and Dean. That surfer music from California."

Les Anglais turn to each other in astonishment at his knowledge. Greg's turn to show the whey. He drops the spoons for snapping fingers above his head.

"Play some Ricky Martin. Add some jalapeños. We'll call that Testa Rossa."

Mais oui, for the striking redhead Ferrari models from two great periods of

Enzo influence. Even more flame with the addition of Latino fame. Aldert, the Kembers, even Max are all into the fun. *Gran Turismo Omologato.* John remains in astonishment at his partner's run-down on cheesy names. Curly Top has his foot down on the accelerator, beating through the bushes.

"We can use some bark from the hawthorn bush. Make … Say Woody." Thoughts move to the thorny bushes along the eastern fence line. "Have a Woody Harrelson testimonial backed by 'What Would You do?' by The Dogg Pound from the *Natural Born Killers* soundtrack. That would give it some firm texture with a bark rind."

Everyone but the unfamiliar Kembers grinds to a stop at the thought of the scatological lyrics. The Kembers are stunned that Curly Top knows anything about hawthorn bushes. Greg stops all doubts in their tracks.

"Just kidding. But that's not all folks." Pedal to the metal, Greg rides on, *le chef chauffeur.*

"As for our triple cream …" (He gives a double nod of acknowledgement to Serge.) "Our grand prix triple cream calls for the name of 'Three on the Tree.'"

Serge, like Michelangelo and his massive blocks of stone, feels a cheese call out his name. This auto term, *dee three tree,* he has never heard before. Greg is auto incredulous that any farm boy has never shifted ye olde three-gear standard shifter branching out from the wheel.

"Three gears off the steering wheel," he clarifies. Left hand on the imaginary wheel while the right hand makes like a sideways wiper blade, with his face saying you-should-know. "Three on the tree."

Greg continues with a cockeyed glance that in local terms is referred to as the half-dumb look. *Et oui,* Serge reflects back in a look *demi-stupide.*

Serge searches his idiom index without a reference point in either French or English slang. *"Quoi?"*

Jimmy taps on the brakes of a long and successful introductory evening, touching the young *fromager*'s arm.

"Tomorrow, you will understand. You will get a lift in my '53 tomorrow."

Serge lights up in the dark night to a morning ride in a '53. His mind rewinds on vintage models, *et quoi? Mon Dieu,* this is earlier than Jan and Dean. Three on the tree — it must be a pickup, but cars had the shift too? No matter, anything '53 will be good.

Big surprise.

"We'll be going to the Sunriser," Jimmy says.

Big breakfast? How could life be better, but let's be certain.

"Quoi?" Serge asks.

Greg's *en français,* confident in switching onto newfound local knowledge. *"C'est la place de café et chit-chat de tous le trucs. Pour les gens de la village."*

Barbara interjects local knowledge to translate the horrible high school French. "Serge, his *truc* means Town focking gossip."

Serge dreams of a big breakfast, his arrival in some sort of vintage vehicle, passing under the dirty neon sign at the east end of Town, a new realization of an unrequited dream in a newfound land. He has no interest in gossip, re-confirming some inside details on the place of the full parking lot, in the middle of the afternoon.

"*Quoi?*"

Barbara has the table and floor. "*C'est un cafétéria.*"

Greg, the high-fool graduate in French, can't help himself. "It's *un dîneur*, Barbara."

A stop, for the record. "Listen, Greg. You have high school French; I actually was the high school French teacher. Focking *écoutez-vous* up, buddy. *Dîneur* is a customer, the person eating their foot-long and fries. *Cafétéria, en français*, is the diner where you're making the bacon, eh?"

Jimmy returns to the table to checker-flag the French race with a framed photo of his '53 Ford pickup. It shows Barbara and Jimmy posing with *the* classic truck, a most famous ride with a flashing shark-tooth grille. The truck's fishy history started when Jimmy's dad bought it new off the Dobson lot. Son has kept the apple of his eye fresh and shiny. Thanks to Benny, there's a vast work and storage garage on Thomas Street, where a new tenant waits for the big move. Jimmy's first move in the morning will be to pick up Serge with the Say Cheese farm truck in order to get his vintage dream ride on the road to the *cafétéria*.

Aldert, quiet for most of the evening, breaks the focus on the framed image with a cheesy suggestion.

"Napoleon Bona Part …"

The group turns with a big *quoi?*

"What?"

There's that mile smile from the Shepherd.

"A cheese. Hard ripened. Nutty taste. Napoleon Bona Part."

Another half-dumb group look. Aldert's up off the bench to repeat his version of that back-and-forth, back-and-forth, giddy-up from-the-hip locomotion. "Well, he does his part."

Serge ropes in the role of the humongous goat. "Maybe for *the* big producer in our factory, the name calls to be The General."

Jimmy backs him up, suggests another product. "And a soft cheese, spreadable, with a nice rind finish in the end, maybe a bit of charcoal. Meet Your Waterloo."

John drives ahead, back on the road with a general segue. "General, yes. General Motor … no. Motor Head Cheese, maybe. There could be A-Ford-Able. Instead of St. Jean, how's Chèvre Bel Air sound? *Très jolie,* no?"

Aldert, no longer the quiet man, lightens it up again. "A silhouette of Jimi Hendrix with Crosstown Traffic in a neon type."

Serge, along with the remaining party line, is hesitant on Aldert's idea but flashes a few air riffs.

"Hendrix at full volume in the milk shed," Aldert says.

"*Il y a un* sound system there?" Serge asks.

Group chorus in a half-dumb, *demi-stupide* French connection:

"*Pourquoi?*"

Serge is blustering in a super-duper excited state. He recounts a graduation report. "*Mon stage au College Agricole de Knowlton! Le professeur de fromage.*"

Barbara slows the lecture down.

"*Lentement, mon fils. En anglais.*"

"My professor has a study on the effects of music on aging cheese. How do you say, audio frequency?"

Easy peasy. "Audio frequency," Barbara answers.

"*C'est ça.* He plays the classical, the rock, even the rap at different volumes, during the cheese aging."

Jimmy, the academic, follows the research. "With results?"

"*Certainement.* Higher volume, lower frequency for *demi-fort* cheese."

The Professor has a wry eye on the recent graduate. "You're not kidding. *Ce n'est pas un blog.*"

Serge repeats the results, the evidence, the facts as he knows them. "*Pas. C'est vrai,* for real. Higher volume, higher frequency for soft cheeses."

The party line is connected, alive to the concept to sound and cheese, a segue for a Say Cheese moment. Aldert speaks first. "Music and aging cheese! Who would have thunk."

Barbara adds on. "Focking weird. Hendrix and cheese. That would age me. Anne Murray or Kenny Rogers, maybe."

John rises up. "We have car names already. We don't need music or music names."

Greg dumbs it down to grab everyone's attention to his epiphany. "*Er-r-r-r-r-rrr …*" From his seat, left hand on the imaginary wheel again, off the tree this time, to the floor, right hand on an imaginary shift.

"*Er-r-r-r-r-rr.* Second gear. *Er-r-r-r-r-rrr.* Third gear."

Max is off the mat, to the far side of the porch, standing in retreat.

Bench response is a chorus as Curly tops off the gears.

"Enough."

Greg stops immediately, precipitating a serious pause around the picnic table. "Look, people. We have satellite. ZIT has the F1 channel *and* three Auto Scene channels. More than enough background sound."

Barbara is out of tune. "Focking noise."

John is so impressed with his partner's tenacity on his sound epiphany. Greg turns to the Professor.

"We could manage it, right, Jimmy? Software. Bluetooth. It is a nice-sounding system."

Jimmy doesn't shift to a higher gear. "Can't hear a thing when the milking equipment goes on."

Serge, *le fromager*, balances his thoughts. "Sound for storage and aging. But don't scare the goats."

Aldert the Shepherd joins his new roommate. "Right on, monsieur. *Er-r-r-r-r-rrr. Er-r-r-r-r-rrr.*"

The image of a revving redhead with the prancing horse logo powering the aging process of goat is chilling. John, who accepts the verve and vitality of difference, sniffs out the off-side profit potential right out of the envelope. A man who can see above the fire and fray, past the world's most recognizable brand, Enzo Ferrari's black horse. A play on words, a trick of the eye on symbols, *and* it's cheese, goat cheese.

"I'll look up the registration restrictions on related images, Photoshopping, and proprietary rights. At the same time …" (John does a little *gin-gin-gin* with raised eyebrows over his designer readers) "… a look-see at the broadcast soundtracks. There are statutes of limitations. Can't see a problem with Little Deuce Coupe, and Three on the Tree is pretty generic in auto terms."

The bench group exhales a breath of uncertainty at these possibilities, feeling better under the leadership of such a smart guy, no offense to the Professor emeritus himself. No doubt, Mezcal is giving a glow to the flow. Two rows of picnic table half-dumb faces smile back at the concept promoted by John, their butts too frozen to contribute. No matter, he's on a roll. The group members, one by one, reassess the alcohol intake on the evening: *How drunk am I?* And the hot continues on for calm John.

"Core Vette," he says. "A little something hot in the centre. *Jal*-opy. With a soft nippy spread of …"

Jimmy sixth-senses the need for their sixth refill. An evening review tells us that the first shot lubricates, and the second shifts the party out of first gear. And then from *POCO* in second to third, where naming stuff is refined and resolved. *LOCO*, meanwhile, is the fourth that drives them on into the dark night. *Mon Dieu, et merci* that Jimmy leaves Serge, along with Aldert, off the next round of golden throat-charmers. How crazy can it get? The fifth already has Greg adding personalized licence plates to their goat cheese marketing arsenal.

"4Q EWE," he says to himself.

Heads up, hatches down, on limes and salt one last time, before responsibilities rein in the love-in that evening. "Serge, it was our big surprise."

The morning will come soon enough. John plays *le grand frère* for some fun. "*Votre Maman* told us that *le Petit* loves his *hungry homme* breakfast."

Greg can't help himself, in a female reprisal of Maman in soprano. "*Mon cher petit aime le breakfast.*"

A head-turner for Serge, from Chef Jean to Chef Gregoire. Serge will be up to try this Sunriser at the rise of sun. He has a question for tonight. "When food is on the table, count me in. Why not *Les Chefs* for breakfast?"

John answers. "Serge, Jimmy does the coffee thing at the Sunriser on his own. This will be your time, a show-and-tell time from you, as an introductory guest of his."

John is pointing his thumb back in a half-check at Jimmy. "Buddy, just count on getting your *le grand homme* breakfast."

Serge comprehends the parallels between Town coffee klatches. Substitute *le Grand* for Jimmy and it's just like Tims in Knowlton.

It's quiet all along the party line now, with time out for a look between roommates. Another look from Barbara and Jimmy and a pause bring Aldert and Serge to their feet.

John comes forward for a final *grand frère* gesture. "Good luck in your meet and greet."

Serge hesitates at the top of the porch steps. "But what should I say?"

John reaches out to touch his shoulder in confidence. "Just be yourself."

Serge is sober enough to hold back, but he does not hold back. Speaking with a Country gravel edge, no accent and a smile: "'Allo, may-sewers. Nice to meet you.' Then I wait for *all* the questions — let Jimmy answer them all, eh? And *pour moi, au revoir, à la prochaine*, of course."

Laughs all round finish the evening with a big good-bye. "*À la prochaine. À bientôt.*"

Serge is on the lawn, facing the front porch bunch with the dark spot profiled behind him. "Nothing to lose, all to gain."

The pause-hold button freezes them, profiled by the screen door frame behind. Serge answers. "My father always said that as a joke. *C'est une blague.* Before we cleaned the barn, he says it is in English. It's from a sixties television show, *Les Acres Vertes.*"

Greg can't help himself but still speaks for the group. "No shit."

Serge and Aldert head off into the darkness beyond the soft lights. Barbara calls out first.

"Don't forget your focking iPhone. Get some photos."

And seconds from the partners: "Yes, yes, take your iPhones. More photos for the website. We have Twitter, Instagram and Facebook."

Greg yells out an incomprehensible shopping list into the darkness. "Those photos of the Swiss technicians, you know, the ones taken in the pass-through window? Pose up a super shot like that, both of you in it."

Jimmy, having had his fill of iPhone advice, stands with one thought in mind: *Will the Shark turn over?*

Barbara's stuck on the iPhone line. "Make sure your iPhone is focking charged!"

Jimmy's quick to turn out the porch lights.

Aldert and Serge are back on the concession, in glorious silence under the bellowing canopy with stars peeking through. No words exchanged between the young men, no need for these no-doubt-soon-to-be friends. Serge closes his eyes to feel a full breath of cool moist air, agricultural stuff with that *je ne sais quoi,* just like home. *Mon Dieu,* he must call Papa no matter the time, on his first day. Aldert notices the pace is suddenly up to double time.

In the Century Farm home, upstairs and downstairs, both couples are over the bathroom sinks brushing their teeth. At the same time, in that same moment, they look in the mirror with smiles.

"*Les Acres Vertes.*"

Chapter 15

Most days, Jimmy's stool is at the end of the S-counter beside the kitchen doorway. Today there's a second empty stool. Braedon's got a full house on deck.

Coffee full steam ahead with multiple pots, check.

Stools up, check.

Booth benches full, check.

Angie can hear Braedon's brain gears grind to a halt before he says the words: "Dim-wits are heading for the back corner booth."

The swing kitchen doors blast open with a slap. Braedon's out in full force with the dimmer button in mind for these dim lights. The S-counter heads pivot with a silent mouth count of his long strides. (*"Braedon took four long steps from the kitchen."* In truth it was more than four, but far less than a dozen.)

"Listen up, Ronnie. Donnie, look at me. Quit hiding behind Walter. Listen up, guys. This is shake-hands-and-shut-your-gob time for you."

The stare seems so much longer than just four seconds.

"Or I'll shake my hand down your focking gobs. Do you understand?"

"Sir, yes sir."

Braedon, in over twenty years, has never, ever been called by this name.

With two hands on the booth's tabletop, Braedon is still able to twist his head back to the rest of the house.

"Do we understand?" he says to everyone.

The crowd in the booths and along the S-shaped counter, save for two dummies in the back corner, nod in agreement. Ronnie and Donnie suck up the farthest corner of the very back booth to avoid further attention. Kind of the shit location in the Sunriser. (*"The booth beside the toilets. Appetizing."*)

With a flash of red over the sash of the picture window that overlooks the parking lot, all conversation ceases. The full house turn to the front windows and greasy window entrance. Guy radar activates when special wheels pull up. The roomful in chorus:

"Ni-i-i-i-ice."

On the ladder to in-the-know status, auto knowledge, with its vast umbrella of coverage, is the most common first step up. We're really talking *vintage* car knowledge, the ability to discern the difference between all-original survivor and mere show condition, between Tuesday-night cruiser and garage queen. First-hand experience is what counts here; mere car magazine seen-and-reads are low on the list. (Second level of in-the-know is easy peasy: Maple Leafs hockey. BBQ is in a league of its own.) Today the coffee klatch car purists purr to the sound of number one.

"'53 Shark Tooth."

The pigeons parrot and coo.

"We kno-o-o-ow."

Three words sum it up about anything vintage, collectible or antique:

Condition, condition, condition.

Original, original, original might cover it.

All in house understand the level of auto prestige earned by special appearances.

"Jimmy keeps it to parades and cruise nights."

Talk's cheap, no matter the condition of the vehicle, if you don't own it.

"How did his dad, then Jimmy, keep it so original? They live on gravel?"

An expensive answer, obvious to a true aficionado.

"Floats it to the fair parade. Elsewhere too." The group's vision calls up a twin-axle, slat-floor open trailer with a chained-down red pickup.

In-the-know correction.

"Twin-axle covered trailer with split doors and hydraulic drop ramps." An impressive hum combines with slurps all round the room. A regular adds accumulated information.

"He floats it into Oliver's for an annual detailing. Before parade season. Before storing it, he has Oliver winterize it. Mothballs."

"Mothballs?"

"Keeps the wee critters out. Oliver gets it right with winter storage. Here's his card if you need storage. Toll-free number right here. It's his cell, so call him anytime."

The klatch nod to a solution for the problems of freezing, winter garage cover and those pesky nesting rodents.

Not many have paid gas to carry them down to Daytona or spent on winter rent for a Florida condo. Not many have flown to Miami, blown a wad on a rented car in Orlando or watched a sunset in the Keys. Still, most know the effort, the detail and the cost of classic ownership.

A young man moves the red pilings in the reserved parking spot. The Red Shark backs in to the reserved space. More than enough time for refinement.

There's a touch of culture coming from a stool, centre front, who throws out an artful add-on. This is real up-front, in-the-know stuff.

"Clark Catchpaw used the '53 in his portrait of Tommy Tin."

Everyone in the room, no matter the dimness of their art foundation, is proud of the Town's famous-son artist Clark Catchpaw. No one here has an artistic clue, but they understand to a red stool that walls from coast to coast show off Clarky's work.

"*Metaphoric*," began the list of adjectives voiced-over in a recent TV spot promoting a Catchpaw retrospective at the McMichael gallery. The ad ran in a loop on the flat screen at the downtown Tims. (Everyone in the Sunriser today has had Mrs. Kember, as a Grade 10 English teacher, explain the use of metaphor.)

"*Vast.*"

"*Villainous good.*"

"*Valuable.*"

"*The best Canadian artist for the 21st century.*" ("Why do you say *for* instead of *in* the 21st century?")

And o-o-o-o-h-h-h … Tommy Tin adds value with the undisputed title of Canada's Rocker. That radio playing in the background will have a Tommy tune, if you wait a bit.

That's popular.

The in-the-knows adds a national art fact.

"Hangs in the National Gallery." Just in case: "In Ottawa."

"What does it mean?" someone says. "I know he commands a big price."

Not many in house today have visited any gallery, whether capital, provincial, across an international border or up the street. With today's special guest at the gates, the art vacuum quickly blows out this conversation. No matter, there's time for a commercial pause.

"Goodwell has a fall leaf run to the Ottawa Valley that includes it. There and back by luxury bus."

More is less when the distance spins on the odometer. Why would you go that far anywaysies? Might be worth it for that production of *Samson* in Branson, Missouri, that was recently featured on Goodwell tours list. The wannabe bus guide seconds his bus-mate promoter.

"Those crashing pillars! That was art."

Bus mate gives a satisfied nod to his memory of the bus, there and back in comfort. "Goodwell …"

Someone from the back echoes the group consensus.

"Will you guys shut the fuck up?"

The introduction party is passing the gates from the parking lot. Inside, the art expert nails the Red Shark in a way that everyone can get:

"Tommy Tin says it's his *favourite* art."

A few final grunts of acknowledgement to the iconic Canadian rocker from the shores of Lake Huron.

The door swings open.

Jimmy and Serge swing in together.

"Bonjour." "Bonjour."

Serge gives a royal *le Petit* wave. The room erupts out of *know*-where.

"Go Habs go! Go Habs go!"

The Carey Price is right for the young cheese-maker, who gives a *grand* smile. Maman did recommend an *un grand homme* breakfast. And Serge is dying of hunger.

What a morning welcome! No worries for Barbara — Serge has already got selfies of him, Jimmy and him even, beside the Red Shark. And with the neon Sunriser sign in the background, even.

Jimmy can see the two empty spaces by the kitchen swing door. First a standing thank-you to the packed house. He tips his John Deere cap. Now Serge flashes *le français, lentement.*

"Merci, mes amis. Je suis très content, ici à votre village très beau."

Anywhere, in any language on the planet, pride is not lost in translation.

Salutations all round the S-counter corners, then back to the booths. All round and back, the echo moves *en français.*

"Merci." "Merci, mon ami." "Merci." "Merci."

Ronnie and Donnie keep silent, lost in the sound of peas circling their empty brain-cases. The whole bean group, the coffee klatch, feel satisfied with a bit of high school *parler en français.* Barbara would be proud of their Everest-sized attempt.

"Barbara Kember was my high school French teacher."

"Focking all right."

The pull-ties of the morning at the Sunriser come together without a hitch. No dim-wit or dummy flaps his flaming gums to screw up the welcome. Nary a *couchez-vous* is heard, nor a *shootez le puck* or that untranslatable, horrible word, *tabernac.*

Braedon is out of the kitchen to shake the hand of *le fromager.* Serge is a Gallic natural, pulling the welcome hand toward him, planting a kiss on each cheek. Braedon is surprised in short order before he short-orders his surprise for Serge.

"Bienvenue. J'ai un grand surprise de kitchen *pour toi. Je reviens avec ça."*

Serge flashes the mile smile *en français.* *"Merci, monsieur."*

The big group eyes wait for the two to settle on their reserved stools, after long weeks of speculation and education on team goats, frequency of Greek salads, Swiss state-of-the-art equipment and Montreal design-build plans. Who's the husband? Not the right gathering for that. Here's the cheese-maker, so let's take lots of time to milk the cheese topic dry.

Jimmy's infrequent visits of late are discussed like a school report card. First stool mate says: "Buddy, I've been here five out of seven days a week. It's at least four weeks since I've seen you."

Braedon can correct that. "I'm counting the fifth week."

Second stool voice from across the S-bend of the counter. "Seems more than that. Six weeks this Saturday, I think."

The coffee klatch has never welcomed *un fromager* let alone *un Québécois* to their gatherings. On the stool front left sits the young man who's going to turn this crazy dream into actual goat cheese.

"Think feta, gentlemen." Braedon flies out the swing doors. *"C'est le surprise de chef."*

Serge looks down at a low and wide soup bowl with no eggs, *saucisses* or *patates.*

Braedon looks at the gobsmacked demi-smile of confusion. *"Mon surprise. Poutine de Serge. Mon nouveau plat du dîner."*

Serge is surprised, and still gobsmacked. Braeden points at the brown features.

"Sunriser shoestring fries, brown and al dente, with secret gravy."

"Secret gravy, *pourquoi?*"

Wink. Wink. Wink. "I mixed feta in the gravy."

Serge does not have to look to see the crowd stare.

"Where's the cheese?" they ask. "Where's the feta come from? Imported?"

"No, from Barbara in her old kitchen at the farm. Her and Aldert made it up *très special pour toi.*"

Serge switches from being frozen on his stool to enjoying the sweet taste of fries and gravy.

"Très bon, monsieur."

Braedon flashes his eyebrows at this crossing over to something new.

"Feta. Feta mixed in the gravy. Mm-m-m-m, *c'est mon secret.*"

The lad from Quebec is about to get his taste of coffee dissection and refinement. Someone to his right:

"All the way from Quebec."

Pass on that question, which answers itself. The first big status item realigns the group.

"Parents have a three-hundred quota."

All Serge can manage through one yummy mouthful. *"Oui."*

The silence is impressive. An in-the-know agricultural witness magnifies the point of a huge cow quota into obvious clarity. "You've seen their bulls at the Royal Winter Fair."

A wee whisper of a true farmer follows the head nods in a row. "No shit, eh?"

Only a few in the room ever get to the world-renowned Winter Fair, most often relating to quilts (by the Missus or not), or hubby's bee honey from the unkempt backyard. Where the City public celebrates local vegetable farmers and growers like the Stewarts and the Turners — turning them into an eating fad that needs capital letters, LOCAL — most folks just watch the Royal Horse Show from the comfort of their living rooms.

The significance of a show ribbon, whether it's regarding honey, patchworks or animals, is not lost on folks in Town, Transvaal or the coffee klatch. A ribbon equals back-home bragging rights. But a grand champion, which comes with one hard-to-lift trophy? That's a livestock grand slam. Listen as the voice with the floor goes on:

"A grand champion, from your farm in Knowlton."

Serge keeps any bragging private.

"Oui, monsieur."

Someone creates a few snickers. "Lot of bull to me."

The moment of clarity has now come into view, this Saturday morning. Serge is on the red seat. Now is the time.

Serge is from Quebec, *oui.* Now is the question.

A nation unites in fever at the S-counter, with the expectation from pre-season action. The one solitude peppers Serge like a practice goalie.

"How will your Habs do?"

"Will Price stay healthy?"

"Will they name a captain?"

"How can they keep Bo-jay-bin as general manager?"

Ronnie shoots some puck levity. "Max D instead of Max P. What's the max problem here?"

Half the room have to turn to confirm a dim-wit came up with a clever something.

Serge cannot contain his delight that his heroes, les Habs, are in play at a small greasy diner in rural English Canada. Bobby Bynck adds his altruistic view.

"How can a Molson own a team named after a Molson beer, Canadian, and yet … yet Budweiser, a 'merican beer, sponsors Canadiens games?"

It's a collective half-dumb look rounding the room. Serge is caught between the second and third questions. He's still collecting his thoughts when someone else throws the puck back into play.

"Don't you think the Habs are too small? Who's on first for their power forward? Grumpy, Sneezy or Dopey?"

Serge understands the reference to Disney *et les dwarfs*. The lad is quick but *le nain* quick enough.

An actual hockey wag balances the content.

"Look, back at the Leafs. Big power forwards out of their yin-yang. Our defence could be a little Goofy. Or not so Happy."

Serge digests the intent of all this yip-yap. Most important matter, though, is the super bowl of *Poutine de Serge*. He pushes the remaining fries into the drips of gravy as he polishes off *ce plat incroyable*. With Maman not looking, he's tempted to lick the plate clean, but not this morning with all eyes on him. The final clean comes from the napkin that he pats his lips and beard with. He turns to his host while still chewing the last mouthful and gives him *un grand sourire*.

Jimmy takes the full smile cue and stands up.

"Well, boys, we can eat poutine all morning, but who's going to make the feta for it, eh?"

Braedon tips his white chef cap to the departing pair. *"Merci tous, au revoir, messieurs."*

"Braedon, see you next Saturday morning. Three stools."

The half-dumb look. "Three?"

"The partners. Greg and John. They're up next for introductions."

Jimmy and Serge wave to the concentrated school of ears.

Next Saturday will be … interesting.

Serge *le Grand* Lamontagne, Maman, *et toute la famille Lamontagne* hear all, bite by bite from the introductory barbecue, sip by sip from the Sunriser, and step by step from the train platform to the complete herd and equipment tours. Le Petit saves le Grand barn detail on the milk operation for later. Both father and son are closet car nuts. Milk, cheese, cows, goats and the subject of *les Anglaises* are of little interest to repeat to *les amis* at the Tims in Knowlton. Their conversation centres on the exotic electric car.

"And Papa, the beast whispers its acceleration."

Le Grand keeps transportation practical.

"*Comment?* How does zero to sixty in four seconds work on a farm?"

"No, Papa. We have a quad cab with a serious Say Cheese logo on it. I'll send you a picture."

"C'est un Ford comme chez nous?"

"Mais c'est King Ranch."

"Très bon."

Serge le Petit has inherited the undaunted spirit of farming. When Serge was top-of-class in his cheese-maker diploma program, it was no surprise to his family, school friends or instructors. Easy to work hard at something you've worked toward all your life. So what if it's goats instead of cows, Ontario rather than near home in Quebec — this opportunity is big. The Kember Farm gives him an open canvas for boutique cheese-making. The high-tech equipment waits for his direction in the controlled process that spoils milk and produces wonderful cheese.

The most important homework of his young life so far is making sense of the milk shed. He had little time on the Say Cheese website, which indeed had nothing on it compared with the CAD files that were waiting for him on his arrival. And nothing digital compares with Jimmy live, in his Professor's instruction mode.

"Serge, the cheese we produce will be under your guidance; you will have your stamp on the cheese. You have the great advantage of a milk source right from our farm, allowing us to use unpasteurized product, which lets the wild bacteria play with the taste. You *will* make prizemaking cheese."

Jimmy is standing beside the cheese vat that picks up all the milk from the cup-sucked teats.

"Our capacity is good for now. Easy to double, triple the production."

Faisal and Ozzy sweep, scrub, squeegee, and shift about in the background, so Jimmy has to move in close to be heard.

"Quantity is not our goal. Quality is. But we need to find out what will make that prizewinning cheese, our style, with our characteristics."

Jimmy reaches for a tap on Serge's arm.

"Trial and error, and it begins with you, Serge. You've mentioned some great examples: Camembert, Roquefort, Stilton. I have some funky moulds for blue cheese, but later. *And,* we need to consider Barbara's great Brie experiments in the kitchen."

The list was pre-approved by Jimmy, in short order after Serge stepped off the train, then vetted for registration issues by John the Auditor. Serge's cheese-maker diploma included courses on specialty cheeses and goat and sheep processing.

"Jimmy, have you heard of lemon juice as a replacement for rennet?" Serge asks.

Jimmy nods. "I will introduce you to all *my* secondary agents."

The Professor gets even closer, a little antsy.

"*This* will help give you *your* different styles. You can review my starter cultures, use your own, to find the characteristics that speak to the cheese."

Serge reflects on the past, the future. "I do appreciate the opportunity. Sad on one hand to be far away from home, but happy to be *un fromager*."

Jimmy reflects on cheese. "Faisselle — have you heard of it?"

Serge has to concentrate hard with Faisal and Ozzy working in the background and the multiple ceiling-mounted, hanging televisions. He sees the HD screens as better suited to working with charts and graphs, and the F1 channel is a distraction — all that constant revving with that constant noise. Serge twists his face up, trying to remember the names they talked about the night before: *Little Deuce Chèvre. Was it Testa Rosa? And Three-on-the-Tree — merveilleux.*

"A French cheese, washed rind, raw milk, correct?"

"Yes," Jimmy says. "And John searched it, it's a non-protected name. A super twin, savoury with chives or shallots or sweet with lavender honey."

Serge loves the Say Cheese team's zest for food; this life seems like a dream.

"The same lavender honey Aldert uses on the crème brûlées?"

"*Oui.* These are the different styles that you will give direction to success. The advantage of being part of a start-up for you, Serge, is that it gives you a blank slate to go in any direction. *Le fromager* must give us the best direction."

Jimmy's hand sweeps across the milk shed.

"In the cold room, we can see what's up on the shelves in our sample experiments. Something may impress you, give you … another direction. Even the Swiss technicians left some Gouda mixed with hawthorn berries and bark. It's ripe and ready."

Serge needs to make more notes. Jimmy sees this question on his face.

"No worries. Everything you can think of, ask of … it's all on our database, sorted by my software. Anything else? You need to file your work on your computer in our office, then *everything* will be in the database."

Serge ponders the hard work next. Jimmy's back on tour.

"First, a little time on the office computer to start the first steps in a plan to make prizewinning cheese."

The *fromager* has one thought.

Homework.

Back at the house, John follows the numbers on social media. Lots of questions on the website already, even with little content. More likes on Facebook. Instagram, too, gets updated with the picture progress of the perfect cheese factory. Lots of questions, but one main ask.

"*Where's the cheese?*"

Hundreds of hits build to thousands more who start to follow Say Cheese on the net. Greg keeps a routine with his iPhone on HD camera. He catches the

Shepherd and Jimmy on their rounds and then tags them. The pictures snap off the screen in high resolution. Queenie stands out on the regular routine.

"Smile, Queenie."

"Na-a-a-ah. Na-a-a-ah again. That guy-ya-ya with the eye box."

Sixty-plus ladies behind their Queen on the slate fence line lift their beards. Queenie points her ass end to the iPhone.

"Na-a-a-ah today. Na-a-a-ah. Let's heh-heh-ead to the old oak tree. We fe-e-e-l hungry for some ha-a-awthor-n-n-n. Some wet gra-a-a-ass. Na-a-a-ah."

Greg dekes right and then left on an opposite path around the barn, past Frankie and his pig group.

"I'll be back for you, porky porky."

The porky bunch pay no heed, following the lead from the trough of feed. Frankie is aware of change with the novel appearance of curds. Not just milk, but pails of chewy chewy, basted with more fatty milk.

"This chewy chewy is chewy chewy. Chewy more tasteless, oink, oink."

No straying from the trough as the family buffet stays open.

"Hm-m-m-m. Frankie thinks too much chewy chewy chewy."

The loop around the barn is a photo quarterback sneak. Greg catches the team lineup in full parade. The misty morning is a setup for a panoramic movie short. The goats form a live motion ribbon in the foreground. While he retraces his path to the pigpen, Greg has his work up on all his social media sites, starting with the Say Cheese website. Afterwards a series of Facebook, Instagram and Twitter additions, thanks to the power of ZIT's high-speed service. Greg seems to have the start on handles and hashtags for marketing.

John wants it straight and simple:

#saycheese

#goatcheese

Serge has one suggestion:

#fromagechèvre

Aldert comes up with a few of his own:

#theteamintraining

#Queenie

#QueenofNubia

The Queen quickly gathers seven thousand followers.

This doubles after the first picture of Napoleon. The big fella has his hoofs on Aldert's shoulders. Waist-up shot.

#thegeneral

#Napoleon

The movie of misty goats on the march is an amazing one-off gem. Greg relishes the hundreds of green likes, yellow thumbs-ups and little red hearts.

Watchers chew up the successful double bubble of goats and cheese.

The short clip of the General chomping, stretching, watching — all waist-up

— gets a hundred thousand hits. The close-up reel of Napoleon laying his raspy tongue across Aldert's mile smile is a major hit. Two hundred thousand viewers.

Barbara watches it with Aldert. "How do you stand still with that focking wet meat drooling on you?"

"Focking practice, Barbie."

The masses eat it up, tongue and all. Greg keeps his head. He's patient with his ZIT coverage. He learns that closer to the farmhouse and shed equals better internet speed.

Viewers become familiar with *le fromager de la belle province*, the import Syrian Twins, the Professor on milking, and the hunk, the Shepherd. There's not one John shot, other than under the Management tab.

One thing is apparent and simple. The Say Cheese followers want more Napoleon. Greg whines out over John Capps the frustration of answering dumb questions.

"Can you take a shot of him together with Queenie?"

"Where does Napoleon sleep at night?"

"Does he have a favourite doe?"

"Do goats mate for life?"

"Can Napoleon reproduce dwarf goats?"

John covers this last one.

"Forget dwarf sex. 'The Blue Goat.' We'll have a goat porno site. Easy peasy with our 24/7 power stud and sixty ladies."

"Napoleon will take about thirty-six hours to finish that job. Wham. Bang. Thank you Ma'am."

(The morning breeze carries the regal report back from her highness. The dawn of musk is upon her. *"Na-a-a-ah with Quee-ee-ee-nie you do-o-o-on't. Na-a-a-a-ah. Sti-i-i-ick to the tea-e-e-am."*)

Serge wants to get that right foothold, certify the standing of his product from the milk shed. Barbara wants to show off her back kitchen talent that's been aging in one corner of the big coolers.

Back in the back kitchen, while Aldert experiments with adding new dimensions to his goat-cheese creations, Serge mixes with hand tools while Jimmy watches.

"Take a little whey, sometimes a curd or two. And ..." He winks. "*Voilà*, something different."

"Something brilliant, my son."

"Look at the creation. Then look around us," Serge says. "Lavender honey, cilantro, mint, basil, onion, pork rind, bacon bits, the huckleberries, black raspberries, smoked walnuts, apples and tangerines."

"Tangerines?"

"Comes from the IGA. I was just kidding. One of the few things I like that's not local. But I can find pears and wild grapes. There's funky mushrooms right behind the old oak tree with acorns underneath. Have you had fiddleheads?"

"My mother would steam them," Jimmy says.

"Mine too. Have you ever eaten lilies?"

"Lilies?"

"Great for a Caesar salad. All this are the exotics on the City menu, but I can source all, in season, in our backyards. Let me show you with this."

"I don't care what this is. Just let me taste it, lad."

More and more, Greg is convinced of a social media winner. He focuses on one platform outside of the website: YouTube.

The unwashed do not have to come to us, he figures. Gregzdream goes to them à la digital.

"Say Cheese." Greg uploads another morning farmyard clip. "Voilà, it shows up on YouTube."

John looks over Greg's shoulder as he works. "You want people to know what 'Three on the Tree' cheese is? Easy peasy. Shoot the tasting."

The idea of having Aldert treat creations demonstrated on the Say Cheese website and YouTube emerges out of direct demand. Cooks, chefs, hosts and hostesses, associations and amateur foodies have begun pouring in the requests. (*"Those crème brûlées look amazing. Recipe?"*)

What fantastic dessert can be made with curds? Aldert's Lavender Honey Goat Crème Brûlées.

Greg can't contain himself. "They don't have to taste it. We don't have to make thousands of crème brûlées to get the word out. We will make short movies with real people. Aldert's first guest will be Barbara."

"Focking all right."

Greg licks his fingers with flare for the fare. "Smacker-licking, lip-sucking dee-light, right into the camera lens."

John returns to practical and pragmatic, but in the flow. "Less City alliteration, more Country ill-literation. Don't scare the natives."

And here Greg comes, throwing caution off another set of tracks into the wind.

"Let's have a reality video party. We'll shoot it here on the farm. *Green Acres*–style." Greg has a pre-emptive caution finger up on John. "No legal issues. We'll call it Dusty Roots. Maybe we can invite those two dummies, Ronnie and Donnie, who came for an interview."

"Can we call them The Dustbin Bumpkins?"

"Dusty Roots, please."

"Stick to the tasting shoot," John advises, with the inevitable cautionary finger point. "Don't scare the locals."

The Sunriser crowd have heard all the details, true and false. They have reflected on the smallest of bits and redefined the big picture of things as this nutty and cheesy tale has developed. It's been a natural flow of witnesses up to this second Saturday morning. On the farm, as they're about to leave for the meet and greet, the partners stand on the porch with Jimmy.

"Serious, guys," Jimmy says. "Yes, that includes you, Greg. Serious. So, no carnival arrival in the Red Shark or in an exotic that cries out Citiot."

Greg and John share a hurt look. "Ouch."

"We take the pickup. Look at the licence plate."

John squints toward the driveway. "*Yours to Discover?*"

"No, the side of the plate. F-A-R-M."

"On the plate?"

"Yup. It means that you're farmers now. A pickup is what farmers go to Town in. To the Sunriser."

"We can get a Model T with a rack back!" Greg says. "The Transvaalian Hillbillies."

Jimmy speaks with generational experience on the right step forward for local introductions. "Folks in these parts are not real high-minded. Forget anything 'City,' even if asked, Greg." He leans on Curly Top for a shoulder tap. "If they ask what you like in the City? Just say the Leafs, then tell them you have HD and the Leafs Channel with ZIT. And these folks are not that low-minded either, so no gay-centric humour, Greg."

Greg and John feel weak-kneed from the length of the lecture. At eight-fifteen AM, the three climb into the pickup.

"Jimmy," Greg says from the back seat of the quad-cab. "We should make a recording of the Ford for the cheese. *Err-r-r-r-r-rrr.* Bang. Bang. *Err-r-r-r-r-rrr.* Bangity-bang."

"Muffler. Should have had it fixed."

Easier to announce their arrival with the local flare of exhaust noise.

Bang. Bangity-bang.

The full house peer out the diner's windows like caged animals.

Greg looks out the rear passenger-side window. "They look hungry. Maybe we should have brought donuts? My God, there's that dim-wit Ronnie, with his mug plastered to the greasy front window."

All pickup eyes right.

"He's mouthing some words?" John says.

"Greg. John. The eagle has landed. Saddle up."

Through the glass doors and down the goat hole they go.

Greg throws aces to the full house. "Hello. Hello, St. Marys."

And back in parrot chorus. "Hello there to you too."

John knows his partner has the personality gene. He lets Greg wear the pants on the intro. John follows along with Jimmy with a one-hand wave toward the far end of the S-counter. John could make a detailed sketch of the room just based on all the data he's heard about the place. Now here it is, and here he is.

The man described in the same input stands in front of them.

"Braedon," says the owner. "Welcome, John."

A nod to Jimmy. "Welcome, Professor."

Braedon waves to Greg during a second ovation while his other hand motions John and Jimmy toward two of the red stools.

"Greg." The point to the third stool. Braedon doesn't tarry, to avoid kissing carry-over surprises like with Serge seven days ago.

Short-Order Angie and the Server Sisters watch Braedon's white-flag approach to the City couple.

"Lads," Braedon says. "I have two orders of our new house special, *Poutine de Serge*, coming up."

Angie pulls together the short orders from the fryers and cooktop gravy pan. Braedon winks to Jimmy.

"And a junior order for the Professor."

Jimmy motions to his stomach, with shoulder shrugs.

"No excuses, *monsieur*. You have to try it."

"Excuse me, Braedon," John says. "Did you say poutine?" He motions to his stomach with shoulder shrugs.

"Can't say no to the secret gravy," Braedon says.

Braedon has a hand on each of the partners' shoulders. He moves in close with a whisper. "Barbara's cooktop feta. That's the secret. Now, John, you wouldn't want to disappoint Barbara, would you?"

John knew he'd like Braedon from the start. "You have a focking point, Braedon."

Greg's pointless. "Count me in. Secret gravy with Barbie's feta. Was Serge holding this back on his *amis*?"

At that moment, like Serge the previous week, the three amigos do not have to turn on their stools to feel every eye in the jammed room on them.

From somewhere. "So where's the cheese?"

Greg does an excellent spokesperson. "Right here in this secret gravy on the poutine. Feta."

The crowd likes entertainment. The new show in Town.

"Feta, you can buy at the IGA," Greg continues, "first of the year. Available at the IGA, on the internet and at our farm store."

John wakes up with an incredulous look. Greg leans in real close and quiet. "The coolers and a cash box to start."

The coffee klatch catch an affable, kind scene between the partners. They don't need to hear the words being spoken.

"Who does the dishes? Who cooks?"

"Well, Barbara's been doing a lot of cooking. Preparing goat-cheese treats with Aldert. Right here too, like Braedon has done with the poutine. Good, eh? No — great, eh?"

Greg gestures for hands in applause. He turns back to Braedon, who's standing with the swing doors pushed out. It's a double credit. No, triple. "Have you tried Aldert's crème brûlées? Great, eh? Eh?"

No matter how many tongues have actually tasted this treat, all hands are clapping away. Jimmy and John dig in to the secret gravy smothering the shoe-string fries.

"Say Cheese Artisan Goat Cheese will have all recipes available on our website, Facebook and Instagram accounts. Make an order. Need a great cheese recipe? We want to be your one-stop goat cheese site."

The crowd are all lost sheep after the word *recipe*.

A saviour arrives with a non-cheese, non–food-related, important question on the most important subject.

"Who gets Jimmy's custom-made barbecue when they move into Town?"

"With five horse spit power," Greg says.

"Right. But who gets it?"

"Say Cheese owns the barbecue," Greg answers, "and Jimmy will stay on as Barbecue King. Watch for special events on the website." He lets it rip. "Say Cheese for more public barbecues."

Greg just made that up, and the crowd goes wild with saucy response. John and Jimmy are still on the secret sauce.

Another saviour resurrects the second most popular subject.

"What do you think about those Leafs?"

"With Shanny, Coach and the Kid — or some might say lots of kids — in the dressing room, Go Leafs Go."

This lifts John's and Jimmy's faces out of the super bowl. They turn their stools to a room full of gobs and nobs, aglow at today's entertainment.

"Your cheese-maker loves Carey Price," someone offers.

Greg is a ringer. "Best goaltender in hockey? No."

The room stops.

"No — the best hockey player in the *world*. But." Greg has both elbows on the counter with a hey-who-knows expression. The morning group is in his corner, waiting for the next shot. "But, will he stay healthy? Thirty-two is an old man in sports. And …" (Greg lowers his voice to a still room) "Kind of a small team. Like Snow White's dwarfs."

The room roars in delight. Jimmy and John are stunned buns on their stools. And then, from prehistoric history in the official partner introduction, that other question.

"So who does the dishes?"

"Like any couple, we argue over who does the dishes."

For some strange but rural reason the house applauds the dishes. The house likes natural transparency. Greg has natural likability. Remember, too, Billie Ball has blazed a trail to the Sunriser for years and years.

Now, an indirect question about the electric exotic. (Automobiles, the single most popular coffee klatch topic.)

"What kinda veh-hick-cull are you driving on the farm?"

"Ol' Giddy Up," Greg answers. "Our beautiful quad-cab F250 with 254 Triton V-8. Can pull our trailer with ease."

The coffee cups have drained, bringing Jacqui and Jayne in for refills. In the pause, Greg motions to Braedon.

"Are you interested in joining our movie shoot this Thursday?"

"A movie shoot?"

"At the farm. All the kitchen creations from Aldert out on the porch. Weather permitting."

"Do you have the room there?"

"We can make the room. The food itself is the actor. Need some lady shots and Napoleon, of course. Friends out in the City, in the business, are coming up with a big favour. We're starving for content on our website and social media. Did you see Serge's photos on Facebook?"

"You bet I did. Lots of likes on the Red Shark."

"Well, the Red Shark will be out front on the farm. Great eye candy to bait the cheese products."

Braedon skips the dirty reminder of gravel and floating the shark by trailer from the oversized garage on Thomas Street. He hitches onto something different. "Why not out front here?"

"Here?"

"At the Sunriser. Jimmy doesn't have to trailer it. Park it out front. Here."

"Here?"

"For all the right reasons. Room. Big kitchen. Our help. And the one reason. That diner feel."

John's turn.

"Here?"

"We'll close at four. Ready Freddy in the kitchen, little cleanup out front, anytime after four."

John takes another turn. "Why, Braedon? Why the misery of someone else's party but at your place?"

"Let me count the reasons. My buddy, the Professor. Promoting the Town. Welcoming new people with new ideas. Good neighbours. The reasons are as many as the ladies in Aldert's herd."

Greg smiles. "Any friend of ol' Jimmy is an ol' friend of ours."

"Good friends, then."

"So you would host our media shoot here at the Sunriser?" John asks.

"Better, guys. With all the room, the stools, booths, we can invite a few VIP guests to fill out the scene. Local background."

"In …" John looks at his smartphones. "In five days?" He glares at Greg.

"Hey, guys," Braedon says. "You already have it up, on the go. Change the GPS, that's all. And add a guest list. I'll email you some possible names later today."

Greg turns to the eyes burning holes in the back of his head. He ignores John's question on short-order timing. "Why not? I have a few guests that I — sorry, we — would include."

"My question," Braedon says, interrupting their tense couple moment. "Where's the cheese?"

"Cheese has been problematic." Greg turns from John. "Whey, curd, and lots of goat milk massaged and manicured by Aldert into treasured treats. You have most of what Barbara had in this homemade feta. But Serge is out there." Greg points past the kitchen, southwest. "Our *fromager* is working round the clock on that Swiss equipment. Cheese will not be a problem." The Producer is up on a plan. "Aldert will prep the crème brûlées at the farm. He'll have all his ingredients bagged and tagged. He will need a lot of counter space, the ovens and the warmers clear."

Braedon nods. "And all clean too. We'll organize a little squirt-around and polish-up."

Honest, Greg is not on anything but Greg. Curly Top the clown shuffles backwards to the entrance glass door. "Jimmy, u-end-doh the Shark in de drive-in?"

Jimmy doesn't get Greg's reference, but he plays it as straight as ever. "The Red Shark will be out front."

In five days.

Stop.

Action.

Shoot.

Chapter 16

"The '53 needs to be out front."

Out front at ground zero, on the asphalt parking lot, cleared in expectation of the big shoot, Greg is wearing his Producer cap in a role review, as Chef Braedon rolls his eyes and nods his head. The Producer points to a hulk waving his arms at the corner of the property. His size is magnified in a tent-sized orange jacket with a fluorescent green cross stamped on his back.

"Who's the X-Man?"

"That's Turf," Braedon answers. "Does nothing in life but help others, always available."

"Help?"

"I said help, not work. He's directing customers to the side street. *And* he's available to keep our parking needs organized from the get-go."

Greg is back pointing at ground zero. Braedon beats him to the point question.

"The '53 will be right there. Turf is exact with instructions."

The film shoot has been scheduled for tonight, after the Sunriser's shortened hours to allow for the special shoot. Greg rolls out the repeated details, more to reassure himself than anything else. "Jimmy's adding some extra classics. Buddies from his cruise nights." Greg looks back at the diner's large, greasy windows. "Director Scottie needs the windows papered out. That will cut the reflection, then later, the headlights." Paper also prevents lookie-looks and rubberneckers from gumming up the windows.

Greg's wide hands are squared up, a finger frame-up in a picture that catches the front of the diner. The picture stays framed while the speaker looks back over his shoulder to no one in particular.

"Scottie will sub the parking lot on the green screen. Sounds like a horror movie or something. *The Green Screen.*"

Braedon stares past the finger frame-up, straight ahead to the empty asphalt and the waving X-Man as he imagines the production reeling out in all directions from his diner. Talking to oneself is catching on. "A night to remember."

Greg's on his own, full steam ahead.

"Eh? Some cool, creative stuff, eh?"

Braedon nods in silent thought while Greg is lost in space, anticipating working with Director Scottie. Clang clang, throttle down. "Beam me up, Scottie."

The fun Producer swivels his finger frame back across the empty asphalt, over the waving X-Man, to square up the Sunriser sign. "The neon needs to be green-screened in. We'll get the shots earlier for background options. We'll be right, bright in the limelight under the starry night."

Braedon can barely nod at this point. Greg has been talking up the behind-the-scenes for five straight days. The diner chef has heard about the detailing but has limited Greg to two meetings. The background staging has really slid together in the last twenty-four hours, with Greg onside, outside, ahead of the game.

"My outside guy cleaned the sign, put a little polish on the neon." Braedon is a go-with-the-flow guy. He grooves as the gossip guru, chief bottle-washer, *chef de greasy spoon,* and owner of the most popular caffeine fill-up station in the Town of St. Marys, with local connections better than ZIT. "My regular guy even waxed the floors last night. Shined the chrome. Dusted the team photo frames. Spanky clean for tonight."

Meanwhile, back in the kitchen, never-seen-before delights — alien food for a diner — with Barbara and Aldert in pre-production prep time. "We'll cut some of the focaccia in small squares," Aldert tells her. "Buttered up with a curd, in the oven then out, with a quick toast under the browner. Barbara, you can top it off with a dollop of your huckleberry jam. A touch of the farm mint."

Barbara doubles up on the focaccia. "Let's toast a few more. Add a little of my homemade mayo with a touch of jalapeño. Farm cilantro, eh? That'll put a focking beard on ya, Aldert."

She gets down and serious. "Open-face for the little buggers works great for app tastes. Better opened."

She's a statue with one hand covering her privates, the other behind her head.

"Venus on the half-shell, eh? An exposed beauty for all to see. Those film shots will focking jump off the screen."

Tonight's shoot will feature a major face-off — not just open face, but face up in antsy-pants anticipation and face down for sumptuous experimentation. Aldert takes it up a notch with enthused extras, dewy droppings of drizzle, crayon-coloured squirts and sweet sprinkles for a puffed-up presentation.

"Wow." Interruption by a Curly Top through the diner pass-through window, opposite side. "The shots will focking jump off the screen."

Barbara, surprised, almost slips teeing up the serving platters. "May the platter be with you," she counters, "*not* focking jump off the counter."

"These *will* focking jump off the screen in high definition." She fans a package of colourful napkins from the Buckaroo Store. "Nice touch on sidelines. Let's intersperse sprigs of mint between the apps."

"Why not add a dusting of ground pepper?" Aldert asks her.

Barb adjusts to the question. "First a sprinkle of mint. The full sprigs can be added at that time" — raises her eyebrows — "from my Town herb garden. Thank you, Faye. Some green to focking jump off the screen."

The green leaves parachute from Barbara's scissors into tiny mint bits.

Aldert does a flyover, cracking the pepper. "Fresh mint, olive oil baste, on barbecue goat. Hm-m-m-m."

Barbara plates on autopilot, then slides the platter into the cooler. "Focking mmm-m-m-m, all righty. Until later, my lovelies."

John has pulled the seating plan together with Jimmy consultation the day before. Jimmy knows the personality map.

"No, John. This guy will not sit beside Norman."

"Problem with Norman?"

"No. The wives do not get along."

"That bad?"

"They're cousins but a real pair of skunks. You don't win a pissing match with a skunk. No one wants to sit next to one skunk, let alone two, eh?"

"Aa-h-h-h, right."

John tried to imagine two skunks going butt to butt.

"And here," Jimmy continued, "Norman's suspect nephew Jamie, he's a sit-alone single."

John knew stand-alone, but sit-alone? Jimmy's Sharpie marked an X on a back table in the seating schematic.

"The guilty bench."

"Guilty bench? Suspect?"

Jimmy went quiet. "Suspected of unnatural activities in the back stalls of barns. Caught guilty-handed with a three-legged stool."

John went quiet at the thought of why, why a three-legged stool. He was interrupted in a whisper with the worst of conclusions.

"Bestiality."

John whispered back, not a question but an exclamation. "Bestiality."

Jimmy without question exclaimed an answer anyway. "Goats."

John was impressed with the Professor of Local Knowledge, but had to ask. "Why?"

"I told you. Norman's nephew. Gets a pass."

But goats. John would never think about goats the same way again. He would sit out the Sharpie X decision.

"Moving on," Jimmy said. "These two benches will be for the Knights. Some will leave their cars and say good night. The lot will be clear by midnight. Some will stay for the shoot, but two benches will cover it — put Jamie in here."

Curly Top butted in. "My one suggestion — place the community actors up front. They'll ham it up on the lamb. Sorry, on the goat. Oh, and remember, Braedon's having a date night. Make sure him and the Missus are in the back corner booth."

Now, evening is falling as mirrored dressing tables across Town reflect the community actors making things up. Terry and Carol suit up with reservations.

"Drip."

"Drip?"

Carol rubs nothing off her chin, points to her costume's matching handbag.

"Careful of food drip showing up on camera. Honey, I have stain wipes."

Terry brushes back his Argan-oiled hair.

"Nice pullover sweater, eh? James Dean."

"White. That's a food drip magnet."

Not important to Terry; he shifts on. "Someone said it's a cruise night."

Nothing from Carol. Terry continues. "Braedon and Jimmy are topping the lot up with classics."

Carol is a lover of the arts but has no clue on the car question.

"Cars?"

Across Town in an amazing array of super-sized garages sticking up from small cookie-box homes, the Kruise Knights Club members cast the ingredients for a big night with more than spit and polish for a classic stepping-out.

Sandy has help tonight, so he instructs his son Auggie in the art of auto presentation.

"A drop of vinegar works. Soap leaves water marks no matter what you do."

Auggie stomps through the puddles in his Baby Shark rubber boots. Auggie is almost four.

One block up, two blocks over, Wes has help tonight in the form of his teenage daughter Stacy.

"Doug's Hardware has a drip-free additive. Apply with a sponge. Rinse off."

Yeah, yeah, yeah. Stacy knows the drill; she'll take the ride but hopes to drive.

Six blocks down and over, Elena calls Andrew.

"Jimmy wants us there before four. Reserved spots laid out."

Over and out.

The Knights will ride with pride, the whole eight or ten blocks from those extra-big garages. Carol calling Terry.

"Baby, let's drive through the downtown and back."

Andrew showing off to Elena.

"My Baby is spotless. That's where she'll be. Spotless at the Sunriser."

Go, Wes.

"Why have a classic if you can't drive it around?"

Stacy is okay and ready to drive it too.

And, the Knight who shall remain anonymous, driving that nifty, shifty little '69 Chevelle convertible SS396:

"Baby, baby, after the shoot. I'll take you on a little ride up Lovers' Lane."

"Baby, that's a classic ride."

An anonymous double-lift of the bushiest eyebrows in the entire Town of St. Marys.

"Later, baby."

And for the car that never leaves home, the Garage Queen, owned by older-than-you-think whiny Joe. Hey, Joe, what are you doing with that hose nozzle in your hand?

"Hope I'm not by that deck patio. Smoking drifts over the whole lot. Looks like the Cayuga tire fire on the weekends — sucks if you have to stand beside your vehicle. Swear I can smell smoke in the car the next day."

Does anybody want tasting notes on that whine?

X-Man directs two stake trucks to the side of the diner, incoming from the City, first arrivals. By seven o'clock, the movie lights are up inside the kraft-papered windows.

Barbara has her head out the kitchen back door with a wave to Turf, who's waving about at everything on the move out front. "Looks like a jack-o'-lantern. No, looks like a focking carnival."

The fading sun throws silhouettes of the parked classics across the bottom of the diner front. The neon lights up the Sunriser like a diorama on Queen. People park, people file in, people sit waiting and wondering about a goat cheese video.

It's almost a Fellini movie the way actors, Knights, VIPs and regulars cast about with the City film crew led by Beam-Me-Up Scottie and Curly Top, the Producer.

"Move those lights. That corner, yup. No plug? Try around the patio door."

Braedon just shakes his head at the unfolding drama after his day at the office.

The kitchen team mind their craft despite the BBQ buzz. Barbara exhales with a shrug of the shoulders. "Jimmy's always a hit with the barbecue. But Aldert, you are the star of the evening."

A mile smile is his answer.

The Professor has a worry-free work plan after he finishes parking-lot detail. He's booked two former PhD students with experience on his barbecues.

Braedon's head reverses from his perch, with minutes to go before the start of the shoot. His eyes canvass the room from the kitchen side of the pass-through. Greg will continue as the Producer while Braedon retires from major domo for the evening, on date night.

"Mason dropped the bread at five." Braedon does a Chef Boyardee OK sign and whistles through the finger O. "Hm-mm-mmm-m-m-m. Did the baking this afternoon. Reversed his baking day just for our show."

He looks at the Producer. "You the man in charge, *the* Producer. No worries, me and the Missus will have a ripe good time on the back bench. Make sure Jacqui or Jayne keep our treats a-coming. I'm leaving you with full staff on. Although Charlie goes home at six."

Greg misses the last few words beneath the sounds of raw horsepower; staff on, Charlie gone … the guest line is long. The Kruise Knights reached out to the Kar Kats, the Eh-Ford-Ables and a few odd buddies to back up their classics, all fronted by Jimmy's chromed shark-tooth Ford half-ton. The community actors walk or follow the instructions to park on the side street. Greg the Producer has shown Scottie and the film crew where to unload. He moves past Braedon through the shiny entrance to watch the classics park one by one, row on row. Jimmy controls the lot.

Jimmy on first helps his car buddies fill up the second and third rows of the lot with the tent-sized X-Man based way back and waving about the last few spaces. The Professor is a well-known lifer, someone who was born in the community, lives here, and engages with his generational knowledge. "This way. Yup, back 'er up, Ronnie. The GT500 will be great right here. Nice to see you, Debbie."

Chug. Chug. Chug.

Gee, gosh, golly Miss Molly, a GTO '70 ragtop. A small crowd of neighbours and complete car nuts has gathered across the side street, standing by for show-time, each classic acknowledged with happy chappies' claps.

"Brian. Looking good. You too, Michelle. Nice bob. Back Black Beauty in here."

Pa-tum. Pa-tum-tum. Patum-m-m-m.

"Hey, Joey from the Kats, right? Perfect. That's your spot."

A yellow '74 Super Bee creates a crowd buzz.

Bum. Bum. Bum-m-m-m. Bum. Bum.

Jimmy's off waving toward the entrance, with background applause.

"Lock up, everybody. This way."

Hey, Joe, out there with two hands up in the air.

"Jimmy?"

The answer before the question. "Joe. Leave the top down. Beautiful evening. Let the ragtop shine on."

The vibe is in the air. The Knights, the Kats and the Ables dress mid-century modern period, otherwise translated as *The Jetsons* or *Grease*. A small snobby voice is lost in the buzz about the Super Bee. "Gotta be pre-1970 or ain't even a classic, let alone *vin*-tage."

Their reflections quiver in the sparkling glass entrance as Greg ushers them inside.

"Hello, hello. Welcome to the goat cheese show. Everybody hungry?"

Greg is unsure what to say. He keeps his lines moving to keep the line moving. "Hello, hello. You have a smile, I have a smile. Hungry, eh?" Guests have to smile at the Curly Top's over-the-top welcome. "Moving, moving, moving along. We'll all have a great time, home by nine. Hungry, eh?"

Moving, moving along to their stool positions, the cast of characters and pretend actors fall into place. The coffee klatch regulars are confused at being ejected off their customary seating by amateur actors.

"Todd Tompkins has my stool. He can act?"

"No, set-building."

And a familiar, craggy face:

"Greg, I know Black Aces staff gets a booth."

"Norman. I thought it was just you and the Missus? You're on your stool 'plus one' at the cash register."

Greg takes a breath, remembering that Norman's wife is one of the two skunks he was warned about. He throws charm into the wind. "Hi, Honey. Love your dress. Is it cotton?"

Normy gives Greg's hand a tight squeeze. "Greg. Get me a booth. *Aargh. Aargh. Aargh.*"

Greg catches Braedon's eye with two fingers, a point, and his lips mouthing BOOTH. A quick check-up from the neck up; my God, there's two skunks in the room. Greg turns to wave to minor amateur cast members lined up along the S-counter with those two empty stools. Normie moves on with Honey, having his say, getting his way behind Braedon.

"Love your '57 Sunliner, Normy," someone calls out.

"Aargh. Aargh. Aargh."

Greg turns and turns, now back toward the line coming through the entrance, grasping for control.

"Seating plan. Seating plan, folks. Bulletin board, right? Check it *before* you walk away." Back in reverse: "This way." Not one person is looking at the chart taped to the cash register. Jacqui and Jayne wasted a bucket of highlighters on a schematic Sunriser, with the most readable hand-printed names and instructions, according to the Book of Jimmy.

Greg pushes through to the benches at the back. "Take your seats, please." One bench over, a newbie with the Kar Kats whispers, "Which of the husbands is he?"

His wife comes back in another ignorant whisper. "Husband? He's the wife. Look at him boss us around. And there's no brains under that curly top of clueless. She's in charge."

Hubbie wonders if Lovie is talking about herself. He holds up an imaginary hand bell. "Hear it? Ring, ring, ringing, Boss. Boss. Boss."

"Shut up, Dave. Remember who's the boss, boss, boss at home. I can toss, toss, toss."

The cast of characters are all in place to go. Greg and Scottie the Director decide the level of light inside. The Director has both fingers pointed.

"Scottie will beam up a little light here," the Director says. "Scottie will beam up more light there."

The movie mood is set, the scene is ready to shoot. Braedon turns to the Missus.

"Pretty sweet for our diner. All lit up like a birthday cake, eh, Sweets?"

How sweet? "Diner delightful, dear. Better with just the candlelight. You wouldn't notice the greasy smear marks in the low light, eh?"

"Oh come on. Lefty worked right through the afternoon on the windows, even though they're papered. He even did extra shining on the chrome over the last few nights."

"I'm afraid it would take Lefty thirty straight afternoons to fully clean your operation, dear."

The City film crew is up front and all around, grabbing casual character shots with a classic background.

"Nice rides, Scottie," one crew member comments. "Are we in *Happy Days*?"

Scottie nods. "Look at the chrome trim on the counter. Those red seat stools. *Happy Days.*"

The neon-lit Sunriser pops in the twilight. In, out, in and out the film crew weaves about on the take, with more stool shots, more shots on the booth benches, photo prepping, one lens on Lefty doing the garbage detail and one leftover shot of X-Man fading into the night. On-the-bench casual shots with a classic car background. Sorry — *papered* background for the green screen. Back in the City studio, the classic part will be inserted via digital editing. Whew.

The rest of the production lights fire up, and the room goes still. Out from the swing doors come the real stars of our evening. For no other reason but hunger, the full house erupts into ravenous applause. Scottie's crew gets a camera sweep of the live reaction.

"Matt, get the audience. Those … characters on stools, with the hunk in the background."

Weaving with server experience, Jacqui and Jayne relay from back-kitchen Barbara to up-front Aldert. Braedon stretches his neck up from the bench to watch the service roll-out. And a bit of a reach on what is coming out of *his* kitchen. "Wow. Look at these little toasties. Soft goat cheese?"

Jacquie reaches out with her free hand to smack Braedon away. The Producer backs up the direction.

"No touchy yet, folks." Greg waves the hanky-spanky, his right palm slapping the back of the left. He firms up the cheese parade order. "Folks. Folks, *let* the film crew catch the excitement. Smile, smile! Lots of teeth, folks. It's a happy-chappie shoot."

Greg holds up his finger frame over his pearl-white smile. The Producer sweeps along the S-counter, then up toward the beyond, up to the glory of the cheese gods. The counter cast look back and to their right, while the booth benches face the Producer. Hungry stomachs pull everyone's eyes back toward the kitchen swing doors.

Curly Top, the ringmaster, follows with his ta-dah point toward the kitchen. "It's a movie shoot, folks. Of our *new and wonderful food.*"

The audience is a mixed salad of car nuts, coffee regulars, and a few real characters, along with all the amateur actor nuts on the stools. An ocean of growlers, a wave of howlers wash and slosh in empty stomachs, back and forth from the booths and along the reverse S-counter. Curly Top Captain grabs the wheel of the good ship Sunriser as it flounders. (Greg would later swear to John that he could hear the stomach noises in the full house.) Hands up, emergency stop. "Folks. Soon enough, people. Let's be patient." The hands motion to the film crew. Hands wave down, down to demand quiet. A soft voice speaks to rapt attention. "Folks. The movie is rolling."

Hands shimmy up from shimmy slipper steps as Greg follows the camera trolley. The film crew has maximum height on their mini wheeled platform in order to get a bird's-eye view, stool by stool, plate to plate. Director Scottie covers eye-level reactions with his hand-held HD smartphone. Greg backs up on the action.

"Let's get the most perfect cheesy shots. Right, Scottie?"

Scottie and the film crew are beaming at the frame, live on their digital screens. "This is great stuff, guys."

And voilà, it gets better.

Aldert places the first act of dressed-up plated appetizers on a bare counter. The cameras catch all.

The camera platform trolley rolls parallel to the parade of delicious treats. The crowd is delirious in their joy to Say Cheese. Greg tags along behind the film crew, a natural as he pulls one out of the hat. He plays the full house with an ace, Elvis:

"Thank you, thank you, thank you very much. *Thank you*, everyone."

Greg motions to applaud. A very short clap in confusion. Food, but when? Greg pirouettes over to Aldert; the audience is lost, trying to decipher an unfamiliar character role. Oh, it's Elvis again, maybe, applauding because it's time to eat? Greg fulfills the room-wide consensus.

"You may eat."

The crowd hoovers the toasties down the hatch. Some witnesses would say the cast *snorted* the crispy soft delights. Cameraman Dave pulls back from the view screen to Scottie.

"Mercy me, looks like a scene out of *Scarface*."

Scottie's quick to disagree, injecting his movie pick on drugs overdone. "No, *Rush*."

The Producer is back with his choice. "No, that movie on Sid Vicious."

Aldert and Barbara beam from the kitchen pass-through. Braedon finds the reverse perspective so odd. From the back bench, he notes a few possible improvements: a cleaner entrance, better accessibility, and especially fixing those walls with the cockeyed frames.

"Dear," his wife says. "You need to level them. Then screw them to the wall." (Braedon has a dirty flashback to a time, after hours at the diner, when he and his wife were first dating.)

Opposite side in the kitchen, the little remains on dishes are swept away by the Server Sisters.

Et voilà. Greg nudges Scottie to get a turnaround on the camera trolley. Aldert has returned with course number two. The melted spreadable cheese in phyllo pastry with Barbara's cranberry-blueberry compote, topped with a squirt of chocolate ganache, stuns the room. Greg puts the brakes on. Hands up.

"Folks. Folks, *wait*. Wait *please*. You know the drill." His hands wave up and about in no apparent pattern, with the crowd nodding their noggins in chorus to Miss Direction. "People. People. Wait until Scottie gets his shots."

The camera trolley moves back and forth, avoiding the lip-drool reflections on expectant jaws. Hungry shots up and down the S-counter. The crowd want the word. Their hands are out front, pushing back the imaginary roadblock. "Okay," Greg gives the final word. "Enjoy." Gates open and gone. In ten seconds all the little delights are sucked out of existence. Aldert and Barbara wink at each other in the kitchen.

And then the cavalry arrive.

Jimmy and his student helpers walk in with the complete billy package, carved and on focaccia, the famous Billy on the Bun. Mason's hours-fresh focaccia has been prepped with Barbara's homemade mayo and butter. Condiments are abundant on the counter.

The character cast asks.

"The two squeeze bottles have no labels?"

"Barbara's secret sauces."

And the BBQ in-the-know.

"Secret? On her Facebook page."

And the unwashed newbie to the experience:

"But which one should I have?"

"Both. Cut the bun in half. Apply one to each half."

And the ready-freddie to shove anything in his gob.

"Where's the salt and pepper?"

The clear path from the beginning has always been barbecue. The crowd would be thin and impatient on goat apps, no matter how creative. Barbecue brings in the numbers, and the numbers are insatiable. Billy on the Bun is lined up on the counter as the crowd waits. Sauce strategy has been discussed and chosen. The crowd waits on alert. Greg prepares to fire the starting pistol.

"Folks," he says, "folks … *Enjoy* the barbecue …"

Folks put thumbs down to the bottom of their plates to grip the buns. Greg shouts with thumbs up above the fracas and froth.

"… Condiments as you please. Scottie and crew, please join us. Just eat. No more filming."

The City crew is frozen in the stage lights of a big job well done. They look back. Greg offers up.

"Eat. Please, eat."

In sixty seconds the first set of sandwiches is completely devoured. Greg seizes the moment while the group toothpick the bits from their teeth. (Greg would not allow toothpicks on camera. *That won't look good. Bunch of locals chewing and picking away. Might as well give them a bunch of focking banjos …*")

The room's a tooth-picking jamboree. Greg wonders at the country and western performance in the room. Braedon saddles up beside him. "Barbecue," he tells Greg. "When there's barbecue, everyone's a camp-out Boy Scout."

The leftover-miners drop their splintered wood picks on the plate. They lick, rub, lick and rub their tongues against their teeth with half-open mouths. Satisfaction all round looks up to the Producer, who has hands up, palms facing the kitchen.

"Another great barbecue, Jimmy Kember. Let's hear it for Jimmy."

The word *barbecue* in any sentence brings a room to attention. Hands rise up in appreciation, stained with barbecued billy with not-so secret sauce and homemade mayo. Through the swing doors with a full tray, Jimmy comes out to a sloppy-palms clap.

Serge and the graduate students are already busy readying the last remains for an extra helping of barbecue. Mason left more than enough fresh bread. Jimmy picked the right enough goat.

Jimmy leans in to Aldert. "Number 63. Kept him too long. Balls dropped. *Bang, bang,* he turned into a rutting machine."

Aldert steps in for team recognition. "Yes, Cassius."

"That's a Roman Senator," Jimmy the academic notes. "Should have tagged him from the start, Jimmy. Cassius is a natural at roaming, and no diplomatic senator; maybe a centaur."

Aldert is in sync with his roommate Serge that names do speak. Shepherd and BBQ Professor speak to the standing subjects of young billy. Jimmy has the histrionics. "Hector the son skipped the cut. That does speak to a Greek hero." Jimmy is histrionic. Aldert describes the naming process as genetic, son comes from father, a clone apple falling from the tree.

"Hector came from a-roaming. When your father comes from roaming, son will be roaming too."

He peter-points two fingers in a forty-five-degree angle toward an invisible goat. *Bang. Bang.* Aldert touches two smoking fingers to his lips, with a post-barbecue choice tip. "Cassius could have been a breeder."

Jimmy tips his hand for the barbecue. "A real top leader on the spit and secret sauce."

Aldert studied Shakespeare in high school English. "Sounds more like Julius Caesar and Anthony."

Jimmy switches from a nod to a head shake. "We'll see about two leaders on site. Hector, stage-front paddock far right. Beside him is Napoleon. Napoleon can still rise up for the occasion. The General could mount two, three hundred ladies."

The Shepherd credits the number-one stud with his 24/7 abilities.

"And what will we do for him the next week?"

"And the weeks after."

Both laugh at the efficiency of their lead stud.

Back on the 6th Concession, Queenie agrees by royal decrees.

"*Na-a-a-ah. Na-a-a-ah nee-e-e-ed for three, no-o-or-rr two. The General commands my-y-y-y ladies once a ye-e-e-ar. Na-a-a-ah to fee-e-e-e-ar. Ca-a-a-s-sius was mi-i-i-iy de-e-e-ar. Hector sta-a-a-ays here.*"

Napoleon, sequestered over in the hawthorn-lined paddock, feels the lament of the Queen.

"*Na-a-a-ah. Ca-a-a-s-sius nee-e-e-e-ded more time with Da-a-a-ad.*"

Mary Beth back from school and Serge in from farm chores are both back in the kitchen, helping Barbara fill the small plates for another delicious round.

Beside themselves, Jacqui and Jayne roll their eyes at the level of dishwashing to be done. They acknowledge the most important job in a restaurant, the Dish Pig.

"Damn. Lefty heads home at eight. Look at the dishes."

"Five courses, Jacqui. No plastic."

"Jimmy does not do plastic."

"Right," Jayne frowns. "We'll see where Jimmy is when the dishes need doing."

Aldert and Jimmy deal out seconds of Billy on the Bun. Barbara tops up the secret sauce bottles with no labels. Mary Beth steadies the aim by holding the bottle. Serge leans in between the two.

"We love the red sauce," the *fromager* interjects. "What do you call it?"

"My Focking Secret Red."

"And the other?"

"I call it, The Focking White."

"Barbara, I can catch a bouquet of … tequila?"

Jimenez passes by. *"Andele, muchachos."*

Hunger has dissipated, the ravenous group anxiety changing to a what-could-be-next euphoria. The last buns standing, still so fresh, so stuffed with goodness, disappear, but in five minutes that seem like hours, compared to the second count-off in the first round.

The last traces of barbecue on the plates get finger-wiped clean. Jacqui and Jayne marvel at the shiny plates, which lifts their sinking thoughts on the dirty dishes. Serge gets out front to win the S-counter and booths. Mary Beth clears the condiments. Barbara wipes the grit, grease and grime covering the squeeze bottles. The high school teacher speaks out for clean hands.

"Aren't adults smart enough to bring focking hand wipes to a barbecue?"

Jacquie adds, "Barbara, finger-licking clean."

"Maybe they have pussy-cat tongues, but their fingers! They're dirty dog paws, looking at these gummed-up bottles."

Aldert is now the busiest, back in the kitchen. He has the counter space to bring out the eight dozen red ceramic pots. Braedon arranged the compote-sized bowls as a rental favour from his restaurant supplier.

"They use them for French onion soup," he told Aldert.

"Any onion smell?"

"These people sterilize their stuff."

Serge lines the compotes up row on row, pointing in the direction of the big man with the butane torch in hand at the counter end. The barbecue-converted City film crew are back out front on their trolley, ready to roll and reel in the filming. Producer Greg has the crowd trained to obey like they're Flippy the Seal. It's showtime again.

Best of show.

The Director has the lights down. The big spots are off. Barbara has sent the Server Sisters out with candles. Jimmy subs in on the torch, under Aldert's direction, to touch up the lavender-honey crust. On top of the aromatic burnt sugar, the miracle lad plates his famous goat-milk crème brûlées with a dollop of goat whipped cream. Serge has a long-handled spoon with a small bucket for the huckleberry jam.

Barbara watches over the end-zone lineup of ramekins. "Serge, *une demi-cuil-lère. A tad works.*"

Barbara drops a sprig of her garden-fresh mint on each creamy top. Topping all the goodness and greatness in their cups is the expectation up front. Over the last two years, Aldert's name in desserts has soared. Jimmy auctioned off twelve crème brûlées at the Annual Volunteer Firefighter Barbecue for 250 bucks, first time. He could have auctioned off dozens the next year for double the price. Word got out. The anticipation tonight is palpable.

Scottie and crew catch it all live on film. The platform trolley rolls above the hungry faces down at the counter. Scottie's up close with the hand-held camera. Everyone present will agree that their bellies are full of billy, satiated, ready for no more. But something's in the air tonight. More than the expanding reputation of a treat — it's the aroma.

"It's the lavender honey. Has a bouquet. Heat makes the smell blossom."

"Yeah, lavender-honey crust, but it's triple decker."

"Triple decker?"

"One deck of lavender-honey crust, one deck of whipped cream, topped with huckleberry jam."

The trays of brilliant red bowls flow out from the swing doors. In their cups, each one is a little white head with a jam haircut. This is mirrored by the customer heads with their assortment of bad hair clips, licking their lips. The City crew nod along in film pleasure.

"We're in."

Yes, they're in, in the flow. Alas, not Greg the Producer.

"Folks. Whoa. Stop."

Greg pulls at the trolley crew, motions to Scottie. All the hands across the counter and back benches have picked up the tiny spoons set before them on the Buckatoo napkins.

The chorus sings. *"Yes."*

The Producer hesitates. "No, *no* folks. Please, put the spoons down."

Spoons are still in the air.

"Naughty naughty, folks. No spooning. Remember what Momma says." He wags his finger. "Never pick up till Momma picks up."

Greg turns to the swing doorway, pointing to Barbara. Barbara points back in a rare public moment. "Momma says, Greg's focking right on."

Serge is behind the mantra. *"Maman."*

All spoons return to the Arborite. The hands are still over the spoons.

"No, no, no, folks. Spoons on the napkin."

That's the motion for the commotion over misplacing spoons. Greg acts all aloha-like, waving, reeling in the complete attention of stools and benches. "First things first. We know the drill."

A lack of beer, wine or alcohol does clear the memory for a course-by-course review. Complete attention is on course to the Producer. Greg's fingers are framed over his right eye. He pans the ceramic bench lineup, switching to a macro gesture toward one standalone ramekin. "We need to shoot the set first. Food untouched."

Ring, ring for the film crew. Ding, ding the trolley comes through. Hands up, Greg follows with a room-gathering shriek.

"Please! Please. Wait."

Greg turns with a desperate look.

"Are we ready, Scottie?"

The Director gives a thumbs up with his camera-free hand.

Greg whimpers in relief, holding up two thumbs in response. "Good to go."

Tap. Tap. Crack, Crack.

The little spoons tap at the crusty, lavender-honey topping for a break-through.

Crunch. Crunch.

Add a little of the goat whipped cream. That jam. The crunchy delights.

Slurp. Crunch. Crunch. Slurp.

The surface is cleaned off.

Click. Click. Click. Click. Click.

The little spoons move deeper into the pudding part, ricocheting off the ramekin sides.

A chorus of clicks follows the reverse S-counter and the back booths. Clicking can be heard by the unseen standing-room kitchen gang.

The clicks have scooped the pots clean and now ascend to the rims. On the edge, the clicks beat to a uniform demand. The clicks rise up to a demand for the artist himself.

Aldert appears from the kitchen. Spoons down, hands up, for a solid round of appreciation. Everyone loves our miracle boy. Aldert *is* the pride of Transvaal, Nissouri, St. Marys, the gore of Downie, the surrounding areas, and Mary Beth. The crowd goes all spontaneous, from spoon to mouth. Some sort of primordial chant takes over the room. A call from the rural roots right out of the soul.

"*Oo-o-o-oh. Aa-a-ah. Aa-a-all-dert.*" *Click. Click. Click.* "*Oo-o-o-oh. Aa-a-a-ah. Aa-a-all-dert.*" *Click. Click.* "*Sis. Boom. Bah-h-h.*" *Click. Click.* "*Oo-o-o-o-oh. Aa-a-a-ah.*"

Aldert holds a low bow in appreciation.

The room goes quiet in a dream come true. A group-wide smile of satisfaction settles any memory of hungry anxiety, or that bossy Producer, or my God the stains on your new shirt. Stomachs are bloated full with tasty but unknown goat treats. The diner's silence can't hide the snare beat of tummies that rumble away in a different direction now, pushing through the unimaginable process of digestion.

That's when it happens.

That comfy feeling of after-dinner satiation slips off the tracks to a surprise knock, more a sharp rap that shakes the glass entrance door.

Bang. Bang. Bang.

Surprise! Knock knock, there's someone calling at the grease-free polished door. All that after-dinner glow ceases to flow as local minds turn to the uninvited door banging. Huh? What's that? This is out of character for a food film shoot, even taking into account the mixed herd of amateur actors, local regulars and car nuts. *Bang. Bang. Bang.*

Not a creature stirs. *Bang. Bang. Bang.*

The room gathers together in thought. "What the focking hell is that?" The mood switches in milliseconds to calculation, the what-ifs and why-nots of a night out, the various potential emergencies. The herd runs down the possibilities, but there are no sirens crying, no cellphones ringing or front pockets vibrating. None of that "How the heck did the babysitter contact us?" or "Why's the funeral home on my call display?" Nothing but a mystery to the inside herd on the outside knock in the darkness. Knock, knock, who's there, where's this going, what's happening?

A lightning storm of anxiety rumbles about, with the car nuts among the first to imagine the worst. "The cars!"

This sucks a big chunk of oxygen out of the room, limiting a big crowd to a little whisper. "The cars! Someone's stealing cars."

With two windy words from the Black Aces booth, Norman ignores the panic from the car club participants. "It's Helen." He's convinced that Honey's mother has kicked the bucket at the old folks' home.

Braedon wonders with two words if their teenager has been up to no good. "Car keys?" He pats his pocket. "Where are my focking keys to the car?"

Bang. Bang. Bang.

The room is papered blind, night blind. The Producer picks up the crowd's nervous vibe, so he takes charge. No one hears his whimper up to action.

"Someone should get the door."

The whole room is at attention, loaded up with alarm, looking at him, the Producer. Greg's hands are up, waving toward the entrance. No help from Braedon from his corner.

"Well then," Greg says to himself. "Well then, someone has to."

Bang. Bang. Bang.

It's a tentative tippy-toe stumble to the door. A *voilà* moment for the Producer. Greg pulls open the door, talking as he walks backwards toward the cash.

"Okay, okay, okay. What's the emergency."

The door pulls in two sturdy, tow-headed lads. They stumble in, pulled by enough off-balance power to reach the cash register, where they come to rest beside Greg.

Greg gets a focus on the pair face to face. "My God. Ronnie and Donnie."

Ronnie and Donnie are absorbed with each other in a big laugh-fest. They face the large crowd who are all dressed up. It's wall-to-wall eyes coming back at them.

"Actors," Ronnie says.

Donnie nods. "Actors."

A happy-chappie nod to Scottie and the City crew clinging to the trolley at the bottom of the first twist in the S-counter. Ronnie points out the obvious. "The film guys. From the City, eh?"

Donnie points at Greg. "The Director."

Greg picks up on the point, pointing at his own chest with a head shake. "Me. The Producer." The finger point moves out to Scottie. "Him. The Director."

Scottie is wearing his best fish mouth in surprise stupor. He is trying to figure out this pair who are missing from the script. Dim-wit hands grab and shake for confirmation.

"The Director."

The room is still amid the sound of rolling peas.

Dim-wit eyes have adjusted to the lower light and candles. Donnie gives Ronnie an elbow nudge with exaggerated eyebrow lifts. "Kinda sexy, don't ya think?" His blond unibrow hedge can be seen from the very back booths.

You could hear Donnie's pea rotate around his empty skull in agreement. The interlopers nod. The rest of the locals in the room — regulars, characters, car collectors, kitchen detail and amateur actors — shake their heads in confusion.

Both clowns just ignore the Producer behind them. Ronnie, the leading dummy, begins calling out. "You-who! You-who!"

Donnie echoes. "You-who! You-who!"

The crowd cringe in all directions. The Producer is in shock but can manage two more words. "Hello? Hello."

The lead dummy does an amplifier pick-up to the corners. "Hello! Hello."

"Big night," Ronnie says. The dim light cannot hide the crouching shadow beside Braedon. "Oh, is that you, Mr. Mayor?"

Cheeko whispers to his bench. "What can I say? What can I do?"

Ronnie advances, pointing into the dim light at the back of the diner. "Hello, hello. Who do we have back there?"

Stools, booths, kitchen, and even the film crew cringe with one question. *Is the idiot pointing at me?*

Yes, Norman, he is.

"Hello, hello. Is that you, Mr. Morrison?"

Stormin' looks away with a hand tip to the room. *"Aargh. Aargh. Aargh."* And then he throws out his assessment. "Braedon. Throw the idiots out."

Ronnie is quick to shine the headlights on Norman's bench mate. "Hello, hello. Chef Braedon." Ronnie has hands up and out, praising the flock of Citizens. "*Whole* darn Town's here. Right here at the old Sunriser."

Donnie tugs on the arm of Ronnie's snap-button shirt. "You didn't tell me, Ronnie."

"Tell you what?"

Both look around the packed room then back at each other. Donnie hesitates. "You didn't tell."

Donnie pauses for another look around. Ronnie watches his lips try to form bigger words, bigger ideas that Donnie has difficulty getting out.

"That … we would … that would be doing *it*, doing *it* in front of a bunch of people. Ronnie, they're people that *we know*!"

Ronnie keeps an eye back on the audience reception. "It is called an audience, Donnie. An *aw-de-ants*. We will need to perform in front of *aw-de-ants*. We talked about that, dummy."

Donnie despises that familiar tag, dummy. A dummy stands in front of a full house of known characters. He tries to score points by picking a known winner. "Look, Mary Beth Johnson is in it."

The whole room turns to the beet-faced girl in the swing door.

"Maybe she's the lead?" Ronnie suggests.

Two peas shake with satisfaction.

"*Wow.*"

Donnie and Ronnie do not fail to notice the largest actor in the room, beside Mary Beth in the swing doors. "There's Aldert," Ronnie says. "Maybe they're in it together."

"*Wow.*"

"Maybe we both get a chance milking those huge teats."

Both laugh in an oblivion to the full house of ears.

The room in the after-taste of post crème brûlées, they sit in shock.

Braedon steps up from the bench, directing attention to the frontal assault. He has ownership of the floor. "What do you *idiots* want?"

"We want to oo-dition," Ronnie says.

Braedon is incredulous. "*Audition?* What oo-dition?"

The peas go positive in a dumb chorus. "The oo-dition for the por-no movie."

The perfect storm? A shit fit? A toxic mix?

Or in military terms, it's called collateral damage.

In the room tonight it might be called collateral taint. A nice word it ain't. A super local no-no.

Porno.

"*T'aint me. Wasn't there.*"

"*Ain't catching me with no smut.*"

"*What's your son reading, then?*"

"My son does not look at that."

"Well, he steals porno mags from Dick's Variety."

Every man in the room has seen it, but not one will admit it. Now two dummies have them roped into a stupidity rodeo.

"Kinda of hot in here," Ronnie says. "Think I'll take my shirt off."

"Good idea, Ronnie."

Ronnie shows a little humour as he senses the uneasiness of the audience. "No point taking my pants off — ain't wearing no undies."

The bare-ass humour is lost in translation. Panic ensues.

Walk away. No, run. The more distance the better. Run away with no confession or discussion.

The room gets cleared out quicker than the crème brûlée ramekins. The floodgates open to the side patio, down the washroom hallway to the emergency exit, or along a runway to the exit back of the kitchen, leaving the dish crew hard at it. Normie's booth storms out to the patio. Half the car owners follow; the rest take the closest path left or right. Most stoolies go down the washroom hallway, a few through the swing doors, a few duck out the entrance. The amateur actors in full dress half-hurry home with not-so-secret sauce stains, button loss from too much billy, smudged make-up, and worse — the shame of not making it to the end credits of the film shoot. The regular coffee bunch grind along not far behind, headless with no in-the-know member leadership. Classics do a hard retreat, rubber-marking their goodbyes to a saluting X-Man. The waft of exhausted cars with tailpipes smoking leave behind a Jackson Pollock of oil drips.

Back inside the diner, the odds and sods, the curious and too-slow-to-move remain with the Say Cheese team and Sunriser staff. The City crew cling to the platform trolley. (Their long drive back will be warmed by cold billy sandwiches packed by Barbara. *"No focking focaccia left, so excuse the white bread, boys."*)

The shoot has suddenly reached the end credits.

Ronnie and Donnie pass the empty stools, the vacant benches where fools dare not sit or stand. The service team has disappeared for a last stand at cleaning up in the kitchen. The counters are bare and clean except for one plate with two sandwiches by the kitchen swing doors. With few witnesses, the twins saddle up to this very back tail-tip of the S-counter. One witness watches sideways through the kitchen pass-through window.

"They're eating the focking sandwiches I left for Turf."

Too late for rescue. The white bread fanatics smother their faces with the last mayo-slathered barbecue billy. They hoover, slobber and drip through the billy.

Empty heads with mouths full look up at the frozen film crew. "Hey buddies, gotta biz card? Contact."

In slow motion, Scottie hands over a card.

Ronnie makes the ask. "You guys do porno movies in the City, right?"

Chapter 17

As the weather gets cooler down on the 6th Concession farm, Greg and John enjoy the Great Lake view on clear days with a morning walk around the farm yard. Today the partners are comfy on the reconnoitre in the cool morning with their custom black sheepskin waist-length coats. Goat radar tells Queenie and the ladies that it's not fake fur.

"Na-a-a-ah. Na-a-a-ah. Ours, ladies. Na-a-a-ah."

Max joins the tour of fall changes every day. After the two of the three savour the flavour of John's wonderful cappuccino, Max watches his happy masters. Happy masters, happy Max. This morning, Greg's marketing work has added value to the cappuccinos, which were enjoyed in sample promotional travel mugs.

"Thermal," Greg says. "Made in Canada too."

John nods in appreciation.

"I like the logo. Not just the cups," Greg goes on. "Which are sample, no cost, John. There's also T-shirts, hoodies, ball caps, gift cards, cheese knives, coasters, pens … all on the website."

"Don't forget souvenir spoons and letter openers," John adds.

"Who collects those? Who gets snail mail?"

Greg realizes John is kidding and then jumps into marketing defense.

"Vicki did the logo in felt, started as a one-off but I liked it. Fuzzy Queenie on the cover of our labels."

"Nice," John admits. "Gives a three-dimensional jump in full colour."

"Yeah, cute, right? She can felt up the whole team. Aldert and Serge with Queenie, Napoleon in the background. Then the Kembers in American Gothic pose."

"Why not Greg and John, the poseurs?"

"Don't scare the natives with that," Greg says. "Our felt art is not just a goat head — she's got everything in the picture. Vicki felted the farm house and the barn." He pinches his fingers into an itsy-bitsy. "Noah's mini-ark in barn and paddocks." A backhand point to the collies resting off the front porch. "And them. Our ladies all felted in mini glory. *And,* it's so local-yokel."

John sips his Capp of cheer. "A-a-ah-h-h. The smell of goat shit in the morning."

Greg sees the change of subject as a chance to get away from marketing, marketing and more marketing. "Don't forget the contribution of Frankie and the Wild Bunch to the aroma."

"More like the Mild Bunch," John says, "with that fill of goat whey. Actually, the Wild Bunch are in the freezer now. Bacon for breakfast." A whole bunch of porky volunteers were recently offed to the organic locavore cause.

Greg adds up a cautionary note. "Frankie makes good copy, though. Right behind Queenie and her court."

John audits pork futures and storage. "Two years of breakfasts. My God, the Kembers have big freezers."

John pauses on the thought of thick bacon breakfasts, while Greg can't imagine the farm social media without Frankie. Greg sees the chance to get off the bacon. "Every time I think about those porno lads at the Sunriser," Greg says. "So cheesy."

"Cheesy porno," John laughs. "The dim-wits did scare the natives, terrify the imports and mystify the city crew." He goes falsetto. *"You-who! You-who!"*

"The whole room were focking silent, looking at their feet."

"Except Scottie. He looked like a drowning carp. Our award-winning director thought he'd missed something in the script."

The night seems so much bigger in the replay.

"Ronnie and Donnie should have to wear those yellow X vests. Then everyone would see them coming." Greg holds a Stop hand out. *"Watch out for the dummies. Dummy crossing."*

Both laugh, unable to stop thinking about the P-incident at The Sunriser, and then they say in unison:

"Oo-dition."

John audits the degree of a potential disaster. "We dodged the bullet, the way people shot out of there."

Greg calls it. "That was a real cattle stampede."

It's been a few days now since the Sunriser shoot that devolved into a complete cattle run. The daze of the chaotic incident is now resolving into clarity.

"We got hundreds, hundreds of thousands of hits," Greg says. "Hundreds of thousands. Just from those videos. On YouTube, Instagram, all social media and our website. Scottie did great."

"Scottie beamed up hundreds of thousands of hits."

Greg catches his partner with a John-style euphemism and a cock-eyed look. "Sometimes it's not the path but the journey."

Ignoring the wisdom from the fool on the hill, the Accountant takes over and moves on. "The Sunriser will never be the same for so many eyes."

"Teach them to make cheese for their billy, not eat the BBQ billy that feeds them."

John is lost in partner translation. "Secondsies on the Capp?"

"S'il vous plaît."

While John goes back to the house to make two more John Capps, Greg will catch up with Frankie behind the barn.

This will be a cartoon-coloured photo of one old, fat pig with snoot down, hunting for cobs of corn in his whey. The Producer snaps away on the smartphone camera in pano, taking both still shots and short videos.

"Lots of hits for this."

Frankie does not concur.

"Oink. Oin-oin-oinking silage. Oink. Oink. Too crunchy. Pig food. Frankie wants Master foods. Sweet corn next time. Plee-e-e-e-e-sies. Plee-e-e-e-e-sies."

Frankie blinks his milky pink eyes from the trough. Greg can feel his pangs. "Still remember the curds, eh, Frankie?"

Frankie, for the first time in his porky life, lifts his snoot in acknowledgement to Master. Greg returns the look.

"Frankie hankie wankie, size of a tankie. Frankie. Frankie." Greg's no Citiot on pigs. Do not touch except through a lens for a touching photo.

"Oink. Oin-oin-oinking come in here, Master. Oink. Oink. Master tastes yummy in Frankie tummy. Oink. Oin-oin-oinking come in here."

Those pink eyes go patio-light fluorescent.

Whoa. Greg has never seen Frankie look at him like *that*. "What's going on in that big head, tubby buddy?"

Frankie knows the established morning pass-by routine. Greg takes pictures and video while he waits for John to return with the next round of capps. The pig waits too.

"Master holds one hoof bottom to his eating hole. The other hoof looks tasty. Oin-oin-oinking Master doing his two-hoof-up talky talky."

Greg squeezes his nose with both index fingers. The tips form a teepee-like crown over the nose. The trick? Do not blow. Suck. Suck the air back into the back of your throat. Suck it tight with a herky-jerky rhythm. Master is off to market. *"Snort. Snort. Snort. U-oink. U-o-o-i-i-i-i-ink. U-o-o-i-i-i-i-ink."*

Frankie licks from one side end of his snoot, a conveyor-belt tongue that slathers from one end then lathers up the other side. The snoot is steady while those fluorescent pink eyes dart in a shift back and forth, waiting for Master to come closer, closer. Frankie has always had the smell of tasty human filed as an unknown; he sees gamey hands dumping the whey, sees something that he has a taste for, a human bite. Frankie gives a goofy half smile at Master's practice in pig, creating an attraction between the two.

"Oink. Oink. Master, speak more Pig Latin to me." He gives Greg some dirty barnyard snort-back.

The pig is clear on the next step when Greg drops his hands to his sides. One hand disappears into his jacket to pull out some green apples. The treat loosens the usual boundaries. At that moment Frankie allows Greg to flop his ears, finishing with double tugs.

Frankie smiles. Greg has gone goofy with the pig. Arriving at the pen, John would clap if he wasn't holding the thirdsies two coffees. "The pig *is* smiling. *Look*, Greg. It's smiling."

Greg has pulled back for an in-and-out video of Frankie's goofy gob. "Yes. Yes, I got it."

Yes, Greg has shot the perfect video. "Lots of hits for Frankie piggy wiggy. Our audience would *miss* you, tankie wankie."

Greg has an evil eye for his partner. Frankie has a pink eye for the Master but green apples rotating in his mouth. The other Master audits.

"Greg, we don't grow corn. We pasture goats."

Greg looks so sad. John audits on. "Buddy, the teat has dried up for old fatso here. Time to move on."

Frankie ignores the pair. He has his green apples. Greg has the last words for his partner. He holds his hands in prayer. "He's *our* Frankie."

Frankie chews on. The four-legged barnyard sweeper licks clean any green remnants. *"U-oii-i-i-i-inking apples. U-yum. U-yum. U-yum."*

The Masters walk on about their farm routine.

"We get a lot of mud for October," John says.

The partners have picked up on the peculiarity of rural weather. "Yup. Three seasons of mud. One season of dust."

"Nope. Two of dust, two of mud."

Their routine path leads past the front left paddock for a General heads-up, over to find Ozzy and Faisal in the barn and Serge in the milk shed. Jimmy does short shifts after his coffee at the Sunriser. Barbara is on demand for whatever arises.

The partners turn back from the barn and amble toward the house. "You know, Greg, now that it's past Thanksgiving, maybe it's time to start planning for our Christmas three-in-one open house."

"A Christmas Open House goes debutante? In wedding dresses?"

John smiles at his partner. Here comes The Producer — flood lights switched on, all well-staged too.

"All sorts of choices," Greg says. "Vintage stuff. Couture, *prêt-à-porter*, off the rack. *O-o-o-or* from Harley's Second-Hand."

Billie pointed out the find, a second-hand store supreme, right out of the gate. Out of closet and for sale in downtown St. Marys.

"Greg. It's our first Christmas Open House in Transvaal, it has to be a dressed-up occasion, no?"

"It'll be a real ball, John." He pauses. "What about scaring the natives?"

John covers the local strategy. "Christmas Open House goes formal dress, black tie if you choose. Cheeko, Braedon, Aldert, Normy, Jimmy can have tuxes, if they choose."

"*O-o-o-or* maybe out of the closet for guys in dresses. Okay either way. No dress code other than formal Christmas."

　　　　　　　　　　　　　　　　　　　　　　　　　　　　　

"I do like your little pillbox thing," John admits.

No stopping Greg. "It's wedding-dress time, buddy. Get into the fun runway. We'll worry about the natives after. Who'll be on our invitation list?"

It's a duet doh-see-doh with Max as their plus-one. All witnessed by Napoleon on the left, Queenie on the right, with the herd behind.

"We need embossed invitations," John says. "RSVP."

"Two colours to accent the theme. And a Christmas-themed appetizer menu centred on the billy … the goat, I mean, not Billie Ball."

John interrupts with the bottom line. "Aldert needs to know numbers. Let's not wear him out."

Greg goes on. "Rented flatware, plates and three kinds of glasses — white and white carnations will be glorious — tall candles, the scent of mulled cider, my photos with Santa …"

He stops. "Whoops. Let's get a professional photographer for some cruise ship grip-and-greet photos. You know, welcome aboard." Back up with the finger frame, *snap, snap, snap.* "Guests enter by the photo backdrop, which is set up in front of the staircase."

"Call Pablo and Juanita," John says. "Billie's friends from Theatre Town."

Greg agrees. "They do the web shots for the auction sales plus actor portfolios. They'll mix well."

John's always practical. "Christmas season is big here — we need to book them now. Even faster than confirming Jimmy on the goat barbecue, buddy."

The dream of Wedding Girl needs three essential ingredients for success: a record with the photo flash, billy basting on the barbecue with a splash of not-so-secret sauce, and mouths full of crème brûlées.

Greg reviews the goat order. "Two or three for the team, eh Queenie?"

Royal eyes are on him. *"Na-a-a-ah. Ma-a-a-aster. Na-a-a-ah."*

Napoleon concurs, from the other paddock. *"Na-a-a-ah. One for the tee-ea-ea-m is eee-e-e-e-nough. Na-a-a-ah mor-r-re."*

John does a bit of a double-take as Curly Top gives the Queen a royal ear-flop. Are Queenie and Greg *talking*?

John brings Greg back into the human fold. "Greg."

Greg turns away from Queenie.

"Greg. Green light. Do it, buddy."

Greg beams. John focuses. "I'll cover it all in an Excel budget spreadsheet. You clear, buddy? Green light, but yellow light on the budget."

"Focking clear, partner."

(After four weeks the mispronunciation of Barbara's f-bomb has already gone viral, synced into John and Greg's rural language.)

A few hours later they're finalizing the invitation copy in John's office.

"Make sure you state Saturday with the date," John says. "We do *not* want people driving up the laneway Friday night."

Greg has the half-dumb look. John replies to it.

"People always screw up their dates. They never screw up their *days*."

Greg continues the look. John replies to himself in a questioning voice. "The 14th?" He answers himself. "Is that a Saturday?"

John's second voice answers the first. "Yes, Saturday the 14th."

John switches into an Archie Bunker whine for his perspective on dates. "Sorry meathead, that's bowling night."

Greg is almost caught on bowling night. John keeps his eye on Greg.

"People know their nights by what they do. Saturday night is bowling night."

Greg pipes up, knowing better. "I do *not* bowl."

"It's only a focking example, Greg. No more than three type sizes. Make sure it's one font only. Upper lower case too. People cannot read caps. All has to be classy, classy, classy."

Greg impresses again by making notes. "Embossed, yes?"

"If Trout Creek Printing offers that."

"And nice paper. Parchment style?"

Greg writes "parchment paper" with a question mark on his list. Greg puts his Citiot hat on. "Will they understand RSVP?"

His Citiot partner is more than surprised. "Of course! Think about it. They do have weddings, anniversaries, christenings and such here. It's not another planet."

"Buck and Doe Parties," Greg laughs.

"At the Moose Lodge, too. That's an alien concept."

"I thought it was some sort of goat club get-together at first."

"Beard-trimming courses for the ladies."

Serge is up with Aldert at dawn almost every day at work, notwithstanding the support cast of collies, Queenie and the ladies, and Napoleon in the right field. Faisal and Ozzy work every day except Fridays *("Praise Allah to our employers")*.

Cheese is dialled into the clock marked with dates in Sharpie. Serge can pump out varying sizes with choice of moulds from the Swiss manufacturer. The goat milk comes right from the teats, tubes leading to a heating tank. Here the temperature is maintained at ninety degrees Fahrenheit so the culture can be added. The flavour begins its journey.

The milk cultures quietly for sixty minutes, the time to convert lactose to lactic acid. This is the time for three to join up in the process of cheese.

"Elle travail, la culture. While we wait, Ozzy, you set up the cheese moulds. Faisal, double-check the spout. Clean, clean, clean. I'll line up the trays and drainage mats. Ozzy, make sure there's lots of clamps."

In an hour *le fromager* adds the rennet to coagulate the curd. After another ninety minutes, with a button press, the contents of the tank spill out the spout to fill the ready warm moulds.

One. Two. Three. Four. Next row. Four. Three. Two. One. Repeat. Repeat. Next tray.

The spout shifts like a soft ice-cream dispenser, layering each small pot with the pure curd. The first twelve bowls are filled. Faisal clamps a drainage mat to the top, moving the tray to a stainless steel table, a very special table with no top but a saddle system for four trays at a time. Once the trays are dropped in the slot, Faisal flips the tray in an easy motion. This takes any lifting pain out of a repeated drain. The process flips over many more times. The drain is slow, with soft turns, done with every possible bit of care — babied every three to four hours by the overnight sitter. Greg usually does one very late shift and the first in the dark morning.

Ozzy, back in the process, brings the next tray. Just two trays today. Greg will be happy. Frankie will be even happier with a rare full trough. The next morning the trays from the stainless table are moved back to the Swiss automatic equipment, this time on the opposite end of things. Here the firm curd moulds will march down the assembly line to a vacuum suck and wrap. All this motion is overdriven by the PSB custom sound system and smart televisions. The speakers and screens play the Argentinian Grand Prix, a live start to the F1 season. The sounds of the F1 Channel broadcast out over the teat parade and serenade the aging cheese in the cooler room.

"*Rrrr-r-r-r-rrr. Rum-rum-rum. Rrrr-r-r-r-rrr. Philippi takes the corner wide. Emerson is tight. Rrrr-r-r-r-rrr. Rrrr-r-r-r-rrr. Emerson passes Philippi.*"

F1 on, and on and on, piped in to age the cheese.

Barbara leaves the milk shed well enough alone. "Hate that focking engine noise. Over and over. Poor focking goats."

Each late afternoon the best of Grand Prix race replays are keyed up on the computer to accompany the automatic teat squeezing of the herd.

"Faisal," Serge calls out. "Faisal, off the screen. #67 needs off. #51, bring her on."

Faisal and Ozzy are mesmerized by F1, coming from a world of donkey-slow, shock-less taxis and stinky diesel buses. Quick learners.

"Sorry Serge, it's the first race of the season."

Serge always has some new English phraseology to show off. "It's a replay, Faisal. Knock yourself out later in the office."

Faisal is lost in translation shock. "Ozzy. He means that I shall flagellate myself in the office, later. Punishment for the F1 watching."

Ozzy is the heavy rock twin. "It is what it is, brother. Look to our work as Father would tell us. The work is what is before us."

The vacuum-packed pucks are stored row on chronological row, segregated by varietal.

"This will be our triple-cream Brie," Serge says as he works. "It calls for the name *Three on the Tree*. And I'm aging it for three months."

Faisal and Ozzy have seen the three-on-the-tree standard shift on the steering wheels of Aleppo market delivery trucks. On their break they search out vintage Ferraris on *classiccar.com*, relishing the beauty of the GTO model.

"The Saudi Princes like these cars in their collections."

"They're a Gulf State power and status indicator."

Serge moves on to the next row. "This will be a soft spreadable. We should have it in time for the Royal Winter Fair. It calls for the name *Testa Rossa*."

Serge is on vacuum wrap with the Sharpie today. "And four weeks on this other softy." Texture points, dates, percentages are coded on top in black ink. "We want an edible bloomy rind to develop. It calls for the name *Four on the Floor*."

"Number 34's production is dropping off," comes Jimmy's voice from the office, talking to himself. "There must be a parasite." He'll talk to Aldert in the morning.

Jimmy clocks the Sharpie notes and the rest of the goat cheese minutiae on the office desktop with Vivaldi on the speakers. Digital notes on who, when, how, fat percentage, individual volume and total production worked over in the Professor's software algorithms.

Every day after the walk-around, Greg's morning routine goes digital. John keeps it analog in coffee support. Greg uploads the videos and photos from his phone. He is able to edit them into vignettes of the farm life at Transvaal. When you click on the tabs at *saycheese.com*, up jumps a stable of choice.

"Look." He jabs a finger at the laptop screen. "Already fresh feeds for today. Feed, Frankie, feed."

John looks up from his work. "Great, Greg."

"Frankie hoovers." Hand down for mouse jabs at the tabs. "Let's get some Queenie action."

No doubt about the numbers: the website gets huge lookie-looks.

Greg spends hours on Napoleon's introduction to get the ultimate talking video. As always, he limits the shots to waist-up.

Napoleon seems to talk to the camera lens: *"Na-a-a-ah. Na-a-a-a-pol-l-leon. Na-a-a-ah."*

This perfect video joins a growing library on the website.

For General information, you need to move the mouse to the tab with the goat's head wearing an officious dustpan-shaped military hat. The General snaps to attention, leaning out from the icon. Press the Ta-a-ab above my head. Na-a-ah. Or the search bar.

The head repeats the come-hither to the viewer until action is taken.
Click. Click. Click.

The hits expand to Town and over to Mike's Auction Barn. These social media vignettes are quickly becoming the national equivalent of Aldert's crème brûlées; instead of limited-edition ramekins, though, it's a Super Bowl audience.

The Say Cheese website shows off a future that looks nice and creamy. The likes on the site come rolling in with a passionate eye.

"My kids love seeing Napoleon. The goat team is fun too."

"Queenie licked little Lolo's hand."

WHAT LUCK TO GET FRANKIE IN HIS GOOFY SMILE THIS MORNING reads one caption. HEADS UP TO SERGE.

(Mary Beth wants a copy of that one.)

"Frankie is so cute. Does he ever lift his head? How about a head shot."

"When are you selling the cheese?"

"Are you making feta?"

Aldert and Serge share this one: *"Are your goats organic?"*

The royal answer. *"Grass feed, yah-e-e-e-essss. Na-a-a-ah. Na-a-a-ah."*

THE COLLIES HERDING UP THE LADIES IN LATE AFTERNOON reads the caption on one of Greg's favourites. THE GLOW IN THE FLOW OF THE DAY.

"The sunset shots of the herd under the old oak tree. Wow." (Greg tells everyone that will listen, *"Here's* a super photograph." He doesn't mention all the time he spent tweaking the photo, upping the tint on the sky.)

Goats are organic but what about the product? *"Is your milk organic?"*

And for the royal answer, Queenie. *"Na-a-a-ah. Na-a-ah tru-u-ue, re-e-e-al de-e-e-al. All ho-o-o-ome team teats. Na-a-a-ah doubt."*

"Where will your cheeses be sold?"

Watch for announcement soon.

"Are you doing tours?"

Double-click Tours, click Information tab.

"Can we order the Shepherd's goat milk lavender-honey crème brûlées?"

No point explaining that, unless we open a restaurant, Greg figures.

"Will there be recipes on the website?"

Watch for announcement soon. Which means, John is reviewing proprietary rights and copyright small print, auditing on into the sunset.

"Can we come and pat the goats? Feed them green apples?"

"Can Napoleon come to my birthday party?"

"Na-a-a-ah. Na-a-a-ah, a-a-a ba-a-a-ad idea. Na-a-a-ah."

"Oh God, no," Greg says. "Not Napoleon. That would be like the daylight bombing of Hamburg."

Greg can't believe the number of questions. He tries to answer most sensible stuff with sensitivity. Greg won't answer the "single" questions:

"Is Aldert single?"

"Est-ce que Serge est célibataire?"

Mr. Social Media Marketing Guy answers on behalf of the whole animal farm. Aldert is on call but keeps to the herd. Serge is on call for cheesy questions and

Quebec ones, cheesy or not. *Le Petit* tells *le Grand* that he is embarrassed by stupid questions *en français. Pour les Anglais de la ferme*, he leaves them lost in translation. Some of the strangest of these come all the way from France.

In the stiffest Parisian French, the first one reads, *"Have you tasted this cheese from the goat named 'the General'? A bouquet of worn saddle and wet boots woven in with the spirit of Napoleon himself. A spirit that continues on through the standing herd."*

Greg asks Serge to translate. *Le fromager*'s having fun. "The writer, he thinks the cheese has leathery smell of an old goat with Napoleon having nothing better to do than sire an army."

"And this one?"

The second one is more confusing: *"Napoleon is the most important General in French history, in world history. Does your Napoleon plan to march his cheese out of the province?"*

"How can explain *en anglais*," Serge says. "The writer somehow uses history in the cheese mix to suggest our General would make a successful charge in Quebec."

John has to ask. "Charge? That's at the cash register, right?"

"No. The writer thinks it's some sort of inter-provincial trade attack. The charge of the cheese brigade over the border. Weird, eh?"

Better if the true meanings remain in their stated ignorance. Serge leaves the translation to a partner struggle, heads back to the milk shed.

"Papa, all the technology in the milk shed," he reports later. "It's a distraction from making cheese. Four sources of information. An ordinary computer in the officer, plus three more in the lab."

"*Petit*, four touch screens?"

"Three touch-screen terminals, one desktop with touch screen."

"Impressive. But distracting, *mon fils. Gardez votre knitting.*"

Serge knows the answer. "*Gardez le fromage. C'est le plus important.*"

John, though, is thankful this technology came with the purchase of the farm. He's impressed on the numbers side with website hits. He leaves the content to his marketer. Greg confesses to a few comment deletions. Most of the trash talk relates to the goat stud.

"Can we watch Napoleon mount the team?"

(*"Na-a-a-ah. Come o-o-o-o-over. Na-a-a-ah-thing bu-u-ut standing fence roo-o-o-om."*)

"My goodness, have you measured his tool when fully …?"

(*"Na-a-a-ah. Kee-e-e-eep your hands off. Na-a-a-ah for yo-o-o-u."*) Napoleon does a swing and swagger without even moving a hoof. Did the stud just wink?

"For the Does …" And the deleted question does go on.

Who are these idiots?

"Would you say Napoleon is more a teat man than an ass man? In General, that is?"

("Na-a-a-ah. Napo-o-o-le-o-on loves to get in be-hi-i-i-ind his team. Na-a-a-ah better mou-u-n-n-n-t.")

Greg leaves the stressful small stuff in a folder titled PROBLEMS.

Chapter 18

The boys, sandwiched on the den couch and lost in time, unwind on their Christmas '87 Sega with duelling hand-controls battling out some dim-wit electronic game.

Seven days have passed, an invisible week for the twins, who laid low as the unfortunate incident that's become known as The Night Cheesy Porno Came to Town wound its way from the coffee line, over neighbour fence lines and clotheslines, through the grocery line, and across ZIT lines for a canopy of coverage from Town to Country.

"We got our contacts in the City porno biz," Ronnie says. "We have real b-z-z-z-ness cards."

Donnie's not feeling so confident. "Lie low, brother. Folks need to run their gums off. Then they'll forget all about the whole thing. I told you not to go in. Windows papered and no open sign. Parking lot full … I told you, private. Problem. Braedon was so pissed. *That* nasty look and *not* a single word to us, pointing to the exit."

"We got b-z-z-z-ness cards."

"We got the exit card, too. Won't be able to go back there for quite a while."

"Lie low, brother. Braedon will get over it."

"Lie low with Turf lurking about? Just waiting to lay a beating on us?"

"Maybe one more week to return to the Sunriser, eh?"

"I told you."

"You told me what? Don't eat the monster's sandwiches? Those babies were waiting for us, all dressed up and pretty well no place to go but from the plate to our mouths. How were we supposed to know that they were waiting for Turf?"

"We loves white bread sandwiches, just like Momsie does them."

"Well, Turf sure doesn't like us."

Turf had watched in the horror of it, looking through the clean glass entrance to the plate at the corner counter where an ambush of his dinner was occurring. The lads could hear loud and clear as the flapping X tent headed towards them.

"You slobbering little pecker-heads. Eat my sandwiches, will you. I'm going to kick …"

The twins scurried off stage out of reach of the X-man linebacker, hiding behind the last standing vehicle, Jimmy's '53.

"Eat my sandwiches. I know where to find you two. You're going to be real sorry. I'm gonna eat your lunch …"

Now, the maternal voice of the eternal white-bread sandwich maker hits two hard beats as she calls in her boys. "Ronnie, Donnie …"

The boys, sandwiched on the den couch and lost in time, unwind on their Christmas '87 Sega with duelling hand controls, battling out some dim-wit electronic game. A higher beat above the buzz, zap and bang. *Don-n-n-e-e-e. Ron-n-n-n-e-e-e.*

Controllers down, arses up, and out to the kitchen, where Momsie is butts-up in the refrigerator. Without a glance back at her sons' arrival:

"No eggsies, boys."

Hard to see anything, as Momsie's size blocks any view into the shelves of the retro-attired Admiral fridge.

"Yes, Momsie?" Ronnie says.

"No eggsies for breakfast, boys. Made 'em all up hard-boiled for your lunchies."

With Momsie's butt covering the complete door opening and her head hidden, the bowtie on top of the apron's back forms a circle impression of a ribbon-topped butt-head addressing the boys. "Thought there was another carton," she muses to herself.

"Yes, Momsie?" Donnie says.

"Boys, you needs to go to the IGA for some eggsies for Momsie."

The background soundtrack at this moment would feature a long wail of a wolf crying out into the heart of darkness, the horror of it all.

The lights go off as the fridge door closes, and the boys' minds light up to a free pass from their week in jail.

Mount up, lads.

Before you can say *Vamos, estupidos,* Donnie has the keys in hand, a black fob with a worn-flat, blue-and-silver–embossed Ford logo. In 1985, "Bronco II" could be read in matching silver, a line below the logo. That image disappeared over time, along with the option of two-wheel drive. The current ride is ruddier, with hubs locked to permanent four-wheel drive. Momsie quit turning the hubs to change the drive from two to four wheels twenty years ago.

Brakes on at the back screen doorway. A world opening to the beautiful early-fall evening, but not before serious Momsie goodbyes.

"Boys. Two cartons, pleasies. And youse must check the due date."

Momsie needs smokes too, but she would never trust her boys with cig purchases. *Their love of the nicotine would makes the endsies for themsies,* she tells herself.

Ronnie and Donnie are off, clucking, chuckling and chortling off to the two-tone (three if you count the rusting lower panels) classic Bronco II.

(A round of car-enthusiast in-the-knows can be heard echoing timelessly at the S-shaped counter of the Sunriser:

"That's no classic. Just another dinosaur produced by Ford."

The Ford supporter responds with a list of opposing dinosaurs.

"Aztec. Trailblazer. Jimmy. All from GM?"

A smartass from the back piles in. *"Corvair? Vega? Cimarron? Fiero?"*

The Chev guy sums up the shopping list and moves it along. *"Okay. But they're not classics, either. I am talking four-wheeler classic. Like, Jeep classic."*

The Ford fan sums it up on the positive for the dim-wit family. *"That Ford product is still carrying old Momsie to IGA, the Beer Store and Bob's Dairy Bar."* He looks the room over for some Ford acknowledgment. And then once more. *"We're talking over thirty years. That's classic."*

Someone else takes a quick look to the back corner for any twin dim-wit attendance. All clear.

"Those idiot lads will be the end of that Bronco ride.")

Over the creek, named after that nonexistent fish, stands a bridge that still carries the train twice each direction every day, two early, two at dusk. The only way south to the downtown from this garden neighbourhood — still hampered by the unfortunate incident with a pole cat that gave it its name, Skunk's Hollow — is along the street that runs underneath the Grand Trunk classic 1857 train trestle. There on the downtown's south side is the IGA on Water Street, destination for those eggsies.

Wait — warning flashes — dim-wit thinking is at work now. Ronnie is about to transform the eggsies errand into a gravel run. Donnie should have guessed an ulterior motive when his twin brother did not grab the keys first.

As they pass beneath the trestle, Ronnie's right hand reaches into his upper left shirt pocket, while his left digs for a lighter in his pants. "What's that?" Donnie says.

"Joint."

"Joint?"

"Yeah, I told you Pablo dropped off his special harvest."

"Weed?"

"No, stupid — special harvest, some Perth County Conspiracy."

"I thought the Conspiracy was dead."

"Pablo dedicated this year's crop to their fiftieth anniversary."

"Fiftieth anniversary?"

"Donnie, chill. I'll spark it up."

Donnie turns from dim-wit to sage for the evening stage. "Eggsies first, dummy. Then … we can head out to the 6th."

Every lying cheat has a sixth sense for the route to deceit.

"Baby, let's go out to the 6th. There's the blind half…"

Dirty dog gets kitty cat lured out on a detour.

"AND what do you suppose we'll do there?"

"Baby, it's been a hard day. Nicole been ragging me right through dinner."

"And what do I get out of it?"

Dirty dog has a bone to offer.

"Business trip to Vegas is coming up. Want to come?"

"Come and come, and come."

The gravel 6th Concession also provides a handy lying opportunity for the drunk:

"Honey, I need some cigs; I'll get milk."

"We have milk. You can smoke my cigs, dear. Dear? Dear?" (frown) *"Where's he off to?"*

Then, those desperate lying teens who get off on the gravel concession:

"Why not Lover's Lane?"

"Too much traffic. Baby, the 6th has the blind right."

A blind right — the two tracks through the grass to an old ford on the Thames River, blind right off the first concession crossroads — offers some dead-end privacy. The traffic interruptions are limited to the occasional four-wheeler or cross-trail biker.

"Billy, I can hear a motorcycle."

"Baby, pull the blanket over our heads. We'll pretend we're camping."

The IGA at seven o'clock tonight is super empty, so Donnie takes the opportunity but misses the irony when he pulls into the first available space — handicapped. Ronnie leaves the Conspiracy special harvest on the half-shell, lower dash with the built-in, chrome cigarette lighter. Classic leftover from the seventies, still in operation for Momsie, who does smoke and drive. Real nice option on any gravel run, a convenience for the stoned that pops out ready to spark 'er up when red-hot.

Ronnie remains bright enough in his errand-runner's role, making sure the eggsies are wrapped in the plastic bag, placed sideways on the back-seat floor mat. Ronnie has experience with eggsies sliding off the back seat or the dash, then sitting on them and stepping on them in both back seat and front. The back passenger-side floor is a proven spot for guaranteeing tomorrow's breakfast. Dim-wit returns to the passenger seat, looks to dim-wit driver.

"Spark 'er up?" Ronnie asks.

"Not yet, dummy — the 6th."

Donnie nods his noggin; he gets it. "We can wave at the Kembers and those City guys."

A stupid pair *is* what a stupid pair *does.*

"Ronnie, let's wait till after the farm. In case we sees someone."

Any car enthusiast about Town would recognize this three-tone Bronco II. The blind would likely even recognize the sound of bad bearings rattling down Water to the IGA, then south to the edge of Town.

Swim quarry closed, tennis courts empty, St. Marys constabulary with radar at the opposite ends of Town — it's a clear ride past the cement plant to shake, rattle and roll over the top of Stewart Hill.

"Momsie needs to have Debbie tuned up," Donnie says. "Maybe an oil change too."

The Bronco's right-turn signal makes a popping click reminiscent of bad radio reception in the Country.

"Spark 'er up now?"

"No, dummy. Past the farm. Remember?"

Ronnie has forgotten the pass-by wave agreed upon. He's stuck in a deep reboot, joint in one hand, Maple Leafs logo lighter in the other. Donnie guides the wheel, points the rubber for ruddy ride down the 6th with all senses to the upcoming farm on their left. City folk would call this a rubbernecker; Momsie calls it a Nosey Parker.

In the passenger seat, Ronnie reaches for the radio dial with his Bic hand. "Tunes."

Donnie is looking, looking and looking with both hands on the wheel. He's seen something. "What's that?"

Ronnie is dialled into tunes. "Country King," he says. "Wednesday night is new artist review. It's Darcy John tonight."

Driver Donnie sees something, to his left. Something he has never seen before — something big, whether deer, pig, horse or cow, or …

The dim-wit driver is gobsmacked. He ignores the Kember farm and double laneway. "Is that a … goat?"

At that moment, Darcy John's new hit, *Gravel Run, Gravel Fun*, blasts out of the tiny tinny speakers:

> *Gravel run, gravel fu-u-u-un,*
> *Loose surface, careless fun …*
> *Slip and slide, what a ride,*
> *'Cause it's a gravel run.*
>
> *Gravel run, gravel fu-u-u-un,*
> *Head down to the falling sun,*
> *Shift the gears, heaven's near,*
> *Here we go ba-a-ayy-be-e-e, on a gravel run.*
>
> *Gravel run, gravel fu-u-u-un,*
> *Baby, baby you're number one,*
> *Hop on in, let's get it on,*
> *All this for careless fun,*
> *'Cause it's a gravel run.*

The melody catches Ronnie conducting with his lighter and joint in hand, one foot tapping the floor, the other with a nervous twitch. The mind of the driver, his brother, is running off in the opposite direction, looking at this giant in the paddock. The twins will argue reasons and means forever, but the music is irritating.

Donnie looks left but lashes out right for a slap to his brother's radio hand, a flick on the Bic. With just one hand on the wheel, he allows the loose surface to jerk the car away, toward the ditch. Darcy John lets it loose on the volume as unslapped fingers turn it up.

"*Gravel run … gra-a-a-a-vel fun-n-n, baby …*"

The twins scream. "*Who-o-o-o-o-o-o-a-a-a-a-a!*"

Ronnie drops the dial, grabs the wheel with his finger, fumbling the lighter still in his hand. Donnie brings back his off-wheel free hand. Ronnie leans into Donnie, pushed into a sandwich against the driver door by the off-balance Bronco sliding off the gravel. Donnie screams on his own, realizing there's three hands on the wheel. Ronnie lets go of the wheel and then the dial, holding onto first things first — the important things, spark and joint — both hands up in horror. Who's driving?

"*Aa-a-a-a-a-a-a-h!*"

Donnie forgets the big sighting, both hands on the wheel with their ride heading toward the wood-slat fence. He squeezes the wheel for a steer to the right, resulting in a sideways slide. Tires get some traction and pull the Bronco back up the ditch onto the loose gravel. Not finished — not before the pitted back bumper hooks onto one post on their wild exit, knocking it off a cement mooring. Still standing in a loose stance, the post waves goodbye to the arse-end of the locked-in four-wheel classic, now heading up over the tall grass, skimming the loose surface to the opposite ditch.

"*Aaa-a-a-ah!*"

Both screaming, Ronnie gives a head-shake to the driver. A dim light shines bright for his survival. "Tap the brakes, dummy! It's gravel."

No more ditch, no more dummy brother's bitch, Donnie has straightened it out. The heavily canopied concession does not hide the ping, pang and pong of those worn-out bearings heading down the 6th.

"Spark 'er up, Ronnie."

Twin laughter into the falling sun, for some gravel fun.

Napoleon has watched the loose surface drama unfold on an extra evening munch over some oats and molasses, beside the salt lick in the centre paddock. It's animal nature that he notices the absence of the high-pitched hum of the electric fence. A sweet Country sound he has never experienced — the call of freedom. The General plans his escape: first, wait for twilight; next, call his Queen; third, test the fence.

Napoleon chews away on the clock, polishing the bottom of the treat pan, taking some extra licks on the salt, then a long cool drink before letting out a low hum that drops at the end. *"Hum-m-m-m-m-m."*

A few repeats with no response, so he looks to the waving post and waits. Napoleon wonders if his call of the wild has been forgotten, only heard once a year during mating. The ladies in the barn *are* responding, though, unbeknownst to him. First, they heard an unfamiliar, labouring mechanical beast chomping about outside the fence, off the gravel. Next was the low bass call of the familiar stud. Queenie understands the restless nature of her herd, who will not move without command.

"Laa-a-a-adies. Sta-a-a-ay inside while Que-e-e-eenie will see-e-e-e."

Her Royal Highness knows the direction of concern, with all team noses pointed to the road. She follows with her royal bearded proboscis, through the small opening of the barn door, toward the concession. The pungent scent is near, closing her nostrils as it fills the air.

Napoleon.

The stink says it all.

Closing in, closing in, big balls on the loose. If they were metal, they'd clang his arrival announcement like a set of arnies. She heads toward the smell.

With twilight now here, Napoleon moves on to problem number three, the fence. This time round, no ball-grabbing jump; forget any hair-raising crash and burn. He can move past the stuck thought of that numbing shock of electricity. This time round, no limits, no boundaries, as both hooves push down on the waving post, catching the high grass on the ditch side. *Creak, crack.* With one last hack and whack he puts all his weight down, displacing the one last barrier to freedom. The General tiptoes through the wreckage, heading to the east paddock. The concentration, energy and effort behind that big push have raised his adrenaline to tsunami levels of musk production — the wall of scent that pulls Queenie forward.

Napoleon wastes no time getting the job done, and he's over, on to the greener pasture. Here, he feels no hum or buzz so he completes another big push, ignoring the multitude of creaks, cracks, splits and snaps from the non-electric clapboard fence. This fence falls inwards toward his royal mount. A brush-by of mutual beards as Napoleon heads back for a close-up quaff of the royal sweet spot and then off.

It's off to the ditch and forward, with no rutting. No intercourse, not a sound exchanged between the escape-artist Casanova and his royal Rapunzel.

Napoleon trots off down the concession toward Town, with Queenie prancing behind him. Some innate sense of the dangers of the 6th keeps him sticking to the edges, keeping his path clear of the mechanical beasts' twin tracks on their path forward. Queenie follows, overcome by the exhaust of male musk. She's deaf to any path, blind to any strategy, only following her General's direction. Napoleon has one thing on his mind: a midnight snack. An opportunity for new foods, which include the sugary smell of Robbie Stewart's sweet corn in a patch first farm on the right, in the back pasture with the deer-safe fence.

The goat's unbelievable ability to zero in on scent is like a hound dog's, a hungry wolf's on track for a snack attack. Queenie remains behind him as he knocks through another post and through a large pasture, with no stops, straight through the narrow posts of the high deer fences, exposing a secluded golden buffet.

"Mm-m-m-m."

No matter the raspy husks, the star-crossed lovers munch on across the sequestered field, well past the midnight hour.

Corn — a marvellous taste, sweet and moist — in unlimited supply can loosen up the system, a golden intestinal charmer. By dawn, Napoleon and Queenie will have filled their guts, piling up huge dumps hither and thither.

Now they come beard to beard by the back, centre post of their half-harvested field. No foreplay, no four legs down but hers — Napoleon puts his fore-hooves up on her back without the merest pleasantry.

They rut.

Rut under the full moon in the sweet corn pasture, surrounded by a sugary smell whipped with the pungent odour of musk.

Before long, Her Royal Highness has had enough of the oversized General's input.

"I-i-i-i-i-i-i can smell something."

In truth, Queenie can smell nothing; she simply wanted the stud to pull out and get off, now. The ploy plays out with royal purpose.

Napoleon is off, back on all his fours, with his long beard and snout lifted up into the wind. Yes, it's all about the gut. *"I-i-i-i-i-i-i smell sum-m-m-m-thing too-o-o-o. Faa-a-a-at pi-i-i-gge-e-ee food."*

The General has a vast memory bank of smells, collected over countless idle days passed in his sequestered paddock. He might not see the routines of the Say Cheese farm, but he can smell all — bank on it. He has a long deposit book on assorted aromas from garden greens, weed roots, apple cores, celery tops, tomato bottoms, and broccoli stems taken from the human shelter to the back of the wood wall that hides the ladies. And into the unknown beyond, there's something different. He can't see anything back there, but can sense the scent of a path that leads to another, unfamiliar animal. The pig-g-e-e-e that the masters call to, whose smell is harsh and bitter. Now, he makes a withdrawal on his memory bank; he can smell the source of perfect green pastures in a goat world, a dream come true.

Not lost on any part of the evening is Max, first witness again to an incident in the making. He watched the vehicle dig deep into the ditch a few hours earlier. The beast groaned; it moaned, signalling with a strange and constant, rattling beat. No Max deep thoughts, though — nothing more as the ping-pong sound got lost in the twilight; not his concern. Still, Max was up, alert to home and family. He was soon rewarded for his canine patience. The old dog heard movement, then cracking boards and a crash — the post.

No one-bark welcome or three-bark alarm; Max moaned.

The west paddock was silent, no stud movement, no hum from the fence, and all quiet on the home front. Still a patient dog, Max sensed movement on the concession. Only one thing to do for a dog. Max moaned again. Again, the farmhouse was all quiet. Max lay back down on his mat on the porch.

Now, a movement in the east paddock. Another, greater snap, crack and pop as down goes the clapboard fence. Dog sense spells out trouble.

Max winds up to a wail.

The lights are on in the house, where early to bed complements an early rise. This wail gets Jimmy's tail off the mattress, with Barbara in a two-step behind him, downstairs to the front porch. *Thump. Thump. Thump.* The boys exit their bedrooms at the same time.

"My head just hit the pillow," John says. "What's up?"

No time for answers until downstairs joins upstairs in a pyjama line at the steps' edge. The pyjama party squints into a heart of darkness broken only by two distant yard lights. Max peers up at the sleepyheads around the old Master, gets a head touch.

"What's up, Max?" John asks.

"Could be a fox," Jimmy says. "Coyote, maybe. But they don't like dogs. Raccoon? I'll get some boots on, grab a flashlight, get my shotgun. Have a look-see."

Barbara can't help herself, looking at an extra curly-topped Greg bundled up in his Little Pony 'jamas. Her mental focus, though, remains solid on the situation at hand.

"Don't be focking tripping around with one hand on a flashlight and the other holding a loaded gun, Jimmy."

Curly Top is ready to help. "I'm good at holding flashlights."

Jimmy and John both look at him. Barbara is still staring at the Little Pony garb. Greg is incredulous.

"Boy Scouts," he says. "Flashlights."

Max counts a missed petting opportunity when Master touches other Master's shoulder. "No worries, Greg. I've got this. Give me five minutes and we can all get back to bed."

Barbara backs him up. "Jimmy, we'll wait here on the porch for you."

Jimmy is off with shotgun under his arm, a herky-jerky flashlight shining the way. John and Greg marvel at the depth of Country darkness, even with the yard lights crying out to see. The bobbing flashlight is the last contact before it goes out through the side barn door. The front porch crew strain to find the dusty, dirty barn windows.

"There. Watch there." Greg points to the unknown, past the yard light. "You can see flashes of light. Jimmy's checking it out."

John and Barbara strain in silence to catch the bob and weave of the flashlight.

Before anyone can say Billy Goats Gruff, the follow-the-path light-bob appears again. Jimmy reappears under the second yard light, answering the silent question.

"All good. All the ladies are happy."

The group waits by the steps, ready to return to a good night's sleep.

"I didn't do a count," Jimmy continues. "But everyone seems happy. Not restless."

"Restless?" John asks, but looks to Greg.

"Well, that might be the wrong word. More like they were waiting. I shined the flashlight across the herd. All the ladies were beards down, heads forward to me. Like they were waiting … for me?"

"Waiting?" Barbara frowns. "What about the count?"

"Too dark. Aldert and the twins will get the count during the morning milk. Let's get to bed."

Jimmy is a bit worn down by the previous months of turmoil, decision-making and new directions. Rest now — morning can wait. Barbara motions Greg back inside through the screen door. She has to have another look at his 'jamas.

John makes a last stand on the porch; he gives the sitting dog a head rub. "Max. Buddy. Max want his beddy? Max. Buddy come inside?"

Max looks up at the new Master with his chocolate-fudge eyes but does not move. Max knows that the wrong in the dark has not been righted. Max can also wait for morning, but he will do it on the porch.

John and Greg sleep in separate beds, with the same clear dreams at the wonder of their life changes. Barbara's night lists away with the roll and rock of a restless farmer.

Chapter 19

No need to set the alarm or listen for the nonexistent cock's crow: before dawn, the squirrels scurry through the canopy, the birds buffet at their feeder and flutter in the bath, the herd stands on alert, and Jimmy has his boots on the porch.

Max is at the top of the steps, with a moan for a greeting.

"Still think something's wrong, buddy? What's up?"

Max moans again, stationary, pointing farmyard west.

Jimmy looks, looks and looks, blind to the guide dog's point. His brain comes to focus on an unseen mystery. "Max," he says. "Something happen to Napoleon?"

A General register strikes a chord in the canine memory. The name is Napoleon, he remembers. Max charges off to the fence with his Master in pursuit. Jimmy is in a mystery state of why, not yet encountering the newfound land of how. The state of the fence is the big question in Jimmy's mind, but Max heads along the line of unbroken slats toward the road. That's when the point of disaster appears: the front post, blasted from its mooring. Okay, that helps explain why no electric current. Never would it occur to Jimmy to blame a pair of dim-wits gravel-running. Instead he wonders at Napoleon's power. The waving post is a testament to the power of the number-one stud.

"Napoleon?" he says to himself. "How in the world?"

Max is quick to move up the bushy berm and onto the gravel of the 6th, heading east. Jimmy stumbles up the bank to the road, charging up behind a rather quick old dog. That's when the opposite side of the farm blast-effect becomes visible, with one post blown inwards. Jimmy stops, adds up the battle scene.

"How in the world? Napoleon."

Two fence posts broken? There should be concussion protocol, Jimmy figures, but it's all Napoleon. Max is ready to go, only a smart old dog waits for direction.

"Max, come buddy. Let's not waste time on the spilt goat milk."

He and Max head across the paddock and back to the barn. Nothing more seems out of place.

"Napoleon, what have you done? And Queenie, where are you?"

But Jimmy knows the answer before asking the questions: his two top goats have eloped.

The herd looks up as Jimmy opens the sliding barn door. The ladies wait — wait for their Queen and her royal command. They're not waiting for Jimmy or milking. He secures the barn through the side door, then heads back to the porch with Max. Barbara, tea in hand, is up and ready. John is making a Capp, and Greg is curled up on a chair, all comfy in his flannel Little Pony 'jamas.

"They're gone," Jimmy tells the group.

"Who's gone?" Barbara asks.

"Both Napoleon and Queenie."

"Focking how?"

"Napoleon knocked a post clear off, broke the electric line."

Everyone looks out past Jimmy, imagining the flattened post hidden from their view.

"Queenie?" Barbara asks. "The General cleared another post off the east paddock, and off they went."

"Where?"

"East," Jimmy says. "My bet, we'll find them in Robby Stewart's sweet corn patch."

Barbara's wisdom is limited to the third set of moans. "Max was growling at ten last night. They could be in focking Florida by now."

Greg tunes into the idea of long-distance travel. "Florida?"

"Barbara means goats can travel as fast as a horse or deer, but much farther, like a camel."

John and Greg are painting up this image in their minds. Greg can't help but think about the mega-flop *Ishtar*.

John goes all business, gets analytical about something he hasn't a clue about. "What will we do? We need an emergency plan. Divide responsibilities."

The official farm team of Say Cheese Artisan Goat Cheese springs into action. Everyone turns to the team captain, Jimmy.

"First," he counts his fingers, "I need to call next door. Then repair the east paddock fence. After, I'll drive over to Robby's. Walk out to the sweet corn for a look-see. If nothing, I'll head into the Sunriser and give a report to the coffee crowd."

John and Greg nod, turning to Barbara.

"I'll call Big Bob."

The partners pucker out with an owl hoot.

"Who?"

Jimmy joins in on a chorus of reflection. "The Fire Chief for missing goats?"

"They find missing dogs, cats. Plus raccoons, possums and ducklings in a culvert drain. That happened —"

Jimmy cuts her short. "Barbara."

She nods. "I'll get a Missing notice with photos onto the W.I. and horticultural websites, and Facebook. The notice?"

It's a direct pass to Curly Top in the snuggy 'jamas. Barbara can't get past children's pyjamas on a grown man.

"I'll send out a plea to our newsletter subscriber list," Greg offers. "Put the

same Missing notice as yours, Barbara. What I have in mind for a notice design
—"

Another chorus. *"Greg!"*
Greg's voice drops off as he turns to Barbara. "We can work on that together."
Then the three turn to John, who is head down in laptop thought.
"Well," he says, "sounds like a great to-do list. I'll keep the master copy, and
…"
John raps away at the keyboard. "I'll call Aldert, apprising him. He can update
Serge. I'll also call the *St. Marys Journal* so they can get a story started on their
website. Greg, if you can forward me the Missing notice attachment, we can all
be on the same page."

In case anyone is wondering about absent members of the team, Jimmy
reports. "Serge and the twins will concentrate on milking and making the cheese.
We don't need to take them off task. The collies will stay on the farm to help move
the herd. We don't need a steeplechase — we need a slow pace, no horns blasting,
right Max? We need a slow, smart dog who will follow the trail, not chase."

Greg applies a Max head-scratch. "I'll call Billie Ball to get the Missing notice
up on Mike's Auction website." He has a sudden revelation. "Those goats could
be in Mike's parking lot by now."

Jimmy pulls Greg back from a far-off look through the farm window, toward
Theatre Town. "Goats are not interested in mid-century modern furniture. Their
stomachs direct their path. First it'll be sweet corn — close, ready and stocked up.
Let's try and catch up to them."

John is first off the front porch. He's thinking about but doesn't mention the
big question: what happens if they lose their number-one stud in addition to the
prizewinning Queen of the herd? Greg is second off the porch; he relishes the
level of publicity on a *Thelma and Louise* storyline.

"Thelma works," he says to himself, but Louise? Napoleon is a stud — he has
to be Louie. "Thelma and Louie."

In the kitchen, Jimmy heads for his cellphone; Barbara goes for hers.

"Robby, Jimmy here. Have you seen two goats? Yes they indeed-y-did, Robby
… knocked out the fence. Yes, the big one, Napoleon — he's on the loose. On the
'lamb'? Funny, Robby. Seen some deer have you? Right. Yes. But you are sure they
were deer? Remember, Napoleon is a big one. No, they were deer. Look, can I
drop over and double-check if my goats did head for your sweet corn patch? Yes,
the sweet corn. You'll wait for me in the yard. Yes. Yes, I am on my way. Give me
five. Bye, Robby. It'll be later than five minutes if we keep talking. Yes, talk on the
way back to the sweet corn patch. Yes, indeed-y Robby. Bye, Robby."

Barbara has Big Bob on the line.

"Yes they did, knocked the posts right out, flat on the ground. Yes, the current
was cut. How can you help? They're our number-one goats, Bob, missing. On the
lamb, that's funny, Bob. How can you help? Can I mention cats, dogs, skunks,

raccoons, possums and remember the ducklings in the drain culvert? Yes, Bob, it did make national news. Do I have to mention squirrels, Bob? Yes the squirrel was dead; it was a grass fire. OK? You say that you need a sighting for action. But Bob, you will report the missing goats to the volunteers, yes? We need eyes on the ground. That works, yes; by email and on the Township website. Yes, I will have an attachment to you within thirty minutes. Yes, I will keep you posted."

John's call catches up with Aldert on his way to the farm. John diverts him to the sweet corn patch.

"Robby's will be a good start," Aldert agrees. "Queenie is queen, but of the ladies. Napoleon is in charge, and his stomach and smell senses give him direction. She will follow wherever the General goes." Aldert is direct from the start. "John, we need one phone number and one quarterback to disperse the information from calls."

The ZIT cell line goes off in a flow of static as the two pause in thought, broken thoughts that come together in one reconnected idea. Both say at the same time. "Barbara."

"John, use the Say Cheese number. Barbara will put her grip on everything incoming." It's a clear line of calling. "John, you need to phone Serge for another update. He's just behind me. He'll be in charge of the herd. Who knows where I or Jimmy will end up this morning. I'll discuss all with Jimmy at Stewart's, then call you back."

John sums up. "One phone number. Barbara picks up. Talk to Serge. All good, Aldert."

Curly Top is on his laptop with a rejuvenating Capp from John. He gets the beard-and-shoulders shots up under the big caps in two wide lines:

MISSING:
2 PRIZE GOATS!

He stops himself from mentioning a reward, taking the neighbourly approach of Town and Township.

Napoleon & Queenie,
Say Cheese (Kember Farm) Artisan Goat Cheese prize goats.
*Please call (519) 729-4628 (519-**SAY-GOAT**)*

Greg is a natural on wine cooler recommendations; now he concentrates on his social media expertise. He smiles on all the previous work as he pulls out the loaded and registered file of internet address firepower, drawing on his reserve holster of special email addresses:

saycheeseartisangoatcheese@hotmail.com

"Ouch. That's a memory cramp; something easier to remember."

He debates a second email to be used for adoration of the General on the Say Cheese website:

thegeneralnapoleon@hotmail.com

"People's choice. I'll use both. Greg, buddy, buddy, you are so-o-o-o-o-o clever."

He breaks out into song.

> *Curly Top, Cur-r-r-r-lee Top.*
> *You're da man, Curly Top.*
> *Everything in hand,*
> *Better than a one-man band,*
> *Curly Top, Cur-r-r-r-lee Top.*
>
> *Curly Top, Cur-r-r-r-lee Top.*
> *Your hair glitters,*
> *No point for scissors,*
> *With the floppy mop.*
>
> *For-r-r-r-r Curly Top,*
> *Cur-r-r-r-le-e-e Top*
> *You're da man, under the mop,*
> *It's Cur-r-r-r-r-lee Tah-h-h-h-op.*

From the partner's office:

"Curly Top, stop. You are a distraction — stop. We have goats that need to be caught."

Greg smiles into the mirror hanging on the wall behind his computer. He presses ENTER and the Missing notice is forwarded to Barbara, Billie, John, Aldert and Jimmy.

Serge and the twins are out in the milking shed. Ozzy and Faisal count and double-check on the clipboard and the computer terminal. Easy calculation — it's so obvious Queenie is missing, and the Queen always leads. No Queen — this is a bad dream when it comes to keeping up the percentage of cream. Serge feels a certain tension.

"*Faisal, s'il te plaît, changes cette* channel to Classic Rallys. *C'est une* feature *de Mille Miglia* from *1957.*"

Serge spells the years out in French, which the twins find so alien from their nurture. *Le jeune fromager* continues.

"*C'est plus* mellow *avec Stirling Moss. Il est magnifique. Un moment spécial,* before theez twin and quad carbs *d'aujourd'hui, ces turbos monstres.*"

Moss belongs on a south-facing rock, as far as the twins are concerned. Stirling sounds like silver or some kind of British money. So Moss, along with Mille Miglia in 1957, might as well be on Mars as far as Ozzy and Faisal are concerned. No matter — Faisal, under directions, changes the channel with the hand-held control. It's a washed-out, grainy scene, with Dinky Toy racing cars flashing across from left to right. The faded blue of the Mediterranean hangs like a vast stage curtain over the cliffside drama.

Vuff-vuff-vuff. Rrr-r-r-r-en-en-en-en. Vuff-vuff-vuff. Rrrr-en. Vuff-vuff. Rrrr-en.

"*Moss takes the corner,*" says the commentator. "*PASSING De Portago. Moss is in the lead.*" *Rrrr-en. Vuff-vuff.* "*Un-be-lieve-able, how Moss commands the road. Ramming his gears up to fourth.*"

Rrrr-en. Pow. Rrrr-en, pow, rrrr-en-n-n-n-nnn.

"*My God, Moss is charging ahead, further into the lead. He's … he's heading for … for … our radar tells us … 170 kilometres per hour. And increasing his speed … AND De Portago is glued to his rear.*"

It's all alien and hypnotic to the Syrian lad caught in traffic before the screens.

"Faisal, off the monitor," his brother says. "Let's get milking."

Faisal is back in line with his brother, joining in and moving on with the goat team. "God is my witness, my brother, Allah forgives the infidel. But I ask you, brother, who watches 1950s rally racing?"

"Western marketing," Ozzy says. "Westerners are always into marketing themselves. Allah forgive them for their addiction to social media."

"Allah be my witness," Faisal agrees, "we must forgive them, for what is social and what is media. They know not what they do. But we can bless the Western technology, too, which allows us to make electronic pay transfers back home."

Serge is walking the suction line, double thumbs up for the sign. "Ozzy, cups up on #47."

The twins double down, moving, moving, moving suction cups along a teat parade. "Faisal, close the shed door after … #77."

The line moves on. Faisal is glued to the classic rally retreads.

"Ozzy, we should buy one of these classic cars. The chicks might find it attractive."

"Faisal, there's only two seats. I know which seats are mine. Allah forgive me, but my brother must hitchhike."

Faisal finishes the last of the ladies in the lineup under Serge's gaze while Ozzy moves out to the adjacent paddock with the empty udders. The yard is packed with patient beards waiting for pasture. Between their full, machine-sucked udders and their growling, giant four-chamber guts, the ladies' thoughts of their missing Queen begin to dissipate.

Rrr-r-r-r-r. Rrr-r-r-r-r. Rrr-r-r-r-r.

"Say Cheese, Barbara speaking."

"It's Billie, Barbara. I know you're busy, but pass this on to Curly Top … sorry, I mean Greg. I got the attachments, plus, plus, plus. They're up on Mike's website, plus, plus …"

Barbara cuts to the chase on words, ideas, euphemisms and anything plus straight talk. "Billie, focking can the 'plus.' Get to the point."

"Sorry, Barbara."

The deep breathing, almost panting, can be heard above the static on the ZIT line.

"Barbara, I added the Missing notice to my Facebook page."

"And?"

"Two hundred and forty likes … *and* it's building. *And,* Greg's idea of Thelma and Louie is brill-l-l-liant."

"Billie, listen up. Barbara would like a few sightings, reportings … not star-gazing, or focking navel-gazing on how many social-media hits or likes. *Fah-ah-ah-awk.*"

"Right Barbara, focking onto it."

At the next farm over, Jimmy meets up with Robby Stewart.

"Robby, let's give it a moment here. Aldert will be here in five minutes. Let's wait."

"Jimmy, that's my prize crop. It's the big feature at the B-N Fair next week."

"Robby, let's be realistic. Most of the damage has already been done. Say Cheese will cover those costs. It may not cover your loss of Fair recognition, but nothing will be out of pocket, Robby."

Aldert pulls up in the Say Cheese quad cab, careful on Robby's cheap-ass gradient laneway not to drop a dust plume over the large man's size-fourteen boots. Bare greetings and off to the sweet corn pasture one hundred yards back, tucked behind the silage bin, blocking any view. A route used by four-wheeler bikes, Robby's assorted tractors and the farm truck makes for an easy enough walk with the three and Max on the scent.

"Jimmy, how did these goats get out … on the 'lamb'?"

"Funny, Robby, you did say that on the phone. Look, goats have never *escaped* from my farm — never. So let's just say, there's more to this story. First job, we need to get those goats."

The Shepherd adds emphasis. "The goats are not familiar with the outside world. Their direction comes from the gut — the brain's connected to the stomach. Food pulls them onwards, to your farm, Mr. Stewart, for example — for the sweet corn, that is." Aldert is in the lead, still behind Max. "Look, goat shit."

Robby, a generational mixed-crop farmer, has been trained in the subject of shit since he first emerged from the cabbage patch. Today, though, he finds himself in unfamiliar territory. "Now I've seen cow pies, pig slop, that runny chicken stuff, cat puree and dog pâté." Robby stops in his path, turns back on the group in his path for some sly humour, no shit. "*And* that ain't no horse crap." Max marches on, ignoring the cold heap. "But old Robby has never seen a pile like this."

The rush to the sweet corn has stopped for a reconnoitre on the yellow-speckled browny-green pile. Robby's having a real head-scratch. "It's not like one of those deer doughnut-bits, or a foxy burnt sausage. Raccoons have a reduced, mushy version of the sausage, with seeds and … other stuff. But this seems to have a lot of undigested corn kernels."

Amazing the volcano of discourse that erupts out of poo piles. Robby looks up. "Holy shit."

Jimmy and Aldert are already heads up, assessing the mow-job on five acres of sweet corn.

"Lock, stock and cob," Aldert says.

"Robby, there's still more than half standing."

"It's a mess, Jimmy. You say two goats can do a shear job like this? Man, half the harvest but increased costs to get the crop off. Looks like a big hand job. We'll see?"

Jimmy talks to himself. "They're only after the cobs. They shear the husks off with those raspy teeth."

Robby is listening the way only a farmer does. "How are they on the hawthorn bushes?"

"A combination of a buzz saw and a mulcher. Except they poop like ponies."

"I'm getting the picture," Robby says, nodding. "It's a shit-show with the shear job, but great for pasture fertilizer."

Aldert shows off his recent graduation in herd management. "That's why the goat herd spends less time in the barn than any other stock animals."

Robby gets it. "Shit like ponies."

The Shepherd reworks the image into something more understandable. "More like a soft-ice-cream dispenser. You know how it piles it on, into the cup."

Robby will never look at Bobby's Ice Cream quite the same way, ever again.

Jimmy moves over the crest of the hill, interrupting the buildup of a disturbing image. "Sorry, Robby, we'll have to get you a new fence post."

The neighbour farmer comes up on the rise. "Goat mowed through that, too?"

"Napoleon," Aldert says.

Robby nods, cupping his empty hands. "The big one."

"Napoleon has finished his business here." Jimmy points helter-skelter to the remaining mounds. "They've chowed down most of the night; now they need water. Napoleon will be on to that, and then on to a grand tour to find new foods."

Jimmy points southeast. "They're heading that way. The noise of the cement plant, the Town dump smell will push them farther south, toward Highway 7. There's the pond by the railway bridge. Jay Turner's property. I'll call him."

Robby is in familiar *terroir*.

"Those ditches aren't just for drainage; some are spring feed, too."

Aldert is GPS-confused, although he is picking up local knowledge as the search area expands. He's off looking north, expanding the view, skips to the big picture. "I think we should call the police," Aldert says. "Car hits a goat …?"

"Jimmy, the big one will destroy a car," Robby says.

All three look off past the Constable horizon, toward the far-off hum of the busy provincial highway.

Rrr-r-r-rrr. Rrr-r-r-rrr. Rrr-r-r-rrr.

"Jay, Jimmy Kember here. Have you seen a goat this morning on your property? Deer? No, one big goat? Yes, Jay, you know the difference between deer and goats. You've seen it on Facebook? Beckie showed you. Thanks, Jay. You've got the picture. Call me after you walk back to the pond. Thank you."

Rrr-r-r-rrr. Rrr-r-r-rrr. Rrr-r-r-rrr.

"Chief, it's Aldert. Yes, it's the Shepherd from Say Cheese Artisan Goat Cheese. Thank you, in herd management. Yes, it is about the goats. You've seen it on Facebook. *And* the Town site. *Plus* out on the Town email list *with* the Missing notice. Thank you, yes, that's Greg, the new owner, yes. You met him with Cheeko. And Cheeko has called you, too. Oh yeah, Napoleon is a big one. What more can you do?"

The Shepherd gets to the point. "Chief, Jimmy and I are concerned that the goats will make Highway 7. That would be a catastrophe for traffic. Yes, he is a big one. What can you do? Yes, please do contact the Provincial Police with a safety alert. City radio stations, TV? Great idea, we'll call them. Thanks, Chief. Goats on the lamb … we've hear-r-r-rd that a few times.

Rrr-r-r-rrr. Rrr-r-r-rrr. Rrr-r-r-rrr.

"Chief Sandy, this is Barbara Kember. Yes, it's about the goats. Aldert called you, great. Yes, I know it's on the Town website. Great, you notified the Provincial Police. Yes, and the Highways Department, yes. What else? What else here, Chief, is the need for an Amber Alert. Why an Amber Alert? For children only, of course. Chief, these are my focking kids, so let's get on it."

Rrr-r-r-rrr. Rrr-r-r-rrr. Rrr-r-r-rrr.

"Barbara, you're on my call display. I just got off the phone with the Chief. What can I do? Get off my arse? What can I do? Yes, I know you want an Amber Alert. Not my department. Get off my focking fat ass? Barbara Kember slow down, the mayor does not like that kind of dirty mouth, not from my favourite Grade 10 English teacher. I'm a fair man — the Missing notice is on our website, plus I had staff send it through our email list … okay. Okay. Pull my what staff out of where?

"Barbara, Barbara, sweet Barbara, I'm getting to the Amber Alert. No, I don't need to pull the staff out of wherever for this one. Let me make a few calls. Monster goat wandering down Highway 7 could be problematic. Sorry, Napoleon. You're welcome, Barbara."

Rrr-r-r-rrr. Rrr-r-r-rrr. Rrr-r-r-rrr.

"Barbara, Rita Taylor here. The W.I. ladies are organizing a grid search. Most don't have Facebook or cellphones, but all have a car and binoculars. Yes, eyes on the roads work. Thank you. We will meet up at Brown's Corners Community Hall, divide the map and go. Nobby Knees Ski Hill is loaning us the ski-patrol walkie-talkies. We will report back. You're welcome."

Rrr-r-r-rrr. Rrr-r-r-rrr. Rrr-r-r-rrr.

"Mrs. Kember, Tony Taylor here, Rita's son. Yes, Grade 10 English. No, I wasn't a great student. But I am president of the Stonetown Wireless Radio Assistance Club. Yes, it is a long name, so we cut it short to SWRAC. No, no, not Shrek — S-W-R-A-C — rhymes with rack. The W is silent. I don't know why it's silent. Yes, that's it. The SWRAC point? The point will be Brown's Corners, where we can help coordinate communication with Ma and her driving granny buds. I know she called you. Yes, Edith will be the contact. Yes, my Aunt Edith."

Z-z-z-z-z-z-z-z-z.

Not that electronic buzz ring common to the human herd of cell users; the goats need sleep. Queenie and Napoleon, Thelma and Louie, stomachs full, drain the rain from the nearby ditch. They take a little sleep in the early autumn afternoon sun by a fresh spring, also known as the ditch, and the shade of rustling ash in the wind.

Z-z-z-z-z-z-z-z-z.

Thelma and Louie have knocked off the escape trail for a shady snooze. Big goats can't be seen in the high grass and orange lilies surrounding their oasis respite. The goats have fooled them all. Who's snoozing now?

Robby Stewart, shaking his head, fires up the Rogers mini-loader and throws the gas posthole digger into the bucket with an assorted toolbox. The one-man farmer puts his generational experience to work. First, he checks for extra wire, clippers, shovel and sledgehammer. On second thought, he has that spare post he's been saving in the corner of the drive shed for a future unknown use.

Jimmy's back down the lane and right, off to the Sunriser. Maybe a straight black coffee will relax him, with familiar support.

Aldert turns left on the 6th toward to the farm. He needs to check the status of the farm team, get back to Jimmy. "Aldert," Jimmy said to him as they parted ways, "tell everyone, and bring in Serge, too. Tell them we'll meet at one o'clock."

Rrr-r-r-rrr. Rrr-r-r-rrr. Rrr-r-r-rrr. That's a call from the human side of the herd.

"Barbara, it's Sheila. The horticultural ladies are desperate to help. Sandwiches. Yes. Sandwiches. We'll drop off four big trays, with refreshments for noon. Yes, feed the volunteers. No peanut butter, yes — Serge has a nut allergy. Covered, Barbara."

The sandwiches prove a hungry hit for Day Two lunch; plus, plus two trays of lasagna with garlic bread, warmed up from Braedon's, will get the farm team through to lights-out. A solemn group faces the setting sun off the front porch. Greg suggests a late-harvest Riesling to calm the anxiety, improve digestion and set the mood.

"What are my kids doing out there?" Barbara wonders. "Cold, hungry … scared."

Jimmy makes sense of it. "It's a warm night, they mowed through an entire sweet corn patch. They have to be sleeping it off in some" — Jimmy deletes "ditch" — "soft, grassy stop, under some shelter trees with a spring-fed brook. Nothing scares Napoleon."

The Shepherd, who has been silent to this point, makes a goat relationship point. "*And,* Napoleon is in charge. Queenie has complete control of the herd, but *here* out in the big unknown, she defers the lead to Napoleon."

"That doesn't work in this relationship. Focking right, eh, Jimmy?" She smiles.

"That's why you are number-one go-to person in charge of the farm team — *the one* to find our kids."

Barbara's hand is on her husband's. John rubs Max's brush-cut head. The old dog can feel a tension release, and so does Greg.

"Let's get to sleep," Greg says. "But first, directions, Barbara, for the morning. And I'll top you up."

She's back to the number-one go-to person. "Jimmy?" She now pulls him back into the conversation as his mind rewinds the highlight reel on the big deal of the full day's drama. He comes to with a dawn reaction.

"Well, Capps off to John at the break of dawn." A chuckle rounds out the evening. Jimmy goes on. "We need to review our social media sources, call back to all our contacts; we can redo our to-do list over coffee. I suggest a seven-o'clock start. John?"

John rises up from sofa comfort, yawning and boxing out slow punches. "Capps will be pumping out of the kitchen by seven bells. And breakfast mint tea for you, Barbara dear."

Chapter 20

Next morning, before the first crack of steam out of the Italian Cappuccino machine, Thelma and Louie are leaving their night shelter by the bubbling ditch (maybe a stretch to call it a brook), as dawn rises before them. A night together side by each; no need for a time clock in goat paradise. Napoleon, with a growling gut, reboots in the new smell of an unfamiliar but delicious food. For the first time in the stud's life, the lure of new tastes outweighs the desire for 24/7 rutting. For the first time, Queenie is free in all senses — she just floats along on a sea of freedom. *I see, I follow.* The General came not, saw not, conquered not, but a sensible brain smells the path forward.

They trot off to a greener pasture. This round's a garden plot of cabbages, broccoli, cauliflower and hot peppers. Why do farmers put their treasured crops in secluded corners, like Robby Stewart and his sweet corn, or Jay Turner and his trout pond? On the menu for Day Three is Gerrard Davis's vegetable garden, which can't be seen from his back kitchen window.

Another mow-job in the making, with no pressure of a chase for the two goats on the lamb.

Back on the farm, Barbara fields the first call of the day.

Rrr-r-r-r-r-r. Rrr-r-r-r-r-r. Rrr-r-r-r-r-r.

"Say Cheese, Barbara speaking," Her mouth becomes an exhaust pipe that rattles out the words. "My God, is it you?"

Her mouth closes in a half-dumb look, a look that repeats on all faces in the room. "I know. I know. *That* was *you*, that *you* looked at this morning in the bathroom mirror. Ha. Ha. Funny."

All Capps are off gaping mouths, attention on. "Yes, you. Not a joke."

The room gives a silent-mouthed *Who-o-o-o-o-ooo?*

Barbara cups her cellphone, announces to the farm team. "It's Kent Ward, from ETV."

Barbara's back speaking into the phone, speaking to the long day ahead. "Yes, Kent, I know it's you. You say what? You want to have a live feed from the focking farm?

"Today? A national feed. Yes, I know that means across the whole Country. Live, yes. Well, Kent, you come on out, come up-Country, buddy. See you at noon. You're on the road now. Well, come on up-Country, Kent. Yes, goats on the lamb, we've her-r-r-rd that one — funny, eh? Yes, Thelma and Louie, that's been a big one too."

Rrr-r-r-r-r-r. Rrr-r-r-r-r. Rrr-r-r-r-r.

"Barbara. Billie here. *And,* over one thousand likes on my Facebook page."

"But Billie, no focking sightings."

"Back to you, Barbara."

As Barbara hangs up, Jimmy is up and off.

"I think I need to walk back to Turner's pond. My cell is on."

Aldert will catch up with the W.I. ladies and mobile radio group. "I'm off to Brown's Corners. My cell is on."

John disappears into the kitchen, hiding the damage-related thoughts that are emerging from his dark actuary side. "More Capps, before I clean up."

Curly Top follows. "I could use a cuppa java with luvva from my buddy boy."

Greg faces up to John's strong turn toward him. He knows that stern look.

"Okay then," Greg says. "Bring the Capp to the office. I'm right onto it — social media, our website, their website, Facebook. I'm on it."

"You'd better get the language script-shape and ready for Thelma and Louie too," John tells him, "*before* that old goat Kent shows up. Don't want Barbara dropping the f-bomb on national TV."

Out on the lamb, Thelma and Louie are beards up toward the strong smell of another garden paradise. By mid-morning, Napoleon has ploughed through two more posts, knockouts, and onto another deer fence surrounding Gerrard Davis's vegetable treasures. The goats are unfamiliar with these vegetable treats: leafy broccoli branches, crunchy cabbage coils and creamy cauliflower. The mow-job begins, and goes on and on, like an Underwood typewriter completing a late essay. The sun passes noon, heads toward the west and begins to fade away. The goats mow on, row upon row, no hurry. When they hit the small row of a cold-weather variety of scotch bonnet peppers, they mow through the diges-tional dynamite stock, leaf and pod. So the water clock begins to tick.

Off in the distance, the back roads are busy with the W.I. ladies' tour on fuzzy-sounding walkie-talkies.

"Ethel, two four and out. A twenty-five on the 9th Concession."

"Two four out, and a twenty-five okey-dokey on the 9th."

Adult children should not let aging parents drive.

"No, Ma. It's two four okay, a two-*five, not twenty-five. Jeez, Ma."*

"Shut your mouth, Andy …"

"Andrew, *Ma.* Andrew, *please."*

"Look, Andy, shut your focking mouth. Let's get on with the search, not on these moronic idiosyncrasies of your wireless radio club of savant idiots. I am your Ma, Andy."

"Okay, Ma, let's just drive over to the 10th."

Big Bob is on chore detail on the home farm, his mobile radio on his belt. "Amber Alert, no," the B-N boss tells Chief Sandy. "But we do have a yellow caution on *Map.net.* Department of Highways website has a yellow caution, too. We have our two fire departments, the Town and Provincial police forces, and a D-H truck full of barriers, signs and cones, for whatever case. The coverage is great from both local and national fronts, all at work to catch these goats … on the lamb."

Big smiles from both men.

"And those W.I. ladies touring the back concessions with those crazy SWRAC lads?" Sandy asks.

Bob's smile turns to a frown. "What else could Barbara want?"

At lunch, at least, Barbara will want for nothing. The horticultural ladies again fill that want the way they know best, leaving another day of sandwiches and four large aluminum-covered trays with Kountry Katerer casseroles for supper.

A different train of five-foot-plus and -minus ladies relay the goodies over the porch, in through the screen door, and back to their Texas-sized Lincoln SUV out front. It's a head turner.

"My God, that's Kent Ward."

"Marilyn, don't trip with all that food in your hands."

The milky-faced man in a suit with the mic leans in on the line. "Nice buns, ladies — the sandwiches, that is."

The ladies don't stop on the misunderstanding that the sandwiches were on white bread, not buns. They smile at the pass. Then the tittle-tattle on Kent starts.

"He's a bad boy."

"Him and that weather girl, Robin whatshername."

"She's bad bird. Cheat. Cheat. Cheat on her husband."

"Don't leave that old buzzard out. He's married too."

"An odd-bird duet that can only sing *cheat, cheat, cheat.*"

The summary of facts from an in-the-know closes the curtain on a bad performer. "He's fat and bald, hidden under a cheap toupee. And a lecher from head to boot with his come-hither evil eye; then the Venus flytrap stuns you with his foul breath fronted by awful yellow teeth that will bite you."

Marilyn does not take a back seat on this. "God, Vera, listen to you. For me, he looks great on the tube."

Barbara answers calls and more calls, all of concern but none with actual sightings. She's busier than a one-armed quilt-maker.

Rrr-r-r-r-r. Rrr-r-r-r-r. Rrr-r-r-r-r.

"Barbara, it's Billie. *And,* over five thousand likes on Facebook, twenty-five thousand hits."

"Billie. Any sightings?"

"*And* Mike's website is getting tons of hits too."

"*And* the focking goats, Billie."

"Back to you, Barbara."

Jimmy arrives at Turner's Pond. The pickup with the Say Cheese logo bounces along the grass path, up to a gate. The tall man standing beside a four-wheeler speaks up to the open pickup door. "Jimmy, nothing to report, the dogs would be making a fuss. Nevertheless, let's take a walk back."

Jimmy and Max cross through the gate. "Don't want the animals near the highway, Jay. They mowed over Robby Stewart's sweet corn, seem to be heading this way. Corn will clean out their intestines, make them real thirsty."

"Jimmy, they're on the move, hungry now." For Jay, the goats are eating machines, which opens things up to poop jokes. "Maybe you can direct them over to my south pasture. A day or two would sure add some fertilizer."

The goat farmer, the vegetable farmer, plus one smart old dog make three on a walk about the pond. A no-surprise at first, they take seconds to encounter a different shit — goose poop by the poodle pile. Jimmy is surprised by the turds.

"My God, that's a lot of goose shit. The size of it. Like a small dog …"

A flutter of leopard frogs and two painted turtles who flip off a log start the geese up to moving along in the opposite direction of the dog. Max curls toward the gate, causing a scatter-patter in all directions. Jimmy and Max go back to the farm for lunch. Jimmy wants an information refresh and to catch the Kent Ward show, live at noon.

Serge and the twins get the goats milked and out the shed door — now it's a go for TV cheese. The three make short order of the cleanup; this Kent Ward suit guy is an alien they want to catch. Back to the real cheese after lunch. The *fromager* has less than four weeks to get the cheese up, ready for the Royal Winter Fair. Three weeks later is "Christmas on the Farm," where the prizewinners can be presented to the public. For Serge, it's a make-or-break moment, getting the product ready. "Papa, the secondary agents are new to me. Lavender, wild nettles, hawthorn berry, green apples and black walnut oil are incredible in their influence on what I hope to be my style."

The cheese to be judged needs to age; tasting will come later, he tells his father.

"Thanks to Jimmy and his bag of cheese-making tricks, then throw in his magical software and database library … Your screen tells you when the whole process makes sense. Papa, if there's something wrong? I can tweak any stage of the production, the aging, anything in the process, from my low-ceiling bedroom next door."

One *le Grand* word covers the near future.

"Homework."

Serge is caught on a dream stage at the Royal Winter Fair, with a ribbon-festooned jacket, on national television. His fuzzy focus sharpens when he finds himself in a face-to-face with the twins. Hunger presses the On button. "Faisal, Ozzy, first is lunch, on the porch. *Maman dit,* food keeps your *energie plus.*"

The four hands of goat help hear "lunch," "porch" and "plus," which is enough to get the point across.

Greg hauls some horticultural ladies' white bread sandwiches piled high on a tray back to his tiny desk in the partners' office. He's almost peeing over the exposure excitement. "My God. National news, Thelma and Louie. My God."

Meanwhile John, Barbara and Jimmy are glued to the kitchen television. John the Auditor has learned, here on Day Three, who among the horticultural ladies makes the stunning, mouth-watering egg-salad sandwiches. He takes account of the standing-room-only situation and the ample selection on the counter. *Pick 'em and stack 'em,* he says to himself. He takes off to the front door, calling after Greg, who's stuffing his face in the side room office.

"Greg, come out to the porch."

John grips the screen door handle, jams with his left foot to pry it open. He doubles down, stretching to look back toward the office door. "I have a Capp for you. And I picked out some of those egg-salad sandwiches that Rita Taylor makes. She uses pickle juice for taste, and bits of celery. Yummy, yummy, Greg — nothing better with a John Capp." *Wink, wink, wink.* "Get up, Greg. On the porch, buddy. We need your laptop up on *Noon Live.* And this dumpy-humpy Kent character live on our front lawn."

The partners saddle up on the wicker porch sofa, with Greg's screen tuned to the ETV live news hour. Greg can't help himself as a background commentator on the live action. "The suit is like bad-taste gay. My, my, the poor guy — his head is a peanut."

Greg points at the live screen. "His head is so-o-o-o wide on the television."

John is heads up. "HD, Greg. Shush, he'll be going live soon."

"Look he's licking his lips and brushing back his hedgehog hair … with his wet fingers."

　　　　　　　　　　　　　　　　　　　　　　　　　　　　　　LORNE EEDY

Now John is waving. "Aldert, boys, over here. Egg-salad sandwiches. Rita Taylor's. It's showtime on the Say Cheese farm."

Earlier on the phone, Kent had said that he was on his way, and bingo, here he is, with Barbara. Right out of the ETV van, he's all over the woman from the get-go, firing a battery of old lecher lines.

"Barbara, you look even better in person. Such a refined voice. Have you done broadcast?"

Kent takes a few steps away from the house. "Barbara, over here, with the barn building behind us."

The bad suit holds his boxed fingers up for a test screen pano around the farm. Barbara corrects the course.

"That's the milk shed behind us — barn's over there, Kent."

Can't stop an old woodsman with many arrows left in the quiver.

"Nice hair, I might say, Barbara Kember. You must get your hair done in the City? A beautiful colour, might I add. Do you work out? Must be lonely out here in the … Country?"

Each arrow gets a stern look from Barbara. She wonders if he has a file of naughty farmer jokes too, the lecher.

Each frown gets a bunch of bushy hedgehog eyebrow-raises in turn. The lecher may have a past-due date with the farmer's daughter, but the farmer's wife is still within range.

"Barbara, we go live in twenty."

The television production gets it on with the correct start on a full day of live reports, highlighted by *News at Noon* and the evening broadcasts.

"Live on stage together, eh, Barbara? But, we need to set the stage with the who, why, what and how. Simple stuff for our viewers to comprehend. Who's missing? Why the big concern? What can the viewer do?"

"Got it, Kent."

"One more important question: if we don't find Thelma and Louie, can we set up our trailers on the laneway?"

"You're covered, Kent."

"Linda, over here, give Mrs. Kember a brush-up with some makeup."

"Kent," Barbara protests. A smart young lady with side saddlebags marches toward them. Barbara's head swivels, stops, swivels as Linda holds a mirror in front of her face. "Linda, dear. Barbara needs no focking makeup."

"Yes, ma'am." Linda does not back off but smiles. "Mrs. Kember, you will do great with no makeup, but ma'am. A little brush on the hair."

Linda reaches for Barbara's blouse. Barbara backs up.

"Please, Mrs. Kember, top button needs to be done up."

Linda keeps to a warm smile; Barbara relaxes.

"There we go. I'll let you hold the mirror. Touch with a brush here, little fluff there. You're good to go, Mrs. Kember."

Wham, bang, the farmer's wife takes a good look in the mirror. "Thank you, young lady."

For the first time in a life of teaching, partnership in the Century Farm, leadership in the community, she does not feel in control. Lonely on the farm — how dare he? Left alone on the farm maybe, but the Say Cheese team was on the job. She felt abandoned on a desert island with a mad man chasing her on a corn conveyor belt. She wasn't happy wearing a half-dumb look.

"Barbara, we're coming up. Look at me, not the camera. Johnny might move about, so do not let it distract you from the three questions."

"Wasn't there four?"

"Look at me."

Kent's mouth widens to show row above row of yellow teeth. Barbara has never seen that on the television screen.

"Barbara," he says.

"Kent."

"Here we go."

Kent gives three big hacks, shakes his head into an Elmer Fudd smile, and then looks at the camera with Barbara framed behind his left shoulder.

"LIVE, ladies and gentlemen, boys and girls, from southwestern Ontario, the agricultural heart of our GREAT Country, from the Century Kember GOAT Farm."

Behind the broadcaster's left shoulder, Barbara mouths the words, "Say Cheese Artisan Goat Cheese farm."

Kent cringes on. "The potential of a tragedy unfolds, as two prizewinning goats have ESCAPED, sight unseen for TWO full days."

Barbara holds her hand up with three fingers behind Kent's head. Her mouth forms the words, "Three days."

Kent looks back at Barbara, his hedgerow eyebrows aiming straight at her. "Two goats, on the lamb …" (He shifts back to the camera, leaving Barbara with a cringey face, giving a heavy eye-roll in the background as she fades right again to his left shoulder for a pantomime.) " … lost in the fields south of St. Marys, near the survey DOT called Transvaal. Not Thelma and Louise, but THELMA and *LOUIE*, having a real go-o-o-oat time."

Barbara's still leaning in on the head-and-shoulders broadcast; she shakes her head side to side in slow motion, mouthing their names. "Queenie and Napoleon."

Kent rotates with an instinctive mic zap into the face of his interview prey. "Barbara Kember, WHO are these missing goats?"

Barbara's never a lightning rod for small matters, so she ignores his dumb-ass look, which the audience cannot see. And those yellow teeth.

"Our best stock, Kent. Number one STUD and the QUEEN of the herd."

"How did this adventure start?"

"Napoleon is a very large animal. He's capable of KNOCKING fence posts out."

"Wow, that's an image. So why not just lee-e-ave the gate open? They could come back on their OWN?"

"Goats follow their guts. We're concerned that the pair, unfamiliar with the big world, may wander on the highway. BAD move." Barbara's tick-tock finger pops up, filling the screen.

"Yes, a bad move. Barbara, I understand that neighbours, friends, plus volunteer firemen and police are ON the search."

"Yes, Kent. HELP from all corners, including the horticultural club, W.I. and Stonetown Wireless Radio … the list is laa-a-a-a-arge. And let's not forget the public everywhere, who have responded to our DISTRESS." Barbara looks right into the camera. "Thank you, EVERYone."

Kent stands back as she blows a gigantic kiss.

"Barbara …" He turns his head like an owl back to the camera. "Our viewers want to ask you, Barbara. How can they help?"

Barbara looks into the camera again. "Friends, please be vigilant; Queenie and Napoleon are not dangerous, nothing to worry. Just call the number on the screen or 911. And please, drive safe on Highway 7. They're our kids."

"Thank you, Barbara Kember." The bad suit, head and shoulders fill the screen. "This is Kent Ward reporting, live, from Transvaal, Ontario." He gives the camera lens a stare-down. "We will update YOU, as the story of Thelma and Louie unfolds. TWO goats on the lamb in southwestern Ontario."

His head and shoulders block out Barbara mouthing a different script. He sees her, a look of shock crossing his face as he translates the foul-mouthed words. He's quick to switch to a serious look into the camera lens for the viewers at home. "They could be your kids."

Linda on makeup; Neil, the producer; Johnny, the camera guy; and the gaffer kid with the extended mic all head off to the trailer.

Kent flashes the hedgerow eyebrows at Barbara as he turns to follow the others to the trailer. Barbara turns toward the house, then stops.

"We have a guest bedroom upstairs. If that would be more comfortable?"

She knows right away she's made a mistake. She's opened up her home in a misplaced act of Country hospitality.

"Love to. Love to mount those stairs."

There you have it: vintage Kent repeating his same old lines, live.

By high noon, when the farm team gathers live on the front porch with egg-salad sandwiches to watch the show, the live lines that started the morning off are old news.

Greg points at the laptop. "Look, it's Barbara. Looking good, Mrs. Kember."

Barbara, though, is not looking good in the kitchen, steaming away about tonight's guest.

Chapter 21

With a giddy-up start, the worn, blue, corduroy dressing gown floats across the kitchen floor up behind Barbara. "Some night, last night."

My God, she thinks, he's an ear-whisperer. The slobbering toad is trying to whisper in my ear. Those rotten little yellow teeth next to my …? His hands …?

Barbara has the immediate double axe handle up: wooden-spoon hand crossed with her stainless-steel-spatula hand blocks the inbound. She dishes out some obfuscation. "Yes, the casserole was delicious. And Greg's B.C. Syrah …"

He's weaving, bobbin' his noggin, moving in on his prey. "Wasn't the meat or the big red that I was thinking about." Those eyebrows flash up, down, as he tries again to move closer, closer. "I was thinking about a different kind of big boy …"

Barbara lowers the axe on Kent. Both spoon and spatula hit his chest at the gown's V-opening: *tap, tap, tap.*

"Nothing happened last night. So, don't be thinking about anything. We invited you to use the upstairs extra bedroom, as our guest. We did *not* …"

Tap. Tap. Tap. "… expect … expect you to walk back and forth to the bathroom butt-ass NAKED."

She pushes her tools into his shaggy bad-dog chest. Kent has both hands up in horror.

"My God, Barbie. We are adults."

She puts her tools on standby. She has a bigger thought of horror imagining the ties coming loose on that ratty gown. Kent is having a TV timeout, a commercial break. All wound up, he's ready to wind it out, desperate reeling to catch a line that works to undress this situation. Does the broadcaster blubber a bit? "I do have to mention Walter, on camera, who is amazing. Along with Linda — that gal, she's the miracle worker on how good ol' Kent-boy looks. Barbie, be fair, I do not even have pyjamas to bring, because I do not *own* them. Please do *not* offer me anything like those Little Pony flannels. God save me from Bronies."

He's back. Kent flashes his yellow teeth, flaps the bushy eyebrows. With his eyes *down there*, he's back to the subject at hand. "My little friend likes a walk in Country-fresh air."

Wink, wink, grin, grin.

His puppet-like facial features suddenly grow more animated. "And he kinda likes you, Barbie."

"Shut the fock up, Kent. Your little friend is not a friend of mine."

Mary Beth, bless her soul, waves her cell phone at Barbara from the porch. Barbara marches off to take the pretend call.

The topic is still in hand for ol' Kent-boy. Desperate for the closing line, he's left talking to himself and the big boy. "Kent and Barbie — it has a nice ring, don't you think, big buddy?"

Kent scurries back to the ETV trailer, tight-lipped, tight-fisted, tight-assed and, not to forget, suffering from a tight crotch.

Jimmy gathers everyone, capps in hand, up on the front porch.

"First, thank you all," he says. "Welcome, Mary Beth, who will help Barbara direct the phone calls."

Barbara chimes in. "We can work the second and third business line now, when Billie Ball shows up to help."

Jimmy continues. "Serge and the twins will manage the herd. As for pasture, the dogs will show you all you need to do."

"Sounds good, Jimmy." Serge has eaten his fill of sandwiches; he heads out with Faisal and Ozzy.

"Greg, you can skip the social media unless it's on your phone, with hotspot reception. But you and John, and Max, are with me. We're going to follow the path, so wear hiking boots, no Bermuda shorts, Greg. I will give you a list of things you need, like water.

"And Aldert, we need you up on Highway 7 at the railway bridge. We'll be pushing that way. It will take us most of the day. Six or seven hours if we're lucky. So you can coordinate the W.I. ladies and their radio help. To save all this useless driving around, can you have the ladies just park on 7 with their four-ways on, so they can put their eyes on the fields? Spread them out three or four each side, back from the bridge, say, for two kilometres."

Both Jimmy and Aldert talk to an unseen distant spot behind the barn. "Super idea, Jimmy — that'll slow the highway traffic right down."

"Not everyone has Google or Garmin GPS with all the road cautions. Organize a car shuffle, and contact the horticultural ladies for additional sandwiches, but in lunch bags. Work it out, Aldert."

Action unfolds off the front yard laneway, off the 6th Concession.

"Look at the dust," Kent says.

Linda applies foundation dabs and a brush of rouge.

"Relax, Kent. Wind's blowing the other way."

"The size of those clouds …"

"Sit still."

"Oh, there's Jimmy and Aldert on the porch. Hi, guys …" Everything off the folding chair is flapping: his makeup gown, his wave, his lips and those bushy eyebrows. "You're on in ten minutes, eh?"

"Kent. Sit down and be still. You're on in minutes."

The goats are in a complete daze; the Say Cheese team and friends are spent, after hours and hours on the hunt, and on the farm's front lawn, minutes have become seconds. "Kent Ward from ETV news, LIVE, from the Kember Farm in Transvaal where TWO prizewinning goats REMAIN … on the lamb."

Napoleon and Queenie are up in a photo on-screen, with their names spelled out below in the bar lines, along with contact information. Whoops — the real local in-the-know can see that the names have been transposed. The bronze goat is nameplated as Napoleon while the black one has Queenie underneath.

Up next, a map has a huge red arrow swinging down on a small square dot, Transvaal.

"The community has organized with the HELP of ETV into quite a volunteer force. Let's LISTEN to Gordie Flanagan, one of these HEARTFELT volunteers."

Gordie leans out his window into the camera lens with his *Rogers Does It* baseball cap, both hands out, one working on a cigarette.

"Me and Missus, the Missus had the missing notice on her Facebook, thought we should help out by touring some of this back gravel roads. The missus got the binocs for her birthday. Bought them on special at Doug's …"

"That was local volunteer, GORDIE Flanagan. NOW to the mayor of St. Marys, WHO toured the scene earlier this morning."

There's a shot of Cheeko pointing and talking in a small crowd of Nosey Parkers. He turns to face the mic. "What can I say? We can all come together to help these poor critters. What can I do? I've called upon the industrious team of municipal employees to back me up, a great team from the beautiful Town of St. Marys. Kent, I've called upon everyone to step up, for the goats."

"Mayor Cheeko, is this an official visit?"

"What can I say, Kent."

"Breaking news, the Say Cheese farm team is coming off the front porch. Let's talk to Professor James Kember. Jimmy, what's the plan?"

Aldert exits to the farm truck, and Max follows Jimmy off the steps toward the camera. "The plan, Kent, is simple. The goats have not gone that far. So, we need to retrace our steps. If folks just can take that extra look on their pasture, their land, we *can* bring the kids home."

"Is that why Max is along, tracking?"

Kent reaches in for a head pet.

"*Grrr-r-r-r-r-r-r-r-rrr.*"

Kent steps back with the mic. "Grrr-eat, Max. Good luck on your search, Jimmy."

"Kent, may I remind people on Highway 7 to drive more careful. These goats have no idea of highway traffic."

"Big goats, too."

"Yes they are, Kent."

Jimmy, the partners and Max are off in the Say Cheese quad cab. John and Greg have prepared according to Jimmy's written list, which included one small knapsack shared between them, with two water bottles and two brown-bag lunches and snacks, in addition to two apples. Nice. They have walking sticks, wide-brim hats.

"Guys, no extra weight, so apply the suntan lotion here, well applied, and leave the bottle. Water will be the only bottle you need to carry."

Kent is reaching the end of News Hour live on the farm.

"There we have it folks. GOATS still on the lamb, our very own THELMA and Louie. This is Kent Ward LIVE from Transvaal, Ontario."

Lots of teeth in the lens, to a cut.

"Linda, get me something, I have a headache. I'll be in the trailer."

Back on the trail with John and Greg, the partners have been introduced to all the neighbours, including Robby Stewart, through the Sunriser, IGA and the video shoot. Jimmy and Barbara know everybody, of course. Max leads the way back to the sweet corn; what's not eaten has now been harvested.

Farmer to farmer. "Jimmy, there were cobs on a lot of trampled stocks, so that designated the time to harvest. Not as bad as I first thought."

Max has no interest in a vegetarian menu, but like all dogs would, he has his nose right in a pile of niblet poo. Greg and John have a struggle ignoring the visual facts.

"My God, John, there's dozens and dozens of … piles."

"Aldert told us it looks like soft ice-cream piled in a cup, except no cup. My God, Greg, watch your step."

"One step I will not make is ordering soft ice-cream."

"The yellow chunks are a total turn-off."

Greg pauses. "The colour, if you think about it, is like the avocado-chocolate ice cream at We Scream …"

"Jeez, Greg, now you have me off the hard stuff, too."

Heads down, heads up to the hunt. John is so practical. "The walk will be good for us."

There is a lot of crap to navigate around.

Curly Top vamps a profile of Sophia Loren, a clever play on *Prêt-à-Porter*, with a heads-up poo point. *"Regardez la merde."*

Robby and Jimmy ignore the chit-chat, watching Max head to the broken fence.

"Bit of spring feeds the ditch," Robby says. "They're following it, long grass, there's some nice shady spots …"

"How far?"

"Kilometre, follow the fence lines. The ditch is soggy; the grass has a sharp rasp to it."

"Max, Max. Here, buddy. I'll leash him so …" (Max smiles with a Master head rub) "… so old Maxy won't be running in the muck, chasing a skunk or something. Right, buddy?"

Robby watches and listens, as the three from the farm team with the old dog go down to cross the wet ditch. It's a scripted repeat.

"*Regardez la merde.*"

"Follow the yellow shit trail, eh?"

"You'd think it was the Green Giant having shits in the woods if we weren't searching for Thelma and Louie."

"I'm stuck on Oz. It's the straw-man's dumps."

Now Greg is singing. "*Off the yellow shit road, following a straw-man's load …*"

"Guys, straw-brains, heads up." Jimmy motions to a spot in front of him that looks no different than any spot along the ditch. "You need to step on this rock, then jump here. Or you'll have a soaker."

"What's a soaker?"

"Wet boots for the rest of the day."

The ditch takes them through two more neighbouring properties. The piles of poo are more infrequent, but the group still notices a blasted-out post on both occasions.

Jimmy has his phone up to his ear, walking on. "Stu, Jimmy here. Yes, those goats. Yes, Thelma and Louie. Yes, cute. Not so cute that the fence post has been knocked out on your back fence line. Yes, that is not cute. Yes, I'm looking at the damage right now. Stu, let's get through this today, settle up on any costs tomorrow. We're trying to catch up to the goats. Yes, Stu, they're still on the lamb."

John is the silent calculator, reviewing the pluses and minuses of their crisis plan. Greg is not confident about finding anything but lunch. "Jimmy, nice shade here. Can we have lunch?"

Nothing.

"Jimmy, it's past two in the afternoon," Greg continues. "We need a break. Take my shoes off and dry my socks."

"Now you know what a soaker is, eh, Greg?"

Jimmy stops and canvasses the soft grassy bank with some sun warmth. "Good spot; let's settle down. Maxy, I have your travel water bowl. Daddy will get you a drink."

Jimmy hands the long leash to John. Greg opens up a wax-paper-wrapped sandwich.

"B-N cheese, red onions, homemade pickles and mayo. My special request to Rita. What a gal. Her suggestion for a long hike and a picnic."

As John's hand digs into the brown bag, Greg slaps it away. "No, no, no. Sandwiches first. Greg does the serving. Snacks for later."

John looks at Max, the faithful, intent and patient sitter, who listens ears-up, pointing toward love, the love of treats. "But Maxy, there's something for you. Master Greg packed some treats for you, buddy. *And* an after-lunch chewy stick."

No arguing here. Max smiles with his tongue out, soaking up the great outdoors on trek with the Masters, with treats.

"Greg, these sandwiches, with fresh … white bread. And the mayo, home-made just like your mother's."

"What a sweet thought, buddy."

Another Max moment, ears perked at the sound of *buddy*.

No sooner have the two buddies stretched out to a post-lunch apple, and Max finished hoovering anything presented to him, than the clock starts again. Jimmy and the old dog are up and ready.

"It's been over half an hour," Jimmy says. "We need to get over to Sammy Otto's. His vegetable field goes to the market on Saturdays. It's on a direct path to the pond. Hurry, we need an hour to get there, and the sun is moving behind us."

The partners give him an even zero of a questioning look.

"Eat the apple with one hand, hold the walking stick in the other." Jimmy does a juggling demonstration with his empty hand and his walking stick. "Greg, get your socks and boots on, now."

Jimmy never shouts or yells; he instructs. Max is off-leash, pointing east, toward a possible target for empty goat guts. These two are ready to go.

After another hour of walking, Jimmy's phone rings.

"Aldert. Yes, getting there. We are over at Otto's. They hit his market field. Yes, another mow-job. Two blown-out fence posts, one on the south side, the other on the southeast corner. Yes, away from the highway direction. The dump? I agree, wouldn't like the smell there. Max is pointing that way. Next? We follow them."

He motions silent marching orders with his walking stick for the other two to get going. "But here's the good, and the bad. Sammy insists that we wait till he walks back to check the damage, with me. He has the gall to tell me his dogs have been barking for the last three hours. Busy on his books, he says, radio on, he says. Stay here, he says, and it's five o'clock, I say. Yes, Sammy will whine. Yes, add another fifteen minutes on to any simple conversation. We have to mention that a heart of gold the man has, yes, a heart of gold. But he's pissed at the moment. Yes, I can. See a set of flashers on the bridge, from here, yes. What? That's the police. What? You can't see me even with the binoculars. What's that? A car lineup?"

Big pause. The other two stop in their tracks, waiting for the scoop of hot information. Jimmy redirects them to Max, who's fifty feet up the trail, sniffing and pissing along the fence line.

"The volunteers with four-ways parked behind the W.I. ladies. Right. Lots of Town and Township folk too. You say, for kilometres, both sides?"

Big pause. The other two plus Max march on, still within earshot of half the news.

"Wow. All lined up like that. Look, we could be up to two hours getting to you. Yes, we need to get to the pond first. That's a guess — they will be thirsty. Cut them off from moving any farther toward the highway, or the tracks."

"Same to you. Till then."

The long conversation has taken John and Greg off the count, totalling up another mine-field of ice-cream-soft piles. This time it's chunky chips of green broccoli stems, creamy white cauliflower buds, and ribbons of cabbage. In the far corner of the field, stringy red bits appear, popping out of the poop.

"My God, John, it looks like candy-cane ice cream … without the cup."

All John can do is ask for God's help to purge another horrid ice-cream image. Jimmy's off the phone and caught up; his conversation was a relief, changing the subject from the big count. So far, twenty-seven plops of poo.

"Lined up?" John asks Jimmy. "What's all lined up, up on the highway?"

Jimmy stops walking so the other pair can pause. Max is long gone.

"Seems Thelma and Louie have garnered a ton of support. The W.I. ladies seem to have attracted a bumper-to-bumper following, all stopped with their four-ways on. Seems the ladies' original three-times-two cars in each direction have turned into a whole lineup of vehicles with four-ways on, stretching for kilometres."

Jimmy stacks his closed fists one atop the other, making a pile up. John gets it — they're parking cars. Greg stands quiet. He *can* help himself this time round; he stays quiet about the power of social media in mobilizing a crowd.

"Well," Jimmy goes on, "we attracted some real support from all sorts of people, ordinary folk who are driving out to park their car behind our cars. Everyone with their four-ways on, forming a stationary convoy along Highway 7. Aldert says it's quite a sight."

Jimmy points to a far-off line of bobbing single headlights. "Stonetown Four-Wheelers have volunteered to bring bag lunches and bottled water, and even taxi people to the washrooms at the arena. The parking is chockablock right up to the bridge."

Jimmy goes on. "See the flashers? Two cruisers are keeping the sight lines open for any highway traffic."

Greg lights up. "Yeah, there they are. I see them."

"See the cruiser on the left? It's beside a stake truck with amber flashers."

Greg nods. "Looks like the ETV production truck. You can see the satellite dish on top."

But Jimmy is looking the other direction, waiting for Sammy and his yapping dogs, who are approaching from across the field.

Max announces their arrival even at a great distance. *"Grrr-r-r-r-rrr."*

"Max, sit," Jimmy says.

Sammy and his dogs race in, quiet down, looking past the giant German shepherd. These guys are on autopilot, moving right to the centre of destruction.

"Jimmy, can't say it's a mow-job. Looks like a chop shop. What they haven't eaten, they trampled on —"

Curly Top chimes in with a direct contact underfoot. "My God, Sammy, and what's left over, they shit on."

"That's a conversation stopper," John says. But he's spoken too soon; Sammy is just about to begin.

"I was right in the middle of my book work. Reconciliation, you know, that takes some concentration. Jesse Cook was a great choice for drowning out those yapping dogs." Sammy has eyes down on the dogs smelling the piles of poop. "Those dogs, eh? Tried a little Bob Seger. *Greatest Hits*, you know, fantastic record, and all on ZIT satellite. But *yap, yap, yap …*"

Jimmy's thinking yippity-yap-yap himself, about to burst his patience bubble. "Sammy, we have to beat the failing light, find those goats before it's dark. We need to get to Turner's Pond before they head anywhere near that highway. We covered, buddy?"

"Well, guess so, Jimmy. Hey, I guess I can sleep in for one Saturday, with no product for the market."

Max is up and pointing for Jimmy. The farm dogs move their noses from one pile to the next, back away from the old dog. Sammy, John and Greg head off toward a fixed light show on the highway bridge.

"Kent Ward, LIVE at five for News Hour. HERE, at Highway 7 railway bridge, just south of St. Marys in southwestern Ontario."

Kent sweeps his mic-free hand back, not surrendering in the stare-down with the lens. Viewers will be distracted by the array of flashing lights filling the screen behind Kent.

"IS IT a bridge too far?"

Another sweep with the hand; this time the lens pans a three-sixty on the four-way flashing display.

"PEOPLE here don't seem to think so. Hundreds of vehicles on BOTH sides of the highway, PARKED, with their four-ways, for as FAR as the eye can see. Here's the Shepherd from the Say Cheese farm.

"Aldert, what DO YOU expect to happen?"

The face with no smile fills the screen. "Our farm team is on the trail of the two goats, and they seem to be heading to this point."

"You're a trained Shepherd, Aldert, a herd manager. You did not say heading in this direction; you said this point. Tell our viewers, how DO you know it's *THIS* point?"

Aldert doubles down on the serious look.

"Kent, the goats follow their gut. They will not like the noise from the cement plant or the human smells from our municipal dump. Goats need water, so they should deflect to Turner's Pond, about one kilometre that way. A Grade 10 geography student could draw a conclusion for any search, including our Say Cheese farm, by connecting food stops, with the availability of water, and the highway here. Connect the dots, Kent — that simple."

"What about trains?"

"We notified the freight people. The next passenger trains in each direction will be after eight. Goats will not like the industrial smell of the tracks either, the blast of the horn, the locomotive noise …"

The producer is circling a hand in the air to wrap it up with another pano. The screen scene switches to the big picture, with Kent's voice-over. "Thank you, Aldert, the Shepherd, Say Cheese."

The screen fills with a vertical string of dangling red lights. "What viewers are seeing is the long line of parked cars to the west."

The camera moves to the east.

"Both directions, a red string of flashing beads …"

The producer has his hands high and wide for a wide shot. He mimics the camera, moving side to side, last with a sweep to the west. Here, the telephoto lens pulls back for a close-up on the bridge. As the camera tries to focus, the road looks clear with bushy edges — no lights but the colours of a fading sun in the background.

The producer recognizes prey. "Pan back, Johnny."

No empty road with bushy edges: it's a wide bald head with Bozo side hair-flares. The new angle produces a huffing, puffy red face popping up, heading right into the lens. Kent picks up on the fresh meat with a beautiful segue.

"Quite a site, a TESTAMENT to a small community banding together in TROUBLED times. Here comes the MAYOR of St. Marys. Cheeko, what do you THINK of this vast group of organized volunteers? QUITE a sight."

"What can I say? Quite a sight." Huff, and puff. "This is what makes our rural communities so special. What can I do?" Huff, and two puffs. "Praise their efforts to save these poor goats."

Does Cheeko have a crocodile tear in his eye? The camera drops the mayor, cutting back to Kent's talking head.

"SO we wait. A bridge too FAR? A journey on the WRONG side of the tracks? Stay tuned for breaking news on Thelma and Louie, two goats on the LAMB, KENT Ward, LIVE, on the Highway 7 railway bridge, near St. Marys."

The camera pans east, a ginger slide in fading light, dominated by the beads of four-way flashers. The view shifts to the tracks, a telephoto finish down the tracks, fading out to a commercial break for Dr. Will Pearl and the Pearl Smile Clinic.

"Dr. Will here. Are YOU getting the most smile for your money? Because a Pearl smile …"

Max, not smiling, points east on the trail to water, so the group follows. They leave Sammy in a wonder at a goat's digestive abilities.

"The buggers hoovered up most of my best salsa peppers — a limited edition, hotter than Death Valley."

Jimmy sums up the pace of the chase. "They'll be galloping to get to that pond for a drink." He and the dogs gaze east, on the trail to Turner's Pond.

A faint voice can be heard behind them. *"Regardez la merde."*

Ahead, Napoleon and Queenie speed up to slow down. Bingo, a long soothing drink at the cool, natural-spring pond on the back corner of the Turner property, past the house but near the tracks. The farm team beats the trail closer and closer, struggling and gaining. The goats *have* to stop; those hot peppers are burning a path to pull the plug on more candy-cane ice cream piles. The rush stops, for a clean, four-compartment sweep of Queenie's twenty-five metres of royal intestines and the General's above-average forty metres. No shit, the goats pile it on. Candy-cane ice cream in the softest texture yet is left behind.

Queenie is the first to move; she smells an exotic flavour, ripe squash. Off she goes, leading for the first time. Napoleon's stomach sloshes like a rocky seashore as he catches up. He nudges her to the right.

"Too-o-o-oo much noi-oi-oi-s-s-se. Ea-ea-ea-eat this way."

Queenie straightens up, heads up straight, straight at the railway tracks. *Baa-a-a-a-ad* fencing offers no resistance to persistent goats. Napoleon nips at her back heels to keep her from the industrial grinding of the cement plant, that ear grit from the pounding limestone rock. Napoleon fails to see Queenie's lack of concern for any heard noise. She's down into the sloppy ditch doing, Moses on the frog populace; then with a stutter-step she's up the bank, up onto the rails. She turns right without a General nip, prancing straight down the track, matching her cadence to the ties.

"Thi-i-i-i-s-s-s-s way-y-y to foo-o-o-od."

The royal personage does not wait for permission to go ahead. Napoleon is horrified — the railway tracks smell, a burnt machine extract mixed in with a hint of the foulest human excretions. The General is off the tracks, off the side gravel, but catching up on the lumpy berm. *"Que-e-e-e-nie, of-f-f-f-ff. Ba-a-a-a-ad."*

Queenie is not catching any hint of danger. Napoleon catches a big whiff of the exotic squash, ripe for picking. There's treasure in mind, somewhere up through the burnt machine's gate. He continues off the railway bedding on a bumpy food track. In stride, he passes his Queen, heading to the Highway 7 underpass. This gate funnels his purpose, with an exhaust of pleasurable smells from another vegetable treasure trove straight into his empty gut.

If he looked back, he'd see his Queen in a trot with her eyes closed. Why? Queenie is free — free to eat and drink, free of royal responsibility to the herd, and free of foot. The Queen is enjoying her freedom in the careless splendour of an open trot on a clear path. She smells her General in the lead; she ignores the passing man-machine stench. She's in the splendour zone, in full pursuit, intoxicated by the aroma of some unknown, exotic food. Napoleon's stuck on his gut, which is connected to his nose. Queenie trots on, in a prance at the splendour of it all. If Napoleon looked farther back, past his royal love — way back on the machine tracks over her right shoulder, in the distance — he would see the shine of an unnatural light. The distant horn is both unfamiliar to Napoleon and inaudible to Queenie. The machine is out of the picture, too far back for him to turn and waste time detouring; so full-steam ahead on an empty goat gut.

"This is Kent Ward, LIVE on the Highway 7 railway bridge, south of St. Marys, Ontario. BREAKING news for ETV, the sun is SETTING on our TWO goats, Thelma and Louie, on the lamb at the END of Day 4. The crowd has gathered ..."

A camera pans east along the side of the bridge, with rows of local-yokel lookie-looks, highway-travelling rubbernecks out of parked cars, and the common breed of Nosey Parkers, who can't miss the closest seat to a raging fire. Folks wave to Kent behind his head. Over their heads, as far as the onscreen view stretches into the distance, is a cascade of flashing lights.

"So MANY people that, ALONG with police and volunteer firemen from the Blanshard-Nissouri department, are HELPING to direct traffic."

The lens pulls back for another sweep along the top of the bridge into the crawling traffic, on to Big Bob and the group of fluorescent X-jackets waving, flashing red batons to the windows-down, heads-out creeping drivers.

"Move ahead, please."

The police stand to the sides as silent witnesses, deferring to the volunteers.

"Move ahead, sir."

One more look-alike buddy with *Roger Does It* ball cap and cigarette hanging out of his mouth: "Can you see Thelma and Louie, sir?"

"Not yet, please move along."

Aldert, binoculars up, searches for the farm team, noticing the distant head-lamp. There is too much action noise — from standing crowd to crawling traffic — on the bridge, too far to hear the first blasts of the train horn. He peers again, gets a clear view of the approaching light.

"It's too soon for the ..." He switches to the cellphone, keeping to speaker for better vision.

Rrrr-r-r-rrr. Rrr-r-r-rrr. Rrr-r-rrr.

No time for salutations, it's an emergency call and Jimmy has his foot on the pedal.

"Aldert, we're not quite at the tracks. What about you?"

Aldert is yelling above the masses on the bridge. "Jimmy. Jimmy. Do you see the train? I can see it from the bridge."

"Yes, I see it coming, but no goats."

Greg, John and Max crowd in close to get the latest update.

"Nothing from here either," Aldert says.

"I'll call you when we're on the tracks."

If Aldert had lowered his binoculars to the rail tracks halfway back to the bridge, he could have deciphered the dark form of a fast-moving object heading his way. No one is looking on track. Every one of the heads on the bridge has their shoulders turned to look at Kent Ward and his LIVE report. Live below, under the dying light, the squash-consumed Napoleon passes beneath, without a blink of notice.

"Behind me," Kent continues, "many of the hundreds of volunteers have gathered on the bridge in SUPPORT of the search."

The producer asks the camera guy through the ear buds. "Who are those idiots with the goofy gobs waving at us?"

"Two dim-wits, looks like twins. They've been here since we arrived."

"Okay. Dim the shots off the little shits."

Producer is back with instructions for his talking head. "Kent. The crowd is looking over the side …"

Kent twists like an owl, back from the lens to the crowd.

"Kent, all of them are waving. They're saying something?"

The voice of experience breaks in. "BREAKING news. The crowd have seen a TRAIN coming. They are WAVING for its attention …"

Kent swivels his shoulders to align with his owl head, back to the tracks, his lower back to the screen. "It IS a train, COMING this way. They're screaming, screaming …"

Sound man has the boom mic up, extended, over the crowd in frantic chorus. *"STOP!"*

The camera is off the bridge and on the tracks as it telephotos out to the fast-approaching light. The producer looks at the screen. "Freddy, pan back to the tracks, slow. See it. See it."

The shot is in silence, except for the faint sound — for the listeners at home, thanks to the enhanced TV microphones — of a train horn.

Producer breaks the silence for Kent. "It's a goat. One of the goats. It's running toward us. The train is coming up behind it."

Kent switches to play-by-play. "The crowd continues to scream STOP. The train BLASTS ahead, a mechanical BULL stampeding toward our goat. A bull's-eye target on the tracks. Is it a bridge too far for Thelma, or Louie, on the tracks?"

The City-to-City passenger train has veteran engineers Coffee Chris and Larry Barry up front. The train has been warned of Thelma and Louie's possible path but advised that goats would never go, never *ever* go, onto the rail tracks.

"Look, Coffee, all the lights on the bridge. Some sight."

"Kinda like a red ribbon, eh?"

"Look, there's … a whole bunch of people. A CROWD of people waving. PULL the horn."

"Barry. Written instructions were 'Ease off horns' … NOT to scare the goats."

"Cab lights on, then. We'll smile and wave."

Cab lights off would have worked better for a quicker sighting of Queenie on tracks.

"Barry. ANIMAL. BRAKES."

Engineer has two hands on all stopping power. "It's the goat …"

A short sentence before contact.

The train hits, or rather bumps, the goat up and off tracks, then over sideways to the lumpy but soft berm. Napoleon watches from the tunnel, listens to an echo in the horror; *the horror of it all.* The bridge audiences gasps, a shrill sound heard over the squealing passenger-train brakes, and the crowd freezes to attention. Under the racket and momentary chaos, electric windows slide down and car doors crack open, along the line of light beads, east and west on Highway 7. All captured in a live panoramic sweep on national TV.

Aldert slides down the steep bank, landing in a run ahead of the police and Big Bob. The farm team catches up to a stopped train. Napoleon retraces his steps under a number of lit-up passenger cars with faces to the glass. Human eyes are stuck in the floodlight spot farther back, and no one notices the large goat until Napoleon is standing over his Queen — a cocked-headed lump on the top of the berm — in full spread for the gawking travellers. Maybe things wouldn't have ended in a lump, if the bump hadn't twisted her neck from the fall from splendour in her trot of freedom. The passengers stare down on tragedy without a dry eye.

Maybe it was the one rotten apple, a seven-year-old kid who started to tap his Transformers figure on the glass; maybe it was the gasping from the bridge audience, or the brakes shredding to stop the massive machine, leaving a leftover burnt smell. The yelling police and shouting volunteers in flashy fluorescent vests did not help. Whatever it was, the General has had enough: he stands his ground, up on his back hooves. With the help of the floodlights from the search-and-rescue van and cellphone flashes from the train passengers, TV screens across Canada show off Napoleon in his full glory.

Up front, off their seats, it's the passengers' turn to gasp.

"My goodness, look at the size of ..."

"His everything, it's huge."

"Looks more like a stallion than a goat."

The well-travelled, talkative Ed, the conductor, straddles the train aisle and speaks up over all the backs and shoulders facing the sideshow.

"In St. Marys, because of the cement plant, they call them 'Arnies.'"

A mutter rides the rail car back and forth on the west side.

"Some Arnies ..."

And the Transformers kid. "Jordy, turn your face." The toy tapping stops.

Most people in the bridge audience have heard the rumours on the General size of the stud goat. The gasps turn to *oooohs* as the floodlights expose all. Even at this distance, big is big.

Kent provides the background to a sad scene.

"The train has STOPPED in the tracks of the GREAT escape. The Thelma-and-Louie adventure has come to an END, in tragedy, with the LOSS of one goat — was it Thelma or Louie ...?"

The producer yells into his mic for an earbud message to Kent. "My God. Look at the size of his equipment ..."

The lower halves of screens in homes all across our nation are filled with the full monty of the General's equipment package.

"ETV sources have CONFIRMED the dead goat is in fact THELMA. Louie, her consort and lover, is STANDING over her body. Her General RIGHT to the end, I STAND on guard for THEE, Your Majesty."

Napoleon, back on all fours, puts his head down to anyone approaching. He cries out a snort and snarl at the closing crowd:

"Baa-a-a-a-a-ack-ack-ack-ack

ahh-f-f-f-f-f-fff. Baa-a-a-a-a-ack-ack-ack-ack."

The *ack-ack-ack* is a coughing gun sound. The *ah-f-f-f-f-f-fff* could be attached to an f-bomb.

Above the raucous unfolding, the police commander shouts out, "Sergeant, bring up Al, the sharpshooter."

Aldert, in a super flash, is out front, blocking any official move.

"I'm the Shepherd. He's my responsibility. I can handle this."

Jimmy holds Max, John and Greg back, motioning for quiet. The bridge group goes silent, absorbed in the drama below. Screens are frozen on the large goat guarding a lump, as a young man approaches in front of the police line.

"Aldert, the Shepherd from the Say Cheese farm, has bought A STAY of execution for the overwrought Louie, who has LOST his Thelma. Police were about to PUT DOWN the bereaved goat, DERANGED in his sorrow. Aldert, Shepherd hero, heaven-sent, has STEPPED up to save Louie. His ONE hand is out; he has a … something green in his hand … it's an APPLE. His hand is out; he has NOT moved another inch."

The producer adds in. "He's talking to the goat, Kent."

"Ladies and gentlemen, boys and girls, LOOK close. Our LIVE breaking news coverage shows the good Shepherd talking to the head of his flock. Day four of the GREAT escape that has ENDED, ENDED in tragedy at a bridge TOO far for ONE goat on the lamb, POOR Thelma."

Napoleon walks away from the lump on the berm toward Aldert's apple hand. Jimmy makes a quick move with Greg's picnic blanket to cover Queenie. He cannot help himself thanking God for the ripe tomato design versus anything Little Pony. Aldert is able to get his other hand on Napoleon's collar. Napoleon is relieved to be led in any direction that will get him back to a comfortable pasture and things familiar.

"The Shepherd has Louie BY the collar and is leading him BACK up to the bridge. The crowd is PARTING in silence. No. Wait. They're CLAPPING — everyone is clapping as the big goat and the young man PASS through. And, wait …

"The audience can HEAR the cascade of horns honking UP and down Highway 7. It's SAD; many of these people will think the rescue of Thelma and

Louie a COMPLETE success. They do NOT know this story ended good for one, AND bad for ONE goat on the lamb."

Pause as the camera follows the recalcitrant goat and Shepherd back to the Say Cheese truck.

"Here's Jimmy Kember, for the Say Cheese farm. Jimmy, a day of GREAT joy with the rescue of LOUIE, and GREAT sadness with the LOSS of Thelma."

Jimmy can smile at last. "It's been an adventure, Kent, to say the least, but Say Cheese will continue on as a number-one artisan goat cheese producer. We will always have a place in our hearts for a noble queen, Queenie. The Queen would insist we move on, in good memories."

Chapter 22

The call comes loud and clear, through social media, on broadcast, in print, over ZIT lines and over neighbour fence lines for the need of a tribute to the noble Queen, now lying in rest under the old oak tree in the back corner paddock of the Century Farm. A small ceremony for the Say Cheese team didn't cut the cheese when it came to public demand to lay their feelings of grief to rest. The core support for two goats on the lamb came through the W.I., with Stonetown Mobile Radio as their search partners. Cookbook ladies and wired men reached past the official response of police, fire, ambulance, the *St. Marys Journal* and the Sunriser to a direct up-link with Kent Ward, who updated the world on his live ETV broadcasts. Now, the W.I. has returned to the heart of the matter to lead a charge of the light brigade to organize a tribute to Queenie. The grounds of Town and Country swell with support, a move to action backed by newspaper columns, TV anchors, and self-declared pillars, with their here-I-am hands in the air: the mayor, the pastor and Kent Ward.

Back on the farm, the motion of routine continues with hollow feelings. It's a sleepwalk for the team. Greg uploads tons of pictures from his smartphone and various contributors, touching on Queenie while taking into account the Thelma and Louie tragedy. On field work, Aldert collars up the collies for outside help running the herd, some control in a vacuum of leadership. Inside, Serge and Jimmy reflect on the unsettled herd and on lower fat levels, while the production graph zigs and zags in a drop on the HD flat screens. Jimmy has developed a nervous habit of cleaning his reading glasses to oblivion while squinting for an upswing in the televised instant data. Around home and office, John keeps his routine to Capps and capital, reminding the team to keep on their game. Behind the barn, Frankie's as surprised as a pig can be at the sudden return of his whey. Over the propane cooktop and cherrywood counter, Barbara experiments with kitchen cheese under strange milking circumstances. She's whisking away in a yellow-ware bowl.

"Goodness me, this milk is beating me up."

Frustration interruption: she wipes off her hands before the sixth ring, picks up the phone.

"Yes, Rita, still in the kitchen. No retirement here, making cheese."

Barbara waits, nodding her head.

"Yes. That Brie I brought to the book club. Yes. Whoa."

Head nods.

"I did see the front page editorial in the *Journal*. Yes, Kent Ward mentioned it too. Yes, it was on the night news. Right, the part where he gives a message from behind his work desk. Like *60 Minutes*, right."

Head shaking.

"No. I haven't heard that."

The ZIT side of the conversation goes silent as Rita is going on, and on. Barbara's back in.

"Well, I can't say no. It's a free world. But you did say Cheeko. *He* thinks that he can organize it? And at The Flats? That's right, you said W.I. in charge. Great. And you say Pastor Harlton too — that's all good. But, Rita, you do have Cheeko on a time clock?"

Rita leaves Barbara with the question of how W.I. will do the day.

"That'll work, with Edith Michaels. And a necktie and hook, you say. Now that'll work with *her* in charge."

Edith, AKA the Mighty Mousse — a dual reference to her stature, at under five feet, and her high standing when it comes to chocolate-inspired, prized desserts. A retired GP from the Pleasant Valley Family Medical Clinic, Edith is a dead ringer for Dr. Ruth. If Barbara had a list, she would be a big check on the short list.

"The day will be inclusive. Yes, I like the idea that we are holding an ecumenical service, with all the churches represented. Harlton will speak on behalf of the Stonetown Ministerial Association. Whoa, the pastor himself graces the event."

Barbara's mind wanders off on the choice of the Methodist Hall minister. *Won't need a PA system with Harlton broadcasting the message.* Back on ZIT with Rita, Barbara's swimming in a fast current of details. The community will gather in force at the confluence of the Thames and that creek in a flood-prone park known as The Flats. Barbara catches up.

"And you say it's a blessing of animals. Okay, *the* blessing of animals. More pastor suggestions to be all inclusive. Yes, the Stonetown Farmers Market ends at eleven. Easy segue, I get it. So does the pastor, right. Not Sunday either, not necessary to piss anyone off, eh, Rita? And he adds on a tribute to farming. We could add on a tribute to the Downtown Merchants Association too?"

Pause. Longer pause.

"Rita, just kidding; it's a joke."

Barbara zips it on the ZIT line about adding whiny merchants to whiny farmers. The logic line and the joke line are lost on Rita. Keep to the list Rita's talking about. What a list.

"Okay, okay, that too, all covered. I need to repeat this to everyone here."

Barbara drops the phone to her Say Cheese logo apron, canvasses the room in a moment of real frustration.

"Where's a focking pen and paper when you need to make a list? No matter."

Phone is back up to her ear.

"You say a parade and blessing of animals *with* a tribute to Queenie."

Pause.

"Yes, blessing of *the* animals. I get it. All inclusive ..."

Pause.

"Yes. At the centre of it all, *still Queenie*. Yes, it *is* the W.I. in charge. No, not the two wind-bags, Harlton and Cheeko. W.I. is in charge of the day. And, the Mighty Mousse on the time clock."

The Flats on a dry day, outside of the spring flooding season, has all the advantages for a day of blessing, a day of thanks, a day of tribute for Queenie, her animal friends and farmers. Easy access on a gravel loop around the egg-shaped park, tons of parking, abundant trees to hide the sun, a dumpy pavilion that offers no rain shelter, washrooms for a pour, and a livestock corral with knock-down grandstands used in quarter-horse, 4-H and dog shows. *All* the get-up-and-go an organizer needs right in the centre of Town.

Cheeko cuts the shit. "You could have Noah's ark and its full passenger list in that park, shitting all day."

If the listener doesn't understand, can't stand to listen to or just can't stand the mayor, all okay. His Worship loves to hear himself think.

"What can I say? My parks guy tells me it's all good for the grass. What can I do? My operations guy tells me rain on Sunday will wash all poop away — drain-able gravel."

A question from Town staff stops the mayor in his tracks.

"What can I say? No, Dan is not a weather expert. What can I do? Ask my wife; she's the weather guide." With election year coming up, he reaches out for support. "What can I say? Grass or gravel, we can work with the shit."

Pastor Harlton takes the higher road, a clean path.

"A big day of blessing that brings Town and Country out in the open, together under God's eyes."

Cheeko sets aside the Country as good neighbours; it's the Town that has the votes he needs for next year's election.

The Say Cheese team is front and centre for the blessing of the animals, a tribute to Queenie. They're stuck there for the full agenda, with their farm repre-sentatives; Coca, Gracie and Lizzie all sit guard over a standing, nervous Hector.

They lead the blessed animals through the corral gate to the double circle of plastic chairs, with Cheeko waiting to the side of the podium as Pastor Harlton throws his holy spirit among Noah's representatives.

"Nice doggie. Good boy. Bless you … pig."

The corral is full of animal life, the chairs all occupied and overflowing onto a standing-room of animals and humans. The inside crowd front two sides of the breakdown grandstands jammed with oversized people and small pets. And all life chews with open, fly-catching mouths. People may be chewing on gum purchased at Dick's Variety, while animals may chew on carrots, celery or leftover veggies donated by the Farmers Market. There's mixed results with a small pack of sly dogs who miss nothing.

"Look. Bruce's dog …"

"Prince."

"Well Prince is having a royal chew. He's got gum …"

"Have a carrot. Farmers Market is giving them out."

No idea what Cheeko has packed in his cheeks, Pastor Harlton takes the podium with a full mouth of empty words. He pivots with one hand to the heavens, acknowledging the crowd, with a special nod to the small lady with horn-rimmed glasses, a pencil in her ear and a clipboard in her hand. He looks over his readers.

"Edith Michaels."

You would never know that she was *standing* next to a front row chair — *that* short. The pastor loses his concentration as the small hand holds up a large stopwatch. He turns his head up from the yoo-hoo reminder, both hands on the podium, eyes roll back, back.

"We. We all, *all* of us here start our lives small. Most will grow in our lives — grow big. But …"

Harlton's eyes return to earth; his right hand points at no one in particular. Those unfamiliar with the Methodist Hall minister's style shiver from that glare and stare.

"But all of us start on four; animal *and* human."

Two four-fingered hands do a scary spider reach; then the arms stretch sideways.

"All will grow to balance ourselves in life."

He turns from the left side to the right side of the grandstands.

"Whether you have two legs or four, today we gather to bless the animals, pay tribute to one lost Queen. Gather in the confluence of the Thames, in this fair park we call with affection "The Flats," in the heart of our great Town, with our Country friends. Town and Country that make this great province of Ontario build into the vast nation of Canada. God blesses us, blesses all animal life present, and holds in his palms those not available — or in the case of Queenie, at heaven's gate …"

Something is waving off to the side. He turns to see that short woman with that oversized stopwatch.

"Please welcome the mayor of St. Marys with his message."

Cheeko has watched that short woman instead of listening for the prompt from the pastor. The polite short applause stops. Whoops, all eyes are on Cheeko, who has a dirty look for the pastor as he steps to the podium.

"Thank you, Pastor Harlton, for your introduction."

A political pause over nothing that matters.

"My fellow St. Marysites, *and* I see many of our neighbour Zorrites, Nissourites, Blanshardonians. Yes, I see you waving. The Transvaalites. Ladies and gentlemen, boys and girls and all the animals gathered here, a blessing from our Ecumenical Association."

A turn of acknowledgement to the front-row church pew of men in suits. A waving hand to the sidelines distracts him for the moment as the stopwatch moves back and forth. A politician has the experience and talent to always continue.

"Today …" Hands to the heavens. The audience is already watching a helicopter ambulance skirt the Town, following the rail line. "…Today we gather. Gather in memory, memory of a prizewinning …"

Readers down, eyes up on the crowd.

"… might I add, a national champion. This animal, known to all, far and in between, as Queenie, an animal we are blessed …"

The mayor turns his cheek in a political nod to the pastor.

"Blessed I would say, blessed to have known our Queen, Queen of the goat team …"

The short woman is hopping a bit on one foot with that stopwatch waving about. Worse, she shifts, motioning to a neck slice from her clipboard.

"… who better to address the Queen, to speak to the royal goat, but the founder of Say Cheese himself. Let me bring forward a man who needs no introduction, our favourite son …"

Cheeko turns in an aside to Jimmy.

"Looking more like a grandfather, buddy."

Cheeko's back to the crowd.

"Our favourite son in business education, with a world-renowned reputation, and might I add for our Country neighbours, a visionary of high-tech farming. Without further ado …" (His Worship looks back at the one-hopping stopwatch woman) "… Professor Jimmy Kember."

Cheeko backs off to stand beside the pastor, stage righteous joining stage political. Jimmy waves at the crowd with a smile, turning for a nod and wink at the short lady, Edith, who is also a member of Barbara's book club. Edith signs off to listen in a sit-down demonstration of her confidence. Professor Jimmy, with a background in theatre-style classes at Western University, hotel ballroom seminars on the road and tours of massive barns, has never seen an audience quite like this. Your hometown is always the most difficult audience. Jimmy waits and waves again, while the applause subsides.

"Queenie."

Big pause; the crowd does not stir or peep.

"Queenie is a loss. A shot to our hearts, creating a hole that memories will struggle to fill. The hole is most evident in the heart of Say Cheese Artisan Goat Cheese company. Our Century Farm has lost a personality — not a person — lost a royal personality."

Time for comic relief in a tight crowd.

"Queenie is a goat."

Murmurs of laughter ripple about.

"Queenie is more than any animal, two-legged or four-legged. Queenie *is* a personality, a royal personality. This personality can never be replaced, but she can be remembered, in *our* hearts. Memories to treasure and keep in *our* hearts. Look above the wall of gold ribbons, embossed certificates and silver-plated trophies that Queenie has racked up over the years. Look close, very close, at the goat herd ..."

Jimmy looks south along the confluence of the Thames, downriver toward the Say Cheese farm. The crowd turns south to gather his point.

"Look at the bronze colour mixed throughout the herd, those eyes; look close. Open eyes that are winter blue, like their mother, grandmother, great-grand-mother ... and maybe a bit more."

Some comic relief again comes hither and thither.

"She was, she *is* the Queen in our eyes forever, eyes reflected in the herd on the farm. A future for us, a *future* for prizewinning cheese from the Say Cheese Artisan Goat Cheese farm."

Jimmy has both hands up in the arm.

"Long reign the Queen. Queenie forever in our cheese."

Greg is caught on his front-row seat with the image in mind of a cork-pop off the porch on a fine fall afternoon. *That Sparkler ...* an *a-a-h-ha-a-a-a* moment out of the cooler ... chilled in the fridge, ripe and ready for toasts all round after the official tribute to their lost Queen. He finds his hand rising to the first toast in the sun's reflection. *"Long reign the Queen ..."* He's enjoying his refreshing quaff at a porch wake when the wake-up call arrives.

"Saddle up, Greg."

Aldert's mile smile has broken in his face.

"We're off. Are you okay?"

Greg looks up at the Shepherd, then over to the dissipating crowd; then he sees the back of a tight suit facing a television camera. This last sight provides Greg enough motivation to exit The Flats. Greg heeds the call of crispy toasts, while a familiar voice begins beaming by satellite loud and clear to the world.

"There you have it. The tribute to Queenie, the goat of Thelma and Louie fame, put to rest by Town and Country in the heart of the small Town of St. Marys, here in the confluence of the Thames in this park-like setting."

The head goes right as the shoulders shift to allow a hand swipe. The camera picks up, continuing the sweep around the gravel loop and under the tree canopy. The shot captures the remnants of the crowd on their way out, giving the camera a few waves, and on closer inspection a few middle fingers. Every single step out is careful, mindful of the shit. The camera returns home to the familiar head and shoulders.

"Kent Ward reporting. A tribute service, a service that included a blessing of the animals, spoke to a noble goat — a prizewinning, champion goat — *Queenie*. We spoke with ecumenical representative Pastor Harlton before the ceremony."

As the farm team make their way to their cars, they glance at the ETV monitors. The on-screen view switches to the pastor, recording with a straight look through the lens.

"Kent, blessed are the animals, for that's where our fortune comes in a rural community. City and Country people eat the cheese, drink the milk, and barbecue the meat of these animals. So let's give thanks, a blessing of the animals, for our animals, whether lap dog, guinea pig, Holstein cow, horse, or goat, of course. A special day, with a tribute to Queenie."

The head and shoulders return.

"The pastor did bless over one hundred animals, including dozens of dogs, cats, a few Holstein cows, plus Hector, a beautiful billy goat off the Say Cheese farm. Let's see what Professor Jimmy Kember says about his young stud."

"Kent," Jimmy's recorded voice echoes over The Flats, "as you know, Napoleon, our number-one stud, returned to the farm a changed goat after the loss of Queenie."

Camera turns back to Kent. "The tragedy of Thelma and Louie. Jimmy, who's this to be blessed?"

The camera goes down to one black, standing goat, surrounded by a plethora of dog paws. The view backs up to capture the three collies. Jimmy speaks to the goat.

"Meet Hector — our number-two billy on the Say Cheese farm. Jet black with charcoal eyes, just like his father."

"Jimmy, our viewers will ask: What happens to the famous General, Napoleon?"

"Napoleon has not met his Waterloo quite yet; breeding season comes later."

The camera stays on Hector, but you can hear the smile in Jimmy's voice-over.

"Hector's got big hooves to fill."

Off record and back to Kent, who skips the voter-pandering politicians.

"With Professor Kember's eloquent, heartfelt tribute to his royal champion,

Queenie, came an array of political representatives with greetings for the gathering."

Those are the last words Greg hears as he closes the passenger door of the Say Cheese farm truck. Next thing, the team's holding flutes high in the air, rounds of goodbye toasts to Queenie, hello to making cheese, tasting the last rays of a warm October day.

John reminds the team.

"Lots of stuff to re-sort on the farm, lots to sort coming up. Roles and goals, gentle people."

Jimmy applies the business smarts.

"Settle the herd, the fat content will return; the volume will be up. Cheese will be in the cooler."

Barbara applies home smarts.

"You're tasting my results from the back kitchen. The double Brie works no matter the whey."

Greg tops up the glasses for applause all round.

"Brilliant, Barbara. You are a wonder in the kitchen."

Off food and milk and on to the herd for the Shepherd.

"Well folks, I'm backing the dogs off, for less control of the herd. I had my idea on leadership and the path seems set."

Jimmy knows what Aldert's referring to, but the others give a quizzical look.

"Her daughter Arrow. Queenie's Arrow. She seems a natural to lead."

Aldert pets Max. "No more dogs, but soon enough, eh, buddy?"

Jimmy knows the next question and answer, waits for the group to catch up. John asks:

"And, what about Napoleon? And Hector, number two in waiting?

Aldert has that mile-wide smile.

"As Jimmy said on television, there's a bit of time till breeding season. A little #1 and #2 should do the job, through and through."

Barbara is giving her former student a once-over in true meaning. Aldert widens the smile.

"You know, Barbara, the old 'one-two' …"

Jimmy steps in.

"Napoleon has earned retirement if that's what he wants. Hector seems keen. But, team …" (All glasses are down, heads on the Professor) "… settle the herd, and we can make prizewinning cheese."

Greg has had enough of cheese and of goat breeding for now.

"We need a party," he says. "Our 'Christmas on the Farm' will be a nice reprieve from all this … action." Greg can't help himself. "We will have 'Christmas on the Farm' with a 'Wedding Girl' theme."

Toasts burn another round on the flutes.

Chapter 23

Tap, tap.

> *"O-o-o-o-oooh that smell.*
> *Can't you smell that smell?*
> *O-o-o-o-oooh that smell,*
> *The smell of cheese surrounds you."*

Eyes closed in a relaxing mantra hum, Jaybird wireless headphones plugged into both ears, finger taps keep rhythm and rhyme on the red cooler. Billie has a ballsy cover in mind.

> *"Now they call me Prince Charming,*
> *Can't speak a word for harming."*

Two taps with eyes down on the cooler wrapped tight with bungee cords and Maple Leafs–logo duct tape.

> *"So you'll be all right with Billie.*
> *And Billie will be tight for you.*
> *Hey, you're so cool."*

Head back, tight grip on the treasure chest, and eyes closed to relax. *Tap, tap.* "O-o-o-o-oooh that smell ..."

"Hello? Hello!"

Billie is eyes wide open, held tap-less. The conductor is bent over into his space, close to his face.

"Sir, your ticket please."

"Of course ..."

Scan and *beep, beep. Beep, beep,* the ear-buds go off.

"Arrival to the City in two hours and a half. Can I put your ... cooler ... in the large baggage area up front?"

The noise of the passenger train makes the words inaudible as Billie turns up a nervous tic to an anxious whisper. "Plus, plus, plus ..."

"Sorry?"

Tap. Tap, with no rhythm. The conductor examines the grey Gollum with straw hair.

"Plus, plus fine, right here will be," Billie says.

The conductor leans in more, almost on top of the cooler, a bird prying. "Might fit on the rack …?"

"Plus, plus fine, right here will be."

Conductor draws both fingers, pointing first at Billie, then the cooler. Billie notes nice nail care. He misses the stare-down.

"Plus, if you change your mind …" The conductor's off.

Billie plugs the headphones back in, switches the music channel in search of calm, maybe happy. Not Jimmy Buffett; maybe Pablo Cruise or … Harry Nilsson. He's off to music undercover land with eyes closed. His lips move onto a sweet spot.

> *"O-o-o-o-oooh what a day,*
> *Nothing can stand in my way."*
> *Tap. Tap.*
> *"Now that you're shipped …"*

Billie's phone rang at five o'clock this morning. That call raised his flaxen head for a sharp wake-up off the exposed rough rafter in his low-ceilinged bedroom. He didn't even have time to say ouch before answering his phone.

"It's Barbara," came the voice. "Get up now, and listen up. This is a big emergency."

She was emergency-whispering, marbles in the mouth.

"Plus, plus, Barbara," he said. "You need plus volume."

"OK, Billie. E-mer-gen-cy. Focking get your plus arse out of bed, I'll pick you up in twenty minutes."

"What about work? What about Mother?"

"What about getting your arse in gear? Listen: *E-mer-gen-cy.*"

"Focking got it, Barb. I'll be outside in fifteen."

Eyes closed, Billie keeps a tight grip on the treasure chest. His lips mouth the storyline while he rewinds the reel of this morning's drama.

In Barbara's car all the way from home on The Gore to the cutesy St. Marys Train Station, Barbara gave him the lowdown on the e-mer-gen-cy that came to light in the darkness of the Say Cheese truck earlier that morning, trailer in tow.

"You better use the bathroom here at the train station so you don't have to let the cooler out of your sight."

When he had obliged, Barbara handed him the cooler. "Don't drop the foot-ball," she told him. She gave him a fifty-dollar bill and the written address on a note for the taxi. She turned to go, then remembered, stuffing a brown paper bag in his satchel. "Billie, I packed an egg salad sandwich I made just for you. Even better than Rita's …"

Last words before Billie boarded the train at the crack of dawn. Billie was relieved Barbara didn't sew his name and address in his jacket.

Up front now, the train conductors confer.

"Look. I told you. His lips move, but the eyes! Closed tight, with that visor grip on the …?"

"It's a cooler. With Maple Leafs duct tape and bungee cords."

"Real strange."

"Strange? Go Leafs go."

"I offered to stow it up front here, or above. He does this *plus, plus, plus* thing and says no."

The two conductors continue their gab-fest on another slow day on the train.

"Forget the Leafs, it's the smell. It's like that song, *O-o-o-o-oooh that smell, can't you smell that smell?* The smell of … mystery surrounds him."

"Smell? B.O.?"

"No, something in the cooler."

"It stinks?"

"No, a mystery aroma. Like my basement on a humid summer day."

"Funky."

The first conductor takes time to consider the odour. "Like my lawn smells after I cut it … maybe a little nutty too."

"Maybe it's his lunch. Salami can be real strong."

"No. It's *not* the cooler. He has a brown bag with a sandwich, and some snacks. I smell egg salad."

Conductor number two looks over the shoulder of his work mate. "He can eat and grip at the same time?"

"Amazing what you can do with your right hand."

"Maybe it's lunch or dinner for his sweetheart or his family …"

"Maybe it's dead body parts, a bag of anthrax, or … a bomb. You know, he takes his hands off and *Powee!*" Conductor number one mimes an explosion big enough to engulf number two, who does not second the suggested disaster scenario.

"Lay off the weed buddy, making you paranoid. Let me go have a little sniff."

Conductor number two rolls down the aisle like a bowling ball ready for a strike.

Billie, eyes closed, pinned to a grip on the cooler, mouths the words, *"O-o-o-o-oooh what a day."* His eyes flash wide open, his back frozen to his seat, firmer on the grip with a different bird now prying over him. The nosey bird talks.

"The City. Two more stops. Can I stow your … cooler?"

"Plus, plus, plus better right here." *Tap. Tap.*

On the plus side, the interruption creates an opportunity to eat the second half of Barbara's delicious sandwich.

FOUR HOURS EARLIER …

Jimmy's on the drive, Serge is up front for the ride, Aldert in the back for a snooze with the KeepKool portable refrigerator whirling away, held in place by the fourth seatbelt. Jimmy did the seating. ("Aldert, you're in the back. Try and catch some shut-eye.")

The Shepherd had set up the herd for Faisal and Ozzy who would be incoming at dawn. Barbara would keep her attention on the regular farm routine throughout the day. Now, kept awake by the cooler's whine, Aldert notices something strange. He squeezes his nose to attention.

"O-o-o-o-oooh, that smell!"

Maybe it was Linda's chili last night. Serge sure piled it back. That garlic bread? His roommate has a Frankie appetite. Who knows? Aldert was long gone to the barn by the time the *fromager* hit *les toilettes*. What *is* that smell?

"Jimmy, a touch down on my window, please," Aldert says.

Jimmy is never impressed by over-childproof vehicles, a pain in the farm butt. He releases the automatic child lock. "Locks off. You can adjust it."

The opened window does not provide relief. The cold air merely wakes up the passengers to something gone wrong, very wrong. What can you say?

"Jimmy." And what can you do? "Pull off at the service centre. We may have a problem."

From the passenger side. *"Comment?"*

"O-o-o-o-oooh, that smell. Can't you smell that smell?"

Jimmy takes in a nose draw. "I can. We'll pull off."

Serge is almost over the front seat to the back, points to the lid.

"Flip the bar up," Aldert tells him. Serge is silent.

Aldert looks at Jimmy. "It's a red light. It's on heat, not cool."

"Ayy-eee. Flip the switch for green," Jimmy says. "Open the lid."

Everyone reaches for their child-unlocked window buttons. Jimmy powers the truck and trailer off the exit ramp for an emergency stop. Three windows go down to a flush of cool industrial service centre air.

Jimmy applies the four-ways and parking brake and opens the door all in one motion. He hops out, skips around the truck hood before you could Say Cheese, into the right back seat. "Not good. We need cheese for competition, not a fondue." He looks up at Serge. "Wasn't it on green, cool from the start?"

"Jimmy, I did not check anything, I'm colour-blind. Barbara asked me to put it in the back seat and plug it in. The truck has to start before the fridge starts. Green and red look the same to me. The light was not on at that time." He turns to Aldert. "The fridge was secure with that whirring sound, right? I assumed all was a go."

Jimmy examines the cheese. "We might be able to save the hard ones, but the Brie will be done."

Serge and Aldert ask the same question. "What's next?"

Jimmy starts off. "I'll call Barbara. I think there's a backup already in place, right ready to save our asses."

Serge is next. "I need to visit *les toilettes*. Last night's chili was so good, but …?"

Aldert is the Shepherd. "I'll check on Hector."

Jimmy knows Barbara's social agenda: a book club gathering this afternoon; early train to the City tomorrow. Tonight her soirée friends plan to play cheese judges on the Say Cheese examples for the Royal Winter Fair, and cover some great Greg drops of the grape. The ladies love the wine complemented by local artisan cheese. And then the horse show will take it over the top. Shepherd's pie and greens, with surprise crème brûlées and port to finish off.

"Almost a million dollars in prize money for the equine competition."

"Dressage is great."

"Work horses impress me."

"Is that a triple-cream Brie?"

"Whoops. My wine glass seems to have gotten empty."

Barbara is not expecting an emergency interruption at five in the morning. After the Royal Fair the Kembers are expecting to wind down to move into Thomas Street in the following two weeks, before the Christmas on the Farm party — which will be Greg and John's responsibility alone, at least for the most part.

The phone's sudden ring wakes her up with a clear head.

"What's wrong, Jimmy? You all right?"

"Yes dear."

She's silent, waiting for her husband to say what's right about the dead-of-the-night call.

"Barbie, we have a problem with the cheese in the cooler. Heat."

"Heat? It's a cooler."

"No, the button got moved. To heat."

She's off the bed. "Focking not all right. What do you think?"

Barbara sits silent in the sleigh bed, listening to a quick review on colour-blindness. Jimmy's quick with a plan that restores the promise of a lost weekend with the help of a designated courier. Barbara buys in.

"Right choice, great plan. *Billie.* The train makes sense, one vehicle in the City. Hector, yes. You need to offload him, the trailer and the nasty cheese. 'Fondue Friday,' funny, Jimmy."

Jimmy describes a well-planned City arrival.

"Taxi money?" Barbara clarifies. "Okay, and somebody will be waiting for him at the Empress Gate, yes?"

"Barbara, you are the best partner."

"All good, Jimmy. Things will be all right with the girls coming over. Barbara always has a focking backup plan. See you Friday."

"Love ya Barbie, thank you."

"Yes, I love you too. No, no, don't thank me. Thank poor Billie, it will be a shock for him."

And that's how Billie came to be in the City for a weekend of Royal adventure plus, plus, plus.

First thing on arrival is a run out of the station to grab a cab. Billie's still on the ball, the football, don't drop the football. It's the City, so no one notices the hurry-scurry of Gollum with his straw head whistling in the wind of York Street as he heads off. So what if he has a lover's latch on his lunch cooler? Go Leafs go. Gollum gasps to the finish line of yellow taxis. The right hand releases its grip on the cooler to work the door open, passing the driver the printed address of the correct Coliseum gate as Billie slides in to a quick acknowledgement.

"Ah, the Princess Gate. Well, that's what we call it. Full name is Princess Virginia Gate."

Jose notices something unusual in the mirror review of his backseat passenger and cooler. Go Leafs go, but what is that strange aroma? Not industrial, not traffic, but a barnyard smell, maybe spoiled milk? It's an inside job. He taps his window button.

"Buddy, windows are electric," he tells Billie. "Need any fresh air …"

Billie draws in a big draft of cheese. One word covers the explanation. "Cheese."

Jose can't believe his ears. "Cheese?"

All that can be seen in the mirror is Billie's free right hand pointing down. Billie's pointing at the cooler; Jose think he's pointing down, down, to his butt. He's cut the cheese. All Billie can see is the gobsmacked look in the mirror. He releases the right hand.

"The window I will open plus."

Jose adds two taps to his window button, bookended by looks in the mirror. His passenger stares off in another direction.

Billie is gripped all round, looking out the window as the cityscape blows back big plumes of smoke over a cold November morning. Billie reflects on the City, starting with who will greet him at the Royal Winter Fair drop-off. That's when he comes into focus. He sees Jimmy out of the Princess Gate with both hands high up, clapping. Billie would swear there are plumes of steam rising from the man. Jimmy reaches down to open the door of the cab.

"Welcome to the City," Jimmy says.

Billie looks up from the back seat of the cab to the country-mile-wide smile on the Professor's face. Jimmy looks down on a face that spells relief. Jose, too, receives unnoticed relief by pushing all four window buttons down. For the first time in over three hours, Billie can drop the grip on the football for a hand-off.

Jimmy looks over the duct-taped cooler. "Go Leafs go."

For the first time in his morning daze a light shines in Billie's eyes. With a wee smirk he says, "Go, Leafs, go."

The tall and lean leading man and the smaller straw-haired comic character pass the cheese under the Princess Gate. "So let's go meet the team so far. Aldert's with Hector in the Say Cheese stall."

Jimmy leads the way, turning back to Billie as he brings him up to speed. "Serge is scoping the cheese on display so far. He's pacing too. Called me six times already." Billie is surprised by Jimmy's cover in a bad French accent: *"As Beellee shown up yet?"*

Jimmy stops on a full turn. "Serge *did* want your phone number. Wouldn't give it to him."

Gollum with the straw hair looks up, a fish out of water with his mouth open, gasping for words. Jimmy fills in the blank look.

"Barbara's incoming Friday, John and Greg late tonight. We rented a loft rental just north of the CNE. Barbara got it off the internet. Four bedrooms, so one of them's yours."

"Born on the farm, but I confess, I've never been to the Winter Fair. We cash-cropped and Dad had chickens. No prizes in that."

They move left into a massive building with glass-block trim around the eaves. For the first time on the trip, farm smells overpower any industrial, City or cheese smell. This place does smell like a barnyard — fresh grass and sour milk. Billie's head moves side to side at the wonder of it all — scores of stalls with cows, cows and more cows — and Jimmy has the answer.

"The Cow Palace. All cows in this building. Small animals are next door."

Billie has a Gore of Downie farmer's summary viewpoint. "Size *does* matter."

Jimmy smiles, points to the exit sign. The football swings through the door with more points from Jimmy. "Straight ahead. The poultry building is behind, while the food building is to the left. We need to get to our stall first."

The cooler swings through the large sliding door. The first thing that's noticeable is the smell, a sweet smell contrasting to the sour smell of cow shit. A palace for goats and sheep, stall upon stall.

Billie shuffles into a Michael Jackson moment. "Look, llamas."

Although Jimmy could mention his many visits to South America, he sticks to a local reference point. He wiggles double fingers at each side of his head. Billie thinks, *Rooster?* Jimmy straightens him out. "Alpacas. They look like Curly Top."

Billie stops for a good look at the curly-topped alpacas. One, taller than the rest, looks back at him. "Aaa-a-h-h, he looks like Greg smiling at me."

"No, *she's* smiling at you." Jimmy has his non-football hand up, waving.

Billie wonders why Jimmy's waving at the alpacas. He gives the curly-topped smiling face a second look.

"Aldert," Jimmy says. "There's Aldert."

The Shepherd's head and shoulders appear above the sea of butts and curly tops. He's beckoning to come hither. As Billie and Jimmy catch up with him, the pace speeds up, around a corner and underneath another exit sign, to their arrival at the Say Cheese Artisan Goat Cheese stall. A banner spread across the wall features a side profile of Napoleon's head, piano hat, beard and shoulders. Billie stands in amazement at the mini-barn setup under a banner worthy of a marching band. Aldert addresses the staging.

"That's what Greg does for you — showtime."

Aldert points a thumb back to Hector whose head and beard hang over the gate, this side of freedom.

"He's in my department," Aldert says. "Judging on Friday." He picks up some material off a small table that looks awfully familiar from Mike's Auction Barn. Aldert splays a full hand. "Look at these business cards, and the full-colour brochure."

Jimmy taps his watch. "Look at our time. Grab the registration envelope, let's get going. Serge will be having kittens."

Billie follows the two through the exit as Jimmy explains. "The envelope has all the paperwork we need for the cheeses. Everything pre-approved, pre-registered — plus most important, the labels."

The swinging red cooler passes through steel fire doors into something different again. Billie stops in his tracks.

"Ooo-o-o-oooh, that smell." His head shifts back and forth over the rows of racks and stacks, open coolers, closed freezers, and vast stainless steel counters. The whole building is jammed full of meats, cheeses, fruits, fish and flowers, including a vegetable row and a jarred and pickled section of heaven. "Oooo-o-o-ooh. Nice."

Off in the distance there's another set of waving hands attached to a head and shoulders. Billie recognizes the beckoning fingers of their *fromager*. Off goes the trio from Transvaal, a silent march up to a waving, not-so-silent Serge at the official registration desk.

"Billie, Billie, Bee-lleee."

The *fromager* grabs Billie first for kisses on both cheeks, then he looks at the football — rather, the red cooler. He sits down on the stool and with Gallic relish rips the Maple Leafs duct tape off. He lifts his head. "Lots of competition here. There's some great cheese from l'Estrie."

He has a big smile. "But let the competition begin with Say Cheese here." He stands while he balls up the tape. "There's *Charlevoix* and even Îles de la Madeleine. We have lots of competition."

He points to the brown envelope and down to the packaged cheeses. "We are down to the deadline, so let's get the stickers applied and the correct cheeses entered."

That's how the football was passed, received and run for a score at the Royal Winter Fair. The details can be found in Billie Ball's private dairy.

The rental condo has no view but offers a short walk back to the MotoMotion Coliseum. On Friday morning Billy is first over from the condo.

Inside the big coliseum, which Billie calls Animal House, he passes the long rows of animal behinds leading to the goat section.

"Hey, Hector. What's up, buddy?"

Hector's City accommodation is a metal-and-wood box with walls as high as Troy, though not high enough to limit his beard-over view out onto freedom. Jimmy applies some vet-recommended suave to knock out the high testosterone clogging the air. "This is *not* breeding season. Hector, no butts here, please."

The goat has adjusted to the geography of his adventure, the unknown crowds of humans and Billie up close. Jimmy is the one of only two humans the goat allows to curry with the goat-specific three-hundred-dollar brush.

"Hector," Billie says. "You are such a brush snob."

Hector gets his first ear flop and head scratch of the day. Billie does not touch the suave. That smear job is limited to Jimmy.

After Billie joins the escort of Hector to judging, he's off to check out the rest of the Fair. Like everyone, Billie makes a toothpick round of the sample placements in the IGA Food Coliseum two buildings over. Billie makes notes on the array of carpaccio, sausage, smoked cuts and wienies that goats contribute to.

He talks up his Theatre Town buddies. "David, James, Robbie, Patrick … they'll love the feta-stuffed curry goat sausage. Party, party! When Billie comes back."

The Food Coliseum gives Billie a taste of cheap-eats heaven.

"Nibble of cheese, pop an olive, chew on a pepperette. Whoa."

Back to the Food Coliseum for the umpteenth time, he bird-dogs the free eats for the team.

"That big Italian grocer has barrels of olives to sample."

"The cured wild boar cold cuts are divine. Roll into Little Deuce Chevre?"

"Amish Army has a booth with samples of their vacuum-packed goat salamis. Today."

Serge is left in technological thought as to how the Amish can vac-pack.

After an hour or two of samples, it's time for Billie to fetch the coffee order. John has discovered a passable barista in the Food Coliseum, just down from the goat-cheese section. John's already buzzing.

"Billie. Double espresso capp with 1% Jersey." John has pincher fingers for an itsy-bitsy hand up with a naughty left finger. "A *half* bag of cane sugar. Don't stir."

John continues his buzz with that pinching motion. "Half bag of raw sugar, no less, no more, please."

"Great, John. Jimmy?"

John flips him two twenties. He doesn't ask for change.

All that afternoon, in between official obligations, the Say Cheese team take in all the kiss-ass pomp and red-carpet circumstances of the affair. They make the rounds of the various local and provincial politicians in attendance. Billy tells the team, "They're the same-same as the wild bunch we have back home. Cheeko's head would be at the top of the unwanted poster."

After hours of milling about with Billie, Greg is wearing a why-me expression. The guy's in plus-plus greet-and-meet super mode. He just can't shut up.

Serge and Jimmy leave to confirm their cheeses on competitive display. Aldert is off in the opposite direction.

"Hector will be anxious. Don't need that for the judges. I'll see you back at the stall."

Billie continues milling about with John and Greg, until suddenly:

"*Oo-o-o-o-ook.* My God, it's Wally. *Oo-o-o-o-ook. Oo-o-o-o-o-ook.*"

Greg and John are lost in translation, but Billie has been found. Billie shoots off towards a grey flannel suit, baggy with a puffy red bow tie. The grey-flannel man has teardrop sunglasses over a pale, puffy face, with a stringy grey moustache hanging low. He ain't no Sam Elliott or Lanny McDonald. The matching grey spaghetti of his shoulder-length hair is topped with a silly floppy hat.

Billie turns back with a quick excuse to the abandoned partners. "I spent my formative Saturday mornings with that clown on my TV."

Greg calls after Billie. "A clown? That's what *it* is?" He fails to see the arms. What arms? "What are those? There are no hands? He has … fins?"

All questions are lost on Billie in his rush to capture the attention of Wally the Walrus Clown — the fat walrus who is the host of the dumbest variety show ever seen on television, at least by kids, that is. Today at the Fair, Wally is coming out on Friday morning for an under-the-radar fly-by. His agent apparently has figured that the appearance is low-risk because most children are in school and it's still too early for a drink. Nonetheless, there's a lineup, possibly because of a school bus trip. Billie pushes his way through to grab a selfie.

"Wally! *Oo-o-o-o-ook, oo-o-o-o-ook, oo-o-o-o-ook-a-chew.* I remember you, Wally. I have your colouring books and pocket pinball. I've been to Wally World."

Wally wants a cigarette and needs a snort. *"Oo-o-o-o-ook,"* he echoes, then catches himself. He gives a perfunctory glance to the agitated straw-headed Gollum. "Great, kid."

The Gollum goes frozen in awe. Then the sobered-up drunk walrus does a double-take. As sarcastic as ever a walrus — a walrus clown — could be, he looks down at the hand-rubbing fanatic. "Oh, great, buddy."

Billie waits. Nothing more is forthcoming from Wally. After a few back-and-forth stares, he can't contain the call of Saturday mornings live. *"Oo-o-o-o-ook, oo-o-o-o-ook, oo-o-o-o-ook-a-chew."*

Wally turns his teardrop sunglasses to the next kid in line with a colouring book. He ignores Gollum, who wants an autograph on his arm. "Ne-e-e-ext."

Billie has to catch up with the partners, who have wandered ahead to check out the Fair's featured guest, Prince Charles, who opened the event a few days earlier.

Billie finds Greg hiding behind the heavy security, trying to take an unofficial selfie with the prince in the foreground.

John and Billie stand at the outside of the crowd. "I wish we got to shake his hand," John says. "He's so dry but so charming."

Billie is right onto social media with photos while they wait for Greg. He adds a hashtag (#mygodthosemouseears) and a caption: *"Prince Mickey Mouse gets a vacation pass out of Fantasy Palace."*

The Say Cheese partners have organized a reserved table for the awards banquet on the final night. Front and centre on their round table is a kraft note card with Say Cheese: Winners embossed in large type.

"Whoa," John says. "I thought we had to wait for the sealed envelope?"

Serge has been here before, with *le Grand* and *les vaches*. He leans into his bosses for the real goods. "This means we will stand at podium at some point this evening. Does not say *what* we win. Does not say *premier*, Best in Class, percentage of butter fat. We saw the ribbons yesterday, but no big announcement until tonight."

Eight soft chairs with black slip covers welcome the group.

"Nice setup," Billie says. "Look. There's bottles of wine on our table." He has never seen anything bigger than the St. Pauls Community Hall. His biggest event ever, two years back, had three hundred plus for Mike's brother Brent and his wife Terri's thirtieth. "My God. Look at the size of the room."

The room is large enough for a hundred plus black tables with black slip covers. Holland Marsh flowers and four tall candles on silver-plated towers pop up from the centerpieces.

"Whoa. Putting on the Ritz, guys." Serge is famished after a long day. "Billie, look at the side of beef. They're carving it up just for you and me."

The Say Cheese team are joined by special, incoming, super-surprise guests from *Les Cantons d'Est*. Le Grand and Maman are joining up with their son le Petit for the big night.

"It's not a huge surprise for me because Papa attends every year," Billie told the Kembers when he found out. "But it's still very special for me. "

Aldert has been absent from the Fair for Friday and Saturday. The Shepherd returned for farm chores, covering Friday so the Syrian Twins could attend mosque in the City.

John and Greg made the upstairs guest bedroom with spa tub available for Aldert and his special guest, Mary Beth.

On Thursday Mary Beth told her parents she was heading off to Western for a research weekend in the library. The reality is, she will never leave the double driveway and the 6th Concession.

Tonight at the reserved table, Billie attaches himself to Maman and Papa, filling his usual role as outrageous raconteur of unmentionable private tales in public. No matter the translation, they will provide fresh ears for years and years of often-repeated oral material.

Billie recaps yesterday's famous introductions, starting with the Premier of Ontario. "He's a knock-off for John Candy's not-so-bright, not-so-good-looking younger brother. Or is he something plus, plus out of *The Big Lebowski*? The guy looks like an out-of-shape bowler. My God, he looks like Des Pair."

Pairing up Des, a Theatre Town drama queen, and the Premier is an unpleasant image, a real drag. Greg sums him up. "Plus, he didn't shake my hand."

The more liberal-acting, "calling-card conservative" Mayor of the City was friendlier. "He shook my hand," John says.

Jimmy had met him before. "Gave me a hug. Didn't remember my name but addressed me as Professor."

An ex-Mayor from Mississauga had come out into the room like an elderly Mother Goose followed by a bevy of Mayors from nearby Cities, County Wardens and Township Reeves. She was the ultimate aged piece of cheese. Serge was touched by the octogenarian. "What a sweet little prune-face she is. Shook my hand and introduced me around. Asked me about the goats and cheese. Maman, she's been to l'Estrie."

"She asked me about goats," Billie says. "Had to fake it a bit. Curly Top backed me up."

Greg ignores the questionable nature of the table wine for proposes a toast.

"Here's to the Kembers: Jimmy and Barbara. We didn't just buy the farm. We bought into your lives."

Jimmy goes next. "Here's to *le fromager*, Serge, who got the damn cheese out, into the coolers, with enough aging time to get us here. Here's to Serge."

"Wouldn't be much of a weekend with no cheese and just young Hector," Barbara adds to the double *chings*. "I propose a toast to Aldert, who built the herd to what it is today — who saved Napoleon. He can't be with us tonight, but to the Shepherd."

Another set of rings on the stemware leads Greg to think about tragedy on the winding road to cheese. "Here's to Queenie, mother, leader and royal breeder. We see her in the eyes of the herd every day." A circle of pride brings together the team at the height of their success.

John is the first to hear the announcement that rocks the group. He interrupts the bevy of bubbly toasts. "Listen. It's us."

"The Grand Champion," comes the announcement from the stage. "Best specialty cheese of 2019. Say Cheese."

A momentary calm settles before the surprise storm. Murmurs through the crowd underline the complete shock.

"Say what?"

"Say *what* cheese?"

"Say Cheese, you say?"

The answer comes from the podium. "For Champion Specialty Cheese. *Honk the Horn* from Say Cheese Artisanal Goat Cheese in …"

Bit of a pause heard in a whisper confirming that this place did show up on a map of Ontario.

"… Trans-velle, Ontario."

Billie sits corrective. "Artisan, dummy. Plus, read the map … Trans-*vaal*."

Maman and Papa are as surprised as anyone at how Say Cheese went from zero to sixty in no time for a Grand Prix win. But Serge is in stride with destiny. He stands up and waves about, hugging the Kembers then kissing the partners, then back again to include Maman and Papa. Billie stands up at last to get some of the great love doing the round table.

As the evening continues, Serge translates the unlikely story for his parents.

"It was a gigantic error in production. A cheese from the needles of the hawthorn bush. Who would have ever guessed? Further, it was a cheese that came out of a mistake."

Le Petit explains the genesis of the big cheese mistake, beginning with a change of address from Quebec to Ontario on his driver's license.

"I had to go to the license office to change my address. Barbara drove me."

Le fromager left Greg home alone and the Syrian Twins in charge to finish off the day. Nothing challenging that day, as *le fromager* had the process up and running, almost complete. Just some finishing touches to go.

Greg listens in as Serge recounts in French. "I told Greg the tanks wouldn't be ready for a couple of hours. Ozzy and Faisal had it covered, but they needed help for the curd, draining it. I asked Greg to help them set up, help them fill the moulds, drain. I would be back by dinner."

By that time Greg was no longer helping with slopping; he kept to the huge social media demands of the business. In between tapping the keys and moving his cursor, though, Greg had a couple of cheese rounds of his very own aging in the coolers. Serge did not yet have firsthand experience with Greg's famous ability to disappear into distraction. Greg calls it being a free spirit. When it comes to that fateful day a few weeks back, Serge calls it a catastrophe.

"Papa, when I got back to the farm, Greg had used the triangle moulds for Brie. Papa, *triangle* moulds. For Brie. *C'est tabou.* I said, Greg, Greg, Greg."

Greg jumps in. "I didn't understand at all."

"I told him it's a tradition, *de rigueur* for Quebecois and their Brie. What Greg told me was … *'vive la différence.'*"

Greg laughs. "Of course Ozzy and Faisal would never question their boss."

Right away Greg, bad boy, understood he had broken the rules. He looked to the light side, wearing his marketing hat. He explains to Serge's parents as they struggle to understand. "We'll call it Honk the Horn, I said. Serge was like, *Quoi?*

"Honk the Horn, I said. You know, *beep, beep.* '*Quoi?*' Look, I said, you mash the hawthorn … thorns. I can't say 'honk the thorn,' so … honk the *horn,* car theme, get it?"

Papa turns to Serge. "*Mon fils*, it's errors that are responsible for some of the most important inventions in history."

Barbara smiles at Serge's parents. "A honking great taste, anyway."

Chapter 24

If the same-sex couple could hear the course of conversation rounding the S-shaped counter these last couple of weeks at the Sunriser! Greg and John, as Citiots, could never have imagined the low bar of the full review given by the coffee klatch to the rumoured invitation list. Full comportment and protocol on the topic start with Mull-Over Monday, a few days after the invitations are sent out.

"So, the husbands …"

Braedon's head stretches out the kitchen pass-through. His silent gaze kicks the dim-wit off line. The current dim-wit, a sensible regular, reboots.

"The partners." He looks at Braedon. The head retracts, nodding, into the kitchen. "The partners …" (The dim-wit turns to face a full court, a caffeine-fuelled court that never drinks French press coffee) "… they have sent out invitations. Embossed, too."

Patrons experienced with anniversaries, daughters' marriages, or open houses know the cost of raised type. (*"Never waste that expense on a Buck and Doe. That's a fundraising drunk."*)

"The partners …" (a look back at the empty pass-through) "… have even asked for an RSVP."

Another dim-wit in the back corner booth antes up, a regular coffee orphan with a bench all to himself. "What's an RS … VP?"

A smartass wag interjects. "You know, *I'll get back to you, sweetie.*"

Braedon's neck is out on "sweetie." Attention sit-ups all along the S of the counter and back to the corner booths. Braedon burns his smoke-fired eyes into the smartie's face. The complete silence facilitates the most perfect entrance:

in comes the Pirate Captain on his irregular day for a regular swing onto his reserved stool. Braedon's neck stretches even farther out, stage left, to the amazement of the crowd.

"Stormin', good morning."

Braedon's head returns to his body as he rips out of the kitchen with one fresh black coffee and three bags of sugar.

"Norman," someone asks, "did you get a fancy invite?"

The Pirate Captain knows all but obfuscates.

"What invitation is this?"

"From your City clients on the Kember farm. Some sort of Christmas Open House."

Dim-wit, still in back. "All embossed like you's going to a special 'ting?"

"Special. Yes, it's the Wedding Girl Big Launch Christmas Open House party. *Aargh. Aargh. Aargh.*"

Norman lets the comment flow subside. Today he gets a reprieve from the usual spotlight with the unusual:

"Billie Ball got an invite," Braedon says from the kitchen.

The room of trained wags looks to the pass-through window. Braedon's neck stretches out into the silence. "Myself and the Missus got our invitation. In the mail. Last week, it was."

Braedon doubles down. "My nephew, the social media specialist, will be there. Bringing …" (The silent room waits in anticipation of an announcement) "… his new boyfriend with him. Never seen the dusty concessions of hayseed western Ontario."

"*Aargh. Aargh. Aargh.* A dusting of snow will make them wish for a return to regular dust."

Norman and his audience chuckle at the unspoken Citiot potential of post-function conversation.

The embossed Wedding Girl invitations were hand-delivered to neighbours and friends, mailed off to the distant City world. Firm details were held close, spread thin outside the Say Cheese team.

Cheeko, the mayor; the Chiefs of Police and Fire; Stormin' Norman; and Braedon got invites, along with all their respective Missuses. A few extra Missuses were found to round up the Town list. The Transvaal neighbours, Lochlin and Bonnie Austin, Scott and Cindy Taylor, and Bob and Carol Havermore, all got a door knock by the pair, with their invite. Billie Ball and a few of his theatre friends were mashed into the list to mix it up.

Mary Beth Johnson; Super Agent Man, Stevie; and the wild bunch from the City all got their embossed invitations in the mail.

For the next week, a complete mash of information on Christmas on the Farm drips in along the tributaries of fence lines, porch stops and family gatherings.

The mash has risen to the heights of the greatest soufflé, in all ways. (Fluffy, light and delicious, all the right colours; careful, it might burst!)

"Over a hundred people expected."

The list-hopeful and the listless-hopeless alike have waited for their invitations. Lots of invite speculation.

"Half of 'dem will be politicians."

"The other half are would-be's too."

"Would-be's? Don't you mean wannabes?"

"No. These would be politicians but we no wanna them to be."

The room pauses after the clever line, leaving a vacuum for the dummy in the back to hang himself:

"Half a bunch of dim-wits if you ask me."

The coffee klatch guffaws at the dumb observation. An in-the-know steadies the tiller of truth onward from fiction. "Half will be from Toronto. The other half we know. They're from here."

The in-the-know collects the concentration of the room. He makes an end pass-off, as someone in the know, to a silent invitee. "Yes, lots of politicians, including Cheeko. Right, Cheeko?"

Cheeko, the mayor of St. Marys, slinks lower in a back booth behind the dim-wits, Ronnie and Donnie. His Worship is still contemplating the ebbs and tides of this morning's update on the new lads. He waits it out in caffeine contemplation for an advantageous moment to take the podium. He wonders why the in-the-know gave Stormin' a miss but not him. It's always open season on politicians. Cheeko tips his cup in an acknowledgement over the head of Donnie.

"Cheeko." Norman turns his stool to the back of the restaurant. "Sorry. Did you get an invitation to the Say Cheese party?" All stools in turn recognize the look on his face: *Game on!*

Front-row stools hear a familiar chuckle. *"Aargh. Aargh. Aargh."*

Cheeko sits up for the attention. He tips his cup one more time, right into Donnie's reversed noggin.

His Worship looks at the dim-wit while addressing the full house. "Well, what can you do, I ask you? What can you do?"

Those collected sigh with a group eye-roll, one more time hearing his worn-out mayoral phrase.

His Worship, a full-time observer of Town and Country play, picks on the person who pointed him out. "You bet I did … Gordie."

The voting majority in the gathering nod to Cheeko, putting a silent check in the come-back box. It's the last check the mayor will get this morning.

Braedon can't believe Cheeko's poke on Gord. Gord hates "Gordie" — it has something, a way-back something, to do with Mrs. Snoddie's Grade 10 English class. Some sort of searing embarrassment dished out by that Panda Woman. As any veteran of Stonetown High School will attest, there's a cemetery full of death-by-embarrassment tombstones erected by that woman over the years. So join the club, Gordie. But Cheeko, Cheeko, Cheeko …

Gord, along with the Missus, three sons, their wives and a flock of grandchildren they crowd into Town hockey games — plus a pack of cousins, neighbours, and Gord's fellow workers at the cement plant — represent an electoral college of voting power that you are pissing right off. Plus, plus, Gord, as the resident in-the-know this morning, needs little material for his reply. The master wag comes out with amazing research.

"What kind of dress you wearing, Cheeko?"

Cheeko goes deer in the headlights. How did Gordie know about the dress code for this launch into cheese?

Gord sees the furrows on Cheeko's brow, the squinty eyes of a politician. Gord ploughs farther inward for the fun of it all. "Chiffon or puffy lace?"

As for Cheeko, well, what could he do?

The morning crowd turn to each other with the same answer-itself question: *Ask yourself. What can he do?*

A few witnesses are distracted as they wonder how anyone in this room, this morning or any morning — even Gord, an in-the-know — would be familiar with chiffon or puffy lace? It doesn't stop. Gord goes on.

"Button or zipper back?"

The room ruminates on the subject with the level of hilarity on a low simmer.

Gord does an impression of pinching fingers, which impresses the room. Then the hands make themselves over into mitts, with a little voice, then a big voice: "Those little clips? With those big hands, Cheeko!"

The mayor casts a political eye over the gathering, making a mental list of the total asshole count that day. Cheeko can always pass a bad-boy referral to the Chief and Supercop, Russ. Can always get Booby Dink's ass on another DUI, for starters. Arsehole.

Cheeko sticks to crisis management. He can't believe that Gordie, going on and on like this. He looks to the room for support. The mayor sees nothing but a bunch of pricks, in for a free show.

Gord doesn't stop. "Bra but no panties, Cheeko. Be … risky."

Cheeko makes the fatal mistake of standing up, then freezes as a full-on target. Better than pay TV, the audience sees a TKO on the challenger's mind. Gord hits with his left.

"Great porno movie."

Back with a solid right.

"Think we should call it *Risky Mayor. Worship Hership.*"

The room catches up with the first title, laughing through the second.

Gord goes on to the third. *"The Whoreship Mayorship."* And may the fourth be with the morning group: *"Between the Cheekos."*

From a booth in the back: *"Don't Tax the Latex."*

A counter resident's turn: "How about a horror movie? *Cheeko Freako.*"

A cacophony of mirth on the stools and chaos in the booths follows.

Cheeko does a sneako out the side patio door, out of sight of the rest of the diner.

Braedon is standing without words in the kitchen doorway. Order is restored in moments. Slurping and contemplation return along the reverse-S counter and throughout the back booths. The mayor has moved along. Braedon moves it along.

"Jimmy's doing a goat on the barbecue."

With Greg behind the wheel, Billie's looking for a deal. The girls have gone shopping for dis tress, a trip to Theatre Town in a review of Billie's best in-the-know sources. They're on their third store of the day when Billie makes the announcement.

"I have found it." Hands up, holding nothing but a guess-what smile.

"Found what, Billie?"

He drags Greg by the hand to a rack at the back of the store. "A canary-yellow chiffon piece of art. It could be a Southern Belle gown. It's *my* '57 classic."

Hang up. "That is *not* a wedding dress."

The guess-what smile changes to a who-cares frown from Billie Ball. That stops *that* line of conversation. Billie will be coming out in his own way. He flips it back.

"What's Curly Top wearing? Clowns don't wear dresses."

Greg is gobsmacked. He gathers his thoughts. "A real vintage 1867 Fort Kingston cadet's uniform. A real deal antique. *Should* be in a museum."

Vintage, antique and museum flow forth to catch Billie's appraiser self. He's all Flow Blue by day, but at night he's the girlie dress collector. Billie roots for the show to go on. "Wedding Girl, buddy! You diss my chiffon? You in the pillbox. Gown on!"

Greg tries to stop the train of thought. "Yes, but Billie, not for me. I'm John's bat-boy escort."

Stop the train for Billie. "John *is wearing a wedding dress?*"

"Right, as Avril Lavigne."

Gollum is in chant mode. *"Go-o-o-own on! Go-o-o-own on!"*

The train makes another stop on the vision in dress. "Avril Lavigne?"

Greg blathers it out. "Plus, Billie, don't get stuck on Avril or Marilyn Monroe, Elizabeth Taylor, Grace Kelly, whatever and whoever. One of those princesses."

Greg is stuck in relief, playing his backup excuse for the cadet uniform. "I am the escort."

"So what's Princess Legal Eagle wearing for his coming out?"

Index finger closes Greg's mouthpiece. "Details must not pass my lips."

"I like to give head," Billie says, and Greg steps back. "Head torture, that is. I can do a good Laurie Olivier as the dentist."

Olivier's tooth-extraction scene in the movie *Marathon Man* has dominated Greg's perception forever. Even a dental consultation freezes him up. Greg is gobsmacked by Billie twice in the same conversation. He re-gathers himself to address the topic.

"You will just *have* to ask John for details *yourself.*"

Billie drapes the yellow chiffon gown over his arm. The Open House thing, a Christmas fling, is off on a wing.

Back on Thomas in Town, Barbara Kember takes an adult lead with Mary Beth Johnson.

"There's a vintage shop near Western. Students have little interest in wedding dresses at this point in their lives. We'll have the pick of the focking litter, dear."

Mary Beth is new to Greg, John and Serge but a known factor to the Kembers. This is Aldert's gal. She is loved by Max, Hector, the collies and Frankie, and was dearly loved by Queenie. In fact, the entire goat team hoovers it up when Mary Beth is on the farm. Hector and Napoleon can smell her before she gets out of the car.

"*Na-a-a-ah ba-a-a-ad. Na-na-na-nah ba-a-yybee. C-c-c-c-ome to Na-pol-le-on-n-n-n, you-u-u-u. Na-a-a-ah.*"

Hector from a field afar:

"*Moo-o-o-o-ve, Na-po-le-on. Your-r-r-r-re blocking the vie-e-e-e-w-w-w.*"

The young lady — heck, even that feisty old one — would certainly be grossed out if she could understand the goat conversation.

Mary Beth has finished her nutrition degree at Western and is now a post-graduate. She has walked by the vintage shop many times on her way from the off-campus parking lot. Barbara will bring her inside for the first time. Mary Beth as her shopping date is new to all the fun drama.

"My God, a Wedding Girl party. What fun. What an idea."

"Based on a focking nightmare, dear."

"Barbara, not a real nightmare?"

Barbara leaves Mary Beth lost in space with a reference to Hal from the Kubrick classic *2001*. "Focking right, a Douglas Raine nightmare."

Barbara fills her in on the sad but weird saga of Allin Douglass on his shim-sham glam Friday night parade. Mary Beth has a little laugh with a few tears, hearing a tale of downtown pathos. The night the old pixie went down. Allin, shot down to the gravel ground in his fifties couture gown.

An echo reaches the Sunriser:

"Run this by me again. Dougie who?"

Billie keeps it straight and simple. "Wedding Girl works best."

Since the embossed cards headed out for delivery, Billie Ball in *Who Is Wedding Girl?* has been a popular theatre request, in-house at the Sunriser. (He confesses to his Theatre Town pals: "Never ever have I had such straight interest in a queer tale.")

Not many, not even the in-the-know regulars, seem to know anything about this back-alley incident from many years back. Billie provides a shot, plus a shot or three, thrusting his invisible shotgun at his audience: *Boom. Boom. Boom.* After the boom, the room is busting to ask more questions.

"Where's the Chief on this one?"

"Nowhere to be found; this was long before his time here. We've had two chiefs after Wedding Girl, before this chief. Remember Rocky? And before him, that bad-ass, Joe Bailey?"

The stools work their heads around the current affairs and past history. "Hm-m-m-m."

And someone poses a style question. "What kind of dress was he wearing?"

And there's clarification. "Didn't he have two kids?"

At home in the stone farmhouse, John is fluffing and floozy-ing it up in front of the mirror.

John cannot believe the reflection. It's simply raw — raw silk that shimmers and shakes with the slightest move.

Greg has a direct line. "My God, a black wedding dress." An oddity, no doubt, to anyone in the wedding world. "I wonder what happened to this girl?"

Greg is up front for an audit. "It's not old." Now, back auditing. "Custom or couture? Where's that label?" Greg pulls for a rabbit ear out of the dress. "There's no tag tail, John. No trail for this piece of shimmer, baby. A wedding mystery tale."

John can't see straight without his tiger-tail striped horn rims. Up top, he sticks up straight, though, with a Tintin comb. No makeup, no wig, no eyelashes — not even lifts or pads. Just John in one shimmer of simmer in raw silk.

"What about the Pancha Lauren stilettos?" Greg asks.

No heel appeal for John. "Ouch, no."

Bad taste radar's up for Greg. "Do *not* wear those running shoes."

Comfort beats taste for a standing affair. "The dress is more than long enough."

Uh-oh, radar trap. Bad-taste police. "Do *not* do it!"

"Who will see?"

Who's the witness? Greg is. "I will know. FSP."

"The East German secret police?"

"No, Fake Stiletto Police." Taste triumphs over partnership. "Stilettos or Oxfords, please. Or I will out you." A wink and a smile. "From the FSP."

An audit and a smile. "FSP. That has to be long distance from Transvaal."

John flows back, shiny and shimmery, to the bathroom. Greg is in flow, too, an emotional flow — of love, pride for the two of them. A sense of perfect partner completeness gives him a shiver.

Allin's night out some forty-five years ago is about to align with the Christmas Open House. Stars align, starting on a corner in St. Marys, two blocks up from where the 1965 Larson couture was shot. From their house at the corner of Peel and Jones Streets, the Johnsons can see over the top of the bowling alley — the shooting site — to the upper end of the castle-like town hall.

"That is the most beautiful thing I've ever seen." With the mile smile from Aldert, a tinge of red appears in Mary Beth's cheeks, overshadowed only by her scarlet lipstick.

"You think so?"

"Yes. I know so."

Her eyes flash. "You do?"

The mile smile stretches another mile. "You *are* the most beautiful date in the world."

Eyes smile; smile closes in on a kiss.

Aldert picked Mary Beth up at her home. The Kembers will be by soon to collect them for the Open House. Mary Beth's father keeps them company at the door.

"Wedding Girl. That's quite a theme for a Christmas party."

"Christmas on the Farm." Aldert diverts from any dirt. "They are the best bosses, Mr. Johnson."

Big smile. Mile smile. Keep the smile. The corners of Mr. Johnson's frozen lips open a crack. Aldert steps into the small gap.

"They entered a bunch of Serge's cheeses in the Royal Winter Fair." Big smile for Mary Beth. "A real cheese adventure."

He directs an announcement to the father. "Three had big wins — Grand Prix champions." Mr. Johnson loves cheese, but he's not sure how much credit the boyfriend deserves. "You guys have had enough time to make cheese?"

"Well, just enough time for aging. And we have a few tricks up our sleeves. Remember, Barbara's been making back-kitchen cheese for years. Jimmy has a bag of agents, including bacteria and moulds, and even uses mashed hawthorn needles. Serge has the process down like Swiss clockwork."

Aldert is losing Mr. Johnson. Mary Beth has heard it all again and again. Some nice smiles round the front hall. Aldert decides on a sweet approach. "Remember, this is where my crème brûlées come from."

Mr. Johnson loves Aldert's special treat, but he has not bought into Aldert's community-raised favourite son status. This is his daughter we're talking about; he is not convinced that a Shepherd should be dating the top of the class. Now, that vibe echoes all the way back to the 6th Concession, past the Say Cheese farmstead, to the next paddock west. Hector has some advice.

"Na-a-a-ah right, Mr. Johnson. Na-a-a-ah, Shepherd. THE-E-E-E Shepherd. Na-a-a-ah any bah-ah-ah-etter lad."

Aldert, simply put, is a lovable sheep; but Father sees a dangerous wolf.

Aldert's a smart lad who never focused all on academics. He worked before school and after; homework was a bedside activity. No matter — he excels as the Shepherd, graduating to herd management, with extra time spent on Hector, his love for a future herd, and excelling as Mary Beth's boyfriend. Now the Shepherd, with his recent Herd Management Specialist diploma in hand, is key help for the partners from the City.

But it's all about status for Mr. Johnson, the height of authority as principal of St. Marys West Ward Elementary. The school is on a hill, with a prime office-window view. He is always civil, but he looks down on the Town in general. Aldert's smile thins with each minute of contact with Mr. Johnson. *Thank God I went to Transvaal SS 27, in Town, up till high school*, Aldert reminds himself now.

Aldert is caught off guard by the continuation of the conversation.

"How do you address them?"

Aldert understands the question, but he questions Mr. Johnson's intent. "Address *them*?"

"Your bosses. What do you *call* them, I mean … I suppose."

"How do I *call* them?"

Mr. Johnson is a lot less smart than Mr. Johnson can ever imagine. "I don't mean by phone. I mean partner, husband, wife, boyfriend …"

A quarter-mile smile. "That's easy. Greg and John. They're my bosses."

Mary Beth has a kilometre-wide smile compared to the mile-long surface of her boyfriend's smile. Her father interrupts the moment, detouring to the lights of the approaching SUV.

"Ah. The … Kembers have arrived."

Mr. Johnson, the formal pencil-head, never calls Barbara or Jimmy by their first names. That would denote some sort of recognition from his fool-on-the-hill office window view. Plus, he is sensitive and insecure about the pecking order of teaching status. Jimmy Kember is a full Professor at Western University.

As for the father, no goodbye kiss is expected. Father's a stiff. Mary Beth steps up, the daughter seen as having *the* taste in Town. With her scarlet Mac lips she plants a goodbye kiss silhouette on her father's cheek. (Mary Beth never goes cheap on lipstick, with Mac, or perfume, with Chanel. Of course this high-end taste is limited to trips to the mall in the nearby City after classes. But the Mac exclusive still sets her apart from the herd. She's the only child, the one daughter. Why cheap out?)

Mary Beth's gown casts a glow as it flows across the Johnson foyer. Mrs. Johnson steps up for a few lasting photo shots. Mother knows best on the final touches. "Honey, keep this pulled in. And this pulled up." She winks at Aldert: mission understood. "A gentleman will pull her over to advise on these details."

Best wishes even from the principal pencil-neck for the evening, with a weak salute to his forehead that's interrupted when the horn honks. Mr. Johnson pushes the nib of his pencil head out the half-open door for known confirmation of an arrival. He takes a half step out onto the cement pad outside the door.

"Coming," he barks out with a wave. A principal's fake smile. A forced thumbs-up with the right hand, the left hand pointing out into the beautiful evening. He turns back, answering himself at the same time. "Some sort of rush to get going, eh? No knocking on the door, just a horn announcement."

"Daddy," Mary Beth says, "Aldert is my escort. The Kembers are driving us."

Daddy is looking out the door crack. "Have *they* been drinking?"

Smile. Wave back. Smile back. Wave.

Out in his SUV, Jimmy turns the wipers back on. He squints into the windshield, enabling him to see the pencil-neck's nib head through the crack in the door. "Is that tight-ass waving?"

Barbara waves away. "He's focking smiling too, there, Jimmy boy. Or should I say, girl."

Jimmy gives the Country viewpoint of a pencil-neck. "Tight-ass must have been neutered."

"Neutered?"

"No balls. Look, his head is stuck in a crack."

Barbara knows the drill. She's on the retired-teacher treadmill herself. "No, it's the teacher pension. The closer he gets to that retirement number, the tighter the asshole."

They both laugh at the waving, smiling malcontent. All six sets of ears are ignorant as to the opposite side's muttering. Eyes move on the sparkling light coming through the night. Flowing, rustling, shimmering all the way out.

"Wow," Jimmy says. "Mary Beth sure looks good."

"She looks beautiful. Helped her pick out the focking rag."

Mary Beth ruffles her dress up and over the frosty elements. A soft branch out, a flower floating from the Johnson home.

Emerging from the house behind her, Aldert in a size forty-eight slim-fit vintage Raymonde follows the shimmer to their ride. The Shepherd's size blocks the light from the Johnson front door behind her.

Barbara has seen the prized beauty in the fitting room. Helped her make the right choice. Barbara stepped back into a special time for Mary Beth. She showed her a magazine photo from long ago that pushes the image of Chanel. The double-breasted top with velvet piping and a bead-ball cross-stitch is a stunner. The champagne-pink organza dress is tucked underneath, a shimmering flow. Barbara knew right away in the mirror that this was the one — the dress and the girl.

I'm happy being the focking mother of the bride, she told herself. She looked at the reflection again. "The rag focking fits."

"Barbara, thank you. I love it."

Now Mary Beth floats that rag with cross-toe-point steps down the frosty flagstone path.

"Wow," Aldert says, seeing his date anew as he opens the back door on the passenger side. A good escort shepherds his date to shelter. He moves around to the driver side and slides in. He struggles with the undersized seatbelts. After greetings all round, the Shepherd starts to focus on the unfamiliar driver with Jimmy's voice.

"Jimmy. What's that you got on there, Jimmy?"

The driver with Jimmy's voice is all face forward on the road. The burning X-ray question:

"Jimmy, baby. Wearing something … special?"

Barbara snickers. Mary Beth focuses in on the driver. Aldert hits the target man-on.

"A little something extra-extra for the Christmas party there, Jimmy?"

Pause. Punch. Pause. "Jimmy?"

Eyes ahead as the SUV pulls along Queen Street through the tinsel-lit downtown. A cheesy Christmas background, no better choice for a night to remember.

The questions are still focused in the front seat. "Jimmy. Jimmy, buddy. Would that be silk or could it be felt?"

Jimmy gives a little jump with the cold shoulder tap from behind. In fact, he almost drives into a parked car. The trio cry out. *"Whoa!"*

Barbara looks to the back seat with a left-eye wink.

"Not focking felt. Eh, Jimmy?"

The response is surprising.

"Organza."

Barbara loses it in laughter. Mary Beth and Aldert look forward, smiling, with one question. "Organza?"

The Professor is insistent. "Yes, my *dress* is made of *organza*. Mary Beth does not have a monopoly on organza."

The young couple snicker. The lecture starts from the Prof.

"Mary Beth and Barbara know better. They *both know* that organza is the best in wedding dress material."

Aldert digs deep. "Why would you know something like that? Girl stuff, if not fashion stuff.

"Mary Beth gave me the heads-up on the material of her dress."

"But more important, *why* would you know that fact of fashion, Jimmy?"

The Professor is stuck in lecture. "Well if *you* want to show some support for your bosses, *support* them with their first big party. *Then* read the big type. It's a Wedding Girl party. Wedding dress optional. Black tie required."

Barbara interjects. "Focking slow **down**, Jimmy. Give us your address …" (Barbara turns, smiles, but it's too dark to see the shine) "… address on the focking dress, Jimmy. Not the focking lecture on big type."

Jimmy slows down, quiet and sheepish. "Thought I would support the lads — in dress, yes."

Barbara picks him up for some focking support. "Focking knock 'em out the room, Jimmy. You be the toast of the party."

From the back seat. "Toastette."

The driver gives it the gas. "Focking drop it, people."

The car jumps forward, then slows back. And from the back seat. *"Okay. O-o-o-o-kay."*

A snicker. "Mrs. Dress-up."

Jimmy is all eyes ahead, watching the road and the rear-view mirror. He picks up on a car tracking them along Water Street and continuing south, past the quarry. One eye sticks to the rear-view mirror. The other eye somehow covers his driver-side mirror. If he had a third eye? He would not look to the passengers. He would feel Barbara's big gob staring back at him.

The passengers can see the red lights in the rear-view mirror; they turn at the sight. Group PA announcement on the PD to the obvious. "He's got his focking cherries on …?"

"Jimmy," Barbara says. "Signal on. Slow, slow and pull over; slow. Right here, dear."

"I can't go any slower. I'm doing twenty klicks. It is a community safety zone."

Barbara is slow. "Signal on, dear. Slow down a little more, dear. Slow. Pull the fock over!"

Public address repeat on the obvious. This time it's Jimmy. "He's got his focking cherries on …?"

"Jimmy. Jimmy, relax. You had one beer. One beer while you got … dressed."

The trio break out laughing. The fourth, Jimmy, is about to piss his panties as the SUV pulls to a stop on the shoulder. He grunts away a few mumbling expletives.

Tap. Tap.

"Jimmy. Please open the window."

Tap. Tap.

"Jimmy. Open the focking window."

Jimmy takes forever to lower the window.

"Good evening, Jimmy Kember. Mrs. Kember."

The officer shines his flashlight onto the rear seat. "Hello, Miss Johnson, and Aldert of course. Merry Christmas all."

The three passengers chime in. "Merry Christmas, Officer Russ."

Russ the veteran Town police officer is on the beat tonight. "Everyone is looking … pretty good. Little Christmas party at the farm?"

Quartet reply. "Yes, Officer Russ."

Russ winks back. "Say Cheese."

The quartet reply. "Yes, Say Cheese."

All Jimmy thinks is *please*, please stop the cheese. Jimmy sticks to the seat in silence, stuck in his SUV on the side of the street, playing for a cheese release. Smack, look right as the light shines in his face.

"And, Jimmy, you aren't drinking? Little Christmas cruise? Luc's Taxi provides a great pick, with a drop holiday package. Been drinking, Jimmy?"

Jimmy goes real quiet. The lack-of-support trio help out.

"No, Officer Russ. Jimmy has *not* been drinking."

Barbara leans across to her former bottom-of-the-class student. "Russell. He's focking embarrassed."

Jimmy looks up with sad-little-girl eyes. The oversized cop blocks his window with that flashlight spotlighting him. The police officer nods.

"Thank you, Mrs. Kember."

Officer Russ pulls back to zero more light in on the driver. "Jimmy, no worries. You are looking kind of extra-pretty tonight?"

The trio snicker.

"That dress wouldn't be … organza?"

Jimmy sinks in his seat like the good boat *Proud Mary*.

"My favourite dress material." Russ looks off into nowhere. "Wedding Dress party would not be right without fluffs of organza."

Russ is standing back. He looks down at the driver. "Jimmy. I have to ask you step out of the vehicle."

The Professor is incredulous. "You are gonna search me?"

"Maybe later if you want to get frisky."

Barbara gets in there. "Make sure you bring the focking cuffs, Russ. He loves the focking cuffs."

The trio lose it. Russ waits for calm waters. "Jimmy. If I stop you, this procedure …"

Russ leans in for a smell. Nothing but nice cologne.

Russ holds up official business. "You were going so slow. Then you do this giddy-up; then you push the slow-down button. Slow, faster. Faster, slow. I was getting whiplash. I thought you were drunk."

Jimmy speaks. "Russ. You were right behind me … forever. Who is it, I'm thinking? What are they doing? I couldn't figure it out. Pass me, please. Stop me. But quit tailgating."

"Jimmy. Getting a little anxious?"

"Russ. Driving on a crappy night. Wearing a vintage organza wedding dress? Yes, Officer, I *am* anxious."

Russ ignores him, slows down for some more fun. It's the dress. "Very nice choice."

Barbara and Mary Beth, all ears in the SUV, call out, "Thank you, Russ."

More laughter. Russ holds up the official business again.

"Jimmy. If I stop you, it's the law. I *have* to see you step out from behind the wheel. *I* have to discern if you are inebriated. Same law says I have to see your licence and insurance."

Barbara leans into the talk. "Have it right here, Russell. I'm holding Jimmy's purse."

Jimmy gets out of the car and stands, outed in organza, while fluffs of frozen crystals backlight a snowy fairyland. The insiders rock.

"Russell."

"Yes, Mrs. Kember?"

"Russell," she says. "No cuffs, though. They're at home."

The trio are having a yuck-fest Saturday night live.

Hands up with the dress, a pair of high-top runners take the flow of organza across the parking lot of the swim quarry. Not so easy to escape the notice of the law. Jimmy feels the officer giving his running shoes a Mike Babcock.

"Nice shoes. I am sure you must have the stilettos in your shoe bag. With your purse."

Jimmy straightens up to move toward a drive-off. Russ follows, which leads to more questions.

"Okay. I have seen just about everything in my thirty-five-plus years on the force. I have never seen anything like *this*."

Jimmy forces up some gumption to turn on the officer. Hands down in why. "Like *this*?"

"Like this." Officer Russ tilts his Constabulary fur hat. "*What* a set of gams, boy."

Another Jimmy hands-down flail. "Like that?"

Russ can't stop the off-the-record notice. "Is that pantyhose, or pull-ups?"

Jimmy can't grab the door handle fast enough to get moving again. The dress-up adventure is on low simmer, starting to taste a little off with this unpleasant holiday seasoning.

"Funny. Funny, Russ. Can we go now?"

Jimmy can't lose the tag game. "Get on your way, dearie. Here, I'll give you a lift. No point dirtying the material girl here."

Jimmy swings open the door and slides behind the wheel nice and quick, thanks to the slippery organza. He waits for the postscript from Russ. *Proud Mary* keeps on sinking, anchored by his hold on the steering wheel, his foot ready to hit the pedal.

Russ shuts the door and releases the official line with a goodbye wave, acknowledged by the supporting cast.

"Merry Christmas," he says. "Have a great party."

The trio respond. "Merry Christmas to you too, Officer Russ."

Jimmy waits, sunk, holding on to the wheel anchor. Russ looks down, no flashlight.

"Jimmy."

Jimmy is all eyes ahead.

"Jimmy."

Jimmy curls his baby-deer eyes up.

"Jimmy. One last question."

"What the heck now?"

"Jimmy. Do you buy your lipstick over the counter? The cosmetics floor at the mall? Or does Avon call?"

Chapter 25

Ding, dong. The Christmas on the Farm Open House is on. The first officials of the night to greet you are the professional photographers, Juanita and Pablo.

"Hello, hello. Welcome to Say Cheese, and have a Merry Christmas, please."

Handshake intro from Pablo, kisses intro from Juanita.

The Syrian twins come forward next.

"Faisal will take your coat and shoe bag ..."

One twin goes off to the side guest bedroom. Pablo acknowledges the hospitality gift.

"Yes, Ozzy will relieve you of that. Cheers."

Both photographers stand off to side, indicating the brightly lit set, living room stage west.

"Greg and John would like to give you a Christmas portrait," Pablo says. "Please follow Juanita."

A postcard Christmas diorama surrounds the cherry-surround fireplace with a Citiot fire on the go: fire logs from Doug's Pro Hardware. (Greg does not apologize. "Easy peasy to start, clean up and do it all over again. Small amount of ashes. Good enough on the *feng shui* thing. While wood? Messy, messy, messy. Did I say messy?")

Mexican crèche and tall candles on the mantle; Pez characters, including Santa and Jesus. The trim is holly and ivy, with tiny gold balls from the dollar store. Greg has tacked mistletoe above a small taped X on the maple floor. Pablo value-adds to the festive fizzy spirits, pointing up to the ceiling. "And to set the real Christmas mood, couple kisses."

Serge appears next, to greet you. "Champagne cocktails. *Joyeux Noël, salut.*"

Bang.

Front door opens again, with laughter.

The festive partiers are surprised by the volume incoming through the green door off the porch. The first three newcomers are enjoying something hilarious.

Max has a happy ear up to welcome his friends, Aldert, Mary Beth, the Missus … and the Master.

Max cannot believe how different his old Master seems. And Master is quiet, but the others are not.

Max is both colour-blind and indifferent to clothes, dependent on smell and dog sense. He feels the electric vibe around the young shiny couple and the black-clad Missus. And the old Master is shiny too. Behind the green screen, the green door off the porch, Max feels the current going red-line at the sight of the couture pin-up gown below a wigless horn-rimmed face.

Half the room is surprised by the Professor in drag, while the other half thinks he looks pretty smashing.

The known response:

"Oh my God. Jimmy in organza!"

The unknown question:

"Hello, hello! Hello, cutie. Are you from around these parts?"

His Worship, from the back kitchen:

"I'm telling you. What can I say?"

Des Pair comments with a City twist:

"He must be a Transvaalite!"

Des's car companion sees Aldert standing there:

"Is that the hunk?"

The Pirate Captain surveys the social seascape:

"Aargh. Aargh. Aargh."

Max is stuck on the porch, thinking how different all the Masters and Missuses are tonight. He's had some time to ponder, after seeing Master John in shiny and Master Greg in Boy Scout. Max rustles on the mat, tussles with the mixed vision. The old dog is Maxed out and the night is still young.

Juanita and Pablo escort the quartet to the photo-shooting field, marked by a big X in Maple Leafs–logo duct tape on the living room floor. "Who's on the X first for their photograph?" Three happy faces and one sad-sack doll with an organza pin-up dress.

"Okay," Pablo tells them. "Curl your shoulders to the centre. Tighten up, folks. Look at my right shoulder. No, Jimmy, staring at the lens does not help. Big cheesy smile. *Digame Queso.*"

Say Cheese in Spanish curls Jimmy's lips up a smidgen.

"Juanita, fluff up the organza. Aldert, bottom button open."

"Focking smile this time, Jimmy."

"Barbara, keep still. Your Chanel bunches a bit. Juanita, attention please. Mary Beth, how can we fix perfection?"

Two kilometre-wide smiles, one mile-wide, and a little curl of the lips greet Pablo's right shoulder.

And the band plays on. The green door swings open again.

Again, the perfect Christmas welcome.

Anyone familiar with parties in southwestern Ontario would call tonight's party a normal affair, with the usual gropers, unusually dressed competition, the guy with bad breath, and a left-at-the-oasis friend who calls like an owl. Wise advice from a party companion to counter the social abandonment.

"Just talk to someone."

"Who?"

"How about that Colonel Sanders–looking gentleman."

"Who?"

"By the cheese table, with the mulled cider from the kitchen. Go there, get some cider and talk to someone."

"Who?"

A mix and mash of Town, Country and City ensues. "Who is that man in the pencil-thin gown with the top hat, and all that … fluorescent pink?"

"That's Aaron. From the City. Calls himself The Human Highlighter."

"H-m-m-m-m."

"Who's Colonel Sanders grunting like a toad?"

"You mean the *Aargh Aargh Aargh* guy?"

"Sounds like a Pirate Captain."

A safe path, practised by all in Town, Transvaal and Country, is duplicity: nod your head and keep saying "You're right" in all face-to-face conversations. Hidden meanings, obfuscations, misdirections, and remember that it's all about me, me, me.

So maybe the dress does suck.

"Oh my God, you look beautiful."

The dress owner sucks too?

"Great to see you. Oh my God, where did you get it …?"

These social protocols work for couples, too, and even from across the room. A quick aside to your partner. "Will you look at her …"

You realize that "her" is approaching with *her* partner. They've picked up the wrong signal. "Looking good too," they say.

You give them an up and down on their dresses, with no smiles. "Nice dress."

And then from the other couple: "Well, look at you."

The Kirkton Kountry Katerers, including two of Aldert's aunties, swing through the rooms. The ladies have platters of nephew inspiration from well-hung goats, in the back kitchen cooler. The aunties delegate well-rehearsed instructions from their miracle-boy nephew. Aldert is not just a natural Shepherd; Aldert is the complete natural.

The Kirkton Katerers take care of the kitchen space. They take further care to sample all that passes by.

"I've had Billy on the Bun at the Volunteer Firefighters' Barbecue. I remember good, but his is brilliant."

"My nephew sure can create."

"A natural with a K for Kreative and a K for Kountry. He could be a K-katerer."

"We have to get the recipe on those sauces Barbara makes."

"Focking secret!" Barbara calls out as she walks past, building the myth of her sauce branding.

The beehive of Kirkton women buzz platters about. Each one goes out treat-full, gets wiped empty, and ends up back in the dish sink. A tasty hub in the kitchen wheels out the goodies to the party bunch. Clean platters wash up for stack and pack, and then they're outed again.

The Wedding Girl party, also known as the Christmas Open House, is the perfect marriage of marketing. The embossed invitations received an RSVP from two well-travelled food critics, two cheese-makers and one cheese reviewer. Four ladies from the City who are staying in Town all blog and Tweet. One travel critic for the *Globe* thinks Say Cheese is a high-end Country B & B. That goes all Citiot viral.

"My, my. We can stay on a cheese farm with goats."

"Are there yoga classes?"

"Curds for breakfast?"

The dress-wearing set do not sit down but float around.

The space is wide open with the chairs pushed back. A teepee-shaped Say Cheese sign directs the crowd to the sample spread from the next room. Brochures, green-flagged toothpicks, cheese tools and knives, and napkins stamped Say Cheese surround a pile of wooden cutting boards lined with samples. Greg whispers to Serge.

"We have someone that can brand our logo onto the boards. We need to find a wrought-iron artist."

Serge was quick in anticipating his spot in the Wedding Girl dress-up night. *Le fromager* holds court over the cheese-themed array spread out on the vast dining room table. All night, the samplers are as tight around the table as Frankie and his friends at the troughs.

Serge can answer all the whens, why, hows and wheres of cheese. Even with his mouth full. "This is my soft spreadable."

Le Petit points in his Say Cheese–embossed apron. "Creamy, bloomy rind. With a touch of heat. It calls to me *Testa Rossa*."

To a nibbling reacher at the corner of the table he says, "Have you sampled Aldert's cheese puffs? That's my ripened goat goodness tucked into the Shepherd's jacket of crispy crunch."

When asked the secret of delicious cheese, he says, "Have you seen our sound system in the milk shed?"

Stepping up, Greg makes a point to the white creamy cheese with the red split. "Try the dream ooze. That's a layer of Barbara's jalapeño jelly sandwiched into udder smoothness. The red specks are real ripe jalapeños."

The first baby cheese born on the farm is hawked by Greg next. "This is our first Brie out of the cooler. Please welcome our less-than-three-month double cream, hot and exotic: Testa Rossa."

The pillbox hat rides high in the air. "Testa Rossa's the Royal Winter Fair Specialty Brie Grand Champion."

The pillbox hat swings across to the *fromager*. Munching hands free up for a crumby congratulatory clap.

Serge is quick on the stage, off to the races in a quick pickup, *en anglais*.

He mile-smiles with one hand on the wheel. The other shifts the imaginary gears on the column.

"*Rrr-r-r-r-rrr.*"

Pause.

"*Rrr-r-r-r-rrr.*"

Pause.

"*Rrr-r-r-r-rrr.*"

John tilts his horn-rimmed glasses for an eye-roll at Greg.

One cheese reviewer has eaten through the spread. Another writer has read all the brochures and cleaned his teeth with a toothpick. They pick up the background of a certified *fromager*, a French-Canadian lad from a few kilometres outside Knowlton, Quebec.

"I was expecting a Québec *fromager* to have hockey names," the writer says. "*Boom Boom, Le Rocket.*"

"Copyright," Serge says.

"Ohhh?"

"Copyright. John is a big-time contract lawyer."

The raw silk dress shimmies past again. "Serge is correct about copyright. But we do have all those names registered. *C'est la pointe.*"

Serge limits his engagement with the hungry contemplation and questions of drifting drunks as he sticks with his script *en anglais*. He shifts through his practiced tasting notes. Barbara helped him with the proper English meanings. Serge started out with his smartphone translator, but his host mother, the retired French teacher, is the best.

"And, *monsieur*, the double cream. Testa Rossa will be our entry point under new and specialty goat cheeses, plus the open cheese category. Two out of three wins — not bad for the Royal Winter Fair."

The food critic slobbers down a wad of soft cheese. "Nutty … a touch of butterscotch. What's this?"

"*Exactemente, monsieur.* A brand new product we call, 'Honk the Horn.' Does it blow your horn, *monsieur*?"

The cheese critic talks to the cheese on the table. "Savoury sweet on the palate to complement a perfect charcuterie."

"The tasting note, *monsieur*."

"Butterscotch? *Comment?*"

"I pick the shoots from the hickory thorn bushes."

"Ahhh."

From an invisible bush, Serge finger-picks the small branches with care. Next his hands grind over an imaginary bowl.

"I have hickory thorns." Serge is back to finger-picking a painful tune. *"Ouch. Ouch. Ouch."*

The critic laughs with *le fromager.*

Serge has all the imaginary ingredients mixing in his imaginary bowl. "I mix them with my secret spice, which I add after the culture into the heated milk. An overnight process that leads to four weeks' aging in the cooler. *Plus de temps, plus parfumé.*"

"Parfume?"

"Non. En anglais, c'est flavoured. Not par-fume. Par-r-r-fu-u-may. *C'est une verbe.*"

"Aa-a-h-hh."

"With age comes flavour, but also I need four week to get that bloomy rind. Eat the rind."

"Whoa. A hint of hard butterscotch. Something bold, a tang. Did you use a zest of lemon?"

"Parfait, monsieur, parfait."

Serge points out the next sample board. "For a beautiful cheese spread, two weeks." The audience that has gathered around the critic puts the brain brakes on all the cheesy minutiae. *"Voilà!* My first automobile cheese from the goat."

"Automatic cheese?"

"No. *Auto-mo-be-all.*"

"Aahhh."

Serge speaks up for the cheese. "A smooth beauty — try it. It calls for the name 'Three on the Tree,' don't you agree?"

"Do you play Jan and Dean in the cooler for it?"

"No," Serge says. "Start Channel F1 live, twenty-four hours a day. *Rrr-r-r-r-rrr.*"

"It's great, Serge. *Vous êtes le chef de fromage.*"

Billie Ball and the Theatre Town invitees gobble on the toasties and toast the novelty.

"My God. Huckleberry jam. My grandmother used to make this preserve."

"The curd is more succulent than chewy. The aioli, wow."

"Barbara's homemade mayo, Portuguese olive oil and secret seasoning."

"How do know that?"

"Joey, Joe, Giacomo. I'm a Portuguese boy."

The Theatre Town group watch as three gorgeous ladies with hairy, unshaven faces fall into the room, seeking out their hosts. ("Greg, John. Transvaalia? Our drive was to Siberia.")

"Who are they?" Billie's friend Joey asks.

"The Sevillians, from the City."

"Sevillians?"

"Seville. The lads have a barbershop called The Three Barbers. Sevillians came along later."

"Who's the hunk on the table service?"

"That's Serge, the cheese-maker."

"Where's his date?"

"He's a fresh arrival."

"Billie, what do you think about bringing him around?"

"Is he the hunk that makes these scrumptious savoury treats?"

"No. That hunk is Aldert. He's with the dish over there."

"Hm-m-m-m. Two hunks and one dish."

All night long, Citizens and Citiots find commonality:

"Have to drive to Cambridge for good sausages."

"We have our favourite butcher at the St. Lawrence Market."

"I thought the City was on the Great Lake?"

"There's nothing good on television." (Both rural and City agree: "Netflix.")

"Do these Transvaalites talk anything but hockey?"

"Mention the word 'barbecue.' And sit back and listen."

"I have a great baste and a super secret sauce."

"Mention the secret sauce, and get mobbed by questions and challenges."

"Like what?"

"Like when. When are you bringing your secret sauce around for the challenge? The question will always be whose sauce is best."

"Do not bet any money. And never compete against Jimmy on the barbecue."

"The famous Billy on the Bun. They're serving it in the kitchen. Fresh off the barbecue."

"And their sauce!"

"Barbara will have at least two on the counter."

"What kinds?"

"Focking Red Sauce and the White Stuff."

"Wow."

"Wow? Wait till you get your lips on that toasted focaccia bun."

"What the fock are we standing here for?"

Wait till they load up their plates with Kountry Katerers' red-cabbage coleslaw, warm potato salad and blue goat-cheese potato pie.

Faisal and Ozzy have shifted back from the drive-shed barbecue to top up the flutes, crack a few beers and unscrew another wonderful Greg white.

"These Canadians sure can drink."

"Eat, too."

"Those ladies with the beards polish off two billys each."

"And at least three champagne cocktails each, before the bun."

"And Jimmy in a dress!"

"Allah forgive him."

"And who is that in the balloon dress?"

"Des."

"Des?"

"Des Pair. 'The unhappy fruit.' That's what he told me."

"And what did you say to him?"

"'And may your evening be fruitful. Can I top up your drink?'"

"Brother, Allah forgive us."

"Allah be grateful. Allah blesses us with kind gentlemen for our bosses."

"Let Allah help us top up their sinful drinks. Allah rewards us with the sweet custard."

Over and over all night long, Billie has shared the oral history of the tale of Allin Douglass ("Dougie," for the few in-the-know guests).

Now Billie runs into the packed dining room with a large mouthful of Little Deuce shovelled down with a smidgen of toasted focaccia.

"We … We-dding Gir-r-r-erl pah … pah-artee!"

His lips make a slapping-seal sound that gets a surprise round.

"Wedding Girl party!" Click. Click. Click. Chin. Chin.

Serge, hearing Dougie's tale for the first time tonight, was *un peu* gobsmacked by it. He will get a refresher catch-up from Aldert on tomorrow's rounds (they call it "chores and cheese").

Round the cheese table sample spread, an open book to the potential of Say Cheese, John is the host in full dress as he faces Billie. "Oh my God, I just wanted to tell you how radiant you look."

Billie is flushed. He would say something, but he's just shovelled two more toasties with assorted cheese ooze into his gob.

"Oh my God, where did you get …" John, of all people, is giving Billie the plus once-over. Billie can't help his crumb-laden closed-mouth smile.

Kirkton Katerers continue to buzz in the background. Having warmed it, toasted it, tossed it and served it, now they are washing it. They patrol the guests, marking special favourites.

"Love these …?" Norman points.

"Cheese puffs. With a pork-rind batter — gives that crunch that pops the ooze into a mouthful of delicious."

"Aargh. Aargh. Aargh. Thank you, Donna."

Donna, with her nonstop trays of food, hits Stormin' Norman as a moving target. Norman's bulking up always goes better without his wife. The drunk-enough man in the horn-rimmed glasses and shimmery long gown tracks the food as Jimmy stands beside him.

"Watch Donna," John says. "She sees Honey head in one direction, so she goes the opposite way to find Norman."

"Focking Normy, eh?"

"That's hospitality. The Katerers can really roll out the welcome carpet." John turns to his goat-farming mentor. "Jimmy, you need another drink."

On the kitchen sidelines, raw silk and champagne organza are about to come together under the word *Mistico* on that worn-down Oaxacan street sign.

(The scene will not replay well in Jimmy's memory. *"This finger,"* he'll recall later. *"I just remember this finger. I think real hard about this finger. It's joined to a raw silk sleeve."*)

Now, the index finger attached to John's hand beckons Jimmy's attention to the golden-labelled bottle. John is dazzling as he points with rising eyebrows. Jimmy is amazed at Juan's switch to a feminine mode of address:

"Amiga. Ropa roja bonita. Vengas acá. No faltan saludos muchisimos."

Let's get wasted. Soon they're passing out cut limes and gusano salt. Two gentlemen, *amigas* in dresses, knocking them back. Knocking them out for that Saturday night live dress parade.

Town Mayor Cheeko holds court in the back kitchen, in front of a bunch of returning smokers. He catches them post-smoke, after they come in the back door.

While he pontificates, the mayor can catch the treats on trays coming and going. "Donna. I'll take that last one. If no one else is having it." No question mark as he shovels the treat into the big political hole. Cheeko's mouth is so cavernous that he can talk and chew at the same time.

"A very popular choice," he tells his captive group. "The Katerers are hard to get on your calendar, with your choice of date." Cheeko sweeps his hand behind his head without turning. "Saturday night, too."

An in-the-know returning smoker nods. "The lads must have booked the Kirkton ladies way back when."

There are no dim-wits at the open house, but one returning smoker is extra drunk. "Must have booked a year before."

The others note the continuity problem. "Wow. Booked a year before they bought the farm!"

Blanshard humour, making light of how impossible it is to book the generational wedding, anniversary and banquet favourite go-to ladies.

The extra-drunk empties his half glass with eyebrow lifts. "The lads probably ponied up." His eyes match the eyebrows. *Wink. Wink.* "*Cash* on the side."

The in-the-know steps in. "Not the reason."

"How then, my friend?"

"Easy peasy. Two of the ladies are aunties of Aldert — Dorothy and Donna."

Yes, he can — our community-raised son can open doors everywhere. Family, friends, neighbours, and all the way to infinity and beyond for the lad.

The extra-drunk is one of the Sunriser regulars who gave up his usual stool for an amateur community actor on the night of the big shoot. His foggy brain remembers Aldert, so he rewinds to the porno shoot. Not hard to imagine a connection to Mary Beth in the back seat.

"Hope things open up with Mary Beth in her liftie-titty Wonderbra."

Cheeko and the returning-smoker bunch relish any dirt, no matter how absurd.

But Braedon sticks his neck into the conversation from the inner kitchen doorway. He keeps it simple. "Hey, buddy. Yeah, you. I'm pointing at you."

Braedon doesn't need to stretch his neck into the doorway, but he puts extra jabs on his point at the extra-drunk. "That's Mary Beth Johnson. Shut the fuck up."

At midnight, Aldert and the team begin readying up his crème brûlées. Each Christmas invitee who has first-hand crème brûlée experience, or who is aware of the treat's reputation, has had a growling stomach for more than a while.

From one of the uninitiated: "Crème brûlées from raw goat milk?"

"Prizewinning goats. French *fromager*."

"*Oui*," Serge chimes in, overhearing. "*Dit fromage, s'il vous plaît. And Grand Prix fromage*, too."

Bang. Out from the back-kitchen cooler for counter topping. Jimmy in organza on torch. Barbara and Aldert jamming and dabbing on spoons.

Faisal and Ozzy hold their spoons. Serge fills out on the trays, as server boy.

Worth the wait for late-night crème brûlées, a highlight of a super night, all agree.

Tap. Tap. Tap.

Click. Click. Click.

A nuclear fallout radiates about the house with a background of sucking, slurping, slobbering to swallow the golden hue of lavender goo. Most invitees never will confess to the slippage slop of collateral splatter.

(Proof is not in the pudding; proof is at the dry cleaner. Marlene at Thames 24-Hour Dry and Clean will see a surge in business in the next week. Ten stained white shirts, six wedding dresses and four assorted couture dresses, plus a dozen slobber-stuck ties. Nothing to mull over on Monday for Marlene. Bonus business.)

As Saturday night live on the farm in Christmas mode winds down on the clock before people wend their separate ways, the buildup to goodbye leads to runs to the bathroom.

Cheeko decides that he will finish a Cuban cigar outside while having a piss.

What can you do? he asks himself. *Well, I can do ambidextrous.*

(Well, more important, what does Cheeko do to spark an adventure that will live forever in Town legend — but more about that later.)

  LORNE EEDY

Goodbye kisses and hugs turn into a game of tag round the room into the back kitchen.

Kiss. Kiss.

"Merry Christmas."

Kiss. Kiss.

"Don't you love their house? A little different than mid-century modern, eh?"

"My God. How could they give up that condo with the awesome view?"

"Sorry, I did not introduce myself. Stephen Shoucrelli."

"Wow. Little Stevie. Super Agent Man Stevie. That's you."

"My card. Let's get together back in the City. I can show you what kind of exponential math subtracts that awesome view."

Kiss. Kiss.

"Where did you get that …?"

Aldert warms up the SUV. Mary Beth, who has stayed snow white tonight, escorts a drunk and solemn Barbara to the back seat. At this point, the road home is frozen, with no sign of the Professor.

Mary Beth has Barbara's head on her lap. "Aldert, Barbara's out. No hurry. We can wait, warm and comfy, baby."

Aldert gets back out of the SUV and calls to Max on the porch.

"Max, where's Jimmy?" Max is quick to respond to the familiar word Jimmy. "Maxy. Where's Jimmy?"

Max, smart dog, knows it's a question. The question is about the old Master. Max is up, out on the frosty brown lawn and heading to the east paddock. Aldert sees the dog paws doubling up on sneaker prints. Jimmy's heading east. East toward the new home on Thomas.

Aldert never swears, but this is a private conversation with one old dog. "Fock. Max, Jimmy's going to die of exposure before he turns off the 6th." Max and Aldert agree on one cardinal point.

"Thank God it's not west." West would be a Waterloo with Napoleon. A last stand, no doubt.

With Mary Beth beside him and Barbara in the back, Aldert drives east toward Town. He's guesstimating on a point of contact based on Jimmy's seeming trajectory.

Jimmy is out plodding along as he leaves sneaker tracks across the field. The tatters of the organza wave on the slats of the fence. Small dress bits blow off to the barn and beyond to the old oak tree. Jimmy jumps three fences. He pushes across the arctic surface of the paddock like Shackleton to the South Pole. Instead of turning left, his drunken sense of direction has him climbing one fence too far. The brain behind the steamed-up horn-rimmed glasses reboots to a left after the third climb on the concession boundary fence. The ladies track the course from the barn.

"Na-a-a-ah. Na-a-a-ah go-o-o-od for the Master. Na-a-a-ah."

Inside, John's last memory of Jimmy tonight is the organza dress flashing out the back kitchen door, leaving him with dirty dishes.

"Thank God for the Katerers. I couldn't face a Sunday dirty-dish morning."

John, in auditor auto-motion, counts the steps over to his bedroom. As he rounds the door trim, a last-minute grab takes him by mistake to Greg's super–king-size bed with the electric tilt-up mattress. But not before John catches the silk dress on a bed post.

Greg is heads up on the quilted and tilted mattress, where he watches in disbelief as the dress saran-wraps itself onto the pole. "My God, look at the skivvies on you, lad."

John, stripped to a corset and pantyhose, bounces off the bed post, over the end rail, and flops pop-goes-the-weasel up into bed. A perfect landing beside Greg, who reaches for his earplugs. The Katerers will lock and leave.

In his own way, Napoleon has had the best of festive times tonight. He moves back to his sheltered shed built for winter, a manger full of oats and barley.

"Na-a-a-ah. Na-a-a-ah-t-t-t-t ba-a-a-ad."

Napoleon recognizes the sound of Master's vehicle sitting on the road. At the same time, he can smell Jimmy's scent getting fainter.

The Shepherd sits, responsible, behind the wheel on the frozen 6th Concession. He knows how soon in the morning work comes. Barbara, with her rumpled Chanel, is hidden under a hooded HBC coat, lights out in the back seat.

In the front seat, there's a surprise coming over the neighbours' wire fence.

"Whoa," Mary Beth whispers. "What's that?"

It's a moment like when a dead body is discovered in murky harbour waters. When the body pops up, your heart pops out.

Four hands are up in real surprise. "My God. Jimmy."

Jimmy comes out all rag-tagged deer-me in the headlights. He has rolled over the sagging fence to roll flat face-down into the ditch. He crawls up the slushy bank, two hands clawing, feet kicking up the side of the ditch. At the summit of the climb, a ragged doll stands up, hands up in the light. Aldert is out for a greeting.

"Jesus, Jimmy. Jimmy, pay attention. Get in the car."

Jimmy is blocking out the headlights with his waving palms. He staggers back toward the ditch; the evening has become a bitch. *"Kembers have … wo-o-o-rked this land."*

Jimmy's gone zombie, with both hands stretched out. The walking dead drunk sings.

"This land is my land, this land …"

Aldert has never seen his mentor in this sort of sad shape.

"Jimmy. In the car."

Wave about. Stumble up to the road. Spin down into the ditch. Wave about.

"This ditch is m-m-m-my ditch. This bitch is …"

Problem solved, hands down. Aldert's catcher's-mitt–sized palms extend all fingers out to Jimmy for any good piece of organza. Right hand gets grip. The left moves up Jimmy's back to catch the one remaining strap on his shoulder.

Yank. Twist. Aldert's second mitt pushes in for back support, giving the direction. Pull the strap up and shove the dress straight toward the open back door of the SUV.

From the inside, a piece of drunken incoherence. "I'm freezing. Shut the focking door."

Aldert replies with the final shove from his knee, pushing Jimmy on top of Barbara in a heap. The HBC parka hood pops up.

"Focking what?"

For the back seat couple, the evening ends as a reel-in and a wrap-up in each other's arms.

Back on the road again. Mary Beth sings out the final credits on their Saturday night live in Transvaal.

"This land is your land,
This land is our land.
This land is the land
my Shepherd and I will buy.

So, in this land,
our love will be …
all blessed from high in the sky."

Aldert hits a low note behind his mile smile.

"And the Shepherd sings bass.
There's fifty acres of ours, right nearby-y-y-y."

Happy, happy kilometre-wide and mile-wide smiles move along with loving faces. The front-seat couple shepherd the snoring back-seat bundle home.

The Kountry Katerers lock up, letting the old dog off the front porch mat.

Max has never seen Master like that, jumping fences and all.

Aldert's Auntie Dorothy gives a great ear flop and head rub. "Maxy, you are such a good doggy. Old fella."

Max returns to the fireplace for the fading embers, surrounded by cheesy Christmas décor. He saddles up as close as possible to the grid irons in warm contemplation.

Serge ends up hitching a ride back to Aldert's with Braedon and his wife. All is clean, organized and put in its place by the Kountry Katerers. Upstairs, not a stir, not a shout, but two snoring partners not moving about. The bosses are more than lights out.

Billie Ball's Theatre Town friends bring him home to his parents' house. His friends wonder why Billie is somewhat tossed, his butt bruised, a bit hard and a little wet. The dog-food-faced lad disappears under a hot face cloth for an hour or so, and then he cleans himself up, sweet, warm and comfortable in his spot in the Gore of Downie. He sinks under quilted covers in his drafty upper-floor bedroom with the low ceilings. He waves his snowman pyjama legs to warm up the flannel sheets. His thoughts warm up too, enough to bury the memory of the damaged couture gown. What an evening.

The frosty windows put him in a Willie Wonka dreamland, where he counts down the gumdrop events to the best night's sleep, better than sheep. John, raw in black. Jimmy, effervescent. Those crazy City extras and his friends, including the Human Highlighter, all in dress.

"My God. I had never even seen Mike in a tux, let alone the hunk. Hm-m-m-m."

Right away, Billie has another party theme in mind. He thinks of the worst dresses through time immemorial.

"I have to tell Curly Top."

Billie's dream moves past candy land. He is stuck on staircase musical movies from the 1930s, with swimming-pool choruses; brother-and-sister dance acts that pretend to be nuptials. *Ohhh, the go-o-o-o-owns*, plus, plus.

The last forty years will work, with his experience in choice stock available from Mike's Auctions, area vintage stores, Grandmother's Closet in Town, and the annual swap show in Theatre Town.

Prehistoric comic characters could be fun, but without style. "My God. We don't want Wilma and Fred. Although I am kind of partial to that Barney Rubble."

The bedroom debate continues. Billie muses on the balance between style and just girls having fun.

"*Mary Poppins*? No style, boring. *My Fair Lady*? Style, yes, but boring again. Sheila McCarthy or Frances McDormand in costume? Period stuff? That's too serious."

He thinks of the beautiful dream dresses of the night just past. And then it hits him, *flash*, without a hit on the rafter. What not a party of dress opposites?

Someone else's bad choice put out to pasture and forgotten. Such a bad-time get-up in an ugly dress, we hope, will turn the pumpkin back into a royal party wagon, for plus fun.

Billie pulls down the quilt to see his reflection in the dark skylight. Close above the low ceiling in the big, outside, December winter wonderland, the frosty breezes carry a fresh and different taste of things to come.

An opposite dress party. A party that speaks to its own name. "Dis Tress. Dat Dress."

Dress on.

Epilogue

The S-counter and booths are filled at the Sunriser, and so are the coffee cups. The klatch swings into gear, bringing in the first catch of the day, a volunteer catch who did catch the action — a confessed embossed-invite receiver. *("Eh? Dan will know, eh? Eh? Eh?")*

This four-star "eh?"-lister slides with confidence into the one vacant stool up front.

A lucky day! On the winds of gossip-comportment fortune, a second live in-the-know witness swings open the not-so-greasy glass doors and heads to a back booth. *("Eh? Joey will know, eh? Eh?")*

The coffee-hole gang hang in anticipation. The flood gate swings open.

The first eh-lister swivels to face the second. "Did you see Cheeko?"

The second volleys back, throwing it out to the room. "His Worship? Out there by the fence having a piss? Hello, hello! I had the full porch show."

The seconder pauses. The porch view of His Worship waving and shaking his willy about is an image best left for a more discreet group. Possible harmful exposure of a most definitely hurtful incident.

The first fires it up with the big picture. "The monster goat appears ..."

(Every bench and stool ass is familiar with the Say Cheese character list. The crowd light up at the mention of the most famous member of the team, the sequestered one.)

"... out of the dark dank night."

(Heads shake at the thought, a beast coming out of the shadows. *Oo-o-o-oh.* A star witness has introduced the star performer of the night. A chorus of thought: *"Napoleon."*)

First witness out front creeps his fingers. *Wiggle. Wiggle.* Wiggling those finger tips. "Napoleon moves in." Flashing eyebrows. "Careful like. Double-wire electric fence, folks."

Wiggling stops. The eyebrows are steady to the roomful of ears tuned to a virtuoso performance. Eh-lister points both his index fingers ahead. "The General *knows* the position of *both* wires."

Dim-wit in back corner booth dares to speak. "He knows where *his* wire is, too."

First eh-lister has one eyebrow up — then down for a pano look over the room. All eyes wait for the touch; the fingers feel the invisible wire, the imaginary shock. Braedon imagines a theatre organ in the background pumping up the crowd, rolling, rolling on with lightning and thunder.

The first witness throws more logs of detail on the fired-up interest. One finger up. A-ha. "Cheeko *sees* Napoleon."

The askance look. One eyebrow up. Finger remains to the point. "The monster ..."

(Audience eyebrows rise in concern. Another chorus of thought after the choir master's lead: *"Napoleon!"*)

No one notices consciously, but this time around it's an opposite eyebrow rise from the witness. "Napoleon *sees* Cheeko." The index finger points back to the full house watching in awe. "Cheeko does not want to get his gear near" — the picture could be no clearer — "for fear of the ominous stud lurking in the dark."

First more creepy fingers, then the hands go low, a cup holding arnies. "Everything is going well for the mayor."

And from the very back, this time a mimic. "Well now. What *can* you do? I'm telling you. What *can* you do?"

Guaranteed laugh track. The room sits in expectation, ready-freddy to get back on the Monster track of attack.

The secondsies witness is up now. All stools and bench butts turn to the back corner.

"But ..."

(Braedon stretches out with full neck attention. He's tracking all the complications in the making of a record Mull-Over Monday. Braedon was 87.7% present, there at the party as a witness but not for the pissing genesis of Cheeko's flood.)

"... Cheeko's sucking on this big Havana ..."

Sucking pinched-fingers motion on the second witness's lips. He indicates an untoward path with a wavering stand. (The whole room round the vision out in their minds. A mind chorus of thought waves from side to side, a mind ripple of warning: *Watch* for the *focking* goat, *stupid*.)

Guaranteed drunk Cheeko is *grande stupido*. The audience can see it: the cigar is a one-hand hold-up, with the other hand down-periscope.

"... Not a man to waste the moment. And remember, Cheeko's a leftie."

Leftie? The room switch hands in their minds to get a grip on reality. The witness fingers away with his left hand on his zipper. His right hand has those pinched fingers off to the side with the invisible cigar.

Zipper movement is left on hold; witness lips are right on for an imaginary puff. A clear picture painted for that dank and dirty night.

(The invite-less heads nod to the inevitable. *Slurp. Slurp. Slurp.* Even more than the caffeine hit, it's the dirty details they can taste — and of course the juicy unknown.)

"Cheeko puts his cigar down on the *metal* gate."

(All the Country folk, not to mention numerous adventuresome Town lads and not-so-bright trespassers have an unwanted charge or two in the memory bank. "*O-o-o-oh n-o-o-o-ooo …*")

The seconder adds a surprise point to the tale's current. "No, no." Hands wave palms-forward to calm. "It's *okay!* His hand is dry."

The witness waves a hand about without pinched fingers, no invisible cigar to drop. (The room has an air of disappointment. "*Hm-m-m-m.*")

Wait, waddle and watch the zipper action off the back bench. "So Cheeko pisses away." Widdle-waddle eyes pinched to the audience. "The goat watches Cheeko with his shine in the dark coal eyes."

As Cheeko's having an invisible piss thrown about, acted out by the witness, watch — here he goes, making a ten-leg, both-hands, creepy finger spider walk. "The goat comes a little closer, closer … closer."

Silence.

"BUT Cheeko the Leftie holds his cigar. The right points his shaky wing-wang."

(The booth beside holds up hands to avoid the spray.)

The secondsies shifts both eyes right, both eyes left, right. "Yes, a dark and dank night further clogs up Cheeko thinking." A steady-eyebrows look off to nowhere. Steady on the zipper. "The mayor. He's pissed as a pirate. He grasps on to the wee tiller tight."

All audience eyes watch the tale-telling eyebrows look down, down to the tight fist below.

"As tight as ye can on such a tiny tiller. A real Timmy."

The speaker moves from a waddle to complete hip pivots. "It's a poor aim all round with his dinky." The pivot stops. "But he's streaming away in the right direction. Away from the closing goat and the double-wire electric fence." Eyebrows lift the audience. "Happy, happy? Happy? Not."

(A group head shake to the inevitable.)

"Not on this night."

The secondsies waddles forward, miming some ornate hand-work on his zipper pull. His motion points to his eh-lister partner, who holds up his hands to block the invisible pee. The crowd is having a spasm of mull-over glee.

Not so for old Cheeko.

His Worship, in dark sunglasses, sits in solitary thought in the heart of the downtown, blocks and blocks west from the Sunriser.

Cheeko's happy with better coffee in hand from the Yapping Dog barista two blocks down Queen, and keen with no group conversation to mind. The mayor's liquored memory is dim. The rim of his red, swollen dinky is raw intelligence on some tragedy. He has retreated for convalescence at his town hall office with his feet up. *Ah-h-h-hh,* the microwaveable beanbag massages his crotch. He grits through his teeth at present pleasure from past pain.

"Well now, what can you do? I'm telling you, what can you do."

His tiny wienie throbs. "*O-o-o-oh. Ow-w-ooh.* What can I say?"

What more could he have done that night? Nothing. Tragedy was in the air.

Back in the east end of St. Marys, at the Sunriser, the first witness wavers on his feet in the live re-enactment. "His Worship bobs, shuffles and slobbers back."

The room watches the invisible fence. They can picture the quiet goat in the dark.

The speaker stumbles back from the stools. The bench hold their hands out, waiting to steady the balance. The speaker grunts over his shoulder, through the invisible fence at the dark shadow of the goat.

The room loves a mimic. He grunts just like fat old Cheeko. The speaker keeps his left fingers pinched, the right in a wavy zipper aim. "*Pis-s-s-sss* on you, pony goat."

Somehow, in his drunk delirium, the mayor took general exception to the goat. Cheeko's natural flight instinct was confused by his stupidity, defused by alcohol. The coffee crowd, in their daze at the information pouring in, see a train coming down a tunnel. The porch witnesses that same night saw the same train.

The secondsies is wavering to make a point. He turns to a booth bunch. "Focking goat. I see you looking at me. Focking dumb pony." He's peering ahead, peeing below. "Oh yeah, go ahead — stick your beard on the fence. Here boy, here boy, go ahead take a suck on my cigar. Focking light you up, dumb goat."

First of all, secondsies leaves out ninety percent of Cheeko's stupid lecture to the goat. What can he say? Mayors do go on and on and on.

"Stupid-looking thing. I can show *you*."

Cheeko, in a turn of ultimate bad manners, directs his pee pour to the closing shadow. "See, goat? Cheeko is the man. See Cheeko's big dick? Piss on you, you … goat."

Not a brilliant speech from the one side of the fence. The cigar hand waves to the monstrous goat. The first eh-lister has resumed his review now, coming onto the front porch. The audience already knows the set-up. "A porchful of witnesses break from the party." The fuss and hubbub pull a crowd out onto the porch, joining Max who keeps to his clean mat. Max can't see, but can smell the human and the beast in the shadow of the fence.

"The porch is packed. Most can see Cheeko. All can hear him. But few see Napoleon on the sidelines closing in." The witness is right on the goat. "On the dark side of the Christmas on the Farm that night, Napoleon hears the blah-blah-blah. He gets the gist. *Na-a-a-ah. Waa-a-a-ait and see-e-e-e. Na-a-a-ah bah-h-h-h-ther.*"

The secondsies tags up, with his right hand moving to zipper tugs. The left holds that lightless, timeless cigar. "So here's Cheeko. He's swearing at Napoleon." Hips pivot. "He's finished the last wags of his piss." Stop with a look of shock. "But no, no, no. He can't show the little shrinking-man to the growing audience on the porch …"

                                                    LORNE EEDY

(The live audience along the S-counter and booths wait on a pinched-finger look.)

"… *And* save his big fat Cuban."

(Smiles around anticipate his fate.)

"Meanwhile the goat is dissing it back at him."

No one, not a single stooly or bencher, questions this embellishment. The addition of a goat dialogue? Dogs are painted playing poker, after all, so just go with it.

"Cheeko has brain farts." Another grunt guffaw on His Worship. "He wants to suck on the last stump of that cigar. So he reaches out …"

(The audience put the brakes on train in the tunnel. *"Oo-o-oh no-o-o-oo."*)

"… but he's preoccupied. The right pull on the zipper is not working. So he switches hands for a better grasp." The action is embellished with a mix of left and right hand shuffles. "His piss-drip right hand reaches for the cigar."

The room has a half-dumb look.

"Cheeko is too drunk to wipe himself. His wet fingers place the cigar on the frosty but *wet metal* bar of the gate." (Some back-bencher snickers: *"Dew drop in."* *"Frosty makes tinky-dinky."*) "Bar none. Cheeko had no idea *wet* on *wet* connects the current on the electric fence."

(The room echoes. *"Oo-o-oh no-o-o-o-o."*)

"It's worse."

(*"No-o-o-o-o-o."* All anticipate the consequences.)

"Cheeko has no idea the gate is metal, let alone frosty moist." A look around the room. "Is Cheeko not grounded? No, Cheeko is a pissed hydro pole."

(A laugh with an echo. *"Oh no-o-o-o-o."*)

Fan the flames with secondsies detail. "Zap. The porch crew even saw the spark."

(The uninvited bunch, no witnesses to the incident, nod their heads.)

"The mayor cries out. *Aa-a-a-a-a-a!!* Ow! Ow! Ow, focking *ow!*" The secondsies' hand-play flaps downward from high shoulders to low zipper. "Cheeko reacts. Cheeko's in shock. Cheeko yanks at his zipper."

(Echo from all, enthralling in unexpected zipper bonus news coverage. *"Oh no-o-o-o-o."*)

"No; he misses his tinky-dinky wing-wang. But …"

(Echo of relief. *"Whew."*)

"But …"

(*"Oh no-o-o-o-o!"* Every man in that room has been there. Some time, somewhere, there. Down there, down zipper, up periscope. The wrong place exposed at the wrong time.)

The secondsies forces his lips to puff out. Both hands on zipper. "Catches his bag in the zipper." His lips are out. Big laugh. "The mayor has never ran softer and harder for his political life."

A bigger laugh.

Next, the story moves forward with a segue in an odd direction: fashion. Remember, top diner topics are, not always in this order: food (BBQ), sports (Leafs), and cars (Classics). But fashion? That sobers up the room.

A back-booth calls up a never-before-witnessed fact. The question without the mark. "Never seen Cheeko in a tux."

A comical movie buff in the room buffoons a bit. "Didn't he play The Penguin in *Batman*?"

A few chuckles from comic fans who are troubled by the mixed image of Burgess Meredith and Danny DeVito.

A stumbling deep voice gives the home crowd what they need. Another deep crack at the mayor. "Well, what can you do? I am telling you, what can you do?"

Fashion wears out the Cheeko lines. An opposite-bencher starts down the runway. "How did Billie Ball do coming out?"

More mixed thoughts on fashionable translation. "Coming out?"

"Yeah, he told us that he was really coming out for this one."

The secondsies witness has this covered. Back to the incident.

"Yeah, he came out all right. Answered the flaming call from Cheeko."

The room limits laughter in anticipation of more.

"Billie's on the porch with emergency response in mind. He skids across the damp floor to the dog's water bowl. Grabs it and streaks off across the yard with this ... double dog dish. The water and also wet food." The secondsies gets high and pitchy. "I'll save you, Worship Cheeko. Hang on ..." (Big laughs) "... hang on, Cheeko."

The secondsies returns to his normal voice. "Billie hits the frosty slick lawn going sixty."

The first eh-lister adds on. "Billie flies out in this canary costume. All yellow like, like he's holding a bird bath too."

The secondsies keeps things on track. "It was the dog dish."

First ignores second. "Fell. Did a face-plant in the dog food."

The room is in calamity wonder.

"The whole porch watches the skid, waiting for his feet to go up, then down on his arse. Billie fooled them." Pause, look and punch. "Billie flies forward into a flip, up and over. Ass over tea kettle." A quick breath with one hand held high over the witness's eyes. "But instead, he flew forward. He soars heads up, up to a down."

The eh-lister is up front, wiping his imaginary dress with a face of horror. "He stood up dog-eared with dog food on the face." Makes a few steps with a kick-off. "Billie does a foot stomp. Then he kicks the bowl for a conversion. Bang, he's off to his car with his friends."

Secondsies: "Right behind Cheeko's sorry-ass tail."

Back to the first. "The porch crew is spontaneous in chorus. Singing an unrehearsed ditty. Amazing. Can you remember it, Joe?"

Joey does an opus for the coffee group, breaking out in a solo.

"Good night, Billie. Good night, Billie.
You drove a country mile.
You gave us a smile.
Good night, good night, Billie Ball ..."

More laughs, more claps and a few spoon taps.

Hello, hello, old Billie comes out later in the week to feed the hungry listeners. Yes, on Thirsty-for-More Thursday, Billie's in through the not-so-greasy front door with a grain shovel of participant information.

He breaks out in *his* voice, in good cover fun. *"Good night, Billie. Good night, Billie ..."*

The group gathers up tears of laugher. Billie talks to his audience. "Well, what can you do? It *is* my song. And I'll be happy to dance to it."

All hands gather up in fun horror to block that offer.

After Billie's good entrance on that Thursday morning, the group is satisfied hearing not just a star witness but a star character, beloved. The coffee-klatch consciousness has expanded to include the cheesy and nutty tale of a massive goat, a fat mayor, and a canary flying out with a double dog bowl.

Wow.

Thoughts and talk have moved past feta, Swiss equipment, goat arnies, not-so-secret BBQ sauce, Leafs, *les Canadiens*, a Quebecois cheesemaker, classic cars, an electric exotic, gay ways, and not to forget the question of who's the husband. Billie could sing like a canary on the chiffon dress, and all the other dresses.

"My God," he tells the room. "All those straight men in dresses. I could name names." He saves warm thoughts and fun memories for sleepy nights in his low-ceilinged bedroom. "My God, what a parade. No, what a charade! — for Gay Cheese."